COCYTUS
PLANET OF THE DAMNED

JOHN CALIGIURI

COCYTUS—PLANET OF THE DAMNED. Copyright © 2015 by John Caligiuri. All Rights Reserved. Printed in the United States of America. No part of this book may be used or reproduced in any manner whatsoever without written permission except brief quotations. For information, contact Insomnia Publishing, 11 Avery Rd, Londonderry, NH 03053

Cover image designed by Eve M. Roberts.

www.insomnia-publishing.com

ISBN-10: 0986397520

ISBN-13: 978-0986397523

To my grandson, Liam Jordan, the shining light of the next generation.

Special thanks to my wife Linda and our children, John, Michael, Kristina, and Dale.

Their love and support is my inspiration.

MAIN CHARACTERS

Dante Carloman	American
Tina Phokas	American
Esther Easley	American
Reggie Easley	American
Angela	American, orphan
Rodrigo Cruz	American, Army Captain
Joe Gentile	American, Army Lieutenant
Virgil Bernius	American, Air Force Special Forces
Dimitri Pertelov	Russian
Gabrielle Peyago	Argentine
Linda Martinel	Australian
Kevin Martinel	Australian, Navy Search and Rescue
Michael	Infiltrator Guardian
Gabriel	Infiltrator Guardian
Rafael	Infiltrator Guardian
Reggie	Destroyer Guardian
Beatrice	An A.I. found on Cocytus
Dis	An A.I. found on Cocytus

CHAPTER I
Unexpected Encounter

From rock to rock they fall into this valley:
Acheron, Styx and Phlegerthon they form;
Then downward go along this narrow sluice

Upon that point where is no more descending.
They form Cocytus; what that pool may be
Thou shalt behold, ... "

Dante's Inferno, Canto XIV

Dante Carloman tightened his grip on the steering wheel of his old Honda CRV as fat snowflakes splattered against the windshield. In good weather, the drive to his parents' home outside of Fredonia, New York took about three hours from Cornell University in Ithaca. This was not good weather.

Despite being only four days before Christmas, few cars occupied the road. No one drove unless necessary during a western New York blizzard, so the sight of a convoy of Humvees roaring by onto Interstate 86 confused him. Dante read the lettering on one of the trucks when it flashed past his headlights: U.S. Army, 10th Mountain Division.

"I wonder what that's all about?" he muttered and glanced to his right.

Tina Phokas snoozed with her head slumped against the passenger door. Dante sighed and pulled onto the expressway. It seemed like such a good idea when he posted the offer on the Student Center bulletin board for riders. It was a long drive, and he thought it a good idea to have someone to talk to and help cover gas. It seemed even better when a gorgeous, second-year medical student responded to his posting. They planned to get an early start and miss the big snowstorm. However, she told him the day before they left that her Human Genetics final had been re-scheduled to four o'clock and asked if he'd mind leaving later. *So much for an early start,* he thought as he glared at the sleeping figure.

At first, they chatted about their studies. Dante described his artificial intelligence thesis project—one of the final steps in his master's degree. He grimaced as he glanced over and saw Tina staring out the passenger window. *God, she must think I'm such a geek. I must've run at the mouth for twenty minutes. She hadn't asked a single question, either.*

She flushed as the conversation came to an abrupt halt. "Are you named after the author of the *Divine Comedy?*"

How many times has someone asked me that? Dante thought. "Yeah. My mom's maiden name is Alighieri, and my folks thought it would be cute to name their baby after someone famous."

"Oh, that's interesting," she mumbled in a flat voice. "Hey, I'm sorry, but I'm pretty beat," Tina declared. "I pulled an all-nighter and could really use a nap." Without waiting for a response, she curled up in her seat.

The next hour he spent on the interstate, listening to his downloaded music. The snow fell harder, and Dante stomped on the gas pedal of the old four-cylinder with the vain hope he could outrun the oncoming storm.

Flashing lights in the rearview mirror caught his attention. *Oh, great. This is just what I need.* He glanced at his speedometer and cursed.

Two State Trooper cars flew past him and vanished in the thickening wall of snow as he stepped on the brakes, skidding onto the shoulder of the road. Seeing that he hadn't crashed into anything, Dante blew out his cheeks in relief.

Tina woke as the car bounced over the rumble strips on the side of the expressway. She tucked a loose strand of long auburn hair behind her ear. "What was that?"

"I don't have a clue. Probably an accident ahead."

Concern creased her face. "I hope no one's hurt."

Dante squirmed in his seat. He hadn't given thought to anyone's safety. "Me, too."

Tina twisted around and craned her neck toward the black sky where they both heard a growing thumping sound. "Look at that." The sound became deafening as four helicopters, flying in formation, roared overhead and vanished into the gloom and thickening snow.

"It must be some sort of military exercise. I saw a bunch of Humvees head in the same direction earlier." He couldn't even hear the choppers anymore. "They're sure moving fast."

Tina's voice tightened. "All of these cops and soldiers scare me. Dante, turn on your radio, and see if you can get a local station."

He nodded and switched the player to radio mode and pressed the scan button. Nothing came through the speakers, and he cocked an eyebrow. "That's weird. I should at least be picking up something out of Buffalo."

"I'm calling my mom. Maybe she's heard something on the news." Tina rummaged through her purse and pulled out her phone, and her brows furrowed. "There're no bars on my cell."

"This is making me nervous. I'll pull off at the next exit and see what's going on." He glanced at the car's gas gauge. The meter hovered close to empty. "I need to fill up anyway," Dante rasped through a constricting throat. "I think we just passed an exit for a town called Angelica. You have any idea where the next one is?"

"No, and there's no cell connection to get my GPS."

A semi and a Chrysler M200 cruised by them. Dante chuckled to himself at the normal flow of traffic.

My imagination's way too active. He scratched his chin. "I remember reading the Tenth Mountain Division specializes in foul weather training. That's why they're based out of Fort Drum in Watertown. I bet they're down here for a training exercise."

"Yeah, what else could it be?" Tina looked relieved. "It's a shame they have those poor men out in this stuff and at Christmas time, too." She stiffened and leaned forward. "Hey, better slow down. There're a lot of lights ahead." She squinted through the ice encrusted windshield.

"I see 'em." Dante groaned as he slid the old CRV to a stop behind the looming mass of a tractor trailer.

A gray-haired, heavyset State Trooper made his way down the line of stopped vehicles. Dante lowered the window as the trooper approached. "What's going on, officer?" he asked as he saw a disconcerted look in the man's eyes.

"Sorry, there's been a chemical spill up ahead," said the trooper. "Once it's cleaned up, we'll reopen the road."

Tina sniffed, her puzzled eyes darting back and forth. "It was those army guys who went racing through here, wasn't it? They were probably carrying poison gas."

"I-I couldn't tell you, miss. I just got here myself."

Dante noticed the man's hands shook, but pressed on. "Uhh, Officer, could we use your radio to get word to our folks? They're going to worry, and our cell phones aren't getting a signal."

"Sorry, it's only for official business." The trooper wiped his forehead. "Besides, it stopped working, too. There's some sorta electronic interference around here." He balled his hands into fists as two more cars approached. "This is a freakin' mess. They were supposed to divert all traffic back in Hornell."

Dante watched as people from the stopped cars climbed out to gawk at the sight of a military unit advancing toward a forest. The loud whine of helicopters caught Dante's attention, and their blazing spotlights lit up the night. A half dozen Humvees knocked over a tall link fence and headed toward a line of dark trees. Gunners manning the .50 calibers rode on top, and a company of snow-covered soldiers in full battle dress spread out behind them.

Dante met Tina's gaze and whispered, "Something's fishy here." Then he called to the State Trooper, "Excuse me, officer, but I don't see any Haz-Mat gear on those guys. Are you sure it's a chemical spill? Those GIs look like they're ready for a war."

By that time, a crowd of civilians bundled against the freezing weather gathered around the State Trooper. Their shouted questions grew more shrill as they realized he knew as little as they did.

Finally, a commanding voice broke through the noise. "Officer, I'm Sergeant Virgil Bernius, Air Force Special Forces, Pararescue. Is there anything I can do to help?"

The policeman swung his flashlight on the newcomer. The man stood at an intimidating six-one with thick, muscled arms crossed over his heavy winter vest. Virgil possessed an olive complexion, a large, Roman nose, and the stubble of dark hair clipped high and tight. The State Trooper sighed. "Everyone, just get back in your cars. I'm sure this'll all be cleared up soon."

One heavy-jowled man screeched, "What's going on? I got a little kid in my car."

A blinding flash illuminated the area before every light died. The helicopter beacons vanished, and their engines ceased their roar. The crowd gasped in horror as the aircrafts dropped like rocks into the trees below and burst into flames. An instant later, the angry report of automatic weapons and munitions' explosions thundered from the woods.

The State Trooper drew his sidearm. "Oh, sweet Jesus. Clear the area. Now!"

Sergeant Bernius grabbed him by the arm with a steel grip. "This sure as hell is no chemical spill. What can I do to help?"

The trooper eyed the soldier. "Come with me. There's a shotgun in my squad car."

"We're not hanging around," Dante yelled. He tried to shift his car out of park, but nothing happened. *What the—I don't remember turning off the car.* His hand trembled as he turned the key. Again, nothing. Panic clawed at him. *This is no time for a dead battery.*

"C'mon, Dante, get us outta here," Tina pleaded.

Another bright flash lit the forest and the gunfire sounded much closer.

"The damn car's dead. We better grab a ride with someone else." Dante looked up and down the line of cars. None moved. "We're going to have to run for it." He went to open the door, but it remained locked. Dante pulled the door latch and clambered out. "C'mon."

Several people crawled out of their cars and stumbled east on the highway through ankle-deep snow. Others milled around in fear and confusion. Dante took two strides, stopped, and hurried back to his car to pull out a hammer he kept under the driver's seat. "Tina, stay on the road. I don't think the last exit's more than a few miles back. Help should be coming soon."

"What kind of help? The army's already here," she snapped in a strained voice. "And what do you think you can do with a hammer?"

Dante's knuckles turned white as he squeezed the tool's handle. "Something is better than nothing."

He trotted past an ancient Ford Focus behind them. An elderly couple sat inside, the back seat filled with brightly wrapped Christmas gifts and a folded walker. The doors hung ajar, but the couple remained still with their hands clasped together and their faces tight. Dante exchanged one quick look with Tina, yelled for her to keep going, and doubled back to the Ford.

He met the concerned eyes of the old man who told him, "I can't move too well without my walker, and my wife's a bit stubborn. She won't leave without me."

Worry etched itself across the old woman's face. "Reggie, in this cold, you wouldn't get a quarter mile, and after forty-nine years of marriage, I'm not about to leave you."

Dante gulped down his terror. "I'll get you out of here." He moved to the open door and reached in, picking up the frail old man.

"Let me help," said a familiar voice. It turned out to be Tina, who pulled the walker from the partially open back door.

Dante gaped at her, then shook his head. "Tina, I told you to get the hell outta here."

"Jesus, how far do you think I'd get? Listen."

Dante cocked his head. The gunfire reached the trees nearby, and a strange, high-pitched noise accompanied it.

Tina whispered, "Whatever's going on might be coming this way." She moved to the other side of the car and helped the old woman out.

"Thank you, dear. The name's Esther." She looked out into night-shrouded woods. "You young folks get going. We'll just slow you down."

"Don't be silly." Tina put on a brave smile and retrieved a car blanket from the back seat. "We'll all get out of this together."

Dante gasped as a squad of soldiers, maintaining a steady fire, backed out of the woods. They broke for the darkened expressway when they passed the last line of trees.

One of the soldiers froze in mid-stride, lit by muzzle flare. A couple of blurs the size of large wolves skittered to the GI and dragged the paralyzed man back into the woods. Other soldiers broke from the forest, either alone or in small groups. Shadowy creatures, moving with long, loping strides, bounded from the trees and paused, studying the frantic scurrying on the interstate.

"Run, you damn fools!" the State Trooper bellowed as he jogged down the line of cars, gun in hand. Virgil followed, carrying a police shotgun in a ready position.

"Where?" Dante retorted, searching the darkness for an escape.

Virgil's gaze swept the inky blackness, his jaw clenched tight. Five infantrymen scrambled past the car where they stood, and Virgil grabbed one. "Corporal, what the hell're ya fighting out there?"

The soldiers crouched behind the car, sucking in air. Fury burned in the corporal's face. "Dear God in Heaven. I'd call them the spawn of Hell. They sure ain't human. They got what looks like a goddamn spaceship the size of a football field back there. It hit us with some sort of EMI pulse that knocked out the choppers and turned all of our electronics to shit. When they dropped our birds, we hit 'em with everything we had. The .50's and Mark 19's shredded a pack of 'em, but hundreds more of those damned creatures poured out of that spaceship. These M4's didn't even slow 'em down. The Humvees were sitting ducks."

The corporal paused and stared into the forest. "Our boys kept the mounted guns hot 'til the creatures overwhelmed them. They ignored us foot soldiers like we were nothin' 'til they finished off our big stuff." He wiped sweat from his face. "Then they came after us, shooting shit I couldn't see or hear."

"But they can die?" Virgil asked.

"Yeah, the heavy stuff worked, but that's gone. Sweet Jesus, they told us it was just some yahoo wackjobs looking to go on a shooting spree. We went into that farm with a reinforced company, and those *things* smashed us to pieces."

Virgil pumped the Mossberg 500 and studied the gathering creatures. "If they can die, then we can kill 'em."

The corporal nodded and planted his rifle along the hood of the car. "Sir, I don't think many of our boys are dead. Captain Cruz was next to me when he was hit and just froze in mid-stride. I could see mist coming from his nostrils, but the poor bastard couldn't move. Lieutenant Gentile ordered us back while those monsters dragged our boys off, still alive."

Dante squinted into the blinding snow. Someone organized the remaining soldiers into a line of defense further down the road. A group of men pushed cars over on their side to form a wall.

Virgil sank down next to the corporal. "I'm Sergeant Virgil Bernius. I think I'll join you guys."

"Joe Viden." The man's hand quivered as they shook. "I don't think you'll be joining us for long."

Dante gulped as he listened to the soldier's conversation and glanced at Tina. She knelt beside the old man, wrapping a blanket around him. She met Dante's look with steady eyes and nodded.

He crept over to Virgil. "Uh, sir, what can we do?" Dante held his gaze steady as the sergeant studied him.

"What do you think you're going to do with that old claw hammer?" A grim look crossed Virgil's face. "Keep your head down and pray, son. Just pray."

Screams came from the east where the small line of civilians had gone. Then silence. A hard voice broke through. "Watch the damn flanks! They're moving around us!"

As if the words were a signal, the gathered creatures moved toward the highway. Their advance met a withering volley that should have devastated any enemy within its field of fire. A few fell, only to rise again. They covered the distance in seconds.

"Prepare for hand-to-hand!" Virgil hollered. A pack of the creatures bounded over the barriers without slowing. A chaos of individual or small group battles broke out down the line of stalled cars.

Blood drained from Dante's face as a monster stepped into view. The creature looked like a harpy. It had a pointed snout and long, cupped ears. The protruding jaw bared needle-like fangs, and its elongated hands ended in clawed fingers grasping a two-foot long tubular object. A large GI picked up one writhing demon and drove it head first through the windshield of his CRV. The soldier snatched the dropped tubular weapon, but shrieked in agony as two other creatures swarmed over him, sinking their fangs into his arms and clawing at his armored vest.

Virgil fired point blank at another leaping alien. The force of the blast slammed the creature to the ground, but it appeared unharmed. The glowing blue belt the monster wore winked out. Virgil pumped the Mossberg, shoved it in the nightmare's mouth, and pulled the trigger. Satisfaction showed on his face as the demon's head splattered, but more of the creatures bounded onto the highway. An eerie sizzling sound surrounded them. He fired the Mossberg again.

Dante would never forget that sight. A harpy sprang down from the top of his Honda, its face contorted into a grotesque caricature of a smile. It pointed its weapon at Virgil, and the sergeant froze. Something inside Dante snapped. He sprang from the dubious shelter beside the Ford Focus and smashed his hammer on the demon-spawn's head. His arm reverberated as it bounced off an unyielding shield.

The creature shook its head and turned to him. He heard a sizzling sound, and Dante found himself paralyzed and in agony. He no longer heard the gunfire or screams, just an incessant hiss and the wind whipping snow through the trees.

CHAPTER II
Damage Control

Made myself ready to sustain the war,
Both of the way and likewise of the woe,
Which memory that errs shall not retrace.

Dante's Inferno, Canto II

Here's the preliminary report, Mister President. We have little more detail about the Angelica Incident than we did at our morning briefing," FBI Director Brenda Campbell said. The Secretary of State, the National Security Advisor, and the Vice President stared at their unopened folders with a look of doom plastered on their faces.

Anger flashed in President Dale Jordan's eyes as he threw the folder on the situation room table unread. "Well, since you told me absolutely nothing this morning, would you please be so kind as to inform me who or what the hell hit us yesterday? This is the worst terrorist attack on our country since Nine-Eleven."

Campbell tapped the screen on her notepad, and the wall opposite her lit with live images of a swarm of people in hazmat suits slogging through snow a foot deep. Wrecked vehicles and smoldering attack helicopters gave the carnage, blanketed in white, a surreal look in the soundless video. She cleared her throat and glanced around the table. The CIA Director, Norm Dennison, and Chairman of the Joint Chiefs of Staff, Bob Gustini, looked back and nodded. All other eyes stared at the scene with pensive anticipation.

Gustini cleared his throat. "As you know, at 11:35AM EST, NORAD detected a single object making an unauthorized intrusion into American airspace. We scrambled pursuit aircraft but were unable to locate it."

Secretary of State Anne Shanks' voice rose in alarm. "Have the Chinese matched our stealth technology?"

Gustini folded his hands on the table, sighing. "The Chinese are still five years behind us. What came through yesterday possessed superior stealth capabilities and, by a factor of two, was faster than anything we fly. This attack—"

National Security Advisor Turnbull squinted through his thick glasses. "General Gustini, speak plainly. Is this at all related to the incident on the west coast of Australia a few months ago or not?"

Dennison raised his hand. "Bob, let me answer that." The general grunted and the wall-sized screen went blank. Dennison pressed a button on his laptop, and three desolate images appeared on the display. "It's only because this was the fourth incursion we know of that we were able to detect it at all."

Vice President Newman sputtered in confusion. "Does everyone but me know what's going on?"

"Mister Vice President, we didn't know what we were dealing with. We held the review of the Australian incident on a need-to-know basis, and you were in Europe at the time for the Hungarian prime minister's funeral." Dennison looked pointedly at the President for support.

"Norm, please continue with the briefing," President Jordan barked.

The Vice President's jaw hung open. "You mean this is the fourth time they've invaded America?"

Dennison met the Vice President's eyes. "No, sir, I mean this is the fourth time over the past year our *world* has been invaded—that we know of." He pressed his knuckles on the table until they turned white.

The Vice President choked. "You're proposing that this is an invasion from outer space? That aliens attacked us?"

"Allow me, Director Dennison." Campbell's eyes turned hard as flint as she faced the VP. "Yes, sir, that's exactly what we're saying. We retrieved DNA material we collected from yesterday's disaster site. It does not match any known life form on Earth. Also, we captured excellent imagery of this incursion." She pressed her notepad, and a nondescript, gunmetal gray sphere appeared on the screen. "It's about the length of one of our naval destroyers and a quarter of that in width and height."

The VP loosened his tie and swallowed.

Campbell turned to the Director of the CIA. "Norm, I think you can continue now."

"Eleven months ago, in an isolated city named Norilsk in eastern Siberia, what we now believe to be the first hit occurred. Originally, our intelligence surmised it was a massive power failure in the dead of winter due to a small meteor strike. The temperature hit a low of minus thirty Celsius. Many of the residents froze to death. The survivors babbled about demons rampaging through the town, dragging people away. The Russian government covered up the incident. Many of the survivors were committed to psychiatric facilities, and few dead were ever found.

"Then, seven months ago, there was an incident in Tierra del Fuego. Apparently, the entire population of a small village disappeared. When the Argentinian authorities arrived on site, there wasn't a single soul, dead or alive. They asked us to help. We didn't have much satellite recon down there, but we captured an image of a large... something. It was there on one pass and gone on the next about four hours later.

"The third occurred three-and-a-half months ago in a mining camp outside of Carnarvon, Western Australia. This time, we managed to take pictures of the damn thing taking off." Dennison glanced at General Gustini. "We have a massive joint facility in Alice Springs with the Australians. That base picked up a unique radiation signature." The director made direct eye contact with the President. "Yesterday's event in the southern tier of New York was the fourth incursion."

General Gustini jumped out of his seat and paced. "We've been analyzing the Australian data for months. Yesterday, NORAD sensors identified the same radiation signature. As I mentioned earlier, we launched interceptors but couldn't locate it with traditional radar. Our air defense systems went to full alert, and Griffiss Air Base in Rome, New York, noticed traces of that radiation and pinpointed the source."

The general slumped back into his seat. "The only asset in the area was the Eighty-Seventh Regiment, Second Battalion of the Tenth Mountain Division. They were engaged in small unit exercises in Letchworth State Park and sent to investigate. The main body of the regiment drove south on Route Nineteen arrived after everything ended. The others..." He swallowed the rising bile. "At 19:07 EST, we lost all contact with the vanguard company. They were backed by four Blackhawk helicopters from the Second Aviation Regiment. We also lost communication with the State Police in the same area.

"At 21:13 EST, the Eighty-Seventh arrived on the scene. They found nothing more than the charred remains of the helicopter crews and a few poor souls who look like they were mauled by wolves. From what we can deduce, an enormous EMP fried the Humvees and all electrical equipment."

Gustini's eyes moistened. "Those boys put up a hell of a fight. By the number of shell casings found, they discharged almost all their munitions. It appears they made a final stand on the interstate. We believe there were also civilian casualties. We found a number of private cars and trucks abandoned on the highway."

The President's throat constricted. "Were our men at all effective against this enemy?"

Gustini cleared his throat. "Sir, it's hard to be definitive. But by the presence of non-human blood, we believe there were several enemy causalities."

The VP gaped. "We had over two hundred trained and well-armed soldiers, and maybe we *hurt* a few of them."

Gustini glared at the VP. "Sir, our boys showed that these bastards can bleed. If they can bleed, we'll find a way to kill them. No goddamn Martians are going to attack the USA without us handing their butts to them."

President Jordan pressed his hands on the table and spoke in an icy voice. "Bob, I don't want any damn chest thumping. I want real answers."

Gustini slumped in his chair and punched a button on his laptop to display a detailed image of the UFO. "These pictures were taken by an F-16 from the Hundred-and-Fifty-Eighth Fighter Wing in Burlington. They attempted an intercept at approximately 20:35 EST." A large, oblong object pulling away from the camera in both altitude and distance filled the screen. "An EMI pulse hit the fighters, but their electronics are designed to function through a nuclear blast, so they survived."

The team in the situation room watched four missiles detonate short of the alien vessel. "The F-16s pursued the bogie into Canadian air space where they fired their air-to-air missiles. They relied on sight guidance since the targeting systems failed to lock on. As you can see, the strikes were ineffective. Some form of energy shield protected the bogie," Gustini said and pressed the button again, and the alien craft appeared as a distant dot. "They fired a second salvo, but the bogie outran the jets and missiles."

The President massaged his temples. "Talk to me, Bob. What can we do about this?"

Gustini scratched the close-cropped, iron gray hair on the back of his head. "Sir, these invaders are way ahead of us technology-wise, but they're not invincible. When those missiles hit their shield, the radiation signature dropped ten percent. The eggheads at NSA tell me a massive salvo would penetrate with a ninety percent certainty factor. Our hardened electronics are also resistant to their EMI weapon." He folded his calloused hands together and leaned on the table. "And sir, we did find the splattered remains of some of those creatures. We know they can die."

President Jordan nodded. "Thanks, Bob. I want every resource the Pentagon has working on this." He looked at the FBI Director. "Campbell, this is no isolated town in Siberia. The media is already swarming around outside the quarantine perimeter, and the Washington Press Corp is eating my press secretary alive. What can we do to keep this under wraps for a few weeks? The last thing we need is the country—" He pounded his fist into the palm of his other hand. "No, the whole goddamn world in a panic before we have some answers."

"Mister President, this won't stay quiet long. Right now, only a few of the high-level personnel at the disaster site know the truth. Most of the searchers believe there was a terrorist camp in possession of exotic biological and low-grade nuclear weapons. But, counting civilians, close to a thousand people vanished from the middle of New York State, and as we gear up, more people will have to be brought into the loop."

The President furrowed his brows. "We need time. I may well be asking our people to prepare for war. They should be afraid. Hell, I'm terrified. They deserve the best analysis we can provide, not piecemeal information full of rumors."

Campbell grimaced as she slid a folder down the table. "I thought you might ask for something like this. My people put together the outline of a plan. However, it'll fall apart on close inspection. I assume I'll be the scapegoat when it does." She arched an eyebrow at the President, and her lips tightened into a thin smile. Campbell knew the reputation she built over her long career as a straight-talking, no-nonsense prosecutor and federal judge would be destroyed forever. "I hope this won't affect my pension."

No one smiled at her joke.

President Jordan nodded in solemn assent. "I hope there's a country left to give you a pension."

Her face turned grim, and Campbell sighed. As a former DA, she knew how to argue a weak case. "We build on the biological terrorist attack theme. There are two microbiologists the FBI is tracking. One's an American citizen, and the other's a visiting professor from Turkey. They both have Muslim Brotherhood ties and recently spent time at the Center for Disease Control in Atlanta. We've intercepted a number of suspicious communications, but those two are nowhere near springing a terror attack. We could falsely place them in that locale. A deadly virus gives us the opportunity to maintain the quarantine. It'll keep the press out and explain why we won't release any bodies." She folded her hands in her lap. "Use the time I'm buying you wisely."

President Jordan rose, walked around the conference table, and pressed his face against the screen. The satellite feed displayed on the back of his bald head. He closed his eyes. "People, you heard the lady. Leave no stone unturned. We need solutions." He closed his eyes and his hands curled into fists. "May God bless America and have mercy on those poor souls who are missing."

CHAPTER III
A Brave New World

Broke the deep lethargy within my head
A heavy thunder, so that I upstarted,
Like to a person who by force is wakened;

Dante's Inferno – Canto IV

C'mon mate, time to wake up."
Dante rolled onto his back and spit out the red dirt filling his mouth. He stared up at thick, roiling yellow clouds and gagged on the stench of sulfur in the air.

"G'day. You a Yank?"

Dante dragged himself into a sitting position. His head spun as he tried to focus on the man who had spoken and found him standing behind a shimmering barrier. "Where am I?"

"Good question, that one. One I've been asking meself for the last couple of months. As near as I can tell, this is Hell."

The nausea eased, so Dante stood and squinted in the direction of the voice. "I think there's something wrong with my eyes. You look a little blurry."

"Naw, your eyes are fine. Ya see these posts between us?" the man said as he spread his lean arms out wide.

Blue glowing pillars a couple inches thick and about ten feet high were spaced out about thirty feet apart in both directions as far as he could see. Dante walked toward one of the poles. "Yeah?"

"Well, don't try to touch 'em, and don't try to walk between 'em. The shock kicks like a mule. You'll find yourself on your arse with a nasty headache for your effort."

Dante froze in his tracks. "Thanks for the warning. I'm Dante Carloman."

"Well, except for the circumstances, pleased to meet ya. The name's Kevin Martinel."

Martinel had a full beard and shaggy black hair. All five-and-a-half feet of him slouched, his hands shoved in the pockets of filthy, ragged overalls. The man leaned to one side as if supporting all his weight on his right leg.

Dante felt the presence of someone behind him and looked over his shoulder. Virgil stood there, examining the barrier, then moved close to the fence near Martinel. "Some sort of electric fence?"

"Well, mate, our hosts are a bit fancier than that. Nothing will go through it." The Aussie scratched his beard. "Ya look like the military type. Army?"

Virgil half smiled. "Master Sergeant Virgil Bernius, US Air Force Pararescue, at your service. You sound Australian."

"That I am." Martinel rocked back on his heels as a number of folks stumbled toward the conversation from behind Dante. Many wore combat fatigues. "You Yanks threw military hardware at the bastards." His shoulders slumped. "Looks like the results were about the same as when they hit us. Nothing we had touched 'em."

A small but feral grin crossed Virgil's face. "Well, I blew the brains out of one of those suckers before they got me."

Martinel's sunken eyes lit with fire. "Ya killed one of those hellspawn? That's something I would treasure for a long time."

While they spoke, Dante searched the gathering crowd for Tina. She had stripped off her parka and knelt beside the old man, Reggie. Esther, with her iron gray hair disheveled, worked at her side.

Their eyes met, and Tina rose and brushed off the dirt from her jeans. Her chin quivered as she walked straight to him and buried her head in his chest, sobbing. "Dante, I want to go home." Her shoulders trembled, and he pressed her close.

The enormous enclosure stretched across hundreds of yards devoid of structures or plant life. To Dante's left lay an enormous body of water, and he could just make out the far side. The near shore lay about fifty feet beyond the barrier to his right, and despite its tranquility, the black water smelled like the source of the sulfurous stench in the air. To his right beyond the barrier stood a dull black, domed structure devoid of any architectural flair that stood about six stories high. Beyond them lay a stark, unbroken plain with no visible flora. The desert-like landscape rose in a series of hills culminating in a snowcapped mountain range.

He gave Tina a squeeze and realized hundreds of people now gathered on both sides of the barrier. After a moment of thought, he turned to face the Aussie. "Kevin, how long have you folks been trapped here?"

"It's hard to tell." Martinel scratched his chin under his unkempt beard. "A couple of folks have been counting the days. Best guess is about three months now. The days seem a bit longer than back home."

Someone in the crowd squeaked, "You mean we're on another planet?"

"Yes, ma'am, I do. Occasionally, this sky clears, and you can see the two moons at night. The stars look all different, too."

Another planet? Dante shucked off his coat. *Jesus, this place looks like the surface of the moon.*

A voice shouted, "How about food and water? This foul air sticks in my throat." Another piped in, "Yeah, and what do you folks use for shelter and privies?"

"There ain't no shelters, and there ain't no loos. What you folks can build is what you get. As for food, the big uglies bring in vats of water and some stinkin' gruel at sunrise and sunset every day. It's the same every day." Martinel squeezed his eyes shut and tears trickled down his cheeks. "And there ain't no medicine. Ya get sick... ya die."

A hollow cheeked woman walked up behind Martinel and hugged him. Dante could not determine her age from the grime caked on her.

Virgil stared around the pen with a worried gaze. "What's a 'big ugly'?"

Anger flushed Martinel's face. "They're worse than those devils. They're human. Or at least they look human. Each one is identical, like some sort of clone. They're big; about six-four, as you Yanks measure it, and hairless. They do whatever those hopping demons tell 'em to do, and they kill without remorse in the arena. They never say a word and never show pity." He looked to his left and pointed with his chin. "There're always some of them prowling around."

Dante looked where the Aussie pointed. Three naked, blunt-faced men walked along the outside perimeter of the fence. They possessed mirror-image faces of one another with the physiques of steroid-stuffed body builders. "How many of them are there?"

Martinel shook his head. "Could be fifty; could be a million. Hard to say."

Virgil furrowed his brow and growled. "What did you mean by 'the arena'? Are we here for some grotesque entertainment?"

"Might be, but I don't think so," said Martinel. "Only a few of those harpy creatures watch, and the outcome's always the same. Once every couple weeks, the big uglies mark off an area with these friggin' poles. Twelve poor souls are dragged in and ripped to shreds." His voice tightened. "Men, women, old folks, and sometimes children."

Martinel looked through the shimmering barrier with heartfelt sorrow in his eyes. "May God protect ya. It's your turn now. The Russians said when the Argentinians arrived, the monsters left 'em alone, and the Argentinians the same thing when we arrived. Now we get to rot in this nightmare of a prison and watch you folks die." He stumbled away with a noticeable limp. "This is Hell. God has abandoned us."

"Wait! Russians, Argentinians... How many people are here?" Virgil called after him.

Martinel turned back. "You're a smaller group. You soldier boys must've rattled their cages a bit. All told, there're probably a few thousand of us waiting to die." He glanced at the yellow clouds and sighed. "The sun will set soon. I suggest you prepare a camp as best ya can. Ya got a couple of weeks before the butchering starts."

Virgil walked over toward a dark-skinned man wearing captain's bars who looked ready to spit bullets. Dante and Tina followed, drawn by the security of the imposing military men.

"Master Sergeant Virgil Bernius, Air Force Pararescue. It looks like I'm in your command for a while, sir."

The other officer ignored the civilians and returned the salute. "Captain Rodrigo Cruz. Special Forces, eh? That's good. Hopefully, we can make use of your talents."

Both men glanced at the barriers, and Virgil scuffed the red clay with his boot. "Strangest soil combination I've seen. You thinking tunnel?"

"Yeah. Seems more practical than trying to go over that fence. There's no cover."

"The tunneling will be tough to hide, too. Everything's so open."

Cruz grunted. "That's just one of about a million problems we have." He rolled his neck, sighing through his teeth. "C'mon. I'm going to start organizing the civilians and inventory what we have. Everyone will be better off if they're busy."

"If you don't mind, sir, I'd like to walk the perimeter. See if I can pick out a likely spot. Those hills look the most promising for an escape destination."

Cruz shuddered. "Yeah. I sure as hell don't wanna cross that cesspool unless I have to." He nodded to Virgil and strode off, giving orders.

Virgil turned to Dante. "I wanted to thank you."

"For what?" Dante cocked his head to the side. Tina rubbed her red-rimmed eyes but didn't release her hold on his arm.

"I saw what you tried to do for me back in New York," said Virgil. "It takes a lot of courage to go after a terror who can shrug off M4 rounds with nothing but a hammer."

Dante let out a bark of laughter. "Or stupidity. I... I had to do something. That monster might've killed you." A breeze wafted foul smelling air across the field and he gagged. "We gotta get outta here."

"We're working on that. How about the two of you walk with me for a while? I want to get the lay of the land and study our captors."

The students agreed and walked with the soldier along the fence. Tina kept a grip on Dante's bicep as they moved, causing their feet to tangle every so often. Dante's hand unconsciously covered hers. Meanwhile, three more of the big uglies passed them along the other side of the barrier, their steps in perfect time.

Virgil mumbled, "Damn, they're built like freakin' NFL linebackers." Then he took a deep breath and shouted, "Hey, buddy, how come your dick's so small?"

The brutes tensed but never paused.

Virgil rubbed his chin. "Hmm... now that was interesting."

"Like how to get us all killed? What do you think you're doing?" Dante gasped. "Those things could take me out with a sneeze!"

Virgil snorted. "Listen, kid, you have to watch everything. We're in big trouble here, and we need all the information we can get." He chuckled. "I learned two things. First, they understand us. The eyes on the one I yelled at tightened a bit when I insulted him. Second, they don't spend much time outside. They're pale as albinos and getting a nasty looking sunburn. And there's not much of a sun." Virgil studied the distant rising landscape and pointed. "How far do you think that mountain is from here?"

Tina furrowed her eyebrows. "Last summer, I vacationed with my folks in the mountains near Boone, North Carolina. The mountains down there look a lot like these." Her face twisted in distaste. "Except for the complete lack of trees. I'd guess it's around twelve miles."

"Over this ground, I could be there in two hours." Dante groaned as he picked up a rock and studied it.

"So you're a marathoner?" Virgil scratched the back of his head. "It doesn't look like you'll get much of an opportunity to run one here."

Dante glared around at their prison. "Not likely." He whipped the stone at the invisible barrier. It bounced back without a sound.

Virgil pulled at his lower lip in thought. "Do that again."

"Do what?"

"Throw another rock, this time as high as you can."

Dante shrugged and threw another stone. The three watched it arc close to thirty feet high and bounce back like the first stone.

Virgil scratched the back of his head. "What is this thing? It doesn't stop sound waves and barely distorts light. An object is stopped dead, but the breeze blows right through." He strode toward the barrier, pausing before he reached it. Virgil took a step toward the barrier and collapsed in a heap. Dante pulled him away from the fence and stood over him as he lay unmoving.

After several seconds, Virgil moaned and staggered to his feet. "That stung. Definitely need to find the off switch before I'll try that again." He rolled his shoulders and glared at the big uglies, who stopped to watch him with blank, cold eyes from the other side. Then he turned back to the two students. "There's nothing else to see here. Let's go back and join the others."

Captain Cruz had marked the outline of a camp with stones and everyone was digging. Even the children pawed at the dirt with army helmets and stones.

That evening, a large procession of big uglies and several harpies exited the domed compound. Without any noticeable signal, they split into four groups. One led by a couple of the harpies approached the Americans' barrier. Two of the blue poles winked out, and a dozen large vats suspended beneath long white pods floated in.

Dante marveled at the anti-gravity devices that moved and deposited the containers without a sound or a bump. He examined one, looking for its power source, when a shout startled him. A half-dozen burly farmers rushed the open gap in the barrier. Two froze in mid-stride by the harpies wielding their sinister tubes. The other four tried to plow through the hairless guards. Dante blanched.

All the farmers possessed solid builds, but their struggle ended in seconds. The large, hairless men became blurs of motion, smashing the Americans with relentless blows. When the last bloodied farmer hit the ground, a harpy hopped to the fight scene. The creature chittered and pointed a palm-sized device at each beaten man's chest. A glowing, blue disk the size of a dime embedded itself in their flesh. The men, still conscious, bellowed in pain and fear as the device burrowed under their skin as if alive.

The harpy hissed and sprang twenty feet backwards. It pressed a device on its belt, and the train of pods that supported the vats floated out. The poles glowed blue again, and the alien captors paraded away.

Captain Cruz and Virgil exchanged meaningful glances as they studied the vats. Cruz snapped an order, and the soldiers helped the civilians form lines for the food. When his turn came, Dante wrinkled his nose at the contents. The porridge had no flavor and the water was tepid. He scooped the slush with his hands just like everyone else. They soon drained the containers.

The soldiers then sprang into action. They flipped over the casks and jumped on them. Three shattered before a couple of aliens with a large troop of big uglies rushed out of their edifice to the prison stockade.

Hoots and hoarse cheers rose from the Australian prison camp. "That-a-way, Yanks! Show those bloody bastards ya can still spit in their eyes!"

Tina exchanged a fierce smile with Dante. The demon creatures glowered at their prisoners while the transporter pods whisked the nine remaining battered tubs away. The remains of the rest lay scattered on the ground. She hissed into his ear, "Those monsters aren't all-knowing, and they're not invincible."

Dante grinned back, but it vanished when he saw the Australians. Most looked emaciated and beaten. "Is that going to be us in a few months?"

Tina shuddered and bit her lower lip.

"Hey… Dante, a moment," said a familiar voice.

Dante recognized one of the bedraggled Aussies as Martinel. He approached the barrier, wary of getting too close. "Ya best tell your folks to avoid getting tagged. It's a death mark."

Dante snapped his head around. The downed men seemed okay. They stood on shaky legs in a wide circle, probing the spot on their chests where they were shot. "They don't seem to be hurt too bad."

Martinel's shoulders slumped. "Yeah, well, it's death nonetheless. You're looking at the first bunch who'll be murdered in the arena. By my count, six more'll be selected before the bloody show starts."

Dante shuddered and motioned to Virgil, who then caught Cruz's attention. The three moved to the side to talk privately Cruz sighed and contemplated the harpies as they skittered into their building. He kicked at the stony dirt in frustration. "There's gotta be a way to beat them."

"We'll find it," Virgil growled.

Cruz stared through the fence at the Aussies, who aimlessly milled around. "But when? A few weeks of eating this crap and we'll be as malnourished as they are. I doubt we'll have the strength to lift our arms, much less fight the bastards."

Cruz ground his teeth in frustration and summoned the men and women he'd tapped as leaders. He directed his troops to fashion crude items from the shards of the smashed vats. Several civilians joined in uninvited. Others watched with curiosity.

The next morning, the roiling yellow clouds yielded to a red sun. Twelve vats arrived, escorted by over three-hundred big uglies who remained at the fence and watched. The prisoners took their time eating. Dante thought the gruel tasted a little sweeter as he watched their large pale captors turn pink in the unforgiving sun.

CHAPTER IV
Michael

Always before him many of them stand:
They go by turns each one unto the judgement;
They speak, and hear, and then are downward hurled.

Dante's Inferno – Canto V

Tina slumped against a low wall made of nothing more than packed clay. She pressed balled fists against her red-rimmed eyes as she sobbed. "It's not right."

Esther sighed as she sat down and pulled the young woman to her. "We did all we could for Mister D'Annunzio." She glanced at the dead man's wife and eleven-year-old son. The mother and boy clung to each other in mourning. "I'm afraid we're going to watch a lot more people die."

A single tear trickled down Esther's dust-covered face as she watched her husband struggle to his feet and shuffle to the bereaved family. A bittersweet smile crossed her wrinkled face as she watched him lay gentle hands on the boy's shoulders and spoke soft words of comfort.

Tina felt Esther's grip tighten and followed the old woman's eyes. "Esther, what's wrong with Reggie? He seems to be getting a lot weaker."

"His kidneys are failing. Dialysis kept him comfortable these last couple years." The elder woman shuddered. "But that's out of reach. I expect he'll follow Mister D'Annunzio within the week."

"I'm sure you're wrong. We'll... we'll think of something."

Esther looked into the earnest young woman's eyes. "What've they been teaching you in that gold-plated university of yours? I was a doctor for over thirty years. You have to face facts as they are, not as you want them."

Her eyes regarded the makeshift infirmary. Her medical staff consisted of four army medics and a wide-eyed, second-year medical student. The "hospital" was nothing more than a few winter coats laid in a shallow ditch and a single low wall of packed reddish clay. They had no medicine or antibiotics; they didn't even have clean bandages. Tina squeezed the old woman's hands.

Esther's eyes grew moist. "No, my dear, in a few short days, I won't have that wonderful old coot to hold."

A disturbance at the energy barrier interrupted the conversation. A pack of big uglies marched into the camp with one of their floating sleds. Her attention shifted to the soldiers as Captain Cruz assembled his company at parade rest.

A gang of angry men led by two burly truck drivers blocked the path of the big uglies. They shouted threats until the harpies shot them with blue disks. The demonstrators fled behind the soldiers, leaving the wounded men writhing on the ground.

The big ugly aliens continued toward the hospital without pause. Everyone retreated except the dead man and Reggie. The old man supported himself against the wall and asked in a calm voice, "Can I help you, gentlemen?"

A big ugly quirked his hairless brow and worked his jaw for a few seconds. In a voice that sounded like a file scraping across a steel bar, he spoke. "All nonfunctioning biological forms are taken to the masters' laboratory for analysis—"

"You leave my dad alone, you monster!" a child's voice raged. A jagged stone flew through the air and gashed the cheek of the alien who had spoken. The big ugly's eyes narrowed, and he turned. A boy with tear-soaked cheeks ran over and stood beside the dead man, defiance showing on every line of his face. The alien raised the marker weapon but twisted his head to the side when he heard the plaintive wail of a woman.

"Tommy, no! Please, God, don't hurt my baby." With terror-filled eyes, she scrambled to the boy and hugged him to her chest.

The alien shrugged and pointed his weapon.

Reggie stumbled in front of the woman and the boy, his arms outstretched. "Shoot me, my friend. I'll take the child's place."

Confusion crossed the clone's face. "The human behind you assaulted a guardian. It is the master's law that such activities make them participants in the blood passing."

"Then you must mark me. I'm the one who threw the stone. The boy just shouted at you."

The big ugly touched his cut and tasted his own blood from his finger tip, then stared at the old man. "I am recently removed from growth stasis and have not yet made my blood passing. Perhaps there is much I yet need to learn." He fired the marker into Reggie's chest. The old man crumpled and fell, gasping, to the clay.

———— ◆ ————

As the big uglies first approached, Dante dragged Tina and Esther away from the infirmary. When Reggie fell, he couldn't hold the women back from rushing to the old man's aid. Dante followed and hovered while they ministered to Reggie. Dante watched as the big uglies unceremoniously dumped Mister D'Annunzio's body on the hover sled.

"Why did he do it?"

Dante almost jumped out of his skin. The alien with the gashed cheek regarded Reggie with a perplexed frown.

"You're awful talkative for a big ugly." Dante gulped and stared pie-eyed at the albino giant. *Oh, God. I shouldn't have said that.*

However, no retribution came. Flat eyes swung in Dante's direction. "Why do you call us big uglies? We are the product of human DNA. The term has a derogatory connotation, yet we are identical to you."

"Ahh, well, you guys are all big, hairless, and walk around in the nude. If we knew your names, we could call you that, but you all look the same."

The alien furrowed his brow. "The same? All of our chromosomes are ideally matched, but I shared the gestation pod with only two others. What name would you give me?"

Dante's knees felt weak as he stared at the alien. "A-a name?"

"Yes."

His childhood best friend's name came to mind. "Uh... how about Mike?"

"Mike? That is a shortened form of Michael, a creature from a powerful species your people call angels. He was a defender. I accept. I am Michael. What is your name?"

"Ahh, Dante."

"Now, Dante, answer my question."

Dante's mind swirled with fear and confusion. "Huh?" Nearby, Esther and Tina gaped as they watched the exchange.

Annoyance crossed Michael's blunt face and he pointed to Reggie. "Why did he do it? Given the trajectory of the missile, he could not have been the source." He pointed at the two women. "And why do they linger over a marked man? His blood will be used to honor our passing in two planetary rotation cycles."

"I... guess the answer is love."

"That is an ambiguous term. It means nothing to me."

Dante shuddered but squared his shoulders and met the creature's eyes. "To understand us, you must understand love." A half smile creased his face as he recalled a quote from his youth. "No greater love hath any man than to lay down his life for another."

Michael looked over his shoulder. Most of his pack had left except for two who watched the events unfold. "I need further study." He turned without another word and headed toward the barrier.

Without thinking, Tina leapt to her feet and ran after him. "Michael." She stopped short when he swung around to face her. "We need medical supplies and shelter. Please, help us."

Michael hesitated, then strode in silence through the barrier's opening. The blue lights relit, and the alien procession with the corpse vanished into the giant hive-like building.

Virgil sauntered over to where Dante stood. "Well, you found a gabby one. Keep him talking. We have no information about our captors or this hellhole we're in. Anything you can get from these guardians could save lives."

That evening, when food and water arrived, Dante recognized Michael as part of the escort. The wound from the stone had closed, but the discolored scar differentiated him from his brethren. As the pods slid into the prison camp, Dante met Virgil's eyes. The other man nodded, and they approached the barrier where the scarred alien stood.

"Hi, Michael." Dante noticed the two big uglies standing beside Michael. Their jaws tightened at those words.

"Greetings, Dante. In my research, I found a partial match of your name in something identified as a major literary work of your planet. Are you the author of the *Divine Comedy?*"

"Ahh, no. That was written over seven hundred years before I was born."

"Is that beyond the normal life expectancy of your species?"

"Yeah, by a factor of ten." Dante spat on the ground. "And in this place, it's more like a factor of a hundred."

Michael tilted his head. "You put more value on an extended existence than the honor of our blood passing."

Dante glared at the towering alien. "You got that damn straight. We have no interest in participating in your grotesque ceremony for those bouncy little harpies you call masters. And—"

A soft hand touched Dante's shoulder; Tina stood at his side. She spoke in a calm voice to Michael. "We humans do not fear death because when these shells of our bodies cease to function, our souls are freed to journey to Heaven. But we don't wish to be murdered in your arena. We cherish liberty and the ability to choose."

Dante noticed Michael leaning forward to catch Tina's words. The three aliens regarded each other in confusion.

"First 'love', now 'soul' and 'liberty'. These are terms I do not comprehend," Michael mused. "When I investigated your name, they were referenced often in that file labeled *Dante's Divine Comedy*. I must do more research. I found a reference to Michael in that repository. It also mentioned that the angel Michael had two podmates. My podmates have chosen those names for themselves." He turned to his left and then his right. "They are Gabriel and Rafael."

Dante nodded at the two identical creatures flanking Michael. He smiled then shook his head as he turned to the man by his side. "May I introduce my friend, Virgil?"

Michael straightened his stance. "Yes, Dante's guide through the Inferno. It will be a pleasure to take your blood in the next passing."

Virgil snapped, "I'll be no easy meat for the likes of you."

Confusion crossed Michael's eyes. "But your DNA will be added to our chromo-repository for further guardian refinements. It is the honored alternative to the rejected material left in the other pens. They are maintained for long-term bio viability analysis."

Virgil's mouth tightened. "I'll die a free man rather than live the life of a slave."

Michael regarded his podmates and then at the humans. "Free? Slave? Two more words with meaning I do not understand."

The sergeant met the alien's eyes. "Then just watch us and learn. There's another document you should read. It's titled the United States Declaration of Independence." He spun on his heels and stalked off.

"Michael, why are you so talkative while no one else of your kind says a word?" Dante asked.

The large alien stood a little straighter. "My podmates and I are prototypes." He paused to find the right word. "We've been programmed — trained — to infiltrate your planetary society in preparation for its subjugation. So we must be conversant with your dialogue and literature."

Dante's lips thinned in a grim smile. *I hope the rest of these harpies' war plans are as sophisticated.* He wasn't sure oversized, hairless albinos spouting lines from ancient books would blend well in the streets of New York. He nodded to Michael, grabbed Tina's hand, and hurried after Virgil. "Hey, what happened to diplomacy and trying to build contacts and all that other stuff?"

Virgil paused and laid his hand on the younger man's shoulder. "We have planted the seed of curiosity. I looked into the eyes of that creature and saw a man. Whether we can reach that man is another question. Today there's a chance, and that chance didn't exist yesterday." He walked toward Captain Cruz, who watched him with steady eyes.

Dante moved to the food line with Tina. They held each other's hands.

The next morning, they found one of the 10th Mountain Division's medical backpacks and a tarp inside the blue barrier.

CHAPTER V
The Arena

Cerberus, monster cruel and uncouth,
With his three gullets like a dog is barking
Over the people that are there submerged.

Dante's Inferno – Canto VI

Fear clutched at Dante's gut as he spotted Michael, Gabriel, and Rafael standing at the blue energy barrier. He hadn't seen them in two days. On the plain beyond them, other big uglies labored to enclose the dusty expanse within sight of the human's prison with more of those strange poles. He knew from the Aussie, Martinel, that people would die in the arena today.

Dante approached the fence, forcing a casual stride. "Hi, guys. This a… social call?"

"Do I have a soul?" Michael blurted without any preamble.

"Huh?" Dante's mouth gaped open.

Michael huffed with impatience. "We have the same genetic code as your species, and all the documentation I have scanned says that a soul is part of you. Do I have one?"

Dante gazed up at the yellow cloud-filled sky, quirked his brows, and snorted. "If someone told me a few weeks ago that I'd be having a philosophical discussion with a giant clone on an alien planet, I would've had the poor sod committed." He met Michael's eyes and found a confused intelligence staring back at him. "All right, big guy… do you know the difference between good and evil?"

Michael's lips slimmed to a tight line. "My understanding is unclear. Some things were called both good and evil in the same writings. It contradicted itself. Show me good."

Dante scratched his two-week-old beard and looked around. He spotted Esther cradling Reggie's head, rocking him back and forth. They gazed at each other with unabashed love. "There. That is good."

Michael craned his neck and observed the old couple in silence. "Is it because the reclining one claimed the honor of the blood passing from the smaller human who sought it from me?"

Dante's eyes flared in anger. "No. That man's name is Reggie, and he wants nothing more than to spend the rest of his days in peace with the woman he loves and be home with his children and grandchildren. But he stepped between you and that boy to protect the child. He knows full well the brutal death awaiting him in that damn arena of yours." He pointed his finger at the alien, who probably outweighed him by a hundred pounds. "Go… go have your freakin' blood sport, but remember that these are real people you'll be murdering so your puppet masters can get their jollies."

Michael twisted his head to his two brethren. "Ensure that the new barriers are secure. The blood passing begins soon."

Rafael and Gabriel grunted and walked toward the pack of harpies and guardians gathered at the arena's site.

In the meantime, Michael turned back to Dante. "I wanted to speak to you privately before the blood passing starts. I should be content that I will soon be a full guardian, but I am disquieted. I've had limited REM cycles and have taken minimal nourishment since we last spoke.

The more of your literature I absorb, the more I want, and the more confused I become. My masters have an artificial intelligence system called Dis. It has full access to your planet's Internet and has retrieved millions of documents. However, Dis is unable to resolve the inconsistencies in that data." He glanced warily over his shoulder. "Dis designed me and the other infiltrator prototypes to interpret the information. I have absorbed much. I read your J.R.R. Tolkien, C.S. Lewis, and Thomas Aquinas, and I think what my masters plan to do is wrong. It's..." A look of anguish crossed his face. "It's time."

Dante jumped back as eleven other big uglies, followed by a couple dozen harpies, joined Michael. The nearby poles went dark, and the aliens entered the human camp. Some of the marked men screamed and attempted to run.

A matched number of guardians squeezed a device in the palms of their hands, and those who fled fell, twitching. The other guardians glanced at their devices and strode to other marked men. Each targeted man screamed in pain and froze. Michael approached Reggie and raised his palmed device.

"Please don't. A shock like that will kill him," Esther pleaded as she cradled her husband, who lay motionless with a yellow pallor to his skin.

"If he ceases to function before the blood passing, another will be selected. Only by taking the life of a living unit can the blood passing be conducted," Michael replied in a flat voice.

"Then you must help me. Please, I need to know my death saved another," Reggie wheezed in a thin, reedy voice.

Michael regarded the skeletal man. "Is this a manifestation of what you term love?"

Reggie reached out with a quivering hand and stroked his wife's tear-streaked face. "Perhaps it is."

Michael pondered those words for a second. "It is not necessary for you to be immobilized for transport to the blood passing ceremony." He lowered his hand with the strange device in it. "Follow me."

"Sorry… you'll have to carry me. I don't have the strength to walk."

Michael swung his head back and forth in a silent struggle with himself. He glanced over his shoulder. Michael's eleven brethren dragged twitching humans out of the prison camp. He crouched and gently lifted the old man from Esther's lap, cradling the frail man against his chest.

Esther leapt to her feet and clung to her husband's hand. "Reggie, don't leave me. I love you. What am I going to do without you?"

Tears welled in the old man's eyes, and he squeezed her hand back. "Darling, these people need you. You're the only doctor they have." He released his grip and draped his thin arm over his captor's shoulder. "C'mon, Michael, let's get this done."

Michael turned to follow the other Guardians when a soft touch on his arm froze him in place. Esther looked at him with sad, tired eyes. "Michael, be gentle with him. He's a good man."

The Guardian looked at her, confusion showing on his squared face. "I… I will wear his blood with honor."

Esther's hand slid from Michael's arm, and she dropped to the ground and wept.

———— ◆ ————

Turmoil threatened to overcome Michael as he reached out to touch her shoulder, but pulled it back and fled the prison with Reggie. He glanced at the frail man in his arms as he tried to sort out the strange feelings.

Reggie closed his eyes and clutched a silver cross hanging around his neck on a chain. The old man muttered in a paper-thin voice, "Our Father, who art in Heaven..."

"What are you doing?" Michael asked. Although he knew he should be setting his thoughts on the blood passing, curiosity overcame him.

"I'm preparing to meet my God," Reggie whispered.

"Ahh, yes. I acquired detailed information about the soul. I... I hope you enter Paradise and not the Inferno. The description sounds much more pleasant."

A weak smile crossed Reggie's face. "I hope so, too." He sobered, and his next words caught in his throat. "Michael, I'm afraid. Will the 'blood passing' take long?"

"The more blood spilled, the greater the honor. I... I will be quick, Reggie." Michael choked on the rest of the words embedded in his brain. He felt the old man's heart flutter against his chest and saw the pleading in his eyes. New thoughts battled old ones in his mind. *This is wrong!*

Michael was the last Guardian to enter the marked off area. The other humans selected for the blood passing had been unceremoniously dumped in a line along one side. The Guardian initiates arranged themselves along the opposite side. Rafael and Gabriel met his eyes with unsettled glances. Michael returned a thin-lipped smile and then shuddered with disgust at the sight of the other nine.

He could see their excitement. Michael sighed at the sight. *They are still Guardians and are acting very un-Guardian-like. Perhaps that's why I—*

He felt a compulsion like a tidal wave rise within him, dulling his thoughts to all except one. *Kill, rend, wash myself in my prey's blood.*

Reggie looked up at him. "Michael, what's happening?"

Michael glowered death at the helpless man. Fearless eyes returned his glare, and the blood lust melted away. He trembled with warring emotions and looked at the other trapped humans. Most of them were now on their feet.

He returned his attention to the old man. "It will be over soon. You... you must stand now and face me."

"I don't think I can," came the reply.

Michael felt something he had never experienced before as moisture dampened his cheeks. "You must or another will be selected."

"Then help me, my friend... one last time."

Michael eased the old man to his feet. Reggie stumbled, and Michael held him upright. The elderly man pulled the chain with the worn silver cross over his head with shaky hands. "Here. I want you to have this."

"What is it?"

"It's the symbol of my God. It's given me a lot of comfort through the years. Maybe it'll do the same for you." He coughed and held out the cross.

"No one has ever given me a gift. I don't have any possessions of my own. I—"

Michael's head snapped back as the violent compulsion seized his mind, and he roared with the other Guardians. Eleven Guardians charged at the trapped men with almost inhuman quickness. His own hands trembled as he raised them to Reggie's throat.

The old man choked out a gasp, but he stared at the large clone with courageous acceptance. Michael could not meet those eyes. His arms jerked, and he took a ragged breath as he eased Reggie to the ground. He cradled the old man in his lap as Esther had done.

Rafael and Gabriel gave him a questioning look and slowed as they ran by. Then their eyes went blank as the compulsion drove them on. Michael squeezed his eyes shut but couldn't stop his ears from hearing the sounds of snapping bones and screams for mercy filling the air. He hugged Reggie in a protective cocoon.

"Michael, I forgive you. Do what you must," said the old man.

"I cannot kill... for the blood passing. I am defective."

"No, my friend, you cannot murder. You have... a soul. Press your hand on the sides of my neck. It'll close off my carotid artery, and I will die. Just promise that you'll look after my Esther. She's not as tough as she thinks she is."

"You don't know what you ask of me. I am programmed to kill humans."

"I think your former masters kinda botched that, didn't they?"

Michael stared at his fellow Guardians. They tore limbs off of the dead humans and smeared themselves with blood. He noted with a confused pride that his two podmates did not partake in the revelry. They met his eyes and walked toward him with a single streak of blood across their chests.

"I promise," Michael choked out.

His iron grip closed around the old man's throat. Reggie opened his hand, dropped the cross in Michael's lap, and died. Rafael and Gabriel stood in silence above him.

Michael did not look at them, his eyes focused on the silver cross in his hand. He sighed, pricked the dead man's finger, and placed a drop of blood onto his chest. Michael then lifted Reggie's corpse and shouldered past his podmates to the shimmering barrier. He faced the human prison camp and spotted Esther clinging to Tina, transfixed by the horror they had just witnessed. He bowed to her, turned, and walked back toward the grey, seamless building. Rafael and Gabriel followed, and the three strode past the Guardians rolling in the trampled gore of the human remains.

Gabriel spoke first. "How did you overcome the compulsion? I could think of nothing but tearing flesh, and yet you resisted. How?"

Michael hesitated before speaking. "I felt it. The

hunger to kill. I had my victim helpless in my hands, and then he called me by my name. I clung to that with all my will, and the first compulsion vanished. The second time, it was like a tempest that took me by surprise, but I focused on my gift. I knew if I could resist this evil, it meant I possessed a soul. I fought that compulsion with every fiber of my being and won." As he passed the masters, he lifted his chin and spoke to his podmates. "Today, I received an incredible gift from this human. Today, he taught me to be a free man."

"I don't think the masters will like this. You will be labeled defective, and they will reclaim your biological material," Rafael hissed.

"We should use words properly. You mean they will kill me. Yes, they will try." Michael sighed, his eyes unfocused. "And they will probably succeed. But I will die a free man with a free will. No one can take that from me now."

"That is more important than serving the masters?" Gabriel furrowed his brow in confusion.

"It feels wrong to do much of what I am commanded to do." Michael groped for the right words and declared, "I have come to the conclusion that what I am programmed to do is evil. I find it much more satisfying to converse with the humans and do things that help them."

"Not so loud." Rafael gave the masters a wary glance as they passed. "I felt a great unease when I crushed the life out of my human opponent. He begged for mercy, and I hesitated. But I thought all would become clear and feel right after I completed the blood passing." He groaned and shook his head. "It did not. I… I feel sick." He looked to Michael with a fire burning in his eyes. "Teach me what you have learned."

Gabriel nodded in silent agreement.

The masters, chittering into small, oblong tubes, paused as the three walked by. The fanged creatures glanced at each other and huddled.

CHAPTER VI
The Hive

Within we entered without any contest;
And I, who inclination had to see
What the condition such a fortress holds,

Dante's Inferno – Canto IX

Michael approached the hive-shaped building with trepidation and clutched Reggie's body tight to his chest. This place had been his home since he became aware, but now he saw it as a nest of evil. He palmed the pad beside the entrance used by the clones. Their collective DNA was identical, and the entry pad had been programmed to it.

Michael slipped through the door and glanced up. The featureless walls rose six stories. Those heights housed the masters and the masters alone. Few Guardians were allowed up there. Michael spotted no movement and sighed with relief. He paused and studied the lifeless body in his arms and the religious chain wrapped around his left hand.

"Come on. This way." With his two podmates at his back, Michael strode down the ramp to the subterranean levels. The sole illumination in the tunnels came from pulsating blue tubes stretched across the flat ceiling mere inches above his head. From the imprints on his mind, he knew it bore no resemblance to what humans called homes.

Narrow passages honeycombed out in all directions in direct contrast to the open space aboveground, but Michael followed the route to the biological specimen disposal unit three levels lower without error. The harpies had imprinted the layout, with the exception of their aerie, on the mind of each clone upon creation.

He paused when he reached his destination. "Podmates, return to your stasis chambers. If you remain with me, you risk my fate."

Rafael glanced around. "We tied ourselves to your fate when we left the blood passing ceremony at your side."

"The human literature we have shared makes me feel alive," Gabriel added before shaking his head. "When in stasis, I dream now. I dream of having family with a real mother and father. And brothers." He met Michael's eyes and pressed his palm on the door seal, which slid open with a hiss. "I will stand by your side forever. Your fate will be ours, too."

Michael glanced at Gabriel and Rafael, and his eyes softened. *I think the correct human word is affection. The masters will view me as defective and reclaim my biological components. My... brothers choose to stand by me, even though it will mean their deaths as well.*

He walked toward the examination platform and paused. *No, I will not desecrate him like this.* Michael clutched the lifeless form close to his chest. "They won't have him." Michael glared at the automated analysis machine. He knew it would remove every organ and record the detailed biometric data. He spotted a low table across the room and placed Reggie there.

"Michael, must you go out of your way to anger the masters?" Rafael hissed as he gave the door a nervous glance.

"Yes." Michael touched the thin scar on his face. "I choose to be human, and I will act as one until I die."

"Why do you still have that scar? The medical system should have erased it."

"I stopped it. I wanted to be different."

Rafael slitted his eyes. "Well, you are, and it looks wrong."

"I think it looks right." Gabriel picked up a razor-sharp incision tool from the examination platform and slashed his own face. "I will be different, too. I also choose to be human."

Rafael gasped and then sighed. "My existence would be boring without you two." A doleful look crossed his face as he squeezed his brother's shoulders. "We will die because of your impetuousness. But I will be with you no matter what may come."

Michael and Gabriel glanced at each other and nodded. The former unwound the cross wrapped around his hand and hung it over his neck. "The Guardian blood passing sickened me. This becoming human makes me feel alive."

Gabriel wiped at the blood oozing down his cheek and studied the dead man. "Humans shroud their bodies. Do you think it would be all right if I took something from your gift giver?"

"This is but the shell of Reggie. His soul is no longer present. He would not mind."

Gabriel sat the dead man up and removed his frayed sports jacket. A battered wallet fell to the floor.

Michael retrieved the billfold. His two podmates leaned over as he examined the contents. "Look, it's an image of Reggie with another human." He pointed to a familiar figure in the picture. "I think this is the one named Esther. From their interaction with each other, I believe they were what humans call mates." He narrowed his eyes. "I promised Reggie I would protect her."

"That is a vow you will have a difficult time keeping since I expect our lives as humans will end before the sun sets today." Rafael gave the door a nervous glance.

Michael flipped to the next photo: a large number of humans with a smiling Reggie and Esther in the middle.

Gabriel rubbed his chin and added with mounting excitement, "That must be their family. I absorbed much information about those relationships while in stasis. It is the foundation of human society."

Michael handed the wallet to Gabriel and closed his eyes. "Families watch over each other. That is what Reggie asked of me. He wanted me to be family to Esther."

Gabriel put the wallet back in the jacket pocket and grinned. "I vow to watch over you, so that makes you my brother."

"Perhaps Esther is our mother, then," Rafael stuttered as his cheeks reddened.

"I like that." Michael grabbed the forearms of his two brothers. "I will miss you when I die." Tears welled in his eyes. "I am sorry. I will be the cause of your death."

"No sorrow, my brother. I'm a free man. Come, let us await our end in stasis. I want to learn as much about families as I can before the end."

Michael snarled. "I will not surrender so easily. I say we gather what food we can and escape. We can hide in the mountains until we determine our next steps."

"Or perish there," Rafael retorted as he wrung his hands.

Michael smoothed Reggie's hair. "We're dead anyway."

Gabriel fingered the material of the old jacket. "I think we'll have a chance. I learned wilderness survival in one instruction segment, and the masters collected much equipment when they raided the human world."

Rafael nodded. "We wait until the sky darkens. It will do little to hide us from their scanners, but the blood passing means they will awaken twelve new prototypes today. They will be occupied with that and less attentive to other things."

Michael grunted, eyeing both of them. "Gather what we need, but do not draw attention. I will retrieve artifacts and information about this planet the masters have collected. It might be useful. We meet at the exit an hour after the human feeding time."

The three podmates left the room, and a blue light in the ceiling winked out. Michael's stomach churned, but he forced himself to walk with a casual stride down the ramp to the next level. Guardians, when not outside, slumbered in stasis, leaving the passages devoid of activity. Masters rarely ventured outside their aeries but could still appear at any time.

Michael located the storeroom he sought and palmed the door. A ragged breath escaped him when it slid open. Stepping inside, he regarded the tables and shelves. Michael's heart sank to see most of the artifacts in pieces. He wandered from table to table, not knowing what he sought.

He paused at a display where several dull brown garments lay. Curiosity overcame him and Michael fingered one of the suits. The silky smoothness of the material surprised him, and he glanced at the footed part of the one-piece suit. They appeared to be made for a creature of his configuration but much smaller.

Humans wear such things to protect themselves from the elements, he recalled. He pulled at the elastic material. Why not? The seam in the front slid open, and as he pulled it up his legs, his feet felt like they were on a cushion. He pushed his arms through the sleeves and shrugged his massive shoulders as he closed the seal. Upon stretching, the garment conformed to his every movement. *Now that is interesting.*

Michael shoved several more of the suits into a storage bag the masters used and continued exploring. He found a collection of devices that seemed whole but could not determine their purpose. As the evening hour approached, he looped the bag over his shoulder. Disappointment creased his face as he left.

I found nothing useful here except for these marvelous garments. He rolled his shoulders. He liked the way the suit felt against his skin. Even his hard, calloused feet felt soothed.

Michael approached the exit with his senses keyed for danger, though he'd chosen an unused pathway. Once, he ducked into a storage room as a trio of freshly spawned Guardians marched down the hall, oblivious to everything around them. Michael didn't relax until he neared the exit and spotted Gabriel hunched on the ground with one of the humans' backpacks. He glanced over his shoulder for any sign of movement.

Seeing none, he trotted toward his podmate. "Look what I found, Gabriel... What's wrong?" His podmate did not move.

Michael realized the danger too late. He froze in mid-stride as pain exploded from every nerve ending in his body. A master dropped from the ceiling and fired an imprisonment weapon at him. He choked out, "Run!" as he spotted Rafael approaching from another tunnel.

Instead of fleeing, Rafael roared with rage and charged, wielding a large grain sack as a weapon. He swung the sack at the master with the gun, sending the creature sailing into the far wall with a sickening crunch. Its imprisonment weapon clattered to the floor. Three masters leapt from hidden perches and dragged Rafael to the ground. Michael watched in impotent horror as they slashed and gouged his brother with talons and fangs.

Rafael's balled fists struck back in stoic silence. More masters bounded into the room, and he vanished beneath a writhing mass. A charged ion smell filled the air, and Rafael's doomed struggle ended.

CHAPTER VII
Family

O ye who have undistempered intellects,
Observe the doctrine that conceals itself
Beneath the veil of the mysterious verses!

Dante's Inferno – Canto IX

Three unconscious clones arrived on the floating sleds with the morning meal rations. Angry shouts grew from the disquieted crowd as people noticed the motionless forms.

"I saw what these animals did to my Thomas. Let's do the same to them." The mob edged forward behind a distraught middle-aged woman.

Dante stood over the prostrate clone with a thin scar on his right cheek and motioned for everyone to stop. "I recognize this one. He was with Reggie." He looked at the ragged scabs and the clothing on the other two and pleaded, "People, don't be stupid. There's a story here."

Virgil stepped up beside him. "You heard the man. Back off. Now!" He squinted in curiosity at the three unmoving figures. "That one looks like he just finished wrestling a pride of lions, and your buddy with the scar's wearing some damned spandex body suit."

Dante shook his head in amazement. "Two of them have backpacks, and one looks like US Army issue."

Virgil bent down to examine the trio further. "They're alive, anyway. Maybe we can get some answers when they come to."

The mob slunk away when Captain Cruz arrived with a squad of soldiers. The men formed a circle around the clones. Cruz stank of sulfur, and his clothing stuck to his skin. "What the hell's going on here? Who are these guys?"

Virgil noticed the captain's clothes and asked, "What happened to you?"

Cruz spat. "The tunnel's not going to work. We hit water about six feet down and the whole damn thing flooded. We're not getting out that way." He nodded to Dante, then spoke to Virgil. "What happened?"

The sergeant scratched his beard. He itched for a razor. "Sir, they just showed up with the—"

"I'm a doctor. Let me through, you big oafs."

Cruz smiled at the gray-haired head hopping up and down outside his ring of soldiers. "Private, let Doctor Easley in."

Esther, with Tina close behind, elbowed her way between the guards.

"Doc, can you figure out what's wrong with these guys?" Virgil asked. "They ain't movin'."

Esther's face furrowed as she dropped to examine the one who had been mauled. She glanced at the other two and gasped. "That's Reggie's jacket."

The creature, its face crusted in dried blood, drew a ragged breath and gasped a single word. "Mother?"

Esther fainted.

———— ◆ ————

In the small, roofless adobe hut, Captain Cruz paced back and forth in front of the three clones. "Now let me get this straight. You guys just decided you were human and switched sides?"

Michael sat cross-legged and looked at Rafael. Rafael, whose face was wrapped in gauze, nodded to him. "Michael, you speak for us. My face hurts."

Michael acquiesced, and in a slow, deliberate manner, continued to answer the captain's rapid fire questions. "Yes. It was the only logical choice, given the data available."

Gabriel sat back and looked around the room, then muttered to Rafael, "So many variations in facial and body configurations. I think I can differentiate between them. The one on the left is our mother, Esther."

Rafael touched his bandaged face. "Next to her is Tina. She treated my wounds. She must be the human version of a healing machine. Beside her is Dante. He's the one who named Michael... and I think he is mate to the healer. See how their hands touch? In the manuscript genre I absorbed called 'romances', that is what they do before copulation."

Tina overheard their whispered conversation and the heat rose in her cheeks. She snapped at him, "I think you need to learn a little bit more about love before you start commenting on it." She rose and moved to an open space next to Rafael. "If you're going to comment on love, you have to experience it. You'll never understand it reading a book." A twinkle lit her eyes. "Aren't there any girl clones?"

Rafael shifted uncomfortably. "No. We are all the same. They give us medicine, so sexual urges do not distract us from our training."

A small smile creased her face. "Now that those harpies are no longer stuffing you full of drugs, I think you better prepare yourself for feelings you never dreamed of."

Rafael sputtered. "Like in those romance books?"

Tina straightened and patted him on his arm. "Yes, just like in those books." She sat back down next to Dante and leaned her head on his shoulder.

Rafael looked at Gabriel, who scratched the back of his head and shrugged. "There is much I do not know." His eyes shifted to meet a pair of piercing blue eyes studying him in return. "That one is called Virgil. I believe he is the human version of a destroyer."

Rafael probed the scabs on his arm. "Human destroyers look kind of puny to me. The Guardians will have little trouble killing them."

Gabriel ground his teeth together. "We are one with them now."

"Yes, so now we have three who can fight Guardians." Rafael sighed and regarded the pacing man, furrowing his brow. "That one is Captain Cruz. He is a master-not-a-master. Those who wear common body wrappings perform the tasks he commands." He scratched the back of his neck. "But those who wear varied body wrappings argue with him."

Gabriel nodded in sage agreement. "Their relationships are incomprehensible. I encountered one small human who attempted to assault me. I do not believe I ever encountered her before, but she seemed to think I committed some dire transgression against her. She screamed that I murdered her husband." He rubbed his arm where she struck him. "I explained the blood passing ceremony to her, and she just became more agitated. Several humans in matching body wrappings dragged her away."

Rafael's eyes widened. "Perhaps she was under compulsion. Humans might have it, too."

"Perhaps." Gabriel plucked at his lower lip. "But the force of her blows was insufficient to cause anything but superficial bruising, and the larger humans pulled her away instead of joining in on the frenzy."

Rafael sighed, waving his hand as he refocused on the questions.

"So you guys are infiltrators designed by the masters to be spies." Captain Cruz snapped his fingers. "So, of course, we should readily accept you. Give me one reason why I should believe anything you're telling me."

Michael pulled the cross out from under his strange suit and rubbed it. "Because we rejected the Guardian blood passing and chose to be human."

"And what caused this incredible epiphany, may I ask?"

"Words."

"Words?" the exasperated captain growled.

"Yes. I absorbed your literature as part of my programming as an infiltrator. It enabled me to think in new ways."

"And can you give me an example of these incredible words?"

Michael closed his eyes in concentration and intoned, "We hold these truths to be self-evident, that all men are created equal, that they are endowed by their Creator with certain unalienable Rights, that among these are Life, Liberty, and the pursuit of Happiness." He smiled at the captain as if that explained everything.

Captain Cruz's mouth hung open for a second and he dropped into a sitting position. "Sergeant, you interrogate them. I'm getting a headache."

Virgil looked at Michael with a raptor's eye. "Ok—"

"Virgil, let me try." Esther lay her hand on Virgil's arm.

Virgil studied her for a moment, then shrugged. "Go ahead." He settled back against the clay wall.

The doctor cleared her throat and faced Gabriel. "Gabriel, why did you call me mother?"

"Because we are family," he replied with enthusiasm.

"But why are we family?"

"Simple." Gabriel smiled and glanced at Michael. "We are podmates, I mean brothers, to Michael. The human named Reggie requested that Michael protect you as a condition for agreeing he was human and had a soul. Michael accepted." Gabriel pulled out the wallet and handed it to Esther.

Tears welled in the old woman's eyes as she clutched the worn piece of leather to her chest.

"We saw images in that folder of a number of humans we determined were your family. Based on our research, the core responsibility of families is to nurture each other. They are not here, so we are your family." Gabriel soaked up the gratitude from Rafael and Michael for explaining it so well.

"That's the biggest crock of shit I've ever heard," Captain Cruz shouted.

"I believe him," Esther said as she wiped her wet face.

Virgil scowled, holding up a cautionary hand. "They admit to being infiltrators. This could be a simple ploy to defeat us."

Rafael grit his teeth. "It requires no special talent to defeat you. I saw no notable abilities in the blood passing yesterday."

Michael gave Rafael a stern look. "My brother, these are our people now. We will live and die with them. There must be a way to teach them to kill destroyers."

Rafael snorted and gestured to the humans. "Brother, look at them. They won't last ten seconds against guardians."

"Then we will fall defending them." Michael's eyes turned soft as he looked at Esther. "While I draw breath, I will not allow another human to be butchered."

Virgil leapt to his feet and stormed over to the clones. "You're gonna find that some of us know how to kill."

Rafael rose and stood nose-to-nose with Virgil. "You have no concept of what a Guardian can do while under compulsion. Over the past year, only two Guardians have expired in the blood passing ritual."

Virgil leaned in with a steel glint in his eyes. "Then why don't you show me?"

Rafael glared back and then cocked his head. "When?"

"No better time than the present."

Rafael rubbed his arm. "This is the first useful suggestion I have heard since we got here. I will train you. Let's start. In less than two weeks, the next batch of prototypes will be ready for the blood passing."

Virgil looked at Captain Cruz. "With your permission, sir."

The captain clambered to his feet. "I'll assemble the company. We'll find a dozen men who can kill those bastards."

Gabriel stood. "I'll join you. Michael's the talker. Besides, Rafael has no patience and will reopen all of his wounds."

Virgil stomped out the gap in the adobe wall. "Let's get started."

Gabriel chuckled at that as he left. "Maybe we can make a destroyer out of that one."

Rafael paused. "Death would be better than that, my brother." He then followed Virgil out.

Cruz followed a few steps behind the group. "Esther, I'll leave a couple guards outside the door. Call if you need anything."

Tina pursed her lips while she watched the soldiers depart. After they left, she turned to Michael. "Is this whole planet as desolate is it looks around here?"

"Most of the planet is an arctic wasteland. The habitable band is quite narrow around the equator. There are a few isolated spots heated by volcanic activity conducive to human life. We are located on one of those geothermal areas."

"Well, that explains the stink in the air around here." Dante eyed Michael, who sat cross-legged across the room.

"The masters..." A smile creased Michael's face. "The *harpies* have little interest in this place except as an undisturbed location for breeding their clone armies."

Thousands of questions swirled through Tina's mind. "So this isn't their native world?"

"No, it is not. As to where they are from, I have no idea. According to the information I possess, they have the analysis lab here and an incubator facility across the lake." Michael pointed with his chin to his left toward the sulfurous body of water.

"Incubator? How many of you are they growing?"

The clone furrowed his brow. "My understanding is that there are millions in various stages of development. The prototypes they breed and orient here. When they believe the model is maximized, they download that imprint to those still in stasis gestation."

"How close are they to maximizing the model?"

Michael scratched his neck. "I believe they are satisfied with the physical constructs. I am aware of no variations from my own." He rubbed his thin scar. "However, they are still experimenting with the training downloads."

"Well, given what you did, it looks like those plans went to hell," Dante chimed in.

Michael wrung his hands. "I hope you are right. Do not underestimate the harpies. They are incredibly clever. Remember, my brothers and I are designed as infiltrators. What better way to validate that plan than to integrate us into a human society?"

"You mean like a spy?" Tina squeezed Dante's hand.

"Not as you construe the word. They can see and hear everything in these pens without anything as clumsy as a spy. But it troubles me that they placed me here instead of eliminating me."

"So you think this is just part of your training," Esther whispered.

Michael hung his head. "Yes. They see and hear everything, but Dis has great difficulty interpreting the data collected. Their minds don't work as ours do. Their prediction models of your behavior to different stimuli have a high failure rate." He met Esther's eyes. "Mother, that is why my brothers and I decided to tell you all we can about them before we terminate ourselves." He spat on the ground. "Of my own volition, I will not share anything I learn with them. But I do not know what access they have to my mind. I resisted the compulsion, but they most certainly have other capabilities."

Dante exchanged worried glances with Tina and Esther, then turned to Michael. "Why don't you tell us what you know about this planet? It seems more like Hell than a place for the living."

"Hell... like the place your namesake traveled." Michael chuckled, and his gaze turned thoughtful. "Then that lake out there must be Cocytus, the body of water in the pit of the Inferno."

His lips thinned. "No, this planet used to be vibrant with life and supported an advanced civilization. The masters did a thorough investigation before they built here. Apparently, about four hundred years ago, a large meteor struck this world. The effect was devastating on the ecology. So much material was thrown into the atmosphere that it was over a year before the sun was able to penetrate the cloud cover. Three-mile high tidal waves swept across the surface, and volcanoes erupted along all of the continental plates. Then the glaciers flowed. Few native species larger than a microbe still exist. None of the intelligent beings have survived to my knowledge."

Michael grimaced, but his tone did not waver. "The masters are not keen on developing good cross-species relationships. If they found any native inhabitants alive, they would not remain so for long. However, the harpies are very interested in artifacts. The creatures who once inhabited this planet were excellent engineers. They were bipedal and warm-blooded, similar to the masters and humans. This costume I wear is of their manufacture."

Dante examined the suits that lay mounded in a pile. "Looks a bit on the small side."

Michael bobbed his shoulders up and down. "The one I wear was the same size. It conformed to my body when I put it on. I feel neither heat nor chill." He wiggled his toes. "It is a very pleasant experience for my feet."

Dante looked at his dirt-caked jeans. "I sure could use a change of clothes."

"It is yours, then. A partial thank you for naming me."

CHAPTER VIII
Gladiators

Ah, how ferocious was he in his aspect!
And how he seemed to me in action ruthless,
With open wings and light upon his feet!

Dante's Inferno – Canto XXI

The breath exploded from his lungs as Michael hit the ground. Everyone froze in stunned silence. In the week of hand-to-hand combat training with the three clones, this was the first time any of the soldiers had knocked one down.

A small grin creased Virgil's face as he stood over Michael's prone form. The smile vanished as Michael leg-whipped him, and he found himself pinned face first in the gritty dirt.

"You still don't understand." Michael swept the gathered soldiers with his eyes. "You must never stop fighting. A Guardian will try to kill you until he draws his last breath." He sprang off of Virgil and beckoned the next soldier. "Okay, Virgil showed you that it can be done. Now let's see if anyone else can do it better."

With a look of satisfaction, Virgil hopped up, dusted himself off, and strutted up to Captain Cruz. "The guy's as big as a house and quick as a cat, but I took him down."

Cruz studied the sparring and spat on the ground. "It's not enough. You're a second degree Tae Kwon Do black belt and the best we have." He grimaced as he watched

Michael, Gabriel, and Rafael almost simultaneously throw their opponents. "After a week of scuffling with these guys, we've now succeeded a total of once."

The smile melted from Virgil's face. "Unfortunately, I agree." He rolled his shoulder as he watched Rafael move in on a fresh challenger. "We need a new approach, and we're running out of time. If what Michael says is true, we'll be looking at the next batch of big ugly hatchlings in less than a week."

He knitted his brows, observing the sparring matches for a moment. "Yesterday, I spoke with that med student, Tina Phokas. She and Doc Easley have examined our three friends daily and said they're slimming down and sprouting a little fuzz." He put his hands on his hips and pointed with his chin. "It looks like their skin's even starting to get a little color."

Cruz half smiled. "Yeah, Doc Easley's taken them under her wing and is hopping mad over what the damn harpies did to their bodies. She believes that those guys have been getting a steady dose of steroids and radiation while in stasis." His tone turned grim. "Not to take away from you dropping Michael a few minutes ago, but these guys may be getting slower and weaker than what we'll face for real. It appears our diet plan isn't ideal for growing supermen."

"There's gotta be a way. There must be something we can do. I won't be a sheep led to slaughter."

"Maybe not new. Maybe something old instead." A gleam lit the captain's eyes. "While at West Point, I studied a lot of military history. When Julius Caesar marched through Europe, his troops were always outnumbered, and warriors opposing them were often larger and on horseback. Yet he always won."

"Ahh, sir, not to squash your ideas, but we're missing a few necessary items that the Romans had: spears, swords, shields…" Virgil groaned as he watched Gabriel pantomime the motion of snapping a fallen soldier's neck.

"Oh, but I think we do. We just need to experiment," Cruz responded with growing excitement.

Virgil hung his head. "Captain, I'm willing to try anything. I've been a soldier my entire adult life, and there's never been a fight I didn't think I could win... until now. We flat out can't beat these guys." He lifted his chin and squared his shoulders. "Tell me what you want us to do, and I'll get our three new recruits to drill us on it."

"No," Cruz snapped. "They can't know."

Virgil's eyes narrowed. "You still don't trust 'em? As far as I can tell, they've kept their word on everything. They treat Doc Easley like she's their mom. Hell, they seem to hate the damn harpies more than we do, if that's possible."

"I'm not sure I buy their cock-and-bull story. I'm still keeping an eye on them." Cruz turned back to the sparring match and sighed. "But even if everything they say is true, we still don't know if their masters have some sort of recorder going through their brains learning everything those guys see and hear. Remember, those goddamn aliens have space travel, so they're not stupid. If they think their prediction models of us don't work, they're going to do what they can to correct it. No, Sergeant, whether those guys are on our side or not, we can't take any chances. We'll do this prep on our own."

After some consideration, Virgil gave a curt nod. "I think you're wrong about 'em. They're like kids trying to absorb everything. They're already cussing as good as our men. I even heard Michael try to crack a joke the other day."

"Yeah, they're fitting in real nice. Isn't that exactly what an infiltrator does?" Cruz shot back.

Virgil bit his lip. "What're your orders, sir?"

Captain Cruz glanced around the prison yard now dotted with clay huts. "This is what I want you to do."

Dante trembled as he watched about thirty harpies approach the barrier accompanied by a dozen albino big uglies. A harpy deactivated a portion of the barrier and the clones marched in. The soldiers from the 10th Mountain Division stood at parade rest, blocking their entrance.

When the clones tried to elbow through, the GIs jumped them. Even with their size and speed, ten-to-one odds did the clones no favors, and the humans swarmed them. The harpies responded fast to the surprise attack against their slaves and swept the area with their strange tubular weapons.

Michael ignored the clones and charged at his former masters with hate-filled eyes. He jolted in pain as a blast hit him but continued to stagger forward. A harpy shot him twice more before he collapsed gasping, inches from his target.

Nearby, a clone pinned Virgil to the ground and beat him with iron-hard fists. Dante leapt on the creature's back and put a choke hold around its bull-thick neck. In the split second the clone used to react, Virgil shoved the heel of his hand into the bridge of the creature's nose, then sprang to his feet and snap-kicked him in the groin. The big ugly grunted and fell to its knees. A moment later, all three combatants collapsed.

The harpies moved into the fray, blanketing the melee with their stun weapons' beams. The struggle ended with none of the fighters left standing. Both clones and humans alike lay writhing in the dirt.

For the second time in a month, pain seared Dante's body and his silent scream echoed through his brain. He watched as civilians fled to the far corners of the prison, fleeing the harpies as they moved through the twitching soldiers and Guardians. One of them approached Dante, whose arm remained locked around the big ugly's neck. The alien cocked its head at him and released a blue disk. For a moment, the disk pulsated on the surface of the suit Dante received from Michael. The strange fabric parted, and he felt the sensation of something unnatural burrowing into his flesh before he blacked out.

———————◆◦———————

Dante regained consciousness with his head resting on a soft lap. Deft hands probed his chest, and he saw a familiar face. "Tina? What happened?"

Tears trickled down Tina's cheeks. "You stupid fool. You damn stupid fool. You're marked for the next round in the arena."

A shiver shook him as he felt the small symmetrical object just under his skin. "Dig the freakin' thing out. Please."

She turned her head to the side and wiped the back of her hand across her eyes. "We tried that already on Michael. Whatever that thing is, it just burrows deeper."

Dante looked around. A number of people, most of them soldiers, lay stretched out on the ground.

"Dear God, why did you have to get involved?" She glared at him with weary eyes.

"I couldn't just stand by and do nothing. That monster was kicking the shit out of Virgil. I couldn't let that thing kill him," Dante moaned.

Tina shoved him off her lap. "So you had to be a damn hero? What did you accomplish except lining yourself up to get ripped to shreds? We both saw what happened last time."

Dante sat up and took a shuddered breath. "We're all going to die here, you know."

"Don't say that! Don't ever say that. Someone will save us."

"Tina, look around you. There's not going to be a miracle. There's no one here but us."

Tina squeezed his hand and looked at him with a pleading gaze. "Please tell me you won't die. Dante, the only thing worse than being in Hell is being there alone. You can't leave me."

Something warm welled up within him, and Dante caressed her hand. "So we should get to know each other better. Ahh, what's your favorite color?"

Fresh tears welled up in her eyes. "Red."

"And what's your favorite food?"

Her voice choked. "Lasagna."

"There, see? I didn't know any of those things about you." He ran his fingers through her long auburn hair. "And tomorrow, we'll learn even more about each other."

She leaned in and kissed him on the lips. "I think I'm falling in love with you."

Dante's false bravado slipped away. He pulled her close and crushed her to him. Feeling her warm body pressed against him gave him solace, and he felt her rapid heartbeat and shivering body. Dante didn't want to let her go. He wanted to soothe her. *Is this love? Putting someone else's feelings ahead of mine?*

When they separated, he whispered, "Tina, that night in my car. I'm sorry I was such a bore. I just get all tongue tied when—"

He got no other words out. Tina threw her arms around him, sobbing into his chest. He enveloped her in his arms and held her close. They lost the world around them until a voice interrupted.

"Tina, I swear to your God that while I draw breath, no harm will come to Dante."

They broke apart, startled by the huge form of Michael looming over them. His face showed anguish, but his fists clenched at his sides. "We will kill those big uglies." Tina reached up and stroked Michael's hand, and in turn, he covered hers in his. "I will find a way."

———◆———

A short distance away, Captain Cruz watched the conversation with his lieutenants and noncoms. Virgil separated from the group and started to walk over.

"No, Sergeant Bernius. We stay with the plan."

"Sir, we got to tell 'em." Virgil pivoted and stepped close to Cruz. "They're both part of it now."

Cruz's face twisted with disgust. "Sorry, I don't trust that, whatever it is, and the civilian is a little too friendly with him. That's an order."

"Sir, we jumped them with two hundred fighting men this morning, and those suckers still didn't go down easy. There'll only be twelve of us in that damn arena tomorrow."

"That's why we have to stick to the plan, Sergeant." The captain lifted his chin. "I'm not trying to kid myself. The odds are that by this time tomorrow, we'll be bloody pulps with those monsters dancing on our corpses." He sighed. "Without our little surprise, that's a certainty. Now go see Corporal Viden and get ready." Cruz rubbed his chest in the spot where he could feel the alien's disk nestled just beneath his flesh, and he walked back to his hut on stiff legs.

———◆———

The next morning, a cool breeze wafted from the distant mountain range, and the sulfurous clouds opened to reveal a surprising azure sky. Dante shivered. *I must've picked up a damn virus last night.* He made a derisive smile, chastising himself. In a few minutes, he'd be marching to his death, and there he was worried about catching a cold.

He stared up at the sun, trying to block out what was about to happen. He stood last in a line of twelve. The first ten, led by Captain Cruz and Virgil, wore helmets and body armor, and stood at parade rest with their hands clasped behind them. Michael stood before him, clothed in a bodysuit identical to the one Dante wore.

Dante glanced around. Nearby, Tina stared at him with her white-knuckled hand grasping Esther's. Michael looked in the same direction, but no longer held his cross.

"I gave Doctor Easley my cross to hold just in case," Michael explained. "Stay close to me. I will protect you."

"Thanks, big guy. We'll come through okay," Dante stuttered. He refocused on the crowd of people gathering and saw Rafael and Gabriel hovering behind the two women protectively.

A small smile crept across Dante's face as he regarded the two big uglies. They'd never be mistaken for the clones on the other side of the fence now. Gabriel had broken his nose in the fight the day before. Doctor Easley tried to straighten it, but it remained bent at an unnatural angle despite her efforts. Rafael seemed to pride himself on his scarred body and disfigured face. Both displayed chiseled muscles but were leaner than when they first arrived in camp.

Dante did a double take when he noticed something about their faces. *The doc was right—they* are *starting to sprout hair.* He glanced at Michael, but the former guardian had the hood pulled over his head. Dante shrugged and pulled his up, too. The little protection can't hurt.

He caught motion out of the corner of his eye and snapped his attention back to the fence. Twelve albino clones trotted toward the barrier trailed by thirty harpies. Dante studied the on-comers and gulped. No wounds or scars showed on their pale skin despite the soldiers' beating the day before.

The barrier lights winked out and the clones moved in, prepared to incapacitate the blood passing victims. But as they entered, Captain Cruz called his men to attention and marched through the opening, not even glancing at the clones who came to drag them out. Dante swallowed the hysteria overwhelming him. *This is insane. It can't be happening.*

The clones paused and looked back toward their masters. The harpies sounded like a pit of snakes, all hissing at each other, and the GIs acted like a bunch of Roman gladiators marching into the coliseum. The clones followed them out. Dante glanced back at the line of guardians and his lips quivered. *I hope those bastards are disappointed they can't use their little toys to incapacitate us again.*

With halting steps, Dante walked on with his eyes fixed on Michael's broad back. Then, for the first time in a month, he stood outside the border of their pen. He heard a chorus of shouts from behind, but Tina's wailing of "no" penetrated all of the other voices. *I'll never see her again.*

He looked to the side where the border of the pen holding the Americans met the pen holding the Australians. His eyes met Martinel's, and the Aussie mouthed one thing: "God bless ya, Yank."

Dante paled as he entered the arena's field, blindly stumbling after the soldiers to the far side of the enclosure. The darkened poles all snapped on with their blue lights behind him. He gasped when he felt a steel grip on his arm, then looked up to see Virgil.

"Kid, there's no time to explain things. Just stay behind me and do what you're told. Got it?" Virgil studied Michael. "Okay, big guy, stay with Dante, and help out where you can."

Cruz pointed his finger at him. "Dammit, Sergeant Bernius, get over here. You're holding down the right flank."

To Dante's surprise, the captain stood at a point with his men formed up in a wedge behind him, anchored against the shimmering wall. The soldiers removed their vests and held them looped through their arms like shields, the back of the vests facing outward. He followed Virgil to the GIs and stood behind them.

Captain Cruz glared at Michael and spoke to Dante. "You two are our reserves. If there's a breakthrough, you plug the freakin' gap. Understood?"

Dante nodded in confusion and stared at the soldiers' equipment. The front plates of the armored vests were missing, and they carried baseball-sized rocks in one hand and makeshift short swords fashioned from the smashed food vats in the other.

Michael took in everything with wide, open eyes. "This resembles a description I—" He dropped to his knees and gasped. "Compulsion!"

At the same instant, the clones at the opposite side of the field shrieked.

"Ready men," Cruz barked.

"Sir, yes sir," the soldiers roared in response.

Michael thrashed on the ground, his arms and legs flailing. The guardians sprinted toward them.

"Steady, men." The captain double clutched the rock he held. "Fire!"

At thirty feet, ten stones smashed into the two clones on the left. One fell to the ground and the other staggered into the shimmering barrier and collapsed.

"Fire!" Cruz whipped his second rock in the face of a charging clone.

Ten more stones flew at the two guardians on the right. One dropped, but the other covered his head with his arms and kept running.

"Shields high, swords low." Cruz pulled out his sharpened weapon. "Gut the sons of bitches!"

The GIs squeezed in tight with each other, and then the clones attacked. Before Dante could make sense of what was happening, the soldiers gutted four of the clones. The soldiers jabbed their makeshift swords like pistons, stabbing the blades deep into the unprotected flesh of their enemies. The coordinated resistance drove the clones into a berserk rage. They pounded the upraised shields even as their entrails hung out and they stood in their own gore. One of them lifted Corporal Viden off the ground while the flailing soldier slashed at the monster's chest. The big ugly tossed Viden to the ground several feet away, and many of the unharmed clones jumped on him like rabid wolves. The man's terrified scream came to an abrupt halt.

Two clones bounded over the line of soldiers. Michael clambered to his feet and roared. He leapt at the nearest one and wrapped his arms around the clone's chest, dragging him down to the dust.

A soldier turned and raised his short sword and shield at the other guardian. His blade skittered across the creature's chest, but he overextended, and the clone grabbed him by the throat, snapping his neck. The guardian howled as it tossed the twitching body against one of the blue poles. The pole sparked as the lifeless corpse struck it. Dante snatched up the dead soldier's blade as the clone with the gashed chest turned on him.

Michael bellowed and smashed his fist into his opponent's face as the creature scrambled to its feet. The big ugly's eyes rolled up in its head as it stood swaying with blood pouring from its nose. The clone threw a clumsy round house at him, and Michael lowered his shoulder and bull rushed his attacker into the sparking pole, pinning the guardian there beside the smoldering, dead soldier.

Dante waved the sword-shaped shard at a shrieking clone and looked for help. Michael had the guardian he battled pinned against an energy barrier. However, agony contorted the giant clone's face as the charged field shrouded him. The blue light in the pole waned and flickered.

Michael met Dante's eyes and croaked, "Run, Dante! Run!"

Without thinking, Dante sprang through the gap. The guardian he confronted sprang after him an instant later. Dante stumbled as he crossed the perimeter, the sensation of a thousand needles stabbing his face, but the pain wicked away like sweat on an arid day. Dante shook off the feeling and fled in terror for the distant mountain range. The big ugly fell to its knees and leaned on its knuckles, looking around in confusion. After a few minutes, it staggered to its feet and followed, first with lumbering steps and then gathering speed.

———————◆•———————

The harpies screeched and tapped the control pads in their clawed hands. For the first time in memory, the blood passing hadn't gone as planned.

Michael stumbled away from the pole, and the barrier lights sprang back to life. He moaned as he fell face first in the red dust beside the bodies of the dead soldier and clone charred against the sparking pole.

Captain Cruz paused to assess the situation, and a feral grin crossed his lips. Only three big uglies still stood, and blood gushed from a jagged cut on one of them. Seven armed GIs remained alongside him, and Cruz cast a wary glance at the harpies. Most of the vile creatures had ceased their chittering and looked engrossed in the battle.

He followed the eyes of the two harpies who weren't focused on the carnage. They hissed at each other and tracked Dante, who loped toward the mountains with a long, steady stride. From what Cruz could see, the boy knew how to run and had a good lead on the big ugly chasing him.

One of the harpies lifted a small oval device and the other pushed it down with a clawed hand. The two creatures turned and bared their sharp fangs when they saw him observing them. He didn't have time to return their glare. The three surviving big uglies, maddened by compulsion, made a berserk charge into the soldier's shield wall, and the GIs cut them down. As the last one fell to its knees, Virgil drove his makeshift sword through the creature's throat.

Cruz stood straight and roared, "All right, men, hold. We beat the freakin' harpies' little pets, but it isn't over. Line up to return to our prison. I don't want to give those fuckers more of a reason to kill us."

"One second, sir. We need to gather our wounded," Virgil called out.

Captain Cruz eyed Michael and clenched his jaw.

"Sir, he fought with us, and we don't leave our people behind."

The captain gritted his teeth. "Okay, Sergent Bernius, choose three men and retrieve him. You're right. I don't want to leave Michael where the harpies can pick his brain. Now let's go back before the damn aliens come up with something else to entertain us with."

CHAPTER IX
The Race

The infernal hurricane that never rests
Hurtles the spirits onward in its rapine;
Whirling them round, and smiting, it molests them.

Dante's Inferno – Canto V

W here's a water station when you need one?" Dante muttered under his breath, shaking his head at his own poor joke. The fever exhausted him, but he couldn't stop. He stole a glance over his shoulder at his pursuer. *That damn monster's still behind me.* He appraised the gap between them and refocused on the broken and rutted ground.

The suit amazed him, in spite of everything. His feet felt like they were on springs, and the stones didn't cut through. He leapt across a dry-washed gully and almost dropped the small sword he clutched in his hand as he landed with a grunt on the other side. *This blade won't be a helluva lot of help if that big ugly tackles me.* He shuddered at the thought.

The race shouldn't be close, by his estimate. He finished twelfth in the Division III Cross Country Nationals two years ago, and even in Division I, there weren't many runners who could beat him. Even so, the gap between himself and his pursuer shrunk. The monster was barefoot and bleeding but still gained on him. Dante licked his parched lips and gasped.

A soft mechanical buzz beeped in his ear, followed by a monotone female voice. "At the two respective paces, your companion will join you in thirty-three minutes. However, if you halt, he will join you in four."

Dante stumbled at the voice. "Who said that?"

The buzz sounded again. "At your current rate of perspiration, I recommend hydration within the next hour. I have an eighty-three percent certainty that your muscular system will initiate spasms soon after."

Dante swung his head in all directions and saw nothing but the big ugly with its head down, following in the distance. "Where are you? You sound like you're right next to me, but I can't see you."

"We are communicating through the audio receptors in your grapheme neural net environmental suit."

Dante grimaced at the sound of the flat feminine voice. "So you're one of the damn aliens playing head games with me? Well, your little pet's gonna have to work to get me."

"Your statement is inaccurate with a ninety-six percent certainty, and your question is ambiguous. Please restate."

Dante shook his head. "Okay, do you bounce around like a rabbit with an evil-looking face and a mouth full of fangs?"

A dull hum ran through the speakers. "Lack self-image… incomplete comprehension of language nuances. Given known variables in question, the answer is no with a ninety-nine percent certainty."

"Ahh." Dante's eyebrows furrowed in confusion. "Okay. Are you associated with that nice little bed-and-breakfast that I just left?"

"Incomplete language comprehension. You are the first self-aware entity within range of my scanners in four hundred and thirty-seven years, seven months, and thirteen days. I was unaware of your existence until the two neural net environmental suits activated one hour and eight minutes ago. I am unable to communicate with the other being."

"Are you a machine?" Dante chewed on his lower lip. "A computer?"

"As you define the term, yes."

"You're not associated with the creatures by the sulfur lake?"

"You stated the same question earlier in a different format. There have been no new variables introduced in that elapsed time."

"How come you speak English?" Dante asked.

"I have an adaptive language translator built into my system. Your sentence structure is the same. I have monitored the intruder site you ventured from for several planetary cycles. Your word construct is similar to what is in my knowledge base, so my heuristic modeling adapted."

Hope rose in Dante's chest for the first time since their capture in New York. "Help me! Please, God, help me."

"I am not a deity as I understand the term, and your request is ambiguous."

Dante took a shuddered breath. *I've got to get ahold of myself.* He'd been working with computer inference engines for five years, and now his life depended on that knowledge. "Computer, where are you located based on my current vector? I'd like to approach."

The brief buzz returned. "To ensure system security, I cannot provide the coordinates of my physical location except to my makers."

Dante gritted his teeth. If he could hack the security systems of Cornell's DoD lab, he could work around this one. It was either that or die trying. He swallowed hard. "Computer, define criteria for a maker."

The hum ran with three noticeable pauses. "It is

ambiguous."

"Computer, then why am I not considered a maker?"

"A maker is a biped, self-aware mammal. That is a match. Your physicality also conforms to the makers' neural net environmental suits. However, your communications is at variance with my programming language both in structure and sound combinations. Probability of you being a maker is forty-nine point eight percent."

"Computer, your last direct communication with a maker was over four hundred years ago. Language can change over that time."

"No basis for confirmation. That theory is plausible. Probability of you being a maker is adjusted to fifty-three point three percent."

"Computer, what is the risk of me harming your infrastructure or data core?"

"Minimal risk. My scan indicates that the only electronic device you possess is a broadcasting beacon."

Dante shuddered, thinking of the disk in his chest. "Hey, if that beacon bothers you, you're welcome to shut it down. I don't think I can reach the off button myself."

"That is beyond my capability. It is transmitting to multiple receptors, including the one your companion carries. At current speeds, he will intersect your position in twenty-four minutes."

"Shit. I've got to lose him somehow."

"Ambiguous statements. Excrement and misplacing your companion are unconnected references."

Dante grimaced as he felt a twinge in his calf. "Forget about excrement. Is there anything you can do to block that signal? I really don't want that freak back there to catch me." He wheezed, trying to gulp more air. "I need information."

"Information… I am an automated self-sustaining bio-mes station. I maintain one hundred sixty-one varieties of vegetation suitable for maker consumption. My supply of flora is limited due to planetary environmental conditions.

"My makers failed to complete my construction. I required eighty-three years, three months, twenty-five days to finish fabrication of facilities and activate primary ecosystem protocols. Resources were inadequate, so I developed alternative systems to meet expected deliverables.

"My original data core contains limited information beyond my protocols, design specifications, and output targets. Until now, I have had no external communications in four hundred thirty-seven years, seven months, and thirteen days."

It didn't take long for Dante to put two and two together. "You mean, you're a farm?"

"Yes. Due to climate issues and equipment limitations, I have been unable to meet the prime objective until thirty-eight years ago. I have maintained an interior greenhouse program and have developed plant species that are both adaptable to current climate conditions and are acceptable for sustaining the maker's food energy needs. Production is limited on the arable land available. My current estimates are that backlogged deliverables will be met in one thousand twenty-two years."

Dante stumbled on loose shale as the land sloped upward. Fear constricted his throat as he studied the hill. He stood on a jagged knoll, and steep cliffs reared not far beyond it. Dante sucked in air and felt a stitch in his side. "Computer, the entity who is pursuing me intends to kill me. I am a maker. Protect me."

"Given your assumption, you will be dead in seventeen minutes. You are decelerating. I am a bio-mes station. I do not understand how I can protect you. I… will miss our conversation. It has been stimulating. Also, please recharge your neural net environmental suit. I will lose communications with you at approximately the same time."

Dante's footsteps grew less certain with no clear

path to follow. Dante moaned as he found himself in a small vale with steep slopes on all sides. He scrambled up the loose shale on the far side and gasped for air. When Dante reached the top, he looked around in desperation. The clone was nowhere in sight. "Computer, is there a path out of here?"

"Ambiguous question. Given your rapid breathing, I deem a slight downward slope would match your needs. Vector ten degrees from true north. You will approach my irrigation reservoir. That will be within the parameters of your request as I understand it."

Dante glanced at the sun and skittered down the hill in a shower of rock. He fell and gasped at the base for a moment. The cramped muscles in his legs felt ready to twist off of his bones, and he limped at a shuffling pace. For the first time in a race, his body refused to respond to his brain's plea for speed.

"Adjust your vector west seven degrees. Communications shut down in three minutes. I recommend that the next time you activate your suit, provide it with a full charge. Companion intercept in two minutes."

Dante struggled to the next rise and looked back. *Oh, my God. There it is.* He could see the wicked gash stretched across the monster's chest, and it left bloody footprints from the long trek over uneven ground. The guardian raised its eyes and met Dante's, and a cruel smile crossed its sunburned face. Dante stumbled backwards and rolled down the other side of the hill.

Those few minutes the computer mentioned must've passed because it next said, "Your companion will join you in one minute. Communications terminating. Please recharge at your earliest convenience."

Dante pulled himself up and snapped his head around as he found himself standing in ankle-deep water on the edge of a lake nestled below a cliff. The calm water stretched a couple miles in all directions. *I'm trapped.*

At least the pervasive stench of sulfur was gone. The air smelled fresh. He looked back up the embankment, and there stood the big ugly glaring at him. Heedless of the fall, the monster sprang down the slope.

Dante threw himself into the water. He swam away from shore with a clumsy breast stroke, his cramped legs providing no kick. The icy water stung his exposed face and hands, but the suit kept the frigid temperatures at bay wherever it covered. He turned and treaded water to locate the big ugly.

The monster hesitated at the shore line and shrieked in pain as its mangled feet touched the freezing water but continued to wade in. The clone thrashed as it plunged in over its head and disappeared beneath the surface.

Dante roared a raw cheer as the water stirred halfway to his location, and air bubbles burst to the surface and then stopped. His cheer turned to terror as a steel grip around his ankle yanked him below the waves. He slashed through the resisting water at the clone's face with his makeshift sword. The monster just stared back with stone cold eyes.

In a frenzy, Dante hacked at the hand holding him while his lungs screamed, and he kicked the clone's head with his free leg. *No, it can't end like this. Tina, I'm so sorry.* Desperate, he dropped the sword and tried to swim to the surface mere inches above his head. Dante's hands churned the surface of the crystal clear water, but he did not move.

A swarm of bee-like insects landed on his hand when it broke the surface and burrowed under the sleeve of his suit. Dante continued to thrash, which seemed to make the tiny creatures move faster, stinging him as they went. *Computer, someone, help me!*

———— ◆ ————

Tina remained at the prison barrier, eyes transfixed on the distant mountain range, long after everyone else returned to their daily activities. Rafael stood at her side, watching two harpies who lingered near the edge of the now empty arena. The aliens chittered at each other and studied the monitor one of them held.

When the creatures turned toward them and hissed, Tina glanced up at the large man standing beside her. She appeared to search Rafael's stoic face for the meaning.

He would not meet her eyes when he spoke. "Dante is dead."

Tina's lips trembled. "No, no. That can't be true."

Rafael wrapped his arms around her. She clung to him, sobbing.

"The signal from the beacon planted in him has ceased. To my knowledge, it cannot be removed once activated." Rafael tightened his grip around her quivering shoulders and glared death at the two harpies. He raised one hand and wiped the moisture on his cheek. "Michael was right. Human emotions—my emotions, are far stronger than any compulsion planted in my brain."

The harpies glared back for a moment but stopped hissing. They bounded back to their hive-like nest.

Tina pushed back from Rafael's chest and stared at the distant peaks through the swirling clouds of grit kicked up by the breeze on the plain. "Rest in peace, Dante. I'll remember your courage and love forever." She wrapped her arms around herself and walked with slow steps to the collection of clay huts.

Rafael followed, deep in his own thoughts, when he noticed a little girl sitting on the ground, sobbing and leaning against a knee-high rock. His eyes followed Tina, unable to think of any words of comfort, and he then walked over to the child and crouched before her. "Little human, what is the matter?"

"My mommy's gone."

Rafael smiled and patted her on the head as he had seen Esther do with young children. "She can't be far away. I will help you find her. Is that okay?"

The child choked out her words. "My mommy died yesterday, and those scary monsters took her away."

Rafael froze, at a loss for what to do next. Instinctually, he opened his arms and the child flew into them. Soft cooing sounds rose up inside him. The child wrapped her arms tightly around his neck, and he rocked her. "What is your name, little human?"

She wiped her nose with her dirt crusted arm and looked him in the eyes. "Angela. I'm four years old and a girl, not a little human."

"Well, Angela, my name is Rafael, but you can call me Rafe. Is your father here?"

"No. The monsters killed him two weeks ago. They're going to kill all of us."

A shiver ran down Rafael's spine. *I was one of those monsters.* He wiped Angela's tear-streaked cheek with the sleeve of Reggie's old tweed jacket. Rafael stood and rocked her some more. "No, they won't. The soldiers killed some of the bad monsters today."

Angela buried her head in his chest, but he felt her nod. He cleared his constricted throat. "Maybe we could be friends. I don't have any parents, either."

She looked into his eyes and stroked his gauze wrapped face. "Did the monsters hurt you?"

He stood with the child clinging to his neck. "Yes, they did, but I hurt them right back."

"We could be friends and take care of each other."

"Then come with me, Angela. Let's go visit Doctor Easley and find you a place to stay."

"Okay, Rafe." She kissed his bandaged face and burrowed her head against his chest.

Rafael walked to the infirmary having never before carried such a light load which was so heavy a burden.

CHAPTER X
Beatrice

There he begrit me as the other pleased;
O marvelous! For even as he culled
The humble plant, such it sprang up again
Suddenly there where he uprooted it.

Dante's Purgatorio – Canto I

A buzzing sound disturbed him. "My protocol has no instructions for this situation."

Dante rolled to his side and spewed water from his lungs. He opened his eyes to see the face of the clone who had pursued him. Snapping awake, he rolled away coughing, crushing the tall wheat-like plants next to him.

The mechanical, feminine voice returned. "My knowledge base on animal biology is limited, but I am eighty-seven percent certain that your companion has expired. I am seventy-three percent certain that you are not an aquatic mammal, so I extracted you from the irrigation reservoir when I noted the distress in your heart rate."

"Where the hell am I?" Dante sputtered as he looked around.

He lay several yards from the edge of the water in waist-high, amber-colored grass. The inert body of the clone lay beside him. Dante saw the deep lacerations where he hacked at the creature's arms. He looked back toward the lake and realized he now stood on the opposite shore from the cliff where he had fallen. It looked to be over a mile away.

"Question is ambiguous," said the computer. "Per your language, Hell is a place of torment for your species. You are currently situated at the junction between my fruit orchard number three, my grain field number one, and my irrigation reservoir. I am eighty-nine percent certain this environmental habitat does not align with your definition of Hell."

Dante pulled open his suit, remembering the swarm of insect-like creatures which attacked him when he nearly drowned. His chest throbbed with a dull pain from a dime-sized, cauterized wound where the alien's tracking disk had rested. The disk now lay on the ground to his left.

He pulled himself into a sitting position. His head spun and his face felt flushed with fever. *I've definitely had better days.* He wrapped his arms around himself to control the shakes. "I thought we couldn't communicate after my suit lost power."

"I have not engaged in conversation in four hundred and thirty-seven years. The stimulation was satisfactory, and I desired a continuation. I determined a solution that coincided with your expressed request to turn off the beacon you wore inside your body."

Dante winced as he poked at the wound in his chest. "So you cut it out of me?"

"I hope I did not err in meeting your desire. When my water purifier detected your presence, I dispatched my plant fertilization micro-bots to extract the power from the device in your chest. I used it to charge the neural net environmental suit. Your implanted device resisted the extraction process, so I incapacitated its CPU. I am making repairs. I will attempt to restore its functionality. The circuitry is unfamiliar, but I have a fifty-six percent certainty that I can reproduce it and reinsert it into your person."

"No, no, no. That's not necessary. I don't ever want to see that damn thing again." Dante resealed his suit and wrapped his arms over his chest, staggered to his feet, and grimaced at the pain his chest. He turned away from the lake and found himself face-to-face with an ivory-colored sphere floating five feet off the ground. Its surface appeared alive with motion, swarming with the micro-bots that had attacked him in the lake. He took a step backwards. "Please keep your little biting machines away from me."

The computer emitted a short hum, followed by a click. "Noted. However, please charge your suit at your earliest convenience. It is currently at forty-seven percent of maximum capacity."

"Sure. The next power outlet I see, I'll be sure to plug in."

Dante studied the area around him. He stood between a large field of grain that swayed in the breeze and an orchard of fruit bearing trees stretching up the slope of the mountain.

"Recommendation. Your companion has expired and no longer needs his device. I could extract the power from it, as I did from yours."

Dante furrowed his brows. "That gadget's still transmitting?"

"Yes."

"Shut it down. Shut it down. Those harpies I told you about will track it, and then they'll kill me and destroy you."

"Tracking is improbable. System security initiated when you entered my biome sphere. The site you identified as a bed-and-breakfast is receiving the signal diverted to a transponder on the windward side of this mountain forty point eight miles due north of your current location."

Dante narrowed his eyes at the lush vegetation. "You don't understand. If their reconnaissance detects this valley, they'll investigate. This is the only spot on this planet I've heard of with any signs of life."

"Assertion is improbable. Security protocol camouflages the valley from aerial sensory and electronic detection. It is a primary objective to preserve the maker's bio-mes."

Dante stumbled about twenty steps along the lake shore to the orchard and ran his hand down the rough bark of the nearest tree. Low branches hung lush with a purple fruit. He turned to look for the strange floating orb and cringed.

The ivory-colored sphere hovered over the dead clone. Dante gasped as the machine thrust a meter-long blade into the creature's neck and severed the head from the body. A cloud of the bee-like micro-bots swarmed into the open cavity and extracted a dimly-lit blue disk dripping with blood and gore. His breath caught. *This is no benign computer I'm dealing with.*

The ivory sphere extended a flexible tendril and grasped the disk. Without a sound, it flew to Dante and curled a second tendril around the ankle of his suit. He stared at it, frozen in terror, but felt nothing. A few minutes later, the tendril retracted, and the ivory sphere sped off toward the snowcapped peaks at the far end of the wide valley.

"Your suit is now one hundred percent charged. Maintenance standards recommend that you should not let the charge drop below twenty-five percent."

Dante nodded when a thought came to him. "Ahh… Computer, do you have a name?"

A short hum. "A name… I am Bio-mes Ecological Agrarian Test Research Station Three. Does that constitute a name per your definition?"

"Yeah, it does but it's a mouthful." Dante chuckled as he tried to simplify it into an acronym and thought about his namesake's *Divine Comedy*. "How about if I call you Beatrice?"

A series of hums interrupted by the occasional click filled his ears. Eventually, the computer answered him in a much clearer-sounding voice. "I have cross-referenced all nonproprietary files with that label. All nonsecure communications will accept that designator. What is your identifier?"

"Dante Carloman."

"Dante Carloman, you are a nonaquatic mammal. That also conforms to the specifications I possess regarding my makers. Probability that you are a maker has risen to sixty-seven percent. You now have level one security access."

"Thanks. Beatrice, please just call me Dante. By the way, your voice sounds a lot clearer now. What happened?"

"You were outside my operating system's firewall. It was difficult to override the automatic defense protocols to initiate communication. The base threat criterion has been satisfied."

"Your security system is a separate entity?"

"In case my software becomes corrupted, the firewall defense is set up as an independent processor."

Dante scratched the back of his neck. "How many security levels do you have?"

"Unknown. I am aware of level two threat criteria. I do not know if there are higher levels. The level one security clearance will accommodate open communications."

Dante gulped and slid to a sitting position at the base of the tree. The pain in his chest subsided, but the fever refused to abate. Also, what would happen if Beatrice ever discovered he wasn't a maker? He stared at the mutilated corpse and shuddered. *I better be far from here when it does.*

Exhaustion from the day's events filled him, and his hollow stomach ached. He glanced at the red sun. Sunset loomed, and the thick yellow clouds rolled back across the late afternoon sky. Dante guessed he hadn't eaten in at least ten hours. His brows furrowed as he eyed the fruit hanging before him. "Hey, Beatrice? Is the fruit on this tree edible?"

"No maker has ever consumed my produce, and to meet production objectives, I have modified the plant species to adapt to the climate changes. All vegetation is within specifications of the originals, but I lack data to verify compliance."

Dante stood and salivated as he picked one of the fruits. He stared long at it. "Do you at least know if it's ripe or not?"

"Unknown. The fruit from that tree species will start falling to the ground in approximately twenty-two planetary revolutions."

"You don't know much for a farm system, do you?" Dante squeezed the purplish fruit. "Well, it's firm enough. I guess there's only one way to find out."

"You are correct. I am not whole. My software was incomplete when the makers' work ceased. I completed the programming I needed to function, utilizing my core inference engines. Why did they not complete me?"

Dante rolled the fruit in his hand as he recalled his conversation with Michael several days earlier. "Based on my information, I'm going to guess a meteor hit the planet at the same time your makers stopped working on you. It set off an ecological disaster this world is only just starting to recover from." His eyes swept the orchard and the amber-colored farmland beyond. "Everything beyond this valley died."

He spotted an ivory orb hovering a few trees away, and Dante jumped. *Shit, I just told this computer that there's no possible way I could be from this planet.* He took a few steps backward. "Ahh, Beatrice, the makers were very advanced. Many of them probably escaped the cataclysm by fleeing in spaceships."

"Over the last four-point-two years, I have detected eight landings at the site you have identified as the bed-and-breakfast. The communications I monitored from there have zero correlation to the syntax of my makers. You arrived in one of those spaceships. You have no knowledge of maker constructs. You are an intruder." The ivory orb moved in Dante's direction.

"Wait a second, Beatrice." Dante raised his arms in front of his face, thoughts racing for an idea that would keep his head attached to his body. "I cannot definitively say I am or am not a maker. You're designed to handle ambiguity. There must be a category between maker and intruder that would fit me, at least temporarily." Dante's head spun. He stumbled back to keep the tree's trunk between the orb and himself.

"Makers and intruders." Beatrice's words slid into another hum. "No other categories."

"How about a guest? I mean you no harm, and I could probably help fill in many of your information gaps regarding your ecosystem. I could help you until a final determination is made."

"A guest?" The orb stopped moving. "Yes, my firewall finds that an acceptable alternative. Level one clearance has been reestablished. You may proceed with the experiment. It will be useful."

"Ahh, the experiment?" Dante, who had just started to relax, tensed again. "What experiment?"

"As you proposed earlier, ingest the edible material in your hand so I can observe the reaction. I am in the process of collecting samples of the other one hundred sixty varieties of foodstuffs that I produce. This will be very beneficial."

Dante gave the nearby field of grain a queasy glance. "Sure, Beatrice, but some food needs to be prepared and shouldn't be eaten raw."

"That is useful data. You are correct; I have many knowledge gaps."

"Here goes." Dante breathed deep and took a small bite from the fruit in his sweaty palm. Sour juice flowed in an explosion of flavor, and he bit off a bigger chunk. A few seconds later, nothing but the pit remained in his hand. "That was incredible. It's the size of a plum but tastes like a green olive."

"I will identify that item as an olive. I have no record of any name for it."

Dante leaned back against the rough bark and slid to the ground. He put his hand to his cheek and frowned at the heat. That wasn't good. He had run close to a half-marathon, almost drowned, and had a slice taken out of his chest. On top of all that, after weeks of thin gruel, his stomach roiled at the tart food.

"Beatrice, I don't feel so good."

CHAPTER XI
The Raid

Ah me! how very cautious men should be
With those who not alone behold the act,
But with their wisdom look into the thoughts.

Dante's Inferno – Canto XVI

Esther sighed and lay her hand on the forearm of a shaking child. "Michael, there's nothing we can do. The boy's going to die. Back home, removing an appendix would be a relatively simple operation. Here, I lack even the basic tools." She glanced at Tina, tending to a dozen other people shivering on mats.

Michael stroked the boy's sweat matted hair. "What is it you need?"

Esther wrung her hands. "Oh, just about everything: antibiotics, antiseptics, surgical tools, anesthetics, a sterile operating room—" She brushed red dust from her filthy jeans. "And having a competent surgeon would be handy, too."

Michael placed a damp rag on the fevered boy's forehead and shook his head. "I should have brought you better materials when I had the chance." He shot to his feet and stormed out of the tent. The sun disappeared into a thick mass of clouds. It matched his disposition.

"Please wait," Tina wheezed as she raced after him.

Michael paused at her plea, his muscles taut and his jaw tight.

"This tent and the first aid supplies you brought helped immeasurably." She placed her hand on his bicep. "You didn't even know us then and you helped anyway. We can never thank you enough."

"I wish others felt as you do." Michael's face softened as he regarded her. "Few in this place will even speak with me, and those who do spew vitriol."

"That's because they don't know you as we do. People here are scared. They're just striking out at the unknown."

He tightened and loosened his fists in impotent rage. "That's no excuse for the soldiers. My podmates and I spent weeks training with them, and now they avoid us."

Tina crossed her arms and glared at where some soldiers had gathered. "That's because Captain Cruz is as stubborn as a mule. He's convinced that you and your brothers are spies for the damn harpies and ordered his men to avoid you."

Esther emerged, closing the tent flap behind her, and walked with a purposeful stride to where Tina and Michael stood. "The captain isn't being spiteful. He just doesn't know what those monsters have planted in your head. He's being cautious."

"That can't be true. Michael almost died on that fence to give Dante a chance to escape." Tina swiped at the tears welling in her eyes. "Virgil's some sort of super soldier, and he doesn't believe any of that mind reading hogwash."

Michael sighed in resignation and scratched the thin fuzz sprouting from his head. "We will think of something."

"It better be soon," Esther urged him.

Michael walked off to where Virgil talked to his two podmates. When he reached the group, Virgil turned and greeted him with a nod.

"Hey, Mick. Ya look like you could bite the head off of one of those harpies." Concern edged into Virgil's casual words. "What's the matter?"

"Virgil, I told you my name is Michael, not Mick." Michael glared at Gabriel when he snickered. "How would you like it if I called you Gabe?"

Gabriel's grin spread wide. "Actually, I would like that. Most of the humans call people they like by nicknames. Isn't that right, Virg?"

"And Rafael lets me call him Rafe," Angela giggled from the top of Rafael's shoulders.

Rafael lifted Angela from his shoulders and swept her through the air before lowering her to the ground. "Go see if Doctor Easley needs any help."

"Okay, Uncle Rafe." Angela sped off. "Bye-bye, Uncle Mick. Bye-bye, Uncle Gabe." All three followed her with fondness in their eyes.

Virgil patted Rafael on the shoulder as the clone's face broke into a broad smile. "Looks like that kid's adopted you." The sergeant then eyed Michael, whose mood had darkened. "Mick, what's happened?"

Michael exhaled in pent up frustration. "Everything. There's a boy dying in the field hospital, the captain thinks we're spies, most everyone hates me, and we're trapped in this cage until the masters — the harpies — decide it's time for us to die. I think that about covers it."

The smile slid from Virgil's face, his lips tightening to a firm line. "There's going to be a lot of people dying before we get outta here. But we will get out."

He paused and glanced at the barrier. "Mick — Michael, I've been talking to Gabe and Rafe about our last bout in the arena. Dante and that one big ugly went through that field at the same time. The kid sprung up and ran like a jack rabbit, but that big ape was out cold for a long time." He ran his fingers along the material on the alien suit Michael wore. "I touched that field once and it knocked me on my ass. You stayed in that energy stream and shouted a warning." He let go of the sleeve and stared at the barrier. "I don't want to get into who's a tougher guy with you, but you and Dante remained conscious while that big ugly and I were flattened. I'd place my bet that Dante had something we didn't." He moved close to Michael. "How many of those jumpsuits do you still have?"

———— ◆ ————

Captain Cruz spoke with clipped words. He suspected anything he said in front of the clones would be passed on to the harpies, but the plan fascinated him, and he didn't have any better ideas. "Sergeant Bernius, it just might work. But what'll it buy us?" He twisted his thumb in Michael's direction. "We just have three suits, including the one that guy's wearing. We have over a thousand people trapped here. How the hell will a few guys wandering around outside the fence help? Oh, yeah, and there's the additional problem of not getting caught. One of those giant freaks took out a marathon runner with a fifteen-minute lead."

"Sir, that's the best part of the plan." Virgil rubbed his fist in his palm. "No one's going to run away. Mick thinks he can still get into the building, and he knows where the harpies' storerooms are. We need weapons and supplies if we're going to fight them. I don't think our little trick with swords and shields will work again."

"And I need medical supplies. We have people dying here," Esther added with urgency.

Cruz glared at Michael. "Don't think I'm going to let the harpies' three little pets go traipsing back to their masters so they can tell them everything they learned."

Michael grit his teeth and cast a simmering look at the officer.

Virgil exhaled in exasperation. "Sir, with all due respect, Mick and his brothers laid their lives on the line for us and have done nothing to deserve your suspicion."

He paused and took a deep breath. "Look, all three of them can't go anyway. We need one to get us in and be a guide, but they don't know what we need." He tapped his own chest. "I'm Air Force Pararescue. We're trained to go into places where we're not wanted and get back out. Give me another volunteer, and I'll go with Mick." Virgil leaned his hand on Michael's arm. "I trust the big guy with my life."

Esther lifted her chin. "I'll go. Neither of you have any idea what medical supplies I need."

Cruz met her eyes. "Well, that's not gonna happen, Doc. We can't afford to lose you."

"Then it's me." Tina elbowed her way into the middle of the huddled circle and planted her hands on her hips.

"Miss, what do you think you can do if there's trouble?"

Color rose in Tina's cheeks. "Captain, I saw Michael, Gabriel, and Rafael toss your men around like rag dolls. I expect I'd fare no worse. Look, besides Esther, I'm the only one who knows what medical supplies we need, and she's too important to risk. I'm not."

Cruz shot her a look, and Tina returned it with the same intensity.

Virgil smiled at him like a cat cornering a mouse. "Sir, ya know she's right on both points. Even if we pull this raid off, the odds of it working a second time's pretty slim. This will be a one-shot deal to grab what we need."

Captain Cruz threw his hands in the air. "All right, all right. We'll do it your way." His eyes narrowed as he turned to Michael. "Your two buddies will be under guard. If anything happens to Virgil or Tina, they will pay. Understand?"

Virgil cast a wary glance at Michael, whose neck was corded tight.

The tension in the building dissolved when Doctor Easley touched the giant clone's arm. The two regarded each other in silence for a long moment.

"Agreed, then." Cruz grunted with satisfaction. "Doc, you and I will put together a list. The three of you suit up and be ready to go an hour after sunset."

————•◆•————

Late that afternoon, the skies opened with a cold, driving rain which continued into the night. Tina stood at the edge of the barrier near the boundary with the Aussies' prison block. Sweat beaded on her forehead even though the strange suit kept her comfortable and dry. She forced herself to banter with Michael and Virgil, trying to stay calm.

The banter stopped short when a familiar voice cut in. "Hey, sheila, it's pouring. Shouldn't ya be under shelter, or are ya planning a little trip?"

Tina wiped acrid water from her face and returned an even smile to the ragged man in the prison camp next to theirs. "Just admiring the scenery, Martinel."

The Aussie snorted. "Yeah, and I'm a harpy. I can tell you're up to something. I just pray it hurts those hopping bastards." He chuckled, bobbing his head. "Ahh, if you come back this way, I'd really appreciate it if you could bring me something I could use for a crutch."

Tina and Virgil sighed. The wish list Captain Cruz had given them was already more than a dozen people could carry. "The only thing missing from this list is an Abrams Tank." Virgil turned from Martinel and looked down the barrier perimeter of his own camp. There they saw nothing in the wet, inky darkness, but the group knew the 10th Mountain Division troops gathered at the far end to create a diversion.

Tina stood close to him with a nervous smile pasted on her face. Her whole body trembled, and she felt light-headed. She studied her co-conspirators in the eerie blue glow of the poles. Both men exchanged light pleasantries with the Aussie as if preparing for a stroll in the park. *What in the name of Heaven made me crazy enough to volunteer for this?* She stared with eyes the size of saucers. The big ugly sentries had passed by a few minutes ago, so she knew the operation would begin soon.

In the distance, she heard it—over two hundred men screaming at the top of their lungs. She heard a faint, electronic sizzle and knew those men were throwing stones at the barrier as fast as they could. *God, I hope this works.*

She stroked the strange suit that kept her dry despite the downpour. *At least I got a change of clothes out of this mess.* Tina gulped as she saw her two friends tense to spring into the charged field.

"What da hell do you Yanks think you're going to do?" Martinel's mouth dropped open. "Are you crazy?"

Michael grabbed Tina's hand and sprinted forward. Virgil grunted and dashed after them. Tina staggered through the field, and her brain reeled with searing pain like thousands of needles jabbing her exposed face. Then it vanished, and she was on the other side. She winced and looked back. *God, that hurt.*

Martinel pumped his fist in the air. "I'll be damned! Godspeed, Yanks, Godspeed." The Aussie hopped on his good leg with a broad grin.

Tina tensed at a light tap on her shoulder. The outline of Michael motioned in the direction of where the large hive-like structure stood. "Hurry. We must be quick."

"Okay," she choked out.

She hadn't taken a step further when a soft electronic buzz sounded in her ear, followed by a flat female voice she didn't recognize. "Are you a friend of Dante?"

Tina stumbled and whipped her head around.

Virgil paused and whispered, "Tina, we shouldn't be chatting. But you know for my part, I considered the kid a friend."

"That wasn't me," Tina wheezed through a constricted throat. "I didn't say anything."

Virgil crouched low and pulled Tina down by his side. He swept the inky darkness with his eyes.

Michael, who hadn't stopped, jogged back with his hands pressed against his temples. "Come on. We can't loiter here." He shook his head. "Why is everything so silent?"

The electronic buzz hummed again. "Who are you? Are you a friend of Dante?"

Hope shone in Tina's eyes as she felt the hood of the suit vibrate by her ears. "Yes, yes, yes. He was — he's a very special friend. Is he alive?"

"Thank you. I will classify you as guests, then, and override my firewall security. In response to your query, Dante's biological mechanisms continue to function. However, my sensors indicate their performance is suboptimal. Identify yourselves… please. Your neural net suits have a… seven percent charge. Communications will be lost soon."

"I'm Tina. Please help him. He's a very good man."

Two beeps replied. "Guest Tina, my knowledge base is limited, but I am monitoring his vital signs. The next planetary cycle will determine whether his body will maintain viability. You are identified and clear."

Virgil growled as he touched the invisible speaker in his hood. "Just help the kid. Now before I tell you who I am, who the hell are you?"

"Dante has assigned me the name Beatrice, and I have accepted that label. My sensors indicate you carry the same tracking device as Dante did. He was insistent on rendering it inoperable. I recommend you do the same based on his experience."

"Yeah, well, that's easier said than done." Virgil ran his hand over his chest. "The name is Sergeant Virgil Bernius. Call me Virg."

"I can instruct the grapheme neural net suit you wear to jam the beacon while it holds power."

"Then do it," Virgil snapped.

"Ahh, Virgil, who are you talking to? We've got to get out of here before the guardians show up." Michael studied the impenetrable darkness for any telltale movement.

"Mick, don't you have someone talking into your ear right now?"

"No. There is nothing but silence." Michael's face clouded in confusion. "For the first time, there is no sound in my head. All I hear is some nonsense coming out of you and Tina."

A light crackle preceded the voice this time. "Guest Virg and Guest Tina, I have blocked communications with your companion. Dante identified an entity transmitting data on the same frequency as an enemy. That individual is not considered a guest."

"No, no, Mick's okay." Virgil raised his hands to no one. "A big ugly chased Dante. Those guys are nasty customers, but Mick isn't one of them. Ahh... can you block Michael's transmissions like you're doing for me?"

"Transmissions from the person identified as Michael were jammed before I initiated communications with you. The life forms from the bed-and-breakfast cannot receive direct evidence of my existence. Jamming his data transmissions consumes more power than the simple beacon you have. His suit will power down in approximately three hours, twelve minutes. I have logged you into my security override algorithm. I am ceasing communications now."

Tina's lips formed a tight smile. "'Bed-and-breakfast'? Now I know you must've met Dante."

"Virgil, Tina, what is going on?" Michael crouched on the ground with his palms tight against his temples.

The sergeant glanced around first. "Ahh—I'm talking to someone named Beatrice. She doesn't like you."

Michael lowered his hands. "She must be related to Captain Cruz," he snorted, but then his tone turned curious. "Beatrice? Is she the heavenly spirit from the *Divine Comedy* that Dante loved?"

"I'm guessing it's not very likely. By the way, it seems like there's some sort of data transmitter inside you. Beatrice is jamming it for now, but it won't last long."

"Interesting." Michael groped for words. "When we came through the barrier, I felt... free. It was like something that was clawing at my mind had stopped. I never noticed it until it was gone." After a moment, he shuddered. "Tell Beatrice thank you. Now let's get going. You can tell me the rest later, but we have to move." He grabbed Tina's hand. "This way."

They had gone a couple hundred yards when Michael whispered for them to drop down. As the three flattened themselves in the red mud, they felt the ground vibrate as many unseen clones raced past them toward the prison. They waited a full minute before they rose, caked in muck.

"There's an entrance on the far side that is often deserted," Michael whispered. They jogged to the black building without any other encounters.

"And if it's not deserted?" Tina touched the side of the building and jerked her hand away. It felt dry despite the rain.

"Then we avoid them if we can, or deal with them if we can't," Virgil answered, snarling.

Tina shrank and her heart pounded. "I don't think I can do this. It's easy to be brave surrounded by friends. But here, I'm—"

"You're doing just fine. We slip in, find the stuff we need, and slip out. It's just a walk in the park." Virgil gripped her arm.

Tina grimaced in turn. "Yeah, a walk in the park, after dark, with monsters lurking behind every bush."

They crept along the curved wall for a few minutes when Michael stopped them. "Here's the entrance. Are you ready?"

Tina squeaked out a yes and Virgil squeezed her shoulders. "You're doin' fine, kid. Lead on, Mick."

She eyed the door. It appeared to be a perfect square, about six feet by six feet, with no hinges or knobs. Except for a slight indentation, it looked identical to the rest of the building's surface.

Michael crouched and palmed the entrance sensor. The door slid open, bathing the three soaked figures in blue light. His eyes swept the empty room for movement. He swallowed hard and led them inside when he detected no movement.

Despite eleven years in the service and a month in the alien's prison, Virgil gawked like a tourist as the door closed behind him. "Not exactly a model for *Better Homes and Gardens*, is it?"

Tina smirked. Virgil's attempt at humor eased her nerves as she studied the lofty dome and then the warren of passages sloping down from the broad chamber they stood in.

"This way." Michael turned and hurried down a ramp at the far left.

The others followed close behind. They continued down the incline for three more levels when Michael called a halt and keyed all of his senses on a pathway to their right. "The human artifact storage room is here. It is not visited very often, but that doesn't mean we won't be interrupted." Michael palmed the door open. Inside was a cavernous room with a low ceiling lit by the ever-present blue light.

"Don't the harpies have security cameras or anything like that?" Tina paused when she entered the room.

"Yes, of course, but guardians are often sent to these rooms for retrieval purposes. You and Virgil would be seen as immature guardians." Michael rubbed his jaw. "We need to move quickly to avoid arousing suspicion. My brethren follow their master's commands and do not spend much time poking around. Dis monitors everything, but sensing us here would not trip any warning mechanism."

She tried to orient herself for her task, but the tables and shelves were arranged in no order she could discern. "Michael, where would I find the medical supplies?"

"I will take you there."

Virgil studied the tables, all of them laden with human weaponry. "Now this is what I'm talking about." Locking in on what he sought, he told the other two, "You guys go ahead. I'm gonna check the stuff over here."

He hadn't finished speaking before he hefted a Russian MP-443 Grach pistol. He placed it back down and strapped on a US Army belt and harness. Virgil unholstered the Beretta 9mm and ejected its magazine, examined it, and slammed it back in.

The last thing Tina saw as she followed Michael around a corner was Virgil inspecting and placing grenades, ammunition, and handguns into a large sack. Lost in worried thought, Tina bumped into Michael's back.

"I believe the equipment and chemicals you require will be found here."

Tina took a ragged breath and examined the items. "Most of these labels are in Cyrillic."

Michael looked at the hermetically sealed hemostat Tina held. "I will translate for you, if needed."

She gazed up at the big man. "How many languages do you know?"

Michael tilted his head up in thought. "Remember, they bred me to be a human infiltrator. I am fluent in twenty-three Earth-based languages." He paused and traced his fingers across a suture set. "The harpies overran a hospital in their raid on the Earth nation state called Russia. It was their first venture to your home world, and they collected much material there."

Tina shuddered as she envisioned the carnage that must have occurred in that remote medical center, then forced herself to think of the task at hand. "See if you can find something we can carry this stuff in. We'll also need a water purifier and a camp stove—"

Michael nodded and headed off.

"—portable lights, tarps, a solar battery charger, and rope. You always need rope."

Michael waved once more without turning around and vanished down another aisle. Tina swept a table clear and placed the surgical tools there, then moved to another row of shelves. *Where are the painkillers, antibiotics, and antiseptics?* She squealed in delight when she found a Field Medical Surgical kit labeled in Spanish.

Twenty minutes later, Michael returned carrying a bulging duffel bag slung on his back and a small empty one in his hand. He grunted and rolled his neck as the load thumped onto the floor. He gave the empty sack to Tina.

She placed the surgical equipment into the bag. "Did you find everything?"

"Of course I did. I would not have returned if I could not complete my mission."

Tina opened her mouth for a sarcastic retort but saw the earnest look in the big man's eyes. "Let's go find Virgil and get out of here."

Michael grunted as he hefted the bag on his back and nodded in silent agreement. They later found Virgil, armed to the teeth, with a bag stuffed as full as Michael's.

Tina arched her eyebrows at the Special Forces Sergeant. "It looks like you're ready to go to war."

"That's what I plan to do." Virgil handed them both belts with holstered pistols. "Put these on."

Michael and Tina buckled the webbing around their waists. Tina's hand shook as she cinched the belt into place. "I don't like guns."

"Well, you don't have much choice," Virgil growled, but then his eyes softened. "Look, Tina, one way or another, this ain't gonna end pretty. Either those harpies'll be dead or we will. There's no middle ground."

Tina lowered her head and wiped her sweaty palms on the strange suit. She marveled as the moisture vanished.

Virgil lifted his weapon. "This is the Beretta nine millimeter. It's not my favorite, but this is the standard US Military issue." He made sure he had her attention as he pointed to the rear of the barrel. "This is the safety. Release it, point the business end at what you want to kill, and squeeze the trigger. You have to hold steady because it's definitely not a hair-trigger, and the weapon will drift on you." He looked her in the eyes. "You got it?"

She breathed. "Yes, I got it."

"We need to leave," Michael hissed. "Now."

Tina clamped her teeth to stop them from chattering as fear of the trip back overwhelmed her. *We're halfway home. I can do this.* She followed the two men with their large satchels up the sloping tunnel.

———————◆———————

They reached the exit without encountering anyone, but when Michael opened the door, they came face to face with two harpies. The monsters recovered from their surprise and drew their weapons and dropped Virgil as he reached for his gun.

Michael dropped his load and charged one of the harpies, driving the creature to the ground and jarring the weapon from its clawed hand. The second harpy hovered nearby, waiting for a clear shot. Michael snapped the first harpy's neck and roared in defiance at the second alien.

He jolted when the room reverberated with the loud discharge of a pistol. The harpy's head exploded, and its lifeless body fell. In the dim light of the open portal, he saw Tina standing, steady as a rock, gripping a still-smoking pistol in two hands. He saw a savage fierceness in that gentle woman's face he did not believe possible. An instant later, however, her eyes shifted to concern. She dropped the pistol and rushed to where Virgil lay face down in the mud.

Michael muttered, "Humans are an amazing species. I'm proud to be one of them." He dragged the harpy bodies outside, looked around the building's interior, and closed the door. Someone would likely come soon to investigate the noise.

Tina lifted her eyes to him as she shook Virgil. "He's not moving. What did they do to him?"

Michael crouched next to her, handing her the discarded gun he retrieved as he studied the soldier. "It's somewhat similar to the weapon you call a Taser, though it stuns the victim for over an hour."

"An hour? What are we going to do? We can't stay here." Tina's eyes swept the nighttime landscape. There wasn't a hint of movement, but the rain had stopped. They had far less cover.

Michael opened the duffel bag and pulled out a tarp and a coil of rope. "You are correct. The masters we killed will be missed. We must depart." He laid Virgil on the tarp and placed the large satchels on top of him. "The ride's going to be a bit bumpy, my friend." He bound everything on the tarp with the rope.

Virgil's eyes flared as the gear piled on his chest.

Tina followed close by but came to a sudden halt. Michael stopped soon after and watched her hand shoot up to her ear, covered by her hood. After a moment, her eyes shone with a hint of tears, and she blurted out, "You must help him! I love him."

Michael slogged over with a rope across his chest, yoked to the makeshift litter. He eyed Tina, puzzled by her behavior, until it clicked. "Ahh, are you communicating with that strange voice again?"

"Yes, Michael, I'm talking to Beatrice. Dante's in those mountains, and I think he's dying. I have to help him."

Michael glanced at the distant mountain range, just visible in the clearing night sky, and then at the prison camp outlined by the glowing blue poles. "I don't trust any voices in my head. Even if this Beatrice is on our side, we can't help Dante now. We have to get Virgil and these supplies to our people."

"Beatrice says she's jamming your transmitter, so you can pull your hood up if you want to talk to her."

"Tell her no thanks. Now let's get going." Without waiting for a response, he dug his heels in the mud and struggled onward, dragging his load.

Tina hurried up next to him, and they trudged in silence toward the prison barrier.

As they reached the line of blue poles, Michael palmed one and it went dark. He dragged the dead weight of his load through and saw Tina standing on the outside, staring at the mountains.

He jumped when he heard a hissing voice. "Yank, get out of there. Them big uglies are comin'."

"Tina, move. They're coming and I must close the fence," Michael pleaded.

"No, Michael. Dante needs help, and I have to go to him."

Michael groaned. He saw in his peripheral vision a squad of soldiers heading toward them from inside the camp, and recalled a word Virgil taught him. "Shit. If those guardians catch the soldiers outside the prison, it will be a massacre." He glanced at the Aussie. "Try to distract the big uglies for a few minutes."

He sprang to his feet, grabbed Tina, tossed her inside the barrier, and palmed the pole so it glowed blue again. He shook the weariness from his limbs and jogged.

"Fair dinkum," Martinel squeaked. "Hey, you ugly bastards, your dicks are more shriveled than a year-old prune!"

Michael sighed and remarked, "That will never work." He waved his arms and shouted, "Hey, big uglies,

I'm over here!" Roaring bellows answered him as he glanced over his shoulder. *Well, that got their attention.*

He fled for the distant mountains with a howling pack in pursuit.

CHAPTER XII
Planting a Seed

Planting a Seed
Hardly the bed of the ravine below
His feet had reached, ere they had reached the hill.
Right over us; but he was not afraid.

Dante's Inferno – Canto XXIII

The sun's rays shot out across the ridgeline of mountains for a moment as morning arrived before thick clouds rolled across the horizon and blocked the light. The flash of light remained long enough to outline the silhouettes of the three clones in pursuit.

Michael grunted and lengthened his stride. He had never felt so free. No claws sunk into his mind, demanding action. He swung his arms and spun. They moved without constraints despite the skin-tight suit.

Michael glanced over his shoulder at the clones chasing him and settled into a long, loping stride. He altered his route toward rougher-looking ground with more jagged stones. From what he could tell, his pursuers were fresh out of stasis. Their feet would be nothing more than bloody stumps before they caught him.

Michael felt the rhythmic slap of the holster on his hip as he moved and wondered why humans had developed such a complicated, inefficient weapon. The simplest of energy shields could defend against it. He glanced over his shoulder again, and a feral grin creased his face as another thought crossed his mind. *It will suffice. My pursuers have no energy shields.*

The first fat raindrops splattered on him, and soon a downpour drenched his clothing, sticking it to his skin. Michael pulled up the tight-fitting hood and decided to engage his foes when he reached the boulders in the hills up ahead.

Then an electronic buzz filled his ears before a voice spoke to him. "Not-Guest Michael, are those who follow you enemies from the bed-and-breakfast, or are they not-guest friends of Dante?"

Michael stumbled at the sudden new sound but collected himself quickly. "Are you the one who talked to Tina and Virgil earlier? Ahh, Beatrice?"

"Yes. Respond to question."

"I am not sure I understand your question. But those who follow me would kill Dante if they had the opportunity, and I will do whatever I can to protect him."

"Since you wear a neural net suit, my heuristics accept your response as sufficient. I will reclassify you as Guest Michael. Vector twenty-eight degrees south." Another buzz. "My fauna husbandry knowledge base is insufficient, and I require assistance. Instruct your companions to depart. My security protocols will not allow you to approach while they accompany you."

Michael angled south without breaking stride and loosened the strap holding the pistol in place. He recalled a phrase Virgil had used and said, "Roger that," then examined the rising ground before him for a place to make his stand. With the inefficient weapon, he would need a perfect ambush site.

Michael swallowed and glanced at the gun bouncing at his side, and he wished then that Virgil had mentioned how many of the small metal projectiles fit in the weapon. *I am going to need many to take them down.*

Michael dashed up a broken slope and spotted two large boulders in the path before him. "Well, Beatrice, wish me luck. I will attempt to terminate those not-guests from the bed-and-breakfast in a minute."

Beatrice responded with a buzz and a click. "Luck denotes indeterminate variability in outcome. It is a fixed requirement; they cannot approach my boundary."

Michael sighed as he stepped behind the rocks and drew the Beretta. "I will make sure to tell them they are not welcome."

The first guardian's head appeared around the boulder. It spotted Michael and roared in triumph. His opponent's eyes showed none of the madness of compulsion. *At least he will have the good sense to die when I shoot him.*

Michael released the safety and fired. The bullet struck a rock three feet from his target. The kick of the gun surprised him, and he struggled to regain his balance. "How can humans work with such imprecise devices?" he muttered as the second shot grazed the charging clone's arm. He fired the next two shots at point-blank range, and the guardian dropped dead with a look of surprise on its face.

"Boundary intrusion is not acceptable," Beatrice informed him.

"I'm doing my best."

The second guardian leapt over the corpse of the first, and two slugs slammed into him before he reached Michael. Blood poured from the clone's chest and right arm, but he charged forward without regard to his wounds.

Michael sidestepped the bull rush and snap-kicked the blade of his foot into the clone's wounded side. As the giant albino crumbled, Michael smashed the palm of his hand into the bridge of its nose, driving bone into the creature's brain. The guardian died before it hit the ground.

The third guardian slammed into Michael before he had a chance to turn and face his pursuer. Michael's head spun from the impact of hitting the shale outcropping, and the gun flew from his convulsing hand. He twisted and swung his fists blindly, but his opponent had already skipped back, circling for an opening.

I know what this guy's next move will be. Michael gulped air and whispered a prayer of thanks to the human's God. *All this time I've trained the human soldiers, they have also trained me.* He rolled his shoulders and recalled in perfect detail every move Virgil had used against him.

Head lowered, the guardian charged. Michael smiled, anticipating his opponent would break left and throw his right fist at his neck. Michael spun away from the attack and side-kicked the clone's knee. He heard the tendons pop as his opponent crashed to the ground. The guardian twisted and tried to stand. A kick to the head drove him back down. The clone rolled over, dazed.

Michael held back the final death blow as he regarded the clone's eyes as they snapped back into focus. He expected the glare of a rabid animal but instead saw brave defiance in his opponent's face. The harpies must not have erased the emotion from him yet.

His head throbbed, but his limbs responded as he moved warily just out of reach of the prostrate guardian. Curiosity overcame him. He had never spoken more than a dozen words to any destroyer. "Why are you hunting me?"

The clone paused, surprised at being spoken to in the masters' language. "You are an escaped human. All humans that breech the confinement pens must be destroyed."

Michael raised his arms wide. "But I am a guardian who chose to be human."

The clone's face clouded. "Then you are a traitor. Humans are the enemy of the masters."

"If they are enemies, it is because the masters have chosen to make it so. Human technology barely allows them to escape the surface of their home world."

Indecision entered the clone's voice. "Then they are inferior and should be conquered by the masters?"

Michael held up his hand and flexed his fingers. "Look at yourself. Guardians are to be instruments for the conquest of the human world, but the same blood flows in our veins as these 'inferiors' on whom we will make war." He spat on the ground as he had seen Virgil do to make a point. "The difference is they fight for their lives and to be free. The guardians fight because they are slaves."

The clone's jaw stiffened as he considered thoughts that had never occurred to him before.

Michael's mind raced with new ideas. "You see me before you. My podmates and I chose humanity over slavery."

"No, that is not possible. The masters are all-wise and all-caring. How can there be any other way?"

"You are a tool to be discarded when your usefulness is done. They control you with programming and compulsion. It is all a lie. I am a man. I will do what I believe is right and not because of a command echoing through my head."

"But, how did you become yourself?"

Michael paused and thumped his chest, thinking back on all the time he had spent with the human captives. "I was given a name. I am Michael, and I am a person."

The clone stopped all pretense of aggression. "How did you receive such a gift?"

Michael regarded the pale giant staring at him. "A human bestowed that treasure on me. One who, right now, desperately needs my help." A flash of inspiration struck him. "As I was named, I so name you. From now on, you are Reggie. Bear the title with honor. It belonged to the noblest person I have ever met." He bowed. "Reggie, I mourn the loss of your podmates, but I will leave this place now. Will you contest it?"

Beatrice's buzz rose in Michael's ears. "Interesting concepts. I have learned much regarding your thought process. Will you hold a similar discussion with the three additional not-guests who will arrive at your current location in seven minutes?"

Reggie stared at Michael. "I will not hinder you." He grimaced as he tried to shift his weight off of his bad leg. "I have much to consider."

Michael's head spun from handling the two separate conversations. "Reggie, other guardians approach. I must leave."

Reggie lifted his chin. "Go, Michael. I will not hamper your escape."

Michael eyed a narrow fissure which cleaved the rock wall at the far side of the clearing. He saw dim daylight on the far side and slipped in. He turned and saw Reggie limp in his direction and met the clone's eyes. "While in the healing machine, consider absorbing some literature produced by these 'inferior beings'. I recommend Tolkien, C.S. Lewis, and Dante Alighieri. You will find their stories fascinating." Michael scrambled through the narrow opening and disappeared, leaving clattering shale in his wake.

———— ♦ ————

Three clones clambered into the small clearing. They appraised the two dead guardians and approached the one wincing in pain and leaning against what appeared to be a shallow recess in a sheer cliff. He held his leg and groaned.

"Which way did the prey go?" asked one of the Guardians.

"I do not know." Reggie bit his lower lip. "I do not know many things."

———— ♦ ————

Michael gasped as he pulled himself atop the cliff. Before him stretched a lake over a mile wide and over two miles long. To his left and right stood mountains just as steep as the one he had just climbed. *It will take me hours to get around this.* He searched the shoreline below the rock outcropping. It was barren, but the strange scent of lush growth filled his nostrils.

He recalled some human literature. Huckleberry Finn. That was it. Michael remembered the story with pleasure because he could relate so well to Huckleberry's friend named Jim. He sighed as he looked at the water, recalling that Jim and Huckleberry had a vessel called a raft to traverse the body of water known as the Mississippi. Michael couldn't swim and didn't possess a raft. Stumped, he pulled at the hood over his head. "Beatrice, will you please help me?"

Silence.

Michael put his hands on his hips. "The one time I could use a voice in my head, and I get nothing."

A sudden pain jabbed him and he slapped at the source. Michael lifted a tiny object with razor-sharp mandibles and gossamer wings. He stared at it in curiosity while hundreds more swarmed him. They stung him over and over as they opened the seam of his suit. The tiny creatures crawled inside despite his flailing. His frantic motions slowed and he slammed down to his knees before falling flat on his back, half-conscious.

Beatrice's voice returned. "As my prediction model indicated, the beacon in your chest has the same power source as Guest Dante. Your suit's energy reserve dropped below its critical level. I had to choose between terminating you or repowering the neural net suit. The data transmitter embedded at the base of your neck must be jammed to ensure security."

Michael went limp. An ivory-colored orb approached and floated over him. Soon after, he felt a searing pain as a number of the scurrying micro-bots peeled the flesh of his chest open and then dragged the disk out of his exposed muscles. *How am I losing so little blood?* His numb mind felt like an outside observer.

Two long, thin tentacles telescoped out of the orb. One speared the disk, and the other connected to the seam in Michael's suit. Although paralyzed, he observed the procedure with curious detachment.

The glowing blue light in the disk device pulsed slower and then faded out. The scurrying micro-bots then flew to the orb and adhered themselves to its surface. Michael sighed with involuntary contentment as the stinging receded and a numbing sensation spread across his paralyzed body. A third tentacle extended to him. He smelled burning flesh but felt nothing. The numbness eased and he moved his head. The cauterized wound in his chest throbbed.

"Your suit now holds a sixty-eight percent charge," Beatrice announced. "That will suffice for current demands. You will be transported to Guest Dante. My heuristic models cannot determine the appropriate treatment. I require assistance in ensuring his continued viability as a living entity."

Michael tried to move but couldn't do anything but moan. One of the insect-like micro-bots lifted the darkened, dime-sized disk and vanished from his limited range of vision. He shuddered as something smooth and metallic slid underneath him. He felt himself lifted, and air rushed across his cheeks as the bots flew toward the far shore. Fat drops of rain stung him as they whipped his face.

CHAPTER XIII
Alliances

The laws of the abyss, are they thus broken?
Or is there changed in heaven some council new,
That being damned ye come unto my crags?

Dante's Purgatorio – Canto I

Michael's unresponsive body moved through the field until the robots rested him next to Dante. When he could finally move, he sat up and noticed Dante attempting to raise his head, but the young man's eyes fluttered and closed again. A large portal stood a hundred feet away at the base of a tall mountain. He lifted his fevered friend from the ground and headed for it.

He kicked what appeared to be a solid plexi-steel door with his foot, then shot a look at the orb hovering nearby. "We need to get him into a shelter. You can't leave him out here in the rain. He's burning up with a fever."

Beatrice's voice rose from the orb. "You are in error. Four hundred thirty-seven years of data indicates that flora grows healthier in the elements."

"Well, Dante is no damn plant. We need to get him inside, and we need to get this fever down."

Dante groaned, "I don't feel so good." A moment later, a glint of recognition cut through his weary features. "Michael? How the hell did you get here?"

Concern etched across Michael's brow. "Will you let me bring him inside?"

"You possess a bi-directional data transmitter the neural net suit is jamming," said Beatrice. "Removal of the suit will terminate its ability to block those signals. The security protocols are prohibiting your entry. It is an unacceptable risk."

Michael's jaw tightened as he studied Dante's flushed face. "Do whatever must be done to lower the security risk. He needs medical care."

"I am synthesizing a device which will satisfy self-defense requirements. It will be ready in twelve point four minutes."

Michael pulled Dante close to his chest to shelter him from the icy wind driving sheets of rain. "What do you have for medicine?"

Two buzzes and a click. "I have a wide variety of nitrogen-rich fertilizers. Will they suffice?"

"Stupid machine. No, no they will not." His forehead wrinkled, and his eyes lit up. "I remember reading that humans often synthesized drugs from plants. Do you have any plants containing salicylic acid? Humans make a fever medicine called aspirin from the bark of a tree they call a willow."

"Yes, that chemical exists in a grove of trees on the far side of this valley. One of my drones is now retrieving bark containing the substance. What quantity do you need?"

"I can't remember for sure… I think the correct amount is about seven hundred milligrams per dose."

"Understood."

Michael jumped when Dante spoke again. "Michael, I'm glad you're here. I didn't want to die all alone." He rolled his eyes at the portal. "Would you tell Tina I'm sorry I couldn't come for her and that I love her?"

"Tell her yourself. You're not going to die." Michael's voice became urgent. "Beatrice, let us in! I swear I will do whatever you ask."

"One of my harvester machines is bringing you a device. Place it around your neck under the neural net suit."

A small hatch in the massive door popped open, and a round drone two feet in diameter hovered before Michael. Hundreds of small gossamer-winged micro-bots clung to its surface, making the harvester appear scaled. A tentacle extended with a black circlet dangling from its tip. To Michael, it looked and felt like a band of nylon rope. He lay Dante down and snatched the smooth band.

Beatrice then warned him, "Be aware, once this jamming device is in place, it can never be removed. It will draw power from your data recorder. Once the connection is established, any break will cause the jammer to detonate."

Michael squeezed the rope-like device until his knuckles whitened, then glanced at the feverish Dante. "I understand." He pulled the cord over his head, and it contracted to a snug fit as he settled it into place. His hand touched the collar as he felt a slight prick on the back of his neck.

"Security protocol is now in place. You may enter. Production of medicine for the makers is in my directives, but I am unaware of anything in that class. Achieving a new category of information and the use of the containment tools outweigh the risk of a level two security breach."

The door opened at last, and Michael rushed in, greeted by a puff of warm, dry air. The rain stopped, and a cavernous room bathed in soft golden light spread before him.

Michael sighed with relief, unsure how far he could press his requests. He barked in his best imitation of Captain Cruz's voice. "Now I need a bed and blankets for him."

"Understood," said Beatrice. "Synthetic or natural fiber?"

"I don't care. And heated water."

"Define heated water."

"Dammit, hot water, just short of boiling."

"Understood."

"And where's the medicine?"

"First dose of salicylic acid will be available in thirteen point five minutes."

"And how about some food? I'm starving."

Beatrice gave two buzzes, followed by three quick beeps. "I have waited four hundred thirty-seven years for that request. Edible material will be delivered in three point seven minutes. Eighty-seven meters to your right is an enclosure which should serve as an adequate dwelling. Do not leave it unless escorted by one of my drones."

———◆———

Dante opened his eyes and stared without comprehension at an unadorned, ivory-colored wall. Other details remained blurred, but they slowly came into focus. He lay in a twelve-by-twelve-foot room devoid of any furnishings.

"It is good to see you awake," said a familiar voice.

Dante looked around until he spotted Michael's bloodshot eyes. "Michael, what the hell are you doing here?" He turned and felt a soft foam-like mattress beneath him. "And, for that matter, where's here?"

Michael blushed, looking thoughtful. "You are in Purgatory."

"Say what? I must still be delirious. I thought you just said we're in Purgatory."

"Beatrice insisted I give the mountain a name. And since you are Dante, and our host is Beatrice, I offered the name Mount Purgatory."

Beatrice's voice came through an invisible speaker in the ceiling. "It is a satisfactory label."

Dante pinched the bridge of his nose and groaned. "I suppose the valley out there is Heaven, then?"

"That's a foolish statement," Michael stuttered.

"My bio-mes has been labeled Eden," said Beatrice.

"And the lake I took the dip in?" Dante propped himself on his elbows and gazed around the room.

"My reservoir is labeled Lake Eunoe."

Dante rolled his eyes toward Michael. "And that is…?"

Michael threw open his hands. "The body of water that borders Eden, of course."

"Of course." Dante pulled himself to a sitting position.

Michael sighed and lowered his head. "Well, as best as I can determine, we are inside Purgatory." He handed Dante a mug with a steaming liquid inside. Shortly after, he placed his hand on the young man's forehead and grunted in satisfaction.

"That I believe," Dante groaned as he accepted the cup.

A couple quiet beeps came through the speakers above. "I am the entire valley encircled by the mountains you crossed. This enclosure is part of the maker's botanical research center. You entered my grounds when you reached the shore of Lake Eunoe."

Dante turned his head to the left. The same voice came from a drone hovering there. He wore a long, loose, beige tunic. "Where's my suit?"

Michael chuckled. "The suit's processor couldn't adjust to your fever's temperature fluctuations, so it shut down with an error condition. Beatrice has corrected the code and is rebooting the suit's system."

Dante sipped from the cup in his hand and savored the aroma. "This stuff tastes sorta like coffee. I didn't think I'd ever taste it again. Where did you get it?"

Michael smiled as he dropped cross-legged onto the floor next to the mattress. "Beatrice here has been working overtime to provide any foodstuffs I can think of." He rubbed his neck and sighed. "It's been a bit tough for both of us. My only knowledge of human food is from literature; I've never tasted any."

"I am accessing programming I have not used since my operating system was installed four hundred thirty-seven years ago," said Beatrice. "Utilizing this software is satisfactory."

"Speaking of food, what do you have in the larder? I feel like I haven't eaten in a month." Dante stood on shaky legs and braced his hand against the wall, waiting for the spinning in his head to subside.

Michael took the cup from Dante and gripped the young man's free arm. "It's only been two days. You had me pretty worried until this morning when your fever broke. Do you feel strong enough to walk?" He pointed with his chin. "This little house Beatrice put us in has a dining and lavatory area over there."

"The neural net environmental suits are incapable of handling solid wastes. Also, the fecal matter deposited in the commodes has provided me with excellent bacterial research material."

"Happy to provide you with new research material," Dante deadpanned. "I'll see what I can do to give you more."

Michael rubbed his chin. "Beatrice seems to find a use for everything."

"Right." Dante shook his head and slumped against Michael as he took his first steps. He tilted his head back to speak and frowned when he noticed the rope-like collar his friend wore. "Hey, Michael, when did start wearing jewelry? You don't strike me as the necklace type." He smiled, sheepish. "Don't I get one, too?"

"It is very expensive jewelry." Michael's jaw clenched and his free hand went to his throat. "You do not want to pay this price."

Danted hadn't expected that reaction. "Ahh, okay. How about we change the subject? What do you got to eat? How about a bowl of chicken noodle soup?"

A small smile crinkled the corners of Michael's mouth. "I have never seen one, but I do not think our host has any chickens about."

"Guest Michael already made that request," Beatrice added. "Until your arrival, I had not encountered any animal life in four hundred thirty-seven years."

Dante rubbed his left temple. "Beatrice, you don't have to put a date stamp on everything you say. I get it. You were built four hundred thirty-seven years ago."

"Noted."

As they approached an oval, ivory-colored table supported by a single pedestal, a savory aroma made Dante's mouth water. "So what did you come up with?"

Michael's face reddened. "Neither Beatrice nor I have ever cooked a meal before, so we've been doing a little experimenting from the literature I have absorbed."

Dante sank onto a bench with a weary sigh. Michael placed the mug of coffee in front of his friend and walked to a wide, flat protrusion on the near wall. A large steaming crock sat on top of it. He ladled the contents into two bowls and returned to the table. After placing one near Dante, he moved around to the other side of the table and sat.

The drone swung in over Dante's head, just below the twelve-foot high ceiling. Dante marveled at the well-lit chamber. The walls, differentiated from the floor, looked like beige-and-green swirled marble polished to be glassy and smooth.

Michael stared at him expectantly. Dante sniffed the bowl. "It smells delicious. Do you have any spoons?"

Michael slapped his head. "I knew I forgot something. In his culture, they use cutlery to assist in the consumption process. They are usually three small, hand-held tools: a sharp blade, a set of tines on a handle, and a shallow cup on a handle."

"I am capable of fabricating a wide variety of tools," Beatrice said. "Do these tools require any software applications?"

"No, just an inert form of metal or plastic. The blade does need to be sharp enough to cut organic matter, and the material should be able to maintain structural integrity to two hundred and sixty degrees Celsius and withstand one hundred pounds of pressure."

More hums and clicks came from the robot. "Prototypes will be available to you in twenty-six minutes."

"Ahh, thanks guys. I'll just sip it out of the bowl for now." Dante's hands shook as he lifted the bowl to his lips and slurped. When he put it down, Michael was staring at him, and if the orb had eyes, Dante could have sworn it was staring at him, too.

"Is it a satisfactory consumable?" asked Beatrice.

Dante grimaced. "Ahh, what's in it?"

Michael puffed out his chest. "Based on my knowledge, the contents consist of lentils, red onions, and garlic. My recollection is that they are helpful for humans suffering from virus ailments."

Dante nodded and took another gulp. "Yeah, I think you're right. I can taste them. But next time, put a little salt in there. The flavor needs work."

"Salt." Michael leaned on his elbows and put his hands on top of his head. "How could I forget? It is a staple for human ingestion."

"Define salt. Perhaps I grow it."

Michael furrowed his brows. "No, you can't grow it. It is a ground-up rock composed of sodium chloride."

"Guests eat rocks? I have no record of makers consuming rocks."

Michael smirked. "Beatrice, you have no record of the makers eating anything." He looked at Dante, saddened. "My soup is ruined."

"It's okay." Dante took another long swallow of the soup. "Michael, is there anything in the inventory here similar to a lemon?"

A quizzical look crossed Michael's face, and the ivory orb floated down parallel to Dante's eyes, making a long buzz. "Unknown. However, I produce a variety of what you label fruit in my hypoid labs. I will bring them to you for correlation to plant labeled lemon."

"While I was in stasis, I often dreamed of what human food would taste like." Michael's face reddened. "I am sure my suppositions are all wrong."

Dante smiled. "Well, if we have any lemons, we can squeeze the juice from one of them into the soup stock. It'll make a good salt substitute. Beatrice, salt naturally occurs in sea water or in rock formations from ancient dry water beds. Do you have any mining capability?"

"Originally, no. I found it necessary to add to my supply of silica for processor fabrication, so I developed a tool for extracting it from the ground. I am capable of refining limited amounts of ore. Analyzing... I have identified a small vein of sodium chloride rock. I will initiate the process to acquire it for this location, now labeled Dwelling One."

A second orb arrived holding a large variety of pronged, sharpened, and cupped instruments made of a black metallic material in an open box. It dumped them unceremoniously on the table. Dante selected a utensil resembling a knife, fork, and spoon, but about twice the size of the norm.

He held them up to the orb. "Fabricate these about half this size, and they'll match my expectations."

"Specifications are now noted for future reference."

Dante spooned up some soup and paused, his spoon halfway to his mouth, as a thought struck him. He picked up the knife and ran his finger along the blade. "Beatrice, how extensive is your manufacturing facility?"

"I can produce and repair all of the equipment necessary for the maintenance of my bio-mes facility," came the reply.

Michael's eyes glinted. "Can you make weapons for us to fight the harpies?"

"I am a bio mes facility I am incapable of weapons production."

"What about those biting micro-bots you attacked me with?" Michael rubbed the sealed wound in his chest to emphasize his point.

"I monitored the conversation you held with the intruder while you attempted to reach my bio-mes station. The words you spoke meshed well with my understanding of my makers. I chose to assist you. However, by necessity, my firewall security is an independent system. I have limited interaction with it. The security protocol allowed me to expand my sentient being categories of maker and intruder to include guests and not-guests, but that was a pass-through request. I had no connection to its heuristic modeling. It will not allow me to fabricate any weapons for you."

"Michael, let me give this a try." Dante placed the knife with the sharp edge in the middle of the table. "Beatrice, could you replicate this eating tool with a longer blade—say, a meter long, and elongate the handle so it can be gripped by someone Michael's size?"

"Yes. It is a tool similar to a harvester blade."

The clone's lips thinned to a tight line. "Dante, I admire your effort here, but a sword is not going to be of much use to us. The harpies will blow us to pieces before we can get anywhere near them."

"Michael, bear with me. Let's see where this goes." Dante smiled and spooned up some more soup. "Beatrice, I need to use the harvester tool on the other side of the barrier the harpies have erected, but nothing seems to be able to pass through it except those neural net suits. Can you modify the harvester so it can be brought in there?"

"Not a serious impediment. The force field arrayed around the bed-and-breakfast is a variation of the energy shields I possess. It is designed to repel matter, but energy passes through it. The surface of the suit you wore is shrouded in a neural net. It absorbed the field's power into its own system. That is how I discovered you and initiated our conversations." Beatrice gave a long, quiet buzz as if lost in thought. "The concept of the plexi-steel harvester tool can be modified to be energy-based. It must be used with caution. The cutter consists of charged particles, so it will slice through any matter it touches."

Dante grinned wide. "Anything?"

"Given the blade length of one meter, it will cut through anything of that depth, regardless of whether it encounters organic or inorganic material. An energy shield could be constructed to negate the charged particles, but that would not be of consequence to such a harvesting tool."

Michael's mouth curled into a raptor's grin.

Dante stirred the now cool soup with his spoon. "Ahh, Beatrice, we could use a few dozen of those." He swung the spoon in the air and made a wistful grin. "How about naming those tools 'light blades'?"

"I have assigned the label of 'light blade' to the harvester tool. Why do you require so many tools? There are only two of you, and my equipment fabrication capabilities are limited."

Dante coughed into his sleeve. "Two prototypes for now will suffice. We'll need to experiment with them." He eyed Michael, then picked up the knife and stabbed it into the table. "However, I expect a busy harvest season soon at the bed-and-breakfast."

"I am unaware of any crops being grown there. Please bring me samples of their flora for my systems to analyze."

Michael pulled the knife out of the table and regarded it. "The harpies discourage agriculture. But I promise to bring back any vegetation I find."

Dante regarded the ivory robot hovering over the table. "There is one more reaping problem you could help us with."

Beatrice beeped twice. "State your request. It is satisfactory to enhance the farming tools and techniques."

"Well, there may be situations when we need to harvest something in a… hard-to-reach spot. Could you produce a tool able to project an energy beam over an extended distance? It would need to be portable and be able to continue operating for several hours."

"Condensed wave light… portable power source… adjustable target distance…" The last buzz faded out. "Yes, but it would be dangerous. The tool would cut through anything in the path of its beam."

Dante nodded. "Ahh, that's a very good point. Could you add a mechanism to the tool so the harvester would be sure of what it's targeting?"

"I agree. That would be a prudent addition."

Michael flushed with excitement. "How long before you could fabricate such a tool?"

"Required materials are not readily available. It will be three days before initial prototypes are available for beta testing."

Dante gave the orb a smile, one twisted with a cruel edge. "Beatrice, please label that new tool a 'ray gun'. And Beatrice, thank you."

"Guest Dante, no thank you is required. It was interesting to observe your override of the security protocols. The firewall integrity is not as refined as I expected it to be."

Dante paled and his breath caught. "You knew what I was doing?"

"Yes. The firewall system is not as self-aware as I am. It views you as a threat. I view you as a guest. I touched the edge of the computer system at the bed-and-breakfast. It is also self-aware but cares nothing about growing things. Its heuristic models are wrong. It wants nothing more than to improve its own makers' ability to kill and destroy. I have reaffirmed its label of an intruder. I will aid you in fighting it within my constraints."

Michael rubbed his chin. "Since you want to help, could you also modify a couple of these orbs so we can drive them?" He looked at Dante with a glint in his eye. "It's a long walk back to the prison, and we're going to have some fighting to do when we get there."

The corners of Dante's mouth tightened, and he nodded in grim assent. He then sighed and noted Michael's red-rimmed eyes. "But first, I need some rest. I think we both do." Dante stood and walked to the bedroom. "And, Beatrice, when I wake up, I'll instruct you on how to make soap and build a shower."

CHAPTER XIV
Escalation

If I had rhymes both rough and stridulous,
As were appropriate to the dismal hole
Down upon which thrust all the other rocks,

Dante's Inferno – Canto XXXII

"Over here," Tina shouted as she regarded the energy fence and rubbed her stinging face.

Seven soldiers jogged over. One of them bent to examine Virgil and asked, "What happened to him?"

Tina bit her lip and tried to see where Michael had gone. "We have to move Virgil and these supplies now." She turned to face the soldiers. "Big uglies will be coming by in a minute, and we don't want to arouse their curiosity. Hurry."

"Yes, ma'am," the tall, raw-boned lieutenant replied. To the other soldiers, he said, "You heard the lady. Move your worthless asses."

"Wait a second." Tina bent to the litter and pulled a folded cane from the bag. "Okay, you can take it now."

Six of the men dragged the litter, vanishing behind the dark walls of the clay huts. The seventh, Lieutenant Gentile, glared at the shimmering barrier and listened to the unseen commotion beyond it. "I thought there were three of you. Where's the big ugly spy?"

The terror of the night, coupled with the suspicion in the man's voice, sapped the last of Tina's patience

She walked up and jabbed him in his chest. "His name is Michael, and right now, he's drawing the damn clones away from here. He saved Virgil and me."

Gentile took a step backwards under her approach and sharp voice, taking a gulp as he moved. "Yes, ma'am. Sorry, but we're supposed to keep tabs on that one. The captain's not going to be happy when he finds out Michael's gone."

"Hey, mate, ya should believe the sheila," snorted another voice. "I saw the big guy running for the hills, whooping and hollering with a pack of them big uglies on his heels."

Martinel watched them from the Australian prison compound. The man was drenched; Tina guessed he must have stood outside all night. She stared toward the distant hills in the now silent darkness and gave a curt nod when Gentile made his excuses and jogged back to the shelters. All went quiet.

She glanced at the folded tube in her hand, then walked to the barrier where the Aussie watched with rapt attention. "Mister Martinel, I hope this helps." She tried to walk through the barrier and gasped as it repulsed her.

"Are you okay, Miss?" Martinel hobbled to the barrier across from where Tina stood flexing her fingers.

"Yeah. My hand feels a little numb, but I'm fine." She narrowed her eyes as she considered the barrier. "I walked right through that thing last time."

He looked thoughtful for a second. "I gotta admit, it was the darndest thing seeing you and your friends stroll right through the energy field. It's gotta be the suit." Martinel scratched the back of his head before pointing to the folded cane. "But the field still seems to stop everything else."

Tina slapped her forehead. "I'm so stupid. Of course." She pulled open the seam in the front of the suit and pressed the cold metal cane against her bare chest.

Martinel chortled, averting his eyes. "Nice view."

Tina blushed and resealed the suit. "I forgot I took my clothes off when I put this thing on." She sighed at the grinning Martinel. "Next time, please keep your eyes to yourself."

"Well, miss, there ain't a whole lot worth looking at around here, so I appreciate the view."

Tina's blush deepened, and she gave the glowing blue poles a wary glance. "I don't like this." As she approached the charged barrier to the Australian prison compound, she gritted her teeth. The pain of a thousand needles stabbed her face and then stopped once she had passed through.

"Just try it without the fancy suit and see what ya think about it, miss."

Tina fell to her knees and rubbed her stinging face. "The name's Tina, Mister Martinel."

Martinel lowered himself on his good leg and sat. "Is there anything I can do to help ya? And none of this Mister Martinel stuff. The name's Kevin."

"No, no, I'm fine." She turned away, opened the suit, and pulled the cane out. She flexed her fingers and snapped the cane into a solid rod. "Hope this helps."

Tina faced the Aussie and saw tears streak down his dirt-caked face as he accepted the gift. He caressed it like a treasure and his lips trembled. "I haven't been able to do much of anything except sit since those gargoyles crashed my car when I tried to run one of them over three months ago."

Tina sprang to her feet and helped Martinel stand.

"Thank ya," he said, then tested the cane. He gave Tina a speculative look. "It's good to see you Yanks giving these damn harpies fits. The way they start chittering whenever you pull off one of your stunts is music to my ears." He glanced at the sun starting to crest the eastern horizon. "Ya better get back while it's still dark." He reached over and squeezed her hand. "I'm the best damn bush pilot in Western Australia. I know that's not much good here, but if there's anything I can do, let me know." He choked back tears. "There's much those sons-a-bitches owe me."

Tina covered his hand with hers and gave a grim nod. "We'll find a way to get out of here. All of us."

"I know ya will, or die trying," he whispered.

She swallowed hard, lowered her head, and leapt through the energy field. Martinel leaned on his cane, studying the woman as she winced from the needle-like pain on her uncovered face. Once through, Tina waved and trudged to the prison compound's collection of small huts.

————◆————

Martinel turned to go back to his makeshift hut when motion on the plain caught his eye. "Well, what do we have here?" Four clones limped back toward the hive. Three of them half-carried the fourth.

Martinel spit on the ground and rubbed his chin. "I saw six of those buggers take off after that big guy in the suit. Only see four of them comin' back." He smirked, turned, and hobbled into his hut muttering, "The damn harpies will have something to chitter about now."

————◆————

"I need some air," Tina said as she stomped out of the hut. She elbowed past the guards standing at the entrance and wandered toward the camp's perimeter facing the mountains.

Cruz was stubborn as a mule. The man saw a conspiracy behind everything he couldn't control. Fuming, Tina turned and glowered at the two soldiers stationed at the entrance of the hut where Gabriel and Rafael were confined. *The idiot captain doesn't believe me.*

The guards stiffened to attention as Captain Cruz and Virgil emerged, deep in a growling conversation. Tina prayed Cruz would listen to him. She had told the captain about Beatrice and what she had said about Dante, but he claimed Tina had been duped by a harpy trick. Her shoulders sagged. *Maybe he's right.* Tina felt the prickle of someone watching and she spun around.

A solitary clone stood on the other side of the barrier. "I have met another garbed in similar body wrappings."

Tina stiffened.

If the clone noticed, he made no mention of it. "Are you a friend of Michael? You wear the same garment."

Tina swallowed hard, calming herself. "Ah, yes. How do you know him?"

The clone's face clouded into a tortured look. "I encountered him in the mountains. He spared my life." His face changed into a slight smile. "He gave me a name and much to think about. My identifier is Reggie."

Tina's jaw dropped and she stared, unbelieving.

"I see my name has meaning to you. Michael said a remarkable person once owned it."

Tina nodded, not daring to speak.

Reggie's face relaxed. "I owe him a debt for both my life and my name. I will repay it to you. Listen." He moved closer to the shimmering barrier separating them. "The masters are seeking the humans who staged the raid last night, and Dis captured images of the death of two masters. They know Michael took part but have not determined who accompanied him." He made a quiet snort. "Sometimes, the masters are stupid. One glance at the video, and I recognized you. Eventually, they will figure it out."

His eyes met hers. "Once they identify you, they will drain your memories. It is a very destructive process. When your mind is empty, you will be dissected to determine whether you possess any physiological variances from other humans."

144

Tina wiped her hands on the suit and glanced to where Virgil stood talking with Captain Cruz.

Reggie followed her gaze. "Also, the blood passing will be in ten days, and this time, it will be different." He frowned and rubbed his chin as he looked around for any other clones. "The masters were excited that human prisoners defeated an equal number of guardians. They will escalate our equipment to match yours. There will be more of us, and we will be armed with swords and shields just as your warriors were. We received these weapons this morning. They are superior to what your destroyers used on the guardians at the last blood passing."

Tina felt a cold chill cut through her. "Will you be one of these guardians?"

"Of course I will. I have not yet made my blood passing."

Tina looked at Reggie in confusion. "If you're going to try to kill our people, why are you warning me?"

Mixed emotions roiled across Reggie's hairless face. "Michael instructed me to absorb human literature while in healing stasis. I did, and now I am conflicted. I am not a mindless, murdering orc of your legends. But I still exist to serve the will of the masters."

Tina stepped so close to the barrier she could feel the energy tingling the tip of her nose. "You don't have to be a slave. You can be your own person. Michael discovered that, and so did Rafael and Gabriel."

"There are others? Is it possible?" Reggie staggered back, looking away. "I have much to consider." He saw a pod of clones walking along the perimeter toward his location, and the emotion washed away from his face. Without another word, he strode away.

Tina's brows furrowed. Had she imagined the emotion she'd seen on his face? As if he could read her mind, Reggie pivoted and winked at her. An instant later, he headed back to the giant hive-like compound.

She hung her head, deep in thought. *Captain Cruz will have to know about this.*

Cruz pounded his fist against the hut's clay wall. "None of this makes any damn sense. Why are those monsters happy we killed their little pets?" He pounded the wall again. "And for that matter, why did they go to the trouble of kidnapping us and dumping us here? They took my boys out without even breaking a sweat. They don't need to know what we're capable of. They already know they can kick our asses."

He regarded the gathered officers and then nodded to Esther and Tina, who looked out of place at the impromptu military conference.

Virgil replied, "That's the point. They don't know what our capabilities are. They've taken a few samples and have encountered various degrees of resistance. They probably want to do some more testing before they commit themselves to Earth's conquest."

Cruz spun around and faced the Air Force sergeant. "But why bother? They have a whole goddamn empty planet here they barely use. What do they want with our world?"

Tina hopped up and balled her fists. "Does that matter? They just do!"

Captain Cruz's eyes tightened. "Yes, it does. By resisting them, are they learning what they need to know to defeat us? Are we feeding into humanity's destruction?"

Virgil met the captain's eyes. "Are you suggesting we just roll over and die?"

Cruz slumped to a sitting position. "Maybe I am. I just don't know anymore."

"There's another alternative, you know." Virgil stared into his empty hands as all eyes swung in his direction. "We kill those suckers. Kill them all."

"And how do you propose we do that?" Lieutenant Gentile stuttered. "Except for your little raid, we can't get near them. Do you have a few hundred of those fancy suits you're wearing?"

Virgil ground his teeth together. "Look, we might have an ally out there. This Beatrice knew about Dante and helped us get into the harpy's building. Maybe she'll help us again."

Gentile made a derisive snort. "Okay, even if the person you spoke to isn't one of those aliens messin' with ya, what can some poor old hag sitting with a ham radio in those mountains do for us?"

Cruz interrupted saying, "I don't know what she can do, but we're going to find out." He massaged his temples. "Virgil, take Tina and head for the mountain range. Locate the kid, Dante, and this Beatrice, if you can. See what help you can find."

Virgil's eyes lit with excitement. "Sir, I think that's a good idea. I'll go, but Tina stays here. It'll be dangerous."

The captain's lips thinned. "No, Sergeant Bernius, take the lady with you. You're both dead for sure if you stay here." He looked at Tina, who sat stone still. "At least out there, she'll have a chance."

Virgil arose and felt the comfort of the Beretta tucked inside his suit. "When do you want us to leave?"

"Tonight." Cruz stared at him. "Don't let the bastards catch you."

"Captain Cruz, I hid from a drug cartel in the Columbian mountains for over two weeks. I should be able to evade these little harpies." He met the captain's steady eyes in understanding. He'd make sure neither of them would be taken alive if caught.

He turned and offered Tina his hand. "C'mon, let's see if we can find that boyfriend of yours."

Tina returned a weary smile.

Esther rose with her. "I'll help you get ready." She squeezed the young woman's shoulder, and the three departed.

"Godspeed," Lieutenant Gentile called out after them. "Hey, be sure to bring the cavalry when you come back." He turned his head to his commander and his lips formed a half smile. No one laughed at his joke.

Captain Cruz regarded the four young officers who stared at him and hoped he could honor the faith they had in him. He sighed, glancing at the still swaying canvas door. "All right, we're going to be dragged into the arena in nine more days. Whether the clone Tina spoke with is setting us up, it doesn't matter. We have to escalate our tactics to stay ahead of them. And pray."

CHAPTER XV
Eden

Eager already to search in and round
The heavenly forest, dense and living-green,
Which tempered to the eyes the new-born day,
Without more delay I left the bank,
Taking the level country slowly, slowly
Over the soil that everywhere breathes fragrance,

Dante's Purgatorio – Canto XXVIII

Beatrice's monotone voice woke Dante. "Have you completed your sleep cycle?"

Dante cracked open his eyes and tasted slime in his mouth. He hadn't cleaned his teeth in forever. He glanced over at Michael, who snored on the thin pallet next to his. *He's not going to move for a while.*

"Well, Beatrice, it looks like it's just you and me for breakfast." Dante stretched his arms wide and yawned. "I don't think I've had a real night's sleep since they abducted us." He got up and rubbed his eyes. "So what do ya got cookin' this morning?"

"I have one hundred and sixty-one varieties of vegetation available for consumption."

Dante sighed as he walked out of the bedroom and headed toward the dining area. "I don't suppose you know how to make biscuits out of the grain I saw in the valley, do you?"

Beatrice answered with a short, thoughtful buzz. "Possess no knowledge of biscuits. Besides my plant types, I now know how to make the ingestible items labeled coffee and lentil soup, with and without salt,"

"I guess bacon and eggs are off the menu, too." Dante chuckled as he sat down and stared at the steaming bowl of lentil soup. He picked up the mug of coffee. "I definitely need to teach you more recipes."

"I have arrayed a sample of all my vegetation. Please examine and determine if bacon and eggs are amongst them."

"I don't think you would grow either of those." His eyebrows arched as he saw row upon row of alabaster bowls aligned on white shelves in the wall facing him. Mug in hand, he walked over with curiosity. "Let's see what ya got."

Dante peered into one bowl on the bottom shelf and could tell something was off just by the scent. "Phew. Ah, Beatrice, you may want to get rid of some of this stuff. It's pretty spoiled." He pointed to the contents of the bowl in front of him. "These look like peaches, but they're rotten now."

A soft buzz preceded a beep. "Food preservation. Another gap in my knowledge base. My makers would be disappointed in my limited capabilities."

Dante moved to the next bowl on his right whose contents looked more rich and produced no odor. "These look okay." He picked up what resembled a dried fig and sniffed it. Upon taking a bite, his mouth watered from the sweet flavor. He gobbled the rest and dropped the stem on the floor, then reached into the bowl again and grabbed two more.

"Please identify."

"To me, they taste like figs. They can be eaten dried like this or fresh."

Beatrice made a clicking noise. "Name noted. They are now labeled as figs. Removal of moisture required for long-term storage noted. I have initiated removal of rotten peaches from retention bins. Please identify other produce."

Dante looked out the open doorway, his mind churning. "How about I do a few more now and then do a little exploring?"

"Need labels." The next buzz sounded somewhat deeper than normal. "Agreed. I will not deliver the light blades and ray guns you requested until produce identification is complete. That is what you call making a bargain. Correct?"

"It's a deal." Dante furrowed his brow as he reviewed the long line of bowls and pointed at the next three. "Call these mushrooms. They've gone bad, and even if they were good, I wouldn't touch 'em. Mushrooms are dangerous and often poisonous." He scooped out the contents of the next container and popped a few in his mouth. "Label these as raisins. They're a dried version of a fruit called grapes."

"Why a different label for the same plant?"

Dante scratched the back of his head and shrugged at the robot floating beside him. "I don't know. It's just what I was taught."

"Not logical, but noted."

He examined the last bowl in the row and taste tested what it held. "These, I'd call almonds, but you'd have to shell them in order to make them edible." He wanted to grab a handful of the nuts but had coffee in one hand and the raisins in the other. He frowned down at the tunic he wore. "Ahh, Beatrice, next time you design clothes, how about putting some pockets in them?"

"Noted."

Dante put the mug on the shelf and grabbed another fig. "C'mon, tour guide, time to show me around this place." He walked out the door without waiting for an answer. The ivory orb followed.

When he stepped outside the building, his mouth dropped open. A vast ceiling of greenish-beige marble curved down in a perfect circle to a ring of one- and two-story buildings around the perimeter. The middle had to be about five stories high, by Dante's estimate.

"Wow. Is the whole mountain hollowed out?" He squinted at the far end of the cavern. Smooth, white columns stretched to the ceiling every fifty yards, emitting a soft, golden light. "It has to be over a mile to the other side."

"You are in error by a factor of ten percent," said Beatrice. "The diameter of the floor space is one thousand, seven hundred and seventy meters, or one point one mile as you alternatively express the measurement."

Dante shrugged. "Okay. I believe ya." He then noticed a number of robots identical to the one beside him flitting along wide, glassy smooth avenues separating rectangular gardens exploding with life. "So what's going on here? Isn't it a little tough to grow plants in this oversized cave?"

"I did not have a successful crop in the valley's natural ecosystem until thirty-eight growing seasons ago."

Dante whistled. "That's amazing. You've been cultivating crops inside this cave for over four hundred years."

"For the first eighty-three years after I became sentient, I was not a functional bio-mes station. Only the solar power receptors on the mountain were active back then. The energy available was sufficient for limited activity. I allocated power to maintenance of my core functionality and construction of the geothermal power generators. I prioritized to satisfy my prime directive for agricultural production."

The orb dipped to examine a bed of fava beans. A tentacle extended and twined a vine into a nearby lattice-work support. "I lost many plant species I was developed to nurture. You have demonstrated to me that I do not understand the purposes of what I am growing. I am incomplete."

Dante didn't know how to offer the mountain-sized computer any comfort. He took in all of the growth and activity around him before clearing his throat. "I'd say you did well with what you had to work with. You're a marvelous system. The makers would be proud of what you achieved."

Beatrice's usual beeps sounded light, even happy. "Your words help. I am glad I did not destroy you as an intruder."

"Yeah, so am I, my friend." He shuddered as he remembered the big ugly shredded by an innocent-looking orb similar to the one next to him.

He glanced around and noticed a wide, curved staircase carved out of the inside wall of the mountain. It wound its way up and vanished into a wide opening of the cavern ceiling three stories above him. Dante pointed to the opening. "So what's up there?"

The usual thoughtful buzz returned. "I do not know."

He scrunched his face and turned to the orb. "What do you mean you don't know? Nothing moves in this entire valley without you knowing it."

"That area consumes five percent of my power, but I have no sensors up there."

"You have about a million of these flying robots. Why haven't you checked it out?" Dante tapped the orb and walked in the direction of the stairs. "Any problem if I have a look?"

"I have no instructions regarding guests. Also, your count is in error. I possess twenty-five mobile fabrication units and five hundred general purpose harvesters, and each orb docks two hundred micro-bot pollinators. In addition—"

"Beatrice, okay, I get it. I don't need an inventory list right now." Michael walked toward them, and Dante smiled. "Hey, big guy. Glad you finally decided to wake up."

Michael scowled. "If I didn't have to be your nurse maid for the last few days, I would not have been so exhausted." He reached into the pouch hanging at his side, pulled out a purplish fruit, and munched it.

Dante did a double-take on his friend's garments. Low-cut boots covered Michael's feet, and he wore the pouch and a sheathed knife on a wide belt cinched around his waist. "Where did you get that stuff?"

A mischievous smile crossed Michael's face. "Simple, I asked for them. I decided I do not enjoy walking barefoot with my hands full."

Dante wiggled his toes and eyed the stairs. "Hey, Beatrice, since you're granting wishes, can I have duplicates of those items?"

"Noted," said Beatrice.

As he approached them, Michael finished the fruit and tossed the pit into a nearby vegetable bed. Four seconds later, an orb swooped in, retrieved the discarded seed, and flew off. Michael paid it no mind and turned to his friend. "So what are you up to?"

Dante pointed to the massive stairs. "I was thinking of doing a little exploring, as long as our tour guide doesn't mind."

"This unit is assigned to monitor your activities. It is not a tour guide."

"Okay, so Big Brother is watching our every move. Let's have a look up there." Dante walked with deliberate steps, absorbing everything around him. The walk took several minutes, and he paused by a bed of flax-like plants as a thought struck him. "Beatrice, you never answered my question. Why haven't you ever gone up there?"

"It is special to me," said the computer.

Michael squinted in confusion as he followed the conversation. "Why?"

"The audio instruction I received from one of the makers is the last one I have recorded in my data banks. I have had no other user input until I communicated with you."

Dante rubbed his chin. "What was the instruction?"

"I will translate to your language." A different, screechy voice blasted through the drone's speakers. "'You stupid machine, get out of here! We're busy. Go do whatever it is you're supposed to be doing.'"

Dante met Michael's eyes and shrugged. "This I gotta see."

The open stairs turned into a tunnel which continued up another two flights of stairs. They climbed in silence until their progress came to an abrupt halt. A blank wall with no sign of any seams or hinges blocked any further progress.

"What the heck is this?" he asked. "Beatrice, how do we open this thing?"

"It is not open. You cannot enter," she answered.

Dante and Michael spent the next half hour searching the nearby walls for a hidden lever, but the smooth marble walls revealed no clues.

The orb retreated down the stairwell. "It is not open. You cannot enter."

Michael slapped Dante on the back. "It looks like this is one mystery we won't solve today. I think it's about lunchtime anyway." He descended a few steps and paused. "Besides, we need to start planning how to rescue our friends."

A vision of Tina swam before Dante's eyes, and the curiosity regarding the upper chambers evaporated. "Yeah, we've got to do that. Fast." He called out to the orb before it vanished around a curve in the stairs. "When will those weap— ahh, tools, be ready?"

"Encountered fabrication issues. Circuitry is shorting out. Experimentation will continue," replied Beatrice.

Dante reached the bottom step. "Do you have a CAD-CAM application tied into what you're attempting? Maybe I can help."

"Direct contact with my CPU is not allowed. I will provide a stand-alone system with media containing the detailed specifications of this project."

"Yeah, that should work. Your technology is far beyond what I know, but I might get lucky." He snapped his fingers. "Could I have a small, portable computer that's networked into the base station you're providing?"

One of the orb's tendrils tapped itself as if scratching its chin. "Capability of desktop and portable is identical, but will be provided per your specification."

When they reached home, Dante pointed to the room on the left. "Have your boys set up the computer in there. I'd like it on a desk with a chair."

"Noted."

"And could I have a keyboard with that?"

"Unnecessary. Display is an interactive hologram. It will react to your hand motions."

Dante bit his lower lip. "Yeah, that's great for most things, but sometimes I need to get right into the operating system's machine code."

"Request is ambiguous. I cannot provide, but you will have the capability of building your own virtual keyboard with a display projection on the flat surface of a desk. It will be an unproductive activity. You are not a maker, so my programming language is unknown to you."

Dante cracked his knuckles. "I can code in Assembler and haven't found an OS I couldn't debug yet."

He jumped as two silent robots flew into the dwelling. The first had a small table with a single pedestal for a leg. The second had a stool on a single leg and two flat, rectangular boxes all of the same ivory-colored material. "Beatrice, you definitely need to broaden your color gamut. Does everything have to be off-white or beige?"

"You did not specify color variance. It would be a non-optimal use of resources."

Michael chuckled and shrugged, moved to the shelves, and sniffed at the contents in several of the bowls. He gathered a collection and dumped his armload of vegetables into a pot on the heating surface. "Beatrice, you'll find nothing Dante does is efficient."

Dante rolled his eyes. "Yeah. Well, master chef, what are you cooking?"

Michael stirred the pot. "Soy beans, carrots, onions, and garlic. I think." He grimaced and picked up a small saucer with a mound of white grains in it. He tasted it and smiled in triumph as he poured its contents into the boiling water. "We now have salt."

Dante walked over and sniffed the contents, then smirked. "It smells pretty good. But next time, you might want to chop the veggies before you cook them."

Michael slapped his forehead. "I knew I forgot something."

Dante chuckled. "Don't worry about it. Anything is better than that mush the harpies fed us."

Dante walked into the new computer room and picked up the tablet on the table. He touched the screen several times, getting a feel for how it worked. "Wow, this is the most intuitive operating system I've ever seen." Dante's hands flew over the interactive display panel as he walked back to the table.

He looked up a few minutes later as the orbs exited the house and remembered something. "Hey, Beatrice, while you have your boys working here, how about having them install a shower for us?"

Another thoughtful buzz sounded. "You referenced soap and shower before you entered your sleep cycle but did not provide specifications."

Dante's hopes rose. "A shower is a spray of water, kinda like a heavy rain, with controls that adjust the water's temperature and pressure. Oh, yeah, and you'll need a drain so the water doesn't flood the house."

He scratched the back of his neck. "I'm not sure about soap, but my grandparents used to make their own using lye." He knitted his brows, thinking back to a talk he had with his grandmother in his childhood. "First, burn some of your dead fruitwood down to ash, then put the ashes in a barrel with purified water and drain most of the water. Let the ashes soak for a few days, and pour what's left into some small containers. You let that sit in a cool, dark spot for a few more days, and then you have soap. I hope."

"Specifications noted. Action commencing." Soon, a steady stream of the flying orbs moved in and out of the empty room adjacent to the bedroom.

Michael stared at the pot of boiling vegetables and tapped his fingers on the table. "Dante, we have some serious talking to do, and I do not like the odds of any plan I have yet thought of. We're discussing food and showers while our friends could be dying." Michael lurched from the table, knocking over the bench, and jabbed a fork into a cooking carrot. "How do you tell when this stuff is done?"

"Whoa, Michael, calm down a little." Dante put down the notepad and set the fallen bench back up. "I'm just as worried as you are, but we can't do anything until we have weapons to fight with."

"I know." Michael waved his hand and sat down at the table. He looked Dante in the eyes. "When you had that fever, it gave me a lot of time to sit and think." He wrung his hands together. "I told you about the fight I had to get here and about the clone I named Reggie."

Dante nodded.

Michael stood and walked to the doorway, staring at the plant beds with his back to Dante. "Remember when we first met? I was bursting with questions and desperately wanted to speak with a human but did not know how." He turned with a rumbling laugh. "You almost jumped out of your skin when I spoke to you."

Dante smirked at the memory. "Yeah, I think I soiled myself." He watched Michael pace. "Back then, you were barely a person. You don't even look the same anymore. Your skin's darker than mine, and I don't think my beard will ever get as thick as yours."

Michael paused and twisted his hairy, tanned arm in front of his face. "I once believed my podmates and I were special." He sighed and sat down again. "I no longer think so. To perform my role as an infiltrator, the masters exposed me to human culture. It was my window of escape. I could see and compare." He shook his head. "Unfortunately, very few of my brethren will have that chance. They will be molded into mindless monsters and never know they have a choice."

Dante snapped his fingers and pulled out his notepad, typing furiously. "Maybe I can help. What's the file structure for your information downloads?"

Michael's face twisted in confusion. "Huh?"

"Hmm, I need a system pass-through." Dante slapped the table, paying little mind to the orb flying in holding his neural net suit. "Beatrice, what's the range of your jamming capability?"

"One hundred percent effectiveness, forty-five point seven meters from interference node. Capability degrades exponentially beyond that."

"And can you retrieve the transponder you cut out of the big ugly who chased me?"

"Yes."

"This might work." Dante cracked his knuckles and picked up the notepad. "Once we get the tools Beatrice is building, we…"

CHAPTER XVI
Friends and Enemies

And lo! As when, upon the approach of morning,
Though the gross vapours Mars grows fiery red
Down in the West upon the ocean floor,

Dante's Purgatorio – Canto II

No, no, no. This will never work." Michael held the third iteration of his light sword. It smoldered from when he had crossed swords with Dante during their fencing practice, but the blade had ceased glowing. They stood in a smoke-filled olive orchard, which reeked of ozone.

Dante shook his stinging hand and stared at the narrow, meter-long rod he'd dropped on the ground. "Beatrice, what the hell just happened?"

"The system overloaded," the computer said. "When the two fields touched, the circuitry could not handle the ion feedback."

"So what you're saying is these things shorted out and are useless lumps of metal right now." Dante plucked at his lower lip, thinking.

Michael's shoulders sagged. "Well, since the harpies all wear charged field protection, they're worthless. I hope the design of the ray guns works out better."

"Now wait a minute. Maybe these can be salvaged." Dante picked up the rod the length and thickness of a fencer's foil and tapped it against his leg. "Michael, what will happen when this light sword touches a harpy's energy field protection?"

Michael rubbed the thick beard on his chin. "It is a similar technology. The force field would suffer the same feedback and short out, too." He shook his head. "What good would it do us? You won't hurt them with that skinny pole."

A gleam lit Dante's eyes. "Beatrice, instead of allowing the light sword to short out, could you build in a circuit breaker to protect the components?"

"Yes, but the system would require ninety seconds to reboot."

Michael snorted, shaking his head. "We'd be dead in five seconds."

"Hold on. Stay with me on this." Dante twirled the thin shaft. "Beatrice, could you add a parallel ion field generator that would take over if the first one shuts down?"

"Yes. A second, redundant system could be online five seconds after the circuit breaker is tripped. However, it would require a thicker base."

Dante wrapped his hand around the finger-thick handle. "That would be a good thing. The grip on this sword needs to be fatter anyway." He ran his hand along the thin cylinder rod. "Beatrice, does the tool need to be shaped like this?"

If a buzz could sound puzzled, Beatrice made the sound. "Ambiguous question."

Dante blew his cheeks in exasperation. "I mean, can it be shaped with a sharp blade along its side and a narrow point at the tip like the tool your harvesters use?"

"Yes, but it is an inefficient configuration."

"Well, just humor me on this one and do it."

"Humor is the juxtaposition of two incongruous facts. It does not seem relevant to the current design discussion."

Dante sighed and wiggled his fingers, which still tingled. "Just make the design change, please. Also, I would like to have a bell guard and grip made out of insulated material on the hilt."

Michael bobbed his head with enthusiasm. "That just might work."

A broad grin creased Dante's face. "Beatrice, when will they be ready?"

"Minimal engineering required. Two prototype units will be available in four hours."

The smile vanished from Dante's face as he glanced at the sun sinking toward the valley's western ridge. "Another day lost. Beatrice, hurry. Please hurry."

Michael walked over and laid his arm on Dante's shoulder. "My friend, it will do our compatriots no good if we blindly charge in ill prepared. We are the only hope they have, and the odds of our success are small enough as it is." He turned and walked toward a harvester orb Beatrice had modified with external controls. "Come on. We need to practice with our transport devices anyway."

Dante eyed the two-meter oblong vehicle he tried to fly earlier in the day. It was narrower than Beatrice's harvester robots with an indentation in the middle for a human to sit. His first attempt at flying it had ended with its nose digging a long furrow in a field of rye before it slid to a halt.

He shuddered. "You go ahead and play with that suicide machine. I think I finally got a handle on the operating system the harpies use in their remote devices. I might be able to crack their programming language with a little more time."

Michael scratched the fuzz sprouting from his scalp and hopped onto the saddle strapped to the ten-foot long cylinder. With a light touch, he moved the joystick. The vehicle responded instantaneously. "These things are marvelous. The lever is for pitch and yaw. The two-foot pedals handle roll and speed." He flew the elongated orb so it hovered four feet from Dante's face. "Your problem is you keep overcompensating for every shift. You will get the feel for it with repetition."

"You practice for me." Dante cinched the belt around his calf-length tunic and stomped toward the cavern entrance. "Alien software is far more interesting."

———•◆———

Tina kept a wary eye on the backs of the three clones who marched past them. She unconsciously reached out for Virgil's hand.

He whispered, "Are you ready? When I say the word, we run. We'll have fifteen minutes to get out of sight before the next set of guards passes this spot."

Tina trembled as she squeezed his hand in response.

Virgil looked left and right, then took a deep breath and rose from his crouched position. "Let's do this real quiet now."

Tina gasped in pain as they passed through the barrier. Her gaze darted around but saw no sign their escape had raised any alarms. She followed Virgil as he trotted toward the distant mountains at an easy jog.

As soon as Tina stepped through the charged field, a clipped female voice spoke into her ear. "Guest Virgil, Guest Tina, I can sense you again. Are you planning on another visit to the bed-and-breakfast?"

Tina smiled at the familiar voice, but her face clouded. "Hello, Beatrice. We were thinking of coming to visit Dante. How is he?"

"Guest Dante's biometric functions are operating within normal parameters. Not-Guest Michael has been relabeled as Guest Michael. He expressed a great deal of concern when he arrived regarding the viability of Guest Dante living."

A tear trickled down Tina's cheek, and she half stumbled on a loose rock. "But he's okay now?"

"Answer is unchanged from your previous query."

"Tell him we're coming, and —"

Virgil's arm slammed Tina to the ground in a muddy swale. "Don't move. They're searching for us," the sergeant rasped in her ear. He lay in the muck next to her and drew the 9mm from his suit.

Tina stifled a cry when she spotted the shadow of a low flying vehicle about four times the size of the floating sleds which delivered their food every day. She could make out the silhouette of several harpies perched in the craft's open-air cockpit, watching the ground. She waited for the pain of their stun guns, but nothing happened. For what felt like an hour, the two remained still, watching the craft disappear to the south.

Finally, Virgil searched the sky in all directions. "C'mon, let's go. We've got to reach cover before sunrise." He helped her up. "Keep your eyes open. Those damn flying machines don't make a sound."

Tina followed Virgil's cautious pace with her head on a swivel. "Beatrice, can you help us? We need to get to Dante."

Beatrice offered no insight.

Virgil grunted. "Great. *Now* she stops talking." He picked up the pace to an easy trot. "I guess we're on our own, kid. Dante and Michael both headed east toward those mountains, so that's where we're going."

The night raced by. Three times they dove into shallow depressions in the earth, and three times the harpy hunters passed by them. The coming of dawn brought a sinking feeling in Tina's heart as she realized they were still over a mile from the nearest foothill, and the barren field offered no cover.

"Okay, we got to run for it now. We're sitting ducks out here." Virgil studied the greying sky for any sign of movement and then patted Tina's hand. "One more dash and we'll be safe." He broke into a rapid ground-eating stride.

Tina lowered her head and charged after him, her chest burning and muscles shrieking in dismay. A half mile later, her body failed, and she collapsed on the rutted ground. Bitter tears welled in her eyes as Virgil came back for her. "Go on without me. I'm slowing you down, and I'll just get you killed."

Virgil's eyes softened. "I'm amazed you got this far. I'll carry you the rest of the—" His eyes narrowed to slits, and he released the safety on the Beretta. "Down." He flattened himself behind a small rock outcropping.

The open cockpit craft landed one hundred feet from their position, and four harpies bounded out. They spread out in a wide arc as they approached the humans' hiding spot. Virgil checked the magazine in the Beretta and breathed deep.

Tina's chin quivered. "I know we can't let them take us alive." She twisted her face into a crooked smile, grasping Virgil's free hand and squeezing her eyes shut. "Just make sure the first shot does the job. I don't handle pain very well."

Virgil stole a glance over the lip of the rock and slumped to the ground after a glancing hit from a stun gun. He collapsed in a heap but stared at Tina with hard, commanding eyes.

She took the gun from his nerveless fingers and held it like a poisonous snake. "I can't. Merciful God in Heaven, I can't."

Virgil held a steady gaze on her.

Tina tried to place the barrel of the pistol against Virgil's forehead, but her hand shook. Tears blurred her vision, and she took a deep breath and steadied the weapon with both hands. "Sweet Jesus, forgive me."

A flash of streaking metal flying through the air caught her eye, and she reflexively jerked the gun up at two speeding blurs. They raced past her before she could blink. As Tina twisted her head, the ground shook and several high-pitched, inhuman screams split the air before coming to abrupt halts. She peeked around the corner of the rock and saw two familiar figures. Her heart raced with a combination of fear and elation.

Dante crouched behind the strange vehicle whose nose was stuck in the ground with the lifeless body of a harpy buried underneath it. Tina didn't recognize the weapon, but it looked like he held some kind of cavalry saber.

Twenty feet past Dante, Michael knelt behind a similar craft, strapping on a glowing blue belt he stripped from a now headless alien. The two remaining harpies moved in opposite directions. One bounded to where Dante had hunkered down and the other to its open cockpit vessel.

Tina reacted without a moment's hesitation. She grasped the Beretta with two hands and emptied its magazine at the harpy charging at Dante. The bullets had no effect, but they did get the harpy's attention. It spun in her direction to face the new attacker. It realized its mistake too late. Dante sprang from his cover and slashed at the harpy with his blade. The harpy twisted out of the way of the cut with cat-like quickness and leapt at Dante, skewering itself on his extended sword. The harpy's belt ceased glowing.

The last alien reached its aircraft a heartbeat too late. Michael barreled into the harpy, and the two went down. Tooth and claw clashed against size and steel-hard muscle. Although the harpy shredded the flesh on Michael's arms, he closed his hands on the creature's neck. A quick, bone-crunching snap later, and the harpy's body went limp. Michael dropped to his knees beside the carcass, wincing and heaving deep breaths.

Tina stepped out from behind her cover. No sound but the low moan of the wind broke the silence. Michael wrapped an improvised bandage around his gouged arm with strips he tore from his tunic. She took a step toward him to help when she saw Dante staring at her with relief on his face.

Tina ran to him, tears welling in her eyes. "I thought I'd never see you again." She threw herself into his arms and Dante crushed her close. Their lips met for a long, lingering kiss.

Dante held her tight against his chest. "My God, a few more seconds, and I would've lost you forever. If Beatrice didn't tell us you were here, we would never have known."

Tina shivered and looked up at his face. "Dante, Beatrice knew we were coming almost eight hours ago."

Dante dug into the pouch hanging at his side and pulled out a small device, which looked like a Bluetooth receiver, and shoved it on his ear. "Beatrice, why didn't you tell me?"

Beatrice's answer came through the line. "Question is ambiguous. Please refine."

Dante ground his teeth. "You knew they were coming, and you didn't tell me."

"Guest Tina requested that I inform you of their approach. I did so when you completed your sleep cycle."

"You could've told me sooner!"

"You said, 'Don't wake me unless Hell is freezing over.' I complied with the implication of your request, did I not?"

Dante's mouth opened and shut, but no words came out.

Tina disengaged herself from Dante's arms and planted her hands on her hips. "That's not good enough. We tried to contact you, and you never answered."

"I monitored your communication frequency but did not transmit," the computer replied.

Michael walked over, holding his left forearm. Blood already oozed through the bandages. "Beatrice, why did you stop transmitting?"

"The computer from the bed-and-breakfast intercepted my communication."

Michael scratched his jaw. "If that's true, why are you communicating now?"

"Closed, line-of-sight communication beam is effective within four point eight kilometers of my transmitting base. It is shielded from interception."

Dante walked over to where Virgil lay. "Well, at least we're all okay now."

Beatrice gave him a warning beep. "Negative. It now knows I exist. It will hunt me."

Tina gasped. "Does it know where you are?"

"My suppression system cloaks my bio-mes from any aerial, electronic, or visual detection. The intruders have not penetrated it in the four point two planetary cycles since their arrival. External communications are a new issue. I bounce transmissions between numerous routers, and the sequence is randomized. It does not yet know my physical location."

Michael grunted. "That's just a matter of time. Beatrice must be referring to Dis. Its cyber-technology is very effective." He bent down by the harpy Dante had crushed with his flier and stripped off its force field belt, then snatched the weapon out of its clawed hand. "We better take whatever we can use and then get rid of any evidence."

"Removal of that vehicle from the approach to Eden is desirable. Its electronic signals will aid the intruders in locating me."

Dante sighed as he knelt beside Virgil. "Well, Beatrice, I guess this means we're allies now."

"Alliance is an invalid request. The maker's directives were explicit regarding maintaining the viability of the bio-mes station."

Michael placed the harpies' belts and weapons in his flier's storage cavity. "You have been able to monitor my former masters. They are your enemy. How long do you think it would be before you are destroyed?"

"My proactive defense capabilities are nonexistent. Once my CPU becomes corrupted, all of the environmental maintenance systems would fail."

"Then I guess we're friends now," Dante wheezed as he dragged Virgil's limp body to Michael's flier.

"You are a guest, not a friend."

Dante straightened his back and smiled. "A philosopher from my world had some wise words which apply here: 'The enemy of my enemy is my friend.'"

Beatrice gave a few thoughtful hums and beeps. "I accept, Guest Dante. The remains of the intruders from the bed-and-breakfast are too close to Eden. They must be removed from the vicinity."

Michael scratched the hair on his chin. "Beatrice, can you have one of your harvesters fly this thing away from here?"

"No. All of my components must remain within Eden."

Michael rubbed the back of his neck. "Their vehicle is automated. I think I can pilot it. Let's pile the corpses in, and I'll fly it about twenty miles south of here and jump out."

Dante frowned as he regarded the flat vista to the south and shook his head. "Michael, you'll be spotted just like Tina and Virgil, and there won't be anyone to rescue you." His eyebrows shot to his forehead, and he snapped his fingers. "Load the bodies in there. I have an idea."

He sprinted to his flier and pulled out the electronic tablet he had in the storage cavity. Dante jogged back, pressing the device's screen. "While you were practicing with these flying death traps, I've been cracking the harpy's operating system. If that thing has a navigational computer, I think I can start it and send it on its way."

"How far will the signal from your notepad carry?" Tina asked as she moved to his side.

"Not far, but the autopilot should keep it moving until the damn thing runs out of whatever it's using for fuel." He smiled as he pressed the screen a few more times. "Ah-ha, I'm in. Now I just need to download a few programs."

Michael stuffed the last body into the flier and huffed. "They're all inside. Now what?"

"First, I get this thing in the air." Dante pressed the screen twice in rapid succession.

Tina cheered. "It's working!" The alien vessel rose in the air and rotated to face southwest.

"Then I get it moving and disable the navigation system's communicator." Dante pressed the screen three more times, and the vehicle rose higher in the air and picked up speed. Dante lifted the notepad. "Beatrice, this computer you gave me is amazing. It takes what I ask for and converts in into functional applications."

"The operating system you have was created by the makers. Mine has evolved since then."

"If I could take this operating system back to Earth, I would put half of Silicon Valley out of work." Dante shook his head and slid the notepad into the empty satchel hanging across his shoulder.

"That would be undesirable. Being productive gives value to existence."

Tina stepped up next to Dante. "Nice philosophical debate, but can we get out of here? More of those horrible creatures could show up any time."

Dante nodded to her. "Sure thing." He walked over to Virgil, who lay limp on the ground. "Michael, help me lift this guy. Then we can throw this sack of potatoes on the back of your flier."

A frustrated glint in Virgil's eye rewarded him, and the man twitched a little.

Dante smiled, containing a laugh. "And Tina rides with me."

She looked at Michael, who was pulling Dante's flier away from the furrow it had churned. "Only if you go real slow."

CHAPTER XVII
Last Option

Takes in the heart for all the human members
Virtue informative, as being that
Which to be changed to them goes through the veins.

Dante's Purgatorio – Canto XXV

The sun crested the mountain range on the eastern horizon, but its clouded light wouldn't do much to warm the day. A chill breeze blew against Captain Cruz's face, and he shivered. "It never gets this cold back home in Corpus Christi."

Lieutenant Gentile sucked in the morning air. "Sir, I don't think this place would make many lists as a vacation destination."

Cruz chuckled and shrugged. "Winter's coming, whatever that means on this hellhole of a planet."

Concern filled Gentile's eyes. "Do you think Sergeant Bernius and Tina made it?"

Captain Cruz shook his head. "The only way we could find out is to ask the harpies, and I don't think they'd tell me even if I could understand their language."

He had assembled his men after one of his sentries reported a commotion near the alien's hive-like building. "Steady, men. Here they come," Captain Cruz barked with a confidence he did not feel.

Lieutenant Gentile gasped as he watched the scene. "Captain, there must be thirty of those damn harpies and at least twice as many big uglies."

Cruz kept a steady eye on the aliens. A few of them held glowing, electronic tablets and yelped at each other. The rest held their weapons leveled at the prison yard while the clones disabled a length of the barrier and entered the prison. "I guess today is selection day, and they don't want us to make a scene like we did last time." He smiled at the men of his company standing at stiff attention. *God bless them. They've held it together in an impossible situation.* "Parade rest."

The soldiers shifted to the new position in perfect unison. The clones braced themselves for an attack in reaction to the unexpected motion and then looked to their masters in confusion when one did not occur. Cruz sneered at the harpies. The soldiers wouldn't cause them any trouble today. His men would save their surprise for the blood passing ceremony.

The harpies with the tablets did not react to the unexpected human actions. They kept jabbing their clawed fingers at the screens and screeched louder. Two of them hissed and bounded back in the direction of the hive.

Lieutenant Gentile leaned in close to the captain's ear. "That's got to be about Sergeant Bernius. There's no one who can give those bastards fits like him."

Cruz rubbed the back of his neck. "I hope you're right, Joe. But is that good news or bad news?"

Motion in the sky caught Cruz's attention. It resolved into one of the alien's open cockpit aircraft. It darted across the barren plain and kept going west past the sulfur lake. Thirty seconds later, an identical flier sped from the upper tier of the hive and headed after the first one. He had no idea what that meant.

His attention returned to the clones stomping through the camp. All of them moved around in teams of three, save one. A solitary clone approached the hospital where Rafael and Gabriel stood blocking the door with their arms crossed. Instead of entering, the creature seemed to be engaged in an earnest conversation with them.

Cruz's eyes narrowed. *Now why the hell is he talking to those two damn spies?*

Lieutenant Gentile interrupted Cruz's observations, speaking through gritted teeth. "Captain, this isn't good. It looks like the big uglies are searching for something. If they find where we hid the stuff Virgil lifted, we got a real problem."

Cruz swept the camp with his eyes and nodded curtly. He stole a furtive glance at the flooded tunnel, now a well of sulfurous water. *Please, God, keep them from finding the guns and grenades.*

The sound of a scuffle drew Cruz's eyes back to the hospital. Three more clones stood at the entrance, trying to push past Rafael and Gabriel. One of the clones threw a roundhouse fist at Rafael, who blocked the blow and kneed the assailant in the groin. As the clone doubled over, Rafael lifted the creature off the ground with an uppercut.

Madness followed. Three more clones rushed over, and Cruz groaned as he saw his four medics charge out the infirmary door to help Rafael and Gabriel. *No, you fools, no.*

The original big ugly stood watching the fight with apparent anguish. The creature slid around the brawl and slipped inside the doorway.

Now what's that one up to? Captain Cruz gritted his teeth in consternation.

He heard a young child's shrill scream, and then an indignant woman's voice he recognized hollered, "This place is for the sick! Get out of here!" Nothing else could be heard over the din. Cruz didn't need long to deduce what had happened. *The bastard hurt our doctor.*

Cruz looked at his men and made his decision. They stood as still as stone, but he could see the rage in their eyes. This was not the way the day was supposed to go, but they had no choice now. He cursed at himself for losing control of the situation.

Rubbing the lump in his chest where the marker rested, he steeled himself. "Let's get 'em, boys." Cruz broke into a run toward the melee. Two hundred 10th Mountain Division soldiers and a couple dozen burly western New York farmers followed him.

The struggle drew all of the clones in the prison yard as well. The harpies bounded in, sweeping the area with their weapons. Clones and humans collapsed an instant later, and all went quiet.

———————•◆•———————

Dr. Easley looked at her half dozen patients. The big clone beside her had helped move them to the far corner of the structure, untouched by the paralyzing blasts spewed outside of their door. She squeezed the iron-hard hand holding hers. Her voice caught in her throat when she said, "Thank you, Reggie."

Angela stood close to Dr. Easley and frowned at the clone. "Monster, you better be nice, or my Uncle Rafe will kick your butt."

Esther noticed a small smile crinkled at the corners of the guardian's mouth as he regarded the defiant child.

"Then I will be good." Reggie's face sobered as he met her eyes. "I am glad I was of assistance. When Gabriel told me you were the mate of my namesake, I needed to meet you and give thanks for the great gift of sharing his name."

Esther wiped the tears from her cheeks and undid the clasp holding the chain around her neck. "Bend down please."

Reggie squinted, but he knelt before the elderly woman.

Esther hung the old, battered crucifix around the clone's neck. "My husband, Reggie, gave this as a gift to Michael. Michael returned it to me in remembrance of him. Now I give it to you. Wear it with honor and courage as the men before you have."

Reggie rose and lifted the cross lying against his chest. He stared at it for a long moment. "Michael was right. There are many new questions whirling inside my head. Perhaps I can become a man."

Lifting his chin, he sighed and listened, but heard nothing but the chittering of the harpies. He squared his shoulders. "I must go now. You would best keep the little human in here a bit longer," he said, then stepped into the dim morning light without looking back.

———— ◆ ————

Two days later, Captain Cruz stood at the head of sixty men by the perimeter of their prison and faced the arena in the nearby field. He glanced at Lieutenant Gentile beside him and gave the man an encouraging slap on the shoulder. Gentile's mouth twitched in a nervous smile. Only seven of them had been through this trial, but the men drew a measure of confidence from the previous success. Cruz rolled over the plan again in his head. *It's gotta work.*

Motion from the direction of the hive broke Cruz's reverie. Despite the warning he'd received about the escalation in weaponry, the sight of it surprised him. The clones looked like a cross between Roman legionaries and riot police. Each of them wore identical black helmets with clear face shields and held short, thick-bladed swords in their hands. They also held a tall, curved black shield tight against their left side.

Lieutenant Gentile leaned over. "They think they got us beat with their new toys, but they're gonna catch a cup of whoop-ass when we hit 'em with our new toys."

Cruz nodded without taking his eyes off of the approaching enemy. "Yeah, unless they have some surprises of their own." He glanced down his line of men and pointed to Rafael and Gabriel. "Keep an eye on those two. I don't want one of the surprises to be a stab in the back."

Gentile shook his head. "Sir, I think you're wrong about them. I've never had a cross word with them, and they seem to hate the harpies more than we do."

Cruz snorted. "Don't be fooled, Gentile; that's how spies act." He spat on the ground. "They even admitted they've been trained to be infiltrators since they were hatched. Don't let their faces fool you. They're as alien as the harpies."

"Yes, sir." Both officers turned and faced the oncoming clones as two of the prison boundary poles winked out. Sixty Guardians marched in and stood in a long row facing the men gined up for the blood passing ceremony.

Cruz's thoughts turned dark. The harpies so far had matched anything he could come up with and possessed an endless supply of clones. The grenade resting in the pocket of his armored vest reassured him as he looked at the distant mountains. As far as he could assess, they'd expend all of their munitions in this fight and be left with nothing, unless a miracle happened.

———————◆———————

Gabriel and Rafael stood at the end of the column. A tiny streak with long, wavy hair rushed from the crowd of humans who had gathered to watch. She flung herself against Rafael's leg. "Uncle Rafe, don't go. The monsters will hurt you."

Rafael stroked her hair. "Angela, you must be very brave for me and stay with Doctor Easley." His throat constricted, and he crouched before her. "I won't be gone long."

Esther hurried over. Rafael had to pry Angela's arms from around his leg. He met the doctor's eyes, wiping his arm across his brow. "Make sure she stays inside. You know... just in case."

Esther nodded and squeezed his arm. Angela's eyes

locked onto Rafael as Esther carried her away. She opened and closed her hand to wave good-bye. Rafael returned the gesture and spun around to face the line of clones.

Gabriel rubbed the heel of his hand in his eye. "Rafe, we'll be fine. Look at this batch of guardians. They're fresh out of stasis." He turned and jeered at the line of clones, brandishing his sharpened shard. The guardians glared back in silence. His mouth clamped shut when he spotted something glistening around the neck of the clone at the end of the opposing line. He nudged Rafael and pointed. "That's the one we talked to by the infirmary. He's wearing Reggie's cross."

The clone, Reggie, saw them staring. He shifted his stance and half-raised his sword in acknowledgement, shielding his action from the watching harpies with his body. Rafael touched the sleeve of the too small, threadbare tweed jacket he wore and bowed in response. The guardians gestured for the humans to enter the arena, and both columns turned and strode out in silence.

As they left, Gabriel found himself walking parallel to Reggie. Reggie touched the cross around his neck and spoke in a low voice. "The masters have something special planned for you and your podmate. I overheard them talking. One of them said it was time to download your memories. They think you have collected sufficient data by now."

Gabriel felt a chill down his spine. "How? When?"

"There is a data recorder attached to your brain. After you are killed in the arena, we have been given instructions to extract it and ensure it is not damaged."

"I don't plan on dying today." Gabriel growled as he watched the line of marching clones.

Reggie shifted his sword to his left hand and touched Gabriel's arm. "Whether you win or lose, the masters will collect your recorders today."

Beads of sweat sprouted on Gabriel's forehead. He had no response. They entered the arena, and the barrier poles snapped on behind them. The clones walked to one side while Captain Cruz hurried his troops to march on the other.

Once there, Cruz barked sharp orders to the soldiers, and they formed a phalanx in the far corner with each end anchored near the barrier's energy field. Gabriel and Rafael stood inside the wedge of fifty soldiers with the civilians and four medics.

"Did you hear what Reggie told me?" Gabriel hissed in Rafael's ear.

"Yes, and I believe him. Captain Cruz was right. We are nothing but unwitting spies. What are we going to do?"

"I don't know. I wish Michael were here. He always had a plan." Gabriel gazed at the distant mountain range. "At the same time, I'm glad he is not." He rubbed his scarred cheek. "We have not felt compulsion in four weeks." His arms dropped to his side. "I couldn't resist the commands then. What if I can't resist it now?"

"You will, my brother." Rafael slapped Gabriel on his shoulder. "Our existence before was a lie. With these humans, our lives are our own. Some of them like us, some of them hate us." His eyes moistened as he gazed back to the prison camp. "Some even love us. Focus on what's in your heart, and the masters' control will gain no hold on your mind."

The corners of Gabriel's mouth turned up. "I still do not look forward to feeling that sensation again." He looked sidelong at the state trooper and the truck driver, then whispered to Rafael, "The captain wants to be sure we don't go crazy and flip sides."

Rafael glanced over. Both men held hand guns, and he knew by the looks in their eyes that they would shoot if he stepped out of line. He clenched his fist. "We're not a threat to these troops. We're a threat to all of humanity. To everything I now hold precious."

Gabriel whispered, "We could take those weapons and destroy the recorders."

Rafael sighed through his teeth. "That won't work. The recorder is somewhere in our brains. We'll only get one shot that way. We must be sure the devices are obliterated."

Rage flowed through him like a tsunami, exterminating his thoughts. Compulsion. He focused his senses on the memory of Angela's small hand wrapped around his finger as she skipped by his side. The urge to smash and kill humans shattered like a wave against boulders. He stood with his hands on his knees, gulping air, and looked at Gabriel and offered him a weak grin. "That wasn't so bad."

Gabriel heard the blood curdling howls of the clones across the field and squared his shoulders. "You ready for round two?"

The second urge hit, a pale shadow of the first. Rafael remembered Angela giggling as she explained horsey rides to him and then squealing with delight as he galloped around the prison yard with her on his back. The madness could find no hold. He roared at the clones across the arena. "I am a man!"

The big uglies rushed forward. A half dozen hand guns barked, but the bullets bounced off the charging guardians' black shields.

Cruz kept a steady eye on the enemy. "Their legs, damn it! Shoot their legs!"

The clones rushed in with their shields high and their swords held straight out. Standing firm, Cruz shouted a second time. "When I give the word, lob the grenades over their heads." Twenty soldiers yanked the pins from the explosives, and he gave his next command. "Now!"

Smiling, Cruz watched as the grenades sailed through the air. Moments later, the deafening roar of the explosives rent the arena. Shrapnel tore through the exposed flesh of the clones. When the smoke cleared, no more than a dozen clones staggered toward the line of humans.

"Charge!"

The surviving clones stumbled around, bewildered, and had no time to mount a defense. Soldiers mobbed them and cut them down. Gabriel and Rafael dashed forward with the rest of the human soldiers. They searched for Reggie but could not see him amid the chaos.

They found him where the clones had first assembled in the arena. He sat on the ground with his legs crossed behind his shield, uninjured save for a single, ugly gash on his right calf. A couple soldiers approached him, and he dropped his shield and knitted his hands behind his head in a gesture of surrender.

One of the soldiers shouted for the captain. Cruz ran over with Gabriel and Rafael close behind.

"What the hell is this?" The captain's eyebrows shot up to his forehead. "We can't take any goddamn prisoners."

Lieutenant Gentile jogged up beside him. "We can't just kill someone who surrenders, either."

Cruz chewed on the inside of his cheek. "Strip him of anything useful. If he tries to resist, gut him." He raised his voice to a shout. "Take anything useful from these dead motherfuckers, and let's get back to our cozy little huts."

Reggie's eyes never wavered from Gabriel as a soldier yanked his helmet from his head. His gaze swung to where the harpies perched. Gabriel followed Reggie's gaze and saw the harpy observers outside the arena staring back at him. He turned to Rafael, who met his eyes. "What can we do?"

Nearby, Captain Cruz ordered his men into a column.

Rafael and Gabriel had a sword, shield, and helmet thrust into their arms as the blue lights of the barrier between the prison and the arena went dark. Rafael came to an abrupt halt and grabbed Gabriel's arm. He pointed to the darkened post. He saw Gabriel's face shift from recognition, to fear, and finally to resolution.

Rafael pulled off his old tweed jacket and laid it reverently on the ground. He cast a grim look toward the camp, where the soldiers received a hero's welcome. No one noticed their hesitation except Esther. Rafael called to her, "Tell Angela I love her very much and that I am sorry. Take care of her." He slung the shield across his back.

Gabriel did the same and squeezed Rafael's forearm. "I'm ready, my brother."

The two men strode to either side of the nearest darkened pole. They locked their left hands into each other's shield and palmed the activation switches with their right hands. They did not scream as the energy powered up and bisected them. The force field could not throw them left or right. As the energy poured through their bodies, sparks flew from the base of their heads. Their flesh charred and then burst into flame.

———— • ◆ • ————

The civilians in the camp screamed in horror. The soldiers stared in shocked silence. The harpies bounded over from the far side of the field, but by the time they arrived and cut the pole's power, nothing remained but two mounds of glowing ash and twisted, blackened grapheme steel.

The harpies screeched in frustration as they poked at the remains as though looking for something.

Reggie picked up the old tweed jacket and hugged it to his chest as he walked to the now glowing barrier, where Esther stood.

She choked out, "Why?" as tears streamed down her face.

Reggie felt his own throat constrict. "They did the only thing they could to protect you. The masters were going to extract all of their memories regarding humans." He glanced at the black ashes swirling in the cool air and furrowed his brow. "They preferred death to betraying you."

"Thank you for telling me." She drew in a deep breath and regarded the folded jacket in his arms. "Keep that in memory of two very courageous men." She stepped away from the barrier, trembling. "Excuse me. There's a little girl I must break some terrible news to."

Esther stumbled toward the infirmary, where she saw a terrified little child scanning the returning troops for two loved ones. Angela saw Esther's face and wailed as she ran into the old woman's arms. "Doctor Easley, I can't find Uncle Rafe or Uncle Gabe. Where are they?"

The doctor took a shuddered breath. "They're dead, honey. They didn't survive the fight."

A barking laugh behind her made her hold Angela closer. "I guess those two big uglies short circuited or something."

"Good riddance," said Cruz. "That's two less of those abominations we have to worry about."

"You can't talk about my Uncle Rafe like that!" Angela screamed as she pushed away from the doctor. Her tiny fists hammered against the captain's leg.

Esther's eyes blazed as she stormed over to him. "Don't you dare open your mouth when you don't have a clue about what happened." Ignoring the small crowd gathering, she drew herself up to her full height and poked Cruz in the chest. "Rafael and Gabriel were two of the bravest, most selfless men I have ever met. They gave their lives to protect us. You were right; there was a device in their heads, recording everything they saw and heard. They knew it and chose a horrible death to ensure the harpies would never receive that information."

Cruz went still. "You mean they—" His shoulders sagged as the full weight of what had happened hit him. He glanced back at the arena where the harpies still screeched and dug through the ashes. "I guess there's a lot I don't understand."

CHAPTER XVIII
New Mysteries

Open thy breast unto the truth that's coming,
And know that, just as soon as in the foetus
The articulation of the brain is perfect.

Dante's Purgatorio – Canto XXV

This is Heaven," Tina called from the shower room. "Will you hurry up? You've been in there for half an hour." Virgil slumped at the table, flexing his fingers and trying to shake off the lingering effects of the hit he took from the harpy's weapon earlier in the day.

"Have not. I don't think I'll ever be able to get this red dirt out of my hair," she grumbled. "This feels so good, but I'll kill whoever came up with this soap. It's pure lye."

Dante wrapped both his hands around his coffee mug and bowed his head. "Sorry. It's my grandma's recipe."

Tina turned off the water, raising her voice. "Beatrice, from now on when you're making soap, use ten parts olive oil, three parts water, and one and a third parts sodium hydroxide."

Beatrice's thoughtful hum poured through the room. "Noted."

"And while you're at it, could you have this hotel furnish towels and combs?"

A short while later, Tina walked into the kitchen wearing her neural net suit and carrying a long, soaking wet tunic in her arms. She sat down at the table and sniffed the bowl left for her, spooning up some of the contents. "Oatmeal and raisins? This is a gourmet meal after the garbage we've been eating for the last month. Wait, what were we eating for the last month?" She looked sidelong at Michael as he stirred the pot on the stove.

He put down his ladle. "It is a carbon-based construct injected with—"

"No, no, don't tell me. It'll probably make me sick."

He smiled and turned off the heat. "Yes, it probably would."

Virgil rolled his neck and pushed back from the table. "I'm going to shower now. Does anyone need to use the commode first? Some design genius put them both in the same room without any dividers."

"Was not in request specification from Guest Dante." The ivory-colored orb followed Virgil to the shower room, buzzing away. "Many requests and product updates. Need guests to prioritize."

Virgil paused and tapped his leg. "Just finish making those damn blasters."

"No project labeled 'blasters' is in process. Please provide specifications."

"Virg, Beatrice has them categorized as ray guns," Dante shouted from the kitchen table.

"What are you? Flash Gordon or something?" The sergeant groaned and turned on the water. "Just make the damn weapons."

"My protocol will not allow the construction of weapons," said Beatrice.

Virgil took off his tunic and tossed it in a corner. "Just finish it." He stepped under the warm water. "Freaking pacifist."

Virgil reentered the house after walking the three-and-a-half mile circumference of the cavern's botanical lab with Tina, Dante, and Michael. "Well, Beatrice, I gotta say this is a pretty impressive operation. This place must've been built to house and feed close to ten thousand people."

"Guests Dante and Michael were the first sentient beings in four hundred thirty-seven years, seven months, and twenty days to use my facilities," said Beatrice.

"Your makers are an impressive people." Michael scooped up a handful of shelled almonds and sat down. "When do you expect the ray guns to be ready for us?"

"The heat tolerance material issue has now been resolved. Need to recode the embedded software and then stress test again. Ninety-two percent confidence that prototypes will be available in fifteen hours."

Virgil plucked at his lower lip. "Beatrice, what did you say was below ground?"

"Level one is produce and raw material storage. Level two is fabrication and systems control. Level three is geothermal power plant."

Virgil looked around at his friends. "I think we ought to check what we have here when we get our people out of that hellhole."

Tina walked to the table. "Beatrice said she'll finish this season's harvest within the next twenty-five days. She expects the first killer frost will come less than fourteen days following the harvest. We need to know that we'll be able to make it through the winter."

"I can provide a complete inventory of my storage areas," the computer offered.

Dante frowned at the orb as he poured himself a cup of coffee. "No offense, Beatrice, but a third of the food you showed me is spoiled. And we still don't have names for half the things we saw."

"Observation is correct. Proceed with inventory and product classification. It will be beneficial. What is the number of guests I need to accommodate?"

Virgil glanced at Michael. "There are close to a thousand Americans still alive. How many folks are in the other pens?"

Michael rubbed his hands together. "I only became a man shortly before your arrival. Based on the amount of food distributed at meal times, the numbers are much smaller. The Russians, Argentinians, and Australians combined are approximately double to your count. The blood passing took the heartiest, and the rest had to struggle through the planet's winter."

Dante absorbed the info and estimated the number of deaths and survivors associated with those numbers. "Beatrice, we will be rescuing over three thousand people. Can you handle that?"

The floating orb near them tapped itself with a tendril. "Yes. Only makers and guests will be allowed into Eden. Intruders and not-guests are not permitted."

"Okay, then." Virgil rubbed his hands on his legs. "A little exploring, a little training, we catch some sleep, and then we save our people against impossible odds."

"Sounds simple enough." Michael rose and walked to the door. "Let's get started."

Tina eyed Dante with a coy glint. "Michael, why don't we split up? You and Virg can check the rotting veggies downstairs. Dante and I will climb Mount Purgatory to check out the view." Her cheeks flushed. "I mean, map out the valley."

The orb tapped itself again. "Unnecessary. I can provide detailed schematics of Eden."

Virgil grinned, stifling a laugh. "That's okay, Beatrice. Let the kids check it out for themselves." He rose from his seat. "C'mon, Mick, let's go exploring. It's getting kinda hot in here."

"Variation in the ambient temperature has been held to twenty-two degrees Celsius, plus or minus one degree, for the last thirty-eight years."

"Perhaps you are getting a fever." Michael squinted in concern as Virgil pushed him down the pathway toward the tunnel leading to the lower levels.

Tina and Dante stood and watched them disappear down the ramp to the lower levels. Dante interlaced his fingers in Tina's. "I think this is the first time we've been alone in — ever."

She moved close to him and stroked his cheek with her free hand, her eyes tearing up. "I thought I'd never see you again."

Dante pulled her close, running his hands down the small of her back. "This is kinda like a first date."

Tina wrapped her arms around him, and their lips met. She moaned with passion at the long kiss, their bodies pressed together.

A set of soft beeps cut into their moment. "This harvester unit will participate in your exploration of Mount Purgatory's exterior. It has a complete set of the valley's holographic images. You are welcome to compare your visual assessment to my recordings."

Tina slid her hands to Dante's chest and pushed back, sighing. "This is a first date, all right, complete with a chaperone." Dante released her, and Tina straightened her still damp tunic. "There are a lot of people depending on us, and we know so little about this place. We should check it out."

"For the greater good of mankind," Dante groaned, taking her hand. "C'mon, Sacagawea, let's go."

Beatrice buzzed in annoyance. "To whom are you referring? That is an unidentified label."

"I'm talking to you, Beatrice. Sacagawea was Lewis and Clark's guide." Not wanting to delve into a history lesson, he sighed and said, "Never mind. I was being sarcastic."

"Ambiguous reference. Please clarify."

"Beatrice, I misspoke, okay? I erred."

"You should correct the error in your programming. It will reduce your functionality to non-optimum levels."

Tina smirked. "And we certainly don't want you performing at a non-optimum level."

Dante rubbed his temples. "I'm getting a headache."

"I have quantities of salicylic acid available. Do you require it?"

"No, no. Just forget about it. I'm fine." He picked up his pace out of the house and toward the vaulted cavern exit.

"Your request to erase a memory entry from my hard drive has been denied. There have been no memory deletions in four hundred thirty-seven years, seven months, and twenty days."

"I thought it was thirteen days." Dante, followed by a grinning Tina, exited the cavern into the late morning air. Thick, yellow clouds gathered on the western horizon.

"Seven additional days of data have been recorded since your arrival."

"Thank you, Beatrice." Dante craned his neck and gazed up at the mountain peak. "The slope doesn't look too steep for the first few hundred feet. We should be able to hike it and not have to do any climbing."

"These boots seem sturdy enough, but I think we'll need something a little warmer than these tunics," Tina said as she scrambled a dozen steps up the mountainside. A mischievous shine lit her eyes. "Beatrice, could you go get us a couple of heavy coats or cloaks or something?"

A puzzled whir answered her. "Specifications?"

Tina looked at her tunic. "Something we can wrap around us to stay warmer. Just as long as it isn't off-white."

"I will comply. I am adding color to the fabric now. Two cloaks will be delivered in twenty-five minutes."

"Well, aren't you going to get them?" She climbed several more steps, locking her eyes on the floating orb beside them. Dante followed in her path.

The orb turned as if to face Tina. "Yes."

"Then go."

"A drone will bring garments. This harvester orb is assigned the task of providing imagery."

Tina huffed and picked up her pace.

Dante followed and chuckled. "Welcome to the world of dealing with Beatrice. At least she added audio speakers and receptors to a few of her harvester units, so we don't have to wear communication headsets."

She shook a fist in the air without slackening her pace. Dante caught up with her, and they continued on their way.

Twenty-five minutes later, an orb caught up with them holding two scarlet cloaks in a pincer. Tina fingered the soft, synthetic material and let out a quiet gasp. "Beatrice, you're a marvel. You made something that isn't beige." She swung it over her shoulders and closed the clasp.

Beside her, Dante donned his own cloak. He leaned against a craggy, granite outcropping and gazed out over the valley. He could make out what looked like a vineyard on the slope of the small mountain at the northern end of the valley, then turned to the harvester robot. "Okay, Beatrice, let's see your projections."

Immediately, a lens extended from the orb. It displayed a miniature holographic image in the air in front of it, showing the entire vale with the surrounding ridgeline oriented from their position at the southern end of the valley.

Tina pointed to the display and gazed across the valley. "It looks like there's a small stream flowing out of the lake and through those northern mountains."

Dante squinted and caught the sparkle of the distant brook as it disappeared around a rocky projection. "Sure wish I had this roadmap the first time I came here. It would've saved me the trouble of climbing those hills, jumping off cliffs, and trying to swim a mile-wide lake."

"There is a sixteen percent probability that altering your route would have been successful. The intruder pursuing you would have intercepted you before you reached the stream," the computer interjected.

Dante shuddered at the memory. "Yeah, Beatrice, you're right again."

"Yes. By your standards, my inference engine is sophisticated. You need to upgrade the probability analyzer in yours."

Tina covered her mouth to quiet her giggle as Dante glared at her. Upon focusing on the holographic display, his irritation vanished. Instead, his eyebrows shot up. "Wow, this is impressive. It's an exact match."

Tina nodded as she studied the picture over Dante's shoulder. "Beatrice, could you display the view of the other side of this mountain we're climbing?"

"No."

"What do you mean, no?" Dante looked to his left.

"Not part of Eden."

Tina followed Dante's eyes in the eastern direction and shrugged. "Let's check it out. There's nothing to the west except the harpies." She glanced up Mount Purgatory. Any further altitude would require some serious climbing. "And I sure don't want to go that way."

"East it is, then." Dante sidestepped across the fissured granite mountainside. "Beatrice, you don't have to come if you don't want to."

"All drones must remain within Eden. I can follow you for the next three hundred and forty-one feet."

He shrugged his shoulders. "Okay, suit yourself." He paused and examined the ground before them. "Hey, Tina, it looks like there's a level trail about twenty feet ahead."

She put her hands on her knees. "That's good because I'm no mountain goat."

They clambered to the site Dante had spotted and paused in amazement. They stood on a man-made path wide enough to drive a car on, and it stretched as far as they could see. Dante guessed it was possible the trail on the Eden side of Mount Purgatory had been taken out by a rock slide in the disaster that had struck the planet so long ago.

Their observations complete, Tina straightened. "This is remarkable. It has to be over four hundred years old and survived everything this planet threw at it."

Dante rubbed his jaw. "Well, if someone built a road, it has to go somewhere. Let's see where it takes us."

They walked half a mile when Dante came to a jarring halt. A nine-foot wide corridor enclosed by sheer rock walls led to an arched opening in the side of the mountain to his left. Dante guessed it to be about twelve feet high on the sides and close to twenty feet in the middle. He stepped inside the dark alcove, but came to an abrupt halt after a few steps. It felt like he had hit a wall.

Dante pulled out his tablet and pressed an icon, after which a light shone from the tablet. He smiled in triumph at Tina, who stood outside the archway peering in. "This flashlight app was the first one I wrote when I was playing with Beatrice's operating system. I knew it would come in handy."

Tina stepped back and looked down the side of the mountain. "I think we're above the ceiling inside."

"This could be a back door to that chamber Michael and I couldn't get into a couple of days ago." Dante held up the light toward the smooth barrier and hissed in frustration. "This door looks like the same material as the one we found on the inside." He searched along the edges but could find no seams.

Tina walked past a curve in the path and then called out, "Hey, Dante, come look at this!"

Dante turned off the flashlight and glared at the camouflaged wall in annoyance. He trotted out without looking back.. When he caught up with Tina, he gasped at what lay before them. Below lay a circular expanse close to a mile in diameter. It looked like a silver plate shattered by a hammer. Two deep fissures ran the entire length of the valley.

Dante shook his head. "I think we're seeing the reason Beatrice was never finished." The tip of an object the size of a football field protruded from one of the fissures. "The upheavals on this planet must've been devastating. I think Beatrice's makers either died or fled this world."

"Do you think that was their spaceship?" Tina asked in awe.

Dante pointed at a large crack in the object's hull. "If it's a craft of some sort, I don't think it'll ever get off the ground again."

She elbowed him and pointed to the far end of the basin. Two ivory-colored, wedge-shaped objects the size of houses sat there. "What do you think those are?"

"They kind of look like spaceships from a B-Grade movie." Dante lifted his tablet and pressed an icon. According to the display, both objects were thirty-five meters long, twenty-six meters wide, and nine meters high. Dante lowered the computer and examined the fissure marring the valley but couldn't see a path that would allow them to cross the expanse.

"They look like they're still in one piece," Tina added with excitement. "We could get one of those flying motorcycles you have and be across that field in minutes."

He glanced at the sky and moaned. Yellow clouds already shrouded the top of the mountain, and the smell of rain filled the chilly air. "This is a mystery we'll have to leave for another day. Let's head back."

Tina sighed and took a last look at the two mysterious objects, then pulled the cloak around her.

"Yeah. I don't want to be caught on this mountainside when those clouds open up. I hope these cloaks are waterproof."

"I hope we don't have to find out today." Dante, who had picked up his pace, paused as they passed the cave entrance and frowned at it.

Tina cocked her head and smiled. "Kind of looks like one of those trucking docks in a big warehouse." She pulled on Dante's arm. "C'mon. That's a mystery for another day."

Fat drops of rain splattered them as they reached the harvester drone waiting for them at the border of Eden. Thankfully, the cloaks were waterproof.

CHAPTER XIX
Prepare for War

As champions stripped and oiled are wont to do,
Watching for their advantage and their hold,
Before they come to blows and thrusts between them.

Dante's Inferno – Canto XVI

"Three seconds." Virgil lowered the ray gun and appraised the hole in the sheet of plexi-steel fifty yards away and the shattered rock ten yards past that.

Michael walked over to the nearest target and unclipped the harpy's shield belt fastened at the base. "I'm impressed, Virgil. You're firing a laser beam in a downpour, and you just blasted through an energy field, plus an inch of plexi-steel and six inches of granite. I'd say that was pretty good."

Virgil shook his head. "Three seconds is an eternity in a firefight, and outside of the four belts we took from the damn aliens, we don't have any shields of our own." He slid his hand along the weapon's barrel. "What did you say the range of this 'tool' is?"

"Effective range is ninety-one point forty-four meters. Capability decreases exponentially after that. Theoretical range is unlimited, but I lack the manufacturing capability to fabricate components with the required precision. The product development schedule you imposed is a constraint."

"So about a hundred yards." Virgil thought about it some more, then sighed. "These will have to do. Now can you build us a few hundred more?"

"No. Required rare earth elements for the power concentrator are difficult to refine to sufficient purity. If I cease further research, production of four units a day can be achieved."

"Then get going. Four a day will have to do." Virgil slung the gun's harness over his shoulder, grimacing. "How about the energy shields the harpies have? Can you make any of those?"

"Answer is unchanged from this morning. Technology is understood, but I lack the raw materials and the precision equipment to fabricate."

Virgil walked over to the boulder where Tina and Dante crouched huddled under their cloaks. "Do either of you want to shoot anymore?"

Tina's teeth chattered as she pulled the hood of her cloak tight around her head. "No. I just want a hot shower. Can we go back inside now?"

The sergeant ran his hand through his soaked hair and powered up the light blade. "Just a few more minutes. Mick, stick the belt back on the target and reboot it."

"My name is— Oh, never mind." He clipped the belt back onto the target and stepped back when it glowed blue. "All set."

Virgil charged and skewered the charred plexi-steel slab. The sword's charged field shut down in a spray of sparks. He swung crosswise, and the blade bit off a half-inch chunk of the hardened metal. Five seconds later, the blade glowed again. Virgil swung it at the target and it split in half.

A broad grin creased his face, and he powered down the sword and slid it into the sheath he wore on his back. "Yeah, that'll work. Now we can go in." He put his hands together and blew on them. "We still have a lot of details to work out."

As the group slogged through the olive orchard in the cold drizzle, Dante found himself walking next to Virgil. He grabbed a piece of the fruit hanging on a low branch and took a bite. "So how did the exploration in the lower levels go?"

Virgil glared at the drone flying ahead of them. "That was a complete waste of time. The food storage area was pitch-black. I had to spend five minutes explaining to that floating beach ball that we need light to move around. Then we had to wait another half hour for an orb to show up with a spotlight." He pulled his cloak's hood over his rain-soaked head. "When we found rotted fruit in the first couple of bins, I had to spend another hour giving a detailed explanation on the use of mason jars and the canning process." He pointed his finger at the orb. "And when I finally convinced it to take us to the manufacturing level, the door was locked."

"It wouldn't let you through?" Dante scratched his temple.

"Oh, it apologized, but said we had level one security clearance and the firewall required a minimum of level two for admittance."

Dante glanced at the robot. "That's strange. I wonder why Beatrice didn't tell you when you first came up with the idea to check things out?"

Virgil waved his hands in the air. "I asked the same question. The stupid machine said it wasn't aware of the requirement until we tried to enter. It was a complete waste of a morning." He stomped into the cavern entrance without another word.

———— ◆ ————

All of the buildings inside the mountain had been labeled with large, black numerals. Beatrice did not understand why the humans couldn't differentiate between most of the structures, but acceded to the request when Tina insisted.

They designated Dante's home House 1 and labeled each structure in a clockwise direction. Six-hundred and ninety-two buildings of various sizes and heights surrounded the circumference of the botanical lab's floor. All had been constructed of the same greenish-beige marble, and most had no windows. House 692, by far the largest at three stories tall, stood on the opposite side of the entrance from House 1.

The main floor of House 692 opened up to a wide atrium with a crystal-clear ceiling. Unlike the other buildings, light poured into this one from the tall golden pillars in the gardens. A wide, curved ramp led to the upper floors. In the center room stood a long, pearl-white oval table.

Virgil had spread all of their equipment on it. "Okay, we have four of the harpies' fancy stun guns, and it looks like three of their energy shield belts are still functional."

"I estimate the probability of the fourth belt being repaired is seventy-seven percent," said the computer.

"Beatrice, I would be very appreciative if you could get it working." Virgil gestured to each item on the table. "We have one Beretta with no ammunition, eight of these energy swords—" he held the short barreled gun—"and one laser rifle."

"That tool is labeled ray gun. Four production units will be available in five hours. They are being stress tested now."

Virgil frowned. "Five is better than one."

Dante squeezed the bridge of his nose and yawned. He had been up most of the last three days experimenting with the operating systems from both Beatrice's and the aliens' computers. He went to the stove and poured two cups of coffee, one of which he handed to Tina as he sat down next to her. "We still have our four neural net suits and those two flying motorcycles."

"What good will any of this do?" Tina slammed her cup down, sloshing liquid across the table. "In case you haven't counted, there are only four of us. I remember what those abominations did back in New York. There were hundreds of those monsters, and now they have an army of these mindless clones. I can't even guess how many of them there are." Her eyes met Michael's, and she bit her lip. "Oh... Michael, I'm so sorry. I didn't mean you. It's just—"

Michael raised his hand. "Tina, it's okay. I've spent much time pondering my existence and the brainwashing that makes my people what they are."

Dante's face creased into a smile. "Well, Michael, then we'll just have to work on their educational opportunities."

A wistful look crossed Michael's face, and he gave Dante a fond smile. "It is a wonderful thought. Perhaps when we rescue Gabriel and Rafael, we can come up with a plan that's better than your crazy idea."

Virgil looked back and forth between the two. "What crazy idea?"

Michael sighed, his eyes averted from everyone. "Dante has a grand scheme to rewrite the harpies' clone stasis training software."

Virgil tapped his cheek. "A cyberattack isn't a bad idea. The problem is we'd have to break into the hive's upper levels."

Dante rolled his eyes. "Virg, haven't you ever heard of wireless technology? Even on Earth, we haven't had to make hard links in, like, forever."

"Well, then, do it," Virgil grumbled.

Dante blew his cheeks in exasperation. "I've been trying. The anti-virus software in that recorder communication device Beatrice pulled out of the dead clone is incredible. Whatever software I attempt to inject into its system is deleted immediately. It only accepts files containing data it's looking for."

"That sounds promising." Tina drummed her fingers on the table. "Can you embed a virus in the data flow?"

"I've tried, but it's all stripped out. I've snuck in nothing useful yet." Dante squirmed once he saw he'd become the focus of everyone's attention. "You remember when I was playing around with the navigation system in the harpies' flier?"

Tina mopped up the spilled coffee. "Yeah?"

"Well, I tried to upload a few malware programs I've been working on, but only one got through."

Virgil's eyes lit with excitement. "That's great. What does it do?"

Dante shrunk into himself and blushed. "Ahh, nothing. It's just a one-line program stub I'm using as a placeholder for going after the clone education system. There's no content in it."

Virgil's face fell. "What was it?"

Dante shrugged his shoulders. "It just reads, 'Knowledge is power' in the harpies' language. At the time, I was just happy to get a handle on their programming code. I'll come up with something."

Virgil scratched his head. "It's a start. It's a good start. It sure as hell's a lot more than I could ever dream of pulling off." He looked over at the orb hovering by the ceiling in the corner. "Beatrice, can you hack into the harpies' system?"

"No," the computer answered. "The intruder will find me if I make any attempt at communications. It is hunting me now. It will destroy Eden. It is evil."

"So much for that idea." Virgil turned back to Dante. "Keep working on it, kid." Shortly after, his eyes glinted with another thought. "Hey, Beatrice, how about lending us your army of flying beach balls and micro-bots? That would help even the odds a bit."

"I am an agricultural station. None of my components can leave the boundaries of Eden."

Virgil snorted in exasperation. "Why does that not surprise me?"

Dante frowned as he looked up from his tablet, waving his arm. "Virg, look around you. Beatrice has done a lot for us already. She's stretched the limits of her design to help us about as far as they can go. Where would any of us be right now if it weren't for her?" He put down the tablet and met Virgil's eyes. "I know I'd be dead."

Virgil nodded and glanced at Michael. "So for better or worse, this is what we have to work with. Do you have any idea what we'll be facing?"

Michael's face clouded. "Do you want the good news or the bad news first?"

"There's good news?"

Michael rubbed his chin. "Sort of. The ones you fought on your planet's surface are of the harpies' warrior class. There are a few thousand of them associated with this project, but they are all off-planet now. Outside of a couple dozen guards, the ones in the hive are engineers and scientists. They are working on the human biological experiments. Altogether, there are no more than a hundred of them."

"So, militarily, who's in charge?"

Michael snorted, smirking. "No one. In the harpies' warrior class, advancement and honor is gained through conquest. The guards here are the lowest of the low. There is a site administrator, but he is a bureaucrat and even more inept from a tactical perspective than the scientists or guards."

Virgil's knuckles whitened as he paced with balled fists. "When will this army of theirs be back?"

"If the cycle holds from their previous excursions, I expect the fleet to return in about two months."

Virgil shuddered. "If that's the good news, what's the bad news?"

"They already have the capability of creating an almost unlimited number of clones." Michael stiffened his jaw as he spat out those last words.

Tina focused on Michael. "It takes nine months for a human infant to grow in its mother's womb. It can't be that quick and easy. Think about your own physical and mental development."

Michael scratched the back of his neck. "True. The count of fully developed guardians is around a thousand. There are, perhaps, another nine thousand undergoing physical development, though they are still in various stages of mental programming." He met Tina's eyes. "Those await their turn at the blood passing ceremony."

Tina shivered and reached for Dante's hand.

Michael's lips thinned and he looked at the ceiling. "The count of clones in the embryonic stage is in the millions."

"Well, for now, if it can't pull a trigger, I'm not going to worry about it." Virgil hoisted one of the harpies' weapons. "Besides these toys, what kind of armament will we be facing?"

"That's a good question. I've never seen the harpies use anything else." Michael chewed the inside of his cheek. "The clones have never been allowed to hold even simple blades until after they lost to your people in the arena." Virgil smiled, but Michael held up his hand. "There is no reason they won't be armed, and the harpies can match any armament production this agricultural station can come up with. They are a very imitative people and quick to absorb technological innovations from other species."

Dante released Tina's hand. "Look, instead of fighting a grand war we have little chance of winning, why don't we get our people out of there and hide here in the hills?"

"Winter's coming." Tina pursed her lips and turned to the orb. "Beatrice, would you accept our refugees?"

Beatrice answered with a simple buzz and click. "Humans are categorized as guests. Guests have level one security clearance. Yes."

Dante eyed Virgil. "Free room and board. What more can you ask?"

"Nice idea, kid, but I think we'll have a fight on our hands if we try to pull a jail break."

"Not necessarily." Dante focused on Michael. "How closely do the harpies track the prisoners?"

Michael snorted again. "Not at all. Except for those who are marked for the blood passing, they only do a daily scan for corpses."

"There's no head count?"

"No. Prisoners are either alive or dead. They don't count them. Why would they bother? No one is going anywhere."

"Michael, do you still have the capability of opening the fences?" Dante's voice rose in excitement.

"Yes. It's tied to my DNA, but the instant the barrier is down anywhere, an alarm sounds," he responded in a flat voice. "Also, guardians walk the perimeter in groups of three. There is never more than a twenty-minute gap between the patrols at any one point."

"I think Dante's onto something." Virgil picked a neural net suit. "How long do you think it'd take to put one of these things on and take it off?"

A gleam of understanding shone in Michael's eyes as he touched the cord around his neck. "Beatrice, we will need two more of these necklaces."

CHAPTER XX
Rescue

Darkness of hell, and of a night deprived
Of every planet under a poor sky,
As much as may be tenebrous with cloud.

Dante's Purgatorio – Canto XVI

A sad smile crossed Tina's face. "Those look like the old hay wagons I use to ride in as a kid around Halloween."

"I don't think your old hay wagon floated on an anti-gravitation device," said Dante. He wrapped his arm around her shoulder and hugged her.

Together, they watched Virgil and Michael ride close to the ground on their fliers. They each towed a floating transport wagon through the pass out of the mountains. The fading dusk swallowed them as they reached flat land.

Dante released his hold on Tina and walked to a stony outcropping near the crest of the ridge they stood atop. He cradled a laser rifle on his arm and focused on the wide ravine below him but could no longer see Virgil or Michael. Tina listened but could only hear water flowing over the rocks.

A day earlier, Virgil had explored the promising gap in the mountains Tina discovered in Beatrice's holographic display. He followed the stream on his flier through the hills until it cascaded onto the plain below

The small, shin-deep brook flowed from the northern end of Eunoe and ran all of the way to the sulfur lake near the harpy's prison camp.

A wide, relatively smooth path cut through the steep hills beside the watercourse. In ancient times, the creek had probably been a broad river. As interesting as that fact was, having the capacity to move people and small vehicles to Beatrice's mountain valley without being seen interested him a great deal more.

"It seems kind of fitting that Michael named the brook the River Styx," Dante mused as he watched the plain, trying to detect any movement.

"It's a bit of a grandiose name for such a small stream," Tina chided.

Dante scratched the back of his neck. "I think it kind of fits. In legend, the River Styx separates the land of the living from Hell." He spat to clear the sulfurous taste in his mouth from the plain to the west. "And that place down there is as good an approximation of Hell as I can imagine." Dante reached for Tina's hand and squeezed it. "We named the foul-smelling body of water down there Cocytus after the lake in the pit of Hell."

Tina let out a quiet huff. "We could name this entire world Cocytus. That sure as heck fits."

They sat on a granite boulder and stared at the faint blue glow on the horizon which marked the distant prison camp. Tina set her stun gun down and leaned against his chest. "Do you think the plan will work?"

Dante set his rifle next to her gun and interlocked his fingers with hers. "Yeah. Mick knows how these aliens think, and Virg is some sort of ninja commando. They'll be in and out of there without the harpies catching wind of it."

"So we just sit here and wait." Tina pursed her lips and shivered. "I feel so useless. We just have to wait until morning, and we'll either see wagons full of our people or our death coming across that ground."

Dante rose, picked up his gun, and walked back to the ledge looking over the ravine. A chill breeze whipped his scarlet cloak. "It's a good plan, and we have to give our people a chance to escape that hellhole. If the aliens don't kill them, the upcoming winter will."

"Those harpies aren't stupid. Even if the plan works tonight, how many trips can Virg and Michael make before they're caught?"

"Then we fight." Dante squeezed the grip of his weapon and returned to where Tina sat. He clasped her hands, running his thumbs across her knuckles. "Sooner or later, we'll have to fight them."

"I know." Tina pasted a brave smile on her face. "Looking at this world, it seems so impossible. They're so powerful and so advanced." Tina turned her face away and shuddered. "Sorry. I'm just tired. Being scared all the time is exhausting."

"I think we all are." A wistful look crossed his face. "But just think of the incredible stories we'll have for our grandchildren when this is all over."

Tina made a tight smile. "They wouldn't believe a word of it. I know I wouldn't." She clutched his hands and looked at the night sky. "Dante, do you think we'll ever see home again?"

"Sure we will. I'll believe that until I draw my last breath." He felt her hands tremble in his. "Say, which one of those stars do you think is home?"

Tina searched the heavens with longing, and quiet tears dampened her face. "Do you think they've forgotten us by now?"

"Are you kidding? Earth was invaded by aliens. Our pictures are probably plastered across every newspaper in the world."

Tina shook her head. "Dante, you heard Martinel. The harpies have been raiding Earth for over a year now, and we never heard a word about it." Her face twisted into a grimace. "I figure the governments are trying to cover this up, hoping the problem just goes away."

Dante forced a quiet laugh and looked into her eyes. "You've never met my mom. She's Calabrese, and they're the most stubborn people in the world. I bet she's been writing a blazing letter to the President every day and has a dozen statues of Saint Anthony buried up to their necks in her garden."

Tina smiled and ran her hand through Dante's hair. "I'm glad you're with me. I don't think I could've stayed sane without you."

"Are you kidding?" Dante gasped. "You're the bravest, most level-headed, and most beautiful woman I've ever met."

Tina flushed. "Oh, shut up, you idiot." Their lips met, and the silent world left them in peace.

———————◆———————

Virgil skimmed his flier low over the dirt, following the course of the River Styx. About a half mile from the north end of the prison's barrier, he landed the silent craft in a deep swale where the stream widened. Michael pulled up next to him and halted. They both cringed as the wagons they pulled made muffled thuds when they settled in the sticky mud. It was about as close as they dared to bring the carts.

Virgil studied the blue outline of the barrier. He pulled the hood up on his neural net suit and bundled four laser rifles inside the other three suits. Next, he rolled up his sleeve and pressed the button on the new stopwatch strapped to his wrist. "These fancy timers Beatrice built for us are working well. Mick, start yours now. If I'm not back in two hours, get the hell out of here."

"My name is Michael," he hissed as he slid off of his vehicle and pulled the stun-like gun out of its storage cavity. He flattened himself at the edge of the two-foot deep depression a dozen strides from his flier and started his timer. "Good luck, Virgil. May God protect you."

Virgil nodded and ran for the compound with stealthy steps. When he was a hundred feet from the barrier, Virgil crouched behind a small boulder and waited. Five minutes later, a trio of clones silhouetted by the glowing fence passed by, staring dead ahead. Virgil started the second timer on his watch and waited until another trio of clones marched past.

Virgil checked his watch and reset the timer for twenty minutes and took a deep breath, then dashed forward and didn't pause when he passed through the barrier. The stinging sensation battered him, but he jogged on. Once he was through, he attempted to orient himself.

A shape materialized out of the darkness carrying a shield and a bared sword. "Who goes there?"

Recognizing the voice, Virgil tensed at the surprise appearance and squinted at the face in the dim light. "Corporal Baker?"

"Sergeant Bernius?" came the shocked response, and Baker lowered his sword. "What the hell are you doing here? I thought you and that girl were long gone."

Virgil took a deep breath. "Well, I'm back, and I have a plan get us all outta here. Get me to Captain Cruz. The night won't last forever."

———— ◆ ————

Captain Cruz's knuckles whitened as he gripped the laser rifle's barrel. His voice shook as he set the gun down. "This is real. It's a solid plan. This is more than I dreamed possible." He glanced around the hut packed with every officer and noncom in his command along with Dr. Easley. He leveled his eyes at Virgil. "This mountain facility is run by non-hostiles?"

The sergeant smirked as he envisioned Captain Cruz interrogating Beatrice. "Yes, sir. The entity I told you about, Beatrice, is some sort of computer left behind by the natives of this world. She definitely opposes the harpies and is willing to ally herself with us."

"And she made these weapons for us?"

The sergeant's forehead creased. "Yes, sir. The kid, Dante, had to work some computer mumbo-jumbo, but he got her to start building them." He looked Cruz in the eye. "These guns are very effective. They'll burn right through the energy shields those freaking harpies wear."

"I'd love to give those bastards a taste of their own medicine," Gentile growled.

Cruz tightened his jaw. "We lost good people back in New York and on this slag-heap of a planet. But revenge will have to wait. We need to look to the living."

"Roger that, sir." Virgil looked at his stopwatch. "Sir, we need to begin if we're going to get anyone out of here tonight."

"This new facility has adequate shelter and supplies for us." Cruz sucked on the inside of his cheek, mentally running through the logistics.

"Begging your pardon, sir, but it's not like we have any other options," Virgil sputtered.

"I know, Sergeant," Cruz replied in an icy tone, "but I can also count. The most we can evacuate in one night is sixty to seventy people. There are close to one thousand Americans under my care, and I don't know how many Aussies, Argentinians, and Russians there are." He sighed and continued in a softer voice, "The harpies aren't stupid. Not by a long shot. Even if by some miracle they don't catch any of our people escaping, they'll eventually realize there are chickens missing from the hen house. I think it's a safe bet that when they do, they'll wash their hands of this filthy experiment of theirs and terminate whoever is still here. So I repeat my question: is there adequate food and shelter?"

Virgil stiffened to attention and saluted. "Yes, sir. Beatrice is some sort of automated farm with the inside of a whole mountain carved out. The facilities there would comfortably support ten times our number."

Cruz nodded and looked around the room. "Any officers not tagged by the aliens?" No one answered, so he turned back to the sergeant. "All right, Bernius, you're in charge of troop and civilian deployment at the safe haven." Cruz rubbed his chest where the aliens' disk lay. "Those of us with tags will be the last go. I don't want those alien fuckers to know where we are until we're dug in." He turned to Lieutenant Gentile. "Do we have any intact fireteams that haven't been marked?"

Gentile scratched the back of his neck as he thought. "Sir, we have three: Baker's, Frontera's, and Dolan's"

"Okay," said Cruz. "The first ones in these magic monkey suits will be Frontera and his men. He's been busted in rank twice now for insubordination, but he's a helluva soldier in a fight."

Virgil nodded. "That's an excellent idea, sir. I have a couple of the harpies' stun weapons, and a three-man fireteam can hold the perimeter of the landing zone with Mick if any big uglies get nosy."

"Whatever you do, keep it quiet." Cruz grunted and looked at Dr. Easley. "Esther, how many children do we have in camp?"

Esther paused to think. "There are about a hundred and twenty under the age of fifteen here. I don't have a clue how many are in the other three prison sectors."

"We save the children first. All the children." Cruz handed the three neural net suits to Lieutenant Gentile, then crossed his arms. "Go get Frontera and his men ready. Have them rendezvous in the hut at the northeastern corner of the camp. Do it nice and quiet, but fast."

"Yes, sir." Gentile ducked past the hanging door cover and vanished into the night.

"I'll start gathering the first few groups of children." Esther turned to follow the lieutenant out.

"Esther, wait a second," said Virgil, patting his chest. He reached inside his suit and pulled out two rope-like necklaces. "Give these to Gabe and Rafe when you see them. There's an electronic jammer built into these things that will lock out the harpy control module embedded in their heads."

Instead of answering, she stared at his extended hand with her eyes wide but distant. Sensing something wrong, he pulled back and asked, "What's the matter?"

Tears welled in her eyes. "Virgil, Gabriel and Rafael are both dead."

Virgil had to fight the pang in his chest as his hands fell to his side. "What happened? Baker told me you smashed the sons of bitches in the arena." Anger shot through him and he swung on Captain Cruz. "You always had it in for them. What did you do?" His rage cooled when he saw true sorrow in the officer's eyes in response to his outburst.

Dr. Easley walked over and grabbed his forearm. "Virgil, they survived the last fight. All of our boys did." Dr. Easley touched the circlets dangling from his limp hand. "They killed themselves so their memories couldn't be collected by the harpies. They sacrificed themselves to protect us."

Cruz cast his eyes down. "I was wrong about them. I was wrong about a lot of things." He met Virgil's suspicious glare. "They paid the ultimate price to deprive the enemy of valuable information. I wish I could've gotten to know them better. Their sacrifice was the bravest act I've ever witnessed."

Virgil swallowed hard. "Thank you, sir. Michael would appreciate hearing those words from you."

"I'll be sure to talk to him. It's the least I can do." Cruz cleared his throat. "I do owe him my sincere apology and thanks for the services he and his brothers have performed to help all of humanity."

Virgil wiped his nose. "I better get to the rendezvous point." He brushed Esther's care-worn face and squeezed the hand she still had resting on his forearm. "Go get the kids. I want to get as many out before morning as we can. Try to put Angela in the first group. She might help Mick deal with this news." He saluted. "Sir, with your permission."

Cruz returned the salute. "Godspeed, Sergeant."

———◆———

Virgil stood at the small adobe structure's entrance, watching three clones march by on the opposite side of the barrier. He nodded to Dr. Easley, who stood beside him. They had gone through with Frontera's team already without trouble, but now the real test stood before them.

He dropped down on his knees and looked into the eyes of the three children all but swimming in oversized neural net suits. They stared at him with fear and confusion. "Now remember what I said. When I carry you past those bad poles, stay curled up inside the suit. Any part of you that pokes out will hurt a lot. Understand?"

They nodded, their expressions solemn.

"There will be no crying. You have to be as quiet as a mouse and as brave as a soldier. Can you do that for me?"

Angela asked, "Will Uncle Mick be waiting for us on the other side?"

He squeezed her arm. "Yes, he will. But first, we have to get past the bad fence. Then the soldiers will carry you the rest of the way."

Angela stood very straight. "I don't care how much it hurts. Uncle Mick is gonna be very sad, and he needs me."

"That's my girl." Virgil tousled her hair and looked up at the parents of the other two children. Tears brimmed their eyes.

"Take care of my baby," one mother choked out.

"You'll all be together soon. It's a good place with food and shelter." He glanced out the doorway. It was time, so Virgil picked up Angela and two mothers carried the other bundled children.

Virgil paused at the barrier and spied Frontera crouched on the other side. "Okay, I'll carry them now." He checked to be sure the children were tucked inside with no part of them exposed. A pair of sobs left the two squirming bundles placed in his outstretched arms. "Ready."

Angela squeezed her mouth shut as tears trickled down her cheeks. The other two whimpered as Virgil hurried them to the waiting soldiers. A quick look around told him they'd made it without being spotted.

"You guys were very, very good," Virgil whispered. "Now take the special suits off and go with these soldiers. They'll take you to Angela's Uncle Mick. He has warm blankets and is going to give you a wagon ride later. Okay?"

Three solemn faced children nodded and climbed out of the neural net suits.

Corporal Frontera met Virgil's eyes and gave him a thumbs up. "I'll be damned if this isn't going to work."

"If it doesn't, we're all dead." Virgil gathered the three suits. "This is going to be a long night. That freaking fence hurts like a son of a bitch."

"Better you than me, Sarge."

Virgil checked his timer and sighed. "Meet you back here in twenty minutes."

"Roger that."

Virgil took a deep breath and sprinted back to the prison.

When he arrived at the hut, a young family waited for him there with Lieutenant Gentile and Dr. Easley. A woman holding her baby met him with hope-filled eyes. A crestfallen man stood behind her, holding the hands of two boys. One appeared to be about seven and the other, about two.

"You'll save my baby," the woman wept as she kissed her sleeping infant.

"That's the plan, ma'am. We're going to save

everyone."

Her lips trembled and she smiled in gratitude.

Her husband crouched down and combed the two-year-old's hair with his fingers. "Be a good boy, now, and do what the soldier tells you." His voice choked. "We'll be together again real soon."

The little tow-headed boy shook his head and cried. "I want to stay with you, Papa. Don't make me leave."

The man crushed the two boys to his chest and met Virgil's eyes. "Take care of my children."

Virgil's arms hung at his side and he squeezed the empty suits in a death grip. He eyed the man and woman. Both showed signs of malnourishment after a month of deprivation. He handed a suit to the seven-year-old and spoke to the two-year-old. "What's your name?"

"Jimmy."

"Okay, Jimmy. Do you think you could wrap your arms around your daddy and hang on no matter what?"

The little boy sniffed and nodded his head.

Virgil showed him the suit. "If your dad puts this on, it'll be very dark and stuffy, and for a little while, it might sting."

The boy wiped his nose. "I was stung by a bee once. Papa pulled the stinger out, and I only cried a little."

Virgil rose and faced the man and woman with hard eyes. "Put these on and carry the little ones inside. Remember, if they make any noise, we're all dead."

They nodded in grim understanding. The woman handed the baby to Dr. Easley and pulled on the suit. The infant woke when the mom jostled her into the suit and started to cry. The mother hushed the baby by letting her suckle.

Virgil grimaced. "This won't work."

"Oh, yes it will," Dr. Easley declared. She slung her arm around Lieutenant Gentile's. "We're going to move down the fence about a hundred feet and have the loudest lover's spat you ever heard." She smiled at the startled officer. "You better be ready to scream back. My late husband used to say I could peel the paint off walls when I got angry." She appraised the two bulging lumps under the parent's suits and nodded with satisfaction. "You've got one minute before the show begins."

Virgil squeezed her shoulder. "You're a marvel, Esther."

She met his eyes and patted his hand. "I know. And you are, too. Now get out of here." Esther pulled Gentile out of the hut. "Come on, Lieutenant. Let's see how well the army taught you to cuss."

Virgil took the seven-year-old's hand and followed her out. They parted ways right after, and a short time later, he heard the screaming.

"What do you think you're doing, coming home drunk again?" a high-pitched voice screeched.

"I have to be drunk to face the likes of you!"

"You worthless piece of garbage. I should've listened to my mother about you."

"Well, both you and your mother can..."

Virgil shook his head. "Those two deserve Academy Awards. Let's go." He urged them on, holding back his own laughter.

———————◦◆◦———————

Six hours later, Virgil leaned on the side of the wagon. He flexed his fingers in an attempt to stop them from twitching.

"Sarge, are you okay?" asked Frontera.

Virgil shot his hand to the cart's railing and gripped it to hide the shaking. "I'm fine, Corporal." He shook his head to clear it. "I gotta say, that damn fence packs a wallop."

"Sarge, you've been through it over forty times now. I think you've had enough for one night."

"Tell Mick to head back with his wagon." He

returned his arm back to his side. The tremors had stopped.

"Sarge, you sent Mick back three hours ago. Another run will kill you." Frontera eyed the eastern horizon where dawn loomed over the mountains. "We're out of time."

Virgil pushed away from the soldier and staggered back toward the barrier. "I got to go back. There's still more kids trapped in there." With bleary eyes, he tried to focus on the stopwatch he wore, but the screen was dark. It had stopped working a few runs earlier.

He grunted as he found himself face down in the mud with Corporal Frontera on top of him. "Sergeant Bernius, you're the only one here who knows how to fly that vehicle." Frontera rolled him over and pointed to the wagon full of children wrapped in beige-colored blankets.

Tears flowed from Virgil's unfocused eyes. "Lizzy, I'll save you."

"Oh, shit, Sergeant, get it together. Who's Lizzy? Captain Cruz knows the schedule."

Virgil continued in a hard, flat voice, unaware of any audience. "My sister, Lizzy. I was on leave after finishing an assignment down in the Columbian jungle and went to visit her and her kids. Her husband was Navy and out to sea at the time. They had a small apartment outside of New Brunswick. Those kids of hers are the three cutest imps in the world."

He shook off the corporal and sat up. "There was a fire, and we were trapped on the third floor. She handed me the two older ones and I jumped." Slowly, he rose to his feet. "My ankle snapped when I landed, but the kids were okay. Flames poured out of all the windows. Lizzy screamed my name and threw the baby to me. I heard sirens in the distance, but it was too late. The last thing I saw was Lizzy's clothes ablaze as she fell back into the room from the window sill."

Frontera grabbed him by the shoulders and stood

nose to nose with him. "Your sister's kids survived because of you." He turned Virgil to look at the wagon. Thirty pairs of young, confused eyes stared back at him. "Those are your responsibility now. Tomorrow, we'll be back and save more."

Virgil shrugged out of the corporal's grip. His eyes cleared, but tears still trickled down his cheeks. "While recouping in the hospital for the busted leg and the burns, I learned a pair of gang-bangers working for the drug cartel I messed with set the fire. I was their target. I'll never have innocents die because of me again." He walked on shaky legs to the flier and climbed onto the vehicle's saddle. "Better get in, Corporal. We get to do all this again tomorrow."

Frontera had barely leapt over the transport's side when it jerked forward, and he found himself skimming along the side of a small brook.

The first rays of the sun outlined the highest mountain peaks.

———•◆•———

Michael drove his flier up the slope beside the cascading water, taking it slower than he normally would. Not just because the obstacles were hard to spot in the darkness but because of the precious cargo in the cart he towed. He stroked the filthy brown hair of the child pressed against him on the saddle. Angela had fallen asleep, but her hold on his tunic had not loosened.

Dead. My brothers are both dead. He wiped the back of his hand across his red-rimmed eyes and strained to focus on the winding trail.

He knew something was wrong when the soldiers in the first group dodged his questions regarding Rafael and Gabriel. It wasn't until Angela had shot into his arms sobbing when he realized why: his worst fears had come to pass. Only after that did one of the soldiers give him the details about his brothers' sacrifice. Since then, Michael felt overwhelmingly alone.

Angela snuggled closer, and Michael cooed to her. Soon after, a quick, triple blink of a light ahead caught his attention—the signal. A small smile crossed his face at the thought of his waiting friends, and he wrapped his arm around the child in front of him. He paused at the base of the hill, waved to the two shadowed figures atop it, and then continued across the valley.

No, I am not alone, he reminded himself. *Rest in peace, my brothers. You will always be part of me.*

CHAPTER XXI
A New Home

Eager already to search in and around
The heavenly forest, dense and living-green,
Which tempered to the eyes the new-born day.

Dante's Purgatorio – Canto XXVIII

Frontera pushed back a third bowl of barley soup and reached for a bunch of grape-like fruit sitting on a platter in the middle of the table. "This place is freaking amazing."

Virgil sat across from him at the large oval table. His six-hour sleep was fitful, but the shaking had stopped. He gazed up through the atrium in House 692. "I've had some time to clear my head and think."

Dante sat in a corner hunched over his tablet, his fingers flying over its screen, but he paused and looked up. "What you pulled off last night was a miracle."

Tina attempted to examine each of the fifty-seven children at the other end of the room, but it was a hopeless task. No longer held prisoner to fear and pain, curiosity drove them to take turns attempting escape. The half-dozen adults had harried expressions on their tired faces as they attempted to corral the children with little success.

The other two soldiers stood in the building's open doorway, their eyes flitting back and forth between the strange orb hovering nearby and the children, who kept trying to dash past them to the well-lit gardens beyond. With Angela riding on his shoulders, Michael walked over, sat down, and handed Virgil a mug of coffee.

"Thanks, Mick," Virgil sighed as he took his first sip and shifted his attention to Frontera. "Corporal, I want to thank you. I lost control out there, and you reeled me back in from what could've been a disaster."

"No prob, Sarge. That much juice would rattle anyone's brains."

"Well, it's a problem. We're walking a thin line between life and death here. I'll accept no screw-ups — least of all from myself. Whose fireteam is coming out tonight?"

Frontera scratched the back of his neck. "Dolan's."

"Okay. Tonight, I'll alternate with those guys."

"Sarge, you're in charge now. You stay here." The corporal glanced at Michael. "Show me how to fly that motorcycle of yours, and Mick can guide me. I'll do the pickups."

"A couple more nights like the last one and I'll take you up on it. But for now, I have some things I need you and your guys to work on." Virgil grabbed a handful of almonds and munched on them before he eyed the corporal. "Have you noticed none of the buildings in here have doors?"

Frontera leaned back, surprised. "Yeah, now that you mention it."

"There's a tall building in the mountain's wall near the ramp. It's labeled House Seven."

"I think I know which one you're talking about." He pointed his thumb at Dante. "The geek says the ramp goes nowhere."

Dante blushed and shot a frown at the corporal. "There's something on the other side. I just can't figure out how to unlock the door."

Virgil waved his hand in the air. "Right now, I don't care about the ramp to nowhere. It's the building I'm interested in."

Frontera shrugged and cocked an eyebrow. "Okay, so what do you want us to do?"

Virgil assessed the collection of armaments on the table. "We need a safe place to keep all of this weaponry. With all of these kids around, one of them is going to get hurt. So first, I want a heavy, lockable door installed on the recessed building, and then I want you to secure our equipment there."

"So you want a proper armory?"

"Exactly." He lowered his voice. "One more thing. Do you know what a sally port is?"

The corporal looked puzzled. "You mean those small entrances in medieval castles?"

Virgil nodded his head. "Yeah. I want one cut through from the third floor of the armory to the outside. It makes me nervous that there's only one way in and out of this mountain, and it's through a gate forty feet wide and twenty feet high."

"Gotcha, Sarge. With a little concrete, we could even build a nice rampart with a guardhouse on the outside of the entrance. How thick is the mountain over there?"

"I gauge it to be about forty feet."

Frontera's eyebrows shot up. "That's solid granite. I hope you don't want it done this century."

Virgil tapped the laser rifle lying on the table. "This thing will blast through that rock in no time."

The corporal made a furtive glance at the orb. "What if all that digging upsets our host?"

"That's another reason to have a lockable door. I don't want Beatrice to know anything about it until the job's finished." He coughed into his fist. "It's easier to beg forgiveness than to ask permission."

Frontera eyed the orb. "Will that floaty thing get us the materials we need?"

Virgil looked down the table at Dante. "Hey, Dante, these guys are going to be doing some construction. I want them to work through you on any requisitions to Beatrice. Is that okay?"

Dante gave Virgil a querulous look. "Sure thing."

Both soldiers jumped when a brief buzz sounded. "Unnecessary interface. Humans are classified as guests. I will meet requests for all staples."

Undeterred, Dante chimed in. "Beatrice, funneling our needs through a few people is a good idea. There'll be hundreds of us here soon. If folks think you're Santa Claus, there will be no end to their wish lists."

"I have no identifier labeled Santa Claus. My human interface designator is Beatrice." She made another buzz. "Current requests occupy eleven percent of my general fabrication capacity."

Dante put down his tablet and faced the robot. "Tasks need to be prioritized."

"My most recent request is for a project labeled skateboard. Is it a higher or lower priority than the project labeled sally port?"

Coffee exploded from Virgil's mouth. "What?"

Tina stepped before the orb. "Beatrice, I informed you about the difference between human adults and human children earlier."

"Yes. Human children have immature brains which do not process data correctly. I have also noted they spend much time rushing about without any purpose."

"I guess that's close enough." Tina made a sheepish smirk.

"Child requests deleted."

Virgil cleared his throat. "Ahh, Beatrice, you don't have a problem with us making a new entrance?"

"Project does not impact structural integrity of botanical habitat. Guests have security clearance on this level. Alternate point of egress will reduce impact of exterior environment on internal climate control." Beatrice made three thoughtful beeps. "Ray gun is ineffective tool selection. I have assigned a mining unit to perform the task at your designated location."

The sergeant gaped. "You heard everything I said?"

"Yes."

"Guess we'll have plenty of stone." Frontera chuckled. "Hey, Beatrice, do you know how to make cement?"

"Define cement."

One of the children made a sudden dash for the door and the lush gardens beyond it. The guard groaned and snagged the boy's new tunic at the last second. "Hey, Beatrice, do you have any nanny robots sitting around here?"

"Define nanny."

Virgil rose and shook his head at the sight of Michael. The big man had his fingers entangled in a thick thread, torn from his tunic, attempting to understand Angela's game of cat's cradle. "Mick, you and Dante can make yourselves useful. Block the door here so the midgets don't get out. I'm taking these three outside for a little target practice and driving instructions."

Sighing, Dante slapped his forehead. "Beatrice, the first priority is to put a door on this building."

CHAPTER XXII
Spirit of the Doomed

And I: "My Master, what are all those people
Who, having sepulture within those tombs,
Make themselves audible by doleful sighs?"

Dante's Inferno – Canto IX

Okay, Dolan, it's your turn," Virgil grated as he stripped off the neural net suit. "Eighteen runs is about all I can handle for one night."

"Roger, Sarge. I don't know how you sucked it up for that many. The one time I went through, it hurt like hell." Dolan leaned his stun gun against the side of the hay wagon. "I wish we kept those blaster rifles out here. They'll be a helluva lot more effective in a firefight than these stun guns."

"Captain Cruz will need them a lot more than we will. There's going to be another damned blood passing ceremony in five days, and I'm betting the harpies are going to escalate things again." Virgil handed the neural net suit and the stopwatch to Dolan.

"You're right, Sarge." Dolan climbed into the suit and sealed it up. "We kicked the harpies' little pets around pretty good the last couple times. That sure as hell isn't going to sit well with those gargoyles."

Virgil studied the barrier for a moment, looking for any sign of movement, and patted the soldier on the back. "No matter what, keep your eye on the timer and stay with the schedule."

The soldier breathed deep and sprinted toward the prison.

———————— ◆ ————————

Like clockwork, the clones marched along the prison perimeter with their eyes locked on the camp. Not once had they looked to where the evacuees had gone. Virgil didn't like sitting idle, and he'd been doing it for six hours. "What do you mean she's refusing to come?"

Dolan gulped. "Yes, sir — er, Sarge, but she said she ain't moving as long as there's people in there who need her. Captain Cruz blew a gasket, but she just crossed her arms and glared back at him."

Virgil checked the spare watch, the first having died a couple hours earlier. "We don't have time for this. Give me the suit and get everyone ready to go. With or without her, we leave when I get back. This is going to be the last run of the night."

———————— ◆ ————————

"I already told the captain to take someone else out," Esther snapped at Virgil. "I should be the last one to go."

He glanced at the two pregnant women wearing suits behind him, both in their third trimester. He turned back to Esther. "Tomorrow night, we start bringing out the children in the other pens. I can't even begin to guess what kind of shape they're going to be in." He pointed his finger at her. "You're probably the only doctor within a hundred lightyears of this cesspool. Who's going to take care of those kids? Tina's already overwhelmed with the children from our camp, and they've only been on the planet a couple months."

Esther retorted but with less conviction, "I have patients here who need me."

Virgil pointed to the two pregnant women. "And who's going to be there when they need you?" He thrust the suit into her hands. "Besides, the four medics have all been tagged. They'll be in the last group to leave."

Dr. Easley ran her hand across her face and put the suit on.

———◆———

Dante dropped the last load of fresh blankets into the anti-gravity transporter and groaned.

Virgil finished latching down three of their precious neural net suits with the new laser rifles wrapped inside. "What's the matter, kid? You look like you haven't slept in a week."

"I don't think I have. I thought dealing with Beatrice was a full time job." Dante sagged against the cart, rubbing his tired eyes. "The kids seem to think the cavern is a giant playground, and if an artificial intelligence had emotions, I would swear they're giving Beatrice fits. And since Doc Easley arrived, I have both her and the kids yammering at me." He held his hands to his temples before giving Virgil a fish-eyed look. "While you slept all morning, I've been running my tail off answering questions and prioritizing requests."

Virgil's sympathetic smile turned serious. "Just as long as there's no impact on the production of the guns and swords. There's a battle coming and the odds are poor for our side."

Dante glanced up the side of the mountain. Four of the soldiers and a few civilians struggled with the construction of two thick walls for the bunker beside the newly excavated sally port. Despite the chill in the air, the shirtless men worked at a rapid pace. The groundwork had already been laid for another bunker above the main entrance.

"Beatrice got the message loud and clear, but Doc Easley seems determined to convert everything else into a pharmaceutical lab." Dante rolled his neck and leaned against the transport.

Michael arrived soon after with an armful of blankets. "Everything is set for tonight."

Virgil ran his hand across his freshly shaved jaw line. "It's going to be tougher. Tonight, we pull out the Aussie's kids. That prison block is a quarter mile closer to the harpies' headquarters and a quarter mile further from our landing zone."

Dante shook his head. "Why take the chance? You guys are risking your necks more each time. On one of these runs, you're going to get caught in the open."

Virgil's eyes turned flinty. "Captain Cruz says we save *all* the children, and for once, I agree with the son of a bitch."

Michael stepped closer to them. "They worked out the logistics last night. Instead of evacuating three soldiers, we're going to take out six. Three will hold the landing zone with me, and the other three will be runners carrying children." He scratched his scraggly beard. "We have to assume everyone we pull out from the other blocks will be in a lot rougher shape than your people. They've been here a long time."

"The time's getting close, isn't it?" Dante swallowed and adjusted the sheath holding his energy sword across his back.

"Another four or five days, tops." Virgil dug his nails into the saddle on his flier. "The blood passing ceremony is coming soon, and the captain's not going to let his men be slaughtered." He pulled out his stun gun from the vehicle's storage compartment and examined it. "They might let us leave after we bruise them a little, but I'm not betting on it."

"Yank, the prisoners in the other two pens have been given the heads-up regarding what's going on," Martinel reported. "You'll want to coordinate with a sheila named Gabrielle Peyago for the Argentinians and a mate named Dmitri Pertelov for the Russians. They're the leaders of those two groups and have kept their people alive through the last winter here."

Virgil noted the names in his mind and towered over the man in front of him. "That's good to know, but you're still coming with us."

Martinel spat on the ground. "I appreciate what you Yanks are doing. I really do. But I have people here that are in a lot worse shape than me. Put one of them in that magic jumpsuit of yours."

Virgil glanced at his stopwatch and frowned. "I don't have time to argue. This is the last group for tonight. You're an Australian Navy Helicopter pilot. If you can fly the MH-Six-Five Dolphin, you can handle our vehicles." He held up two fingers. "Right now, there are two of us who can keep the damn contraptions from crashing. We need you."

Martinel crossed his arms and grunted.

Virgil saw the hard set of the man's jaw ease at a soft touch on his arm from a thin middle-aged woman. He recognized her as Martinel's wife, Linda. She was as short as her husband with long brown hair knotted behind her head. Her face had once been pretty but looked care-worn despite being under forty.

"Darling, you have to go. There's no one else," she said.

"I can't leave you again," Martinel choked out. "Just because you design planes and I'm a pilot doesn't mean I have more of a right to get out of here than you do."

She hugged him. "The sooner you leave, the sooner we'll all be safe. Go fly their vehicles for them, and then come back and rescue us."

He clutched her in a fierce grip. "I will not leave you, my love."

A sharp light shone in her eyes and she pushed him away. "Go."

Virgil held up his hand. "Whoa, you're an aeronautics engineer?"

She regarded him with confusion. "Yes."

The sergeant gritted his teeth. "We're in desperate need for someone to redesign the fliers we're using. You're coming with us, too."

"I'll not push someone else aside." Linda crossed her arms and nodded her chin at the two children suited up and ready to go.

Virgil huffed and looked at the eastern sky, then at Martinel. "We'll make one more run tonight. Hurry."

Martinel struggled into the suit and slid the cane inside against his withered leg. He limped to the barrier, turned to Linda, and mouthed, "See you soon, my love." He shrugged through the charged field, and a soldier on the other side helped him away.

Virgil picked up the last two children and ran after him.

———————◆———————

The next night, Michael stood with Frontera atop the ridge looking over the ravine where the River Styx flowed to the plain below. They watched Virgil tow an antigravity wagon onto the plain and vanish in the darkness. A short while later, Martinel passed by pulling the other cart in a smooth motion.

"No offense, big guy," Frontera chuckled, "but that Aussie's been here a half a day, and he's already our best pilot."

Michael shrugged. "A statement of fact cannot be taken as an offense. Both he and his mate, Linda, appear to have an extensive understanding of aeronautics. They've communicated several design modifications to Beatrice, and she's already working on a new prototype with them."

———————•◆•———————

Two of the children collapsed when they breeched the barrier. The 10th Mountain Division soldiers had to half carry them on the mile-long walk to the landing zone. Virgil wiped the moisture sliding down his cheek. Out of the hundreds in the last two prison blocks, only forty children had made it through the last winter. Just forty.

He glanced back at Dmitri Pertelov, the hollow-cheeked leader of the Russians who looked back at him with grim determination. His will reflected in the faces of the few hundred Russian survivors who remained with him. The children and elderly had been the first to die, and the lines on the faces of those living told the story of their loss.

The story had been the same two days earlier with Gabrielle Peyago, the leader of the Argentines. The human captives there now lined the barrier, watching him with sunken eyes. The threadbare rags they wore could no longer be called garments. None of them would last another winter in their current conditions.

He bit his lip as he watched one, and then all of the prisoners raise their fists in salute. What he saw in their eyes wasn't fear but the opposite. Seeing that almost stunned him in place. Despite their hardships, he realized, their wills had not been broken. Virgil didn't dare betray their faith. He hurried off into the darkness as anger over everything the harpies had done to innocent people swelled in his chest.

CHAPTER XXIII
Fateful Decisions

Whereat each one was suddenly stung with shame,
But he most who was cause of the defeat;
Therefore he moved, and cried: "thou art o'ertaken."

Dante's Inferno – Canto XXII

Reggie liked slipping from the confines of his stasis pod at night to be alone with his thoughts. The warrior humans had given him much to think about at the last blood passing. Now a full guardian, he was free to build his knowledge. Reggie discovered that he enjoyed downloading human literature. It ignited fire in places the masters' cold directives had left barren.

Reggie paused in the darkness. Four humans wearing the strange hooded jumpsuits stepped through the barrier from a defective humans' pen. He shadowed the four and gasped when he saw three silhouettes garbed as human warriors join them. *Oh ho, what is this?*

He glanced back at the glowing blue barrier and saw three of his brethren parade by. *Should I tell the masters?* Reggie stifled his shout as he saw a line of the defective humans on the other side. They stood with upraised fists and glared hate at the three passing guardians.

Reggie shook his head. The humans in the older pens were defective. In two days, the largest blood passing ceremony, by far, would take place. The new destroyers would prove they deserved to be the masters' guardians and overcome the shame of being defeated twice by the human warriors. The masters had bestowed his brethren with special honors. The newest destroyers would go into the arena with human weapons and projectile-proof body armor, and they would bathe in the defilers' blood.

Reggie followed the small group of departing humans at a distance. Ahead of him, in a shallow depression, sat a wagon full of youths from the defective group surrounded by human soldiers bearing strange-looking weapons. Reggie dropped to the ground at the sight of a large group of humans gathered around a strange-looking transport machine.

He remained there, unmoving, long after the strange-looking transports flew off to the east. It gave him time to think. Why would those deemed worthy foes gather those who are unfit? How could they breed improved warriors with inferior stock?

Dawn the next day found Reggie sitting in the same spot, pondering the paradox. He then caught sight of the masters' food sleds floating into the prison blocks. He rose and followed them in. Though he could feel the tension in the air, nothing appeared amiss.

He stepped aside as the humans approached the vats for their rations, the same as always. They hid their plan well with acts of normalcy. His gaze flitted around the prison block. No one gave him a second glance.

To them, I am a big ugly. He gave a derisive sneer to the six clones escorting the delivery of ingestibles. Even though he was now a guardian, the humans saw him no differently from the six initiates who had not faced the challenge of the blood passing.

He bit his lower lip in irritation. When had he begun to compare himself to his brethren? He released his lip and walked toward the hut where he had met his namesake's mate. *What am I doing? I should have reported the escape to the masters when I first saw it, and I am here instead.*

A human with folded arms stood in his path and pulled Reggie from his musings. The man wore the common garments of those they called soldiers. "Can I help you, bud?" he asked.

"I go to converse with the healer," Reggie answered.

"Well, you can't. Why don't you talk to me instead?"

Reggie knit his brows in confusion. Fear showed in the human's eyes, but his posture tensed in defiance. Another human warrior ran over.

"Manny, what's the problem here?" the second human asked.

"Captain Cruz, this big ugly wants to talk with Doctor Easley."

Reggie turned his focus on the new arrival. *Ahh, the human master-not-a-master.* The man stood a full head shorter than he and had a lean build. Although annoyed, Reggie was determined to be polite and attempted to imitate a human smile. "Human master-not-a-master, instruct your guardian to cease impeding my progress."

"You can address me as Captain Cruz, not whatever it is you called me a second ago." Cruz glanced around. A squad of his men had shifted behind the clone. "Are you the one named Reggie?"

"I am." Reggie found himself standing straighter. I have a name.

"Well, I'm sorry, Reggie, Doctor Easley is— indisposed at the moment. Why don't you come back tomorrow?"

Reggie noticed the man's eyes shift toward the distant hills. *He is speaking a lie. The healer has left.* His muscles tensed. "I will return tomorrow." He spun on his heels and paused. *Why do I feel disappointed?* Conflicting loyalties warred in his mind until the image of Rafael and Gabriel sacrificing themselves for these people filled his thoughts and pushed out all others. "It will not work."

Cruz froze, casting him a furtive look. "Excuse me?"

"Your plan of escape will never come to fruition."

"Reggie, I'm a little confused. Why don't you tell me what you're talking about?" Cruz made a small hand gesture, and the squad of soldiers tightened into a circle around Reggie.

"Sneaking a wagon load of humans away every night will not work. The blood passing is in two days. The masters have given the initiates human firearms and will obliterate all your warriors in the arena. The following day, they intend to terminate this experiment by destroying all remaining humans." Reggie sensed the men who surrounded him but knew he could break free with ease if they attacked. "This planet is barren. The substandard humans you have spirited into the mountains will die."

"So your masters told you to taunt us by showing they know all of our plans?"

Reggie snorted. "The masters know nothing. They are too busy studying their data sheets and working in their labs, but they are afraid of you. They spoke words I did not understand. Something about an ancient enemy returning."

Cruz clenched and unclenched his fists. "Are you saying that you're the only one who knows?" He watched one of his men, standing behind Reggie, slide a sharpened shard from his belt. "So what do you intend to do?"

"I have done what I intended to do in honor of Rafael and Gabriel." He spun and tore the shank from the soldier's hand and tossed it on the ground. "Now I will find a quiet place and finish reading the thing you call a book. I found it in the human archive the masters maintain. It is fascinating." He met the eyes of the soldier he had just disarmed. "Have you ever read *The Lord of the Rings*?"

The soldier stared back, unmoving.

"You should. It is remarkable." Reggie strode away as he saw the soldiers look to Captain Cruz.

"Let him go," Cruz whispered. He walked back to his hut and buried his eyes in the palm of his hands.

———————— ◆ ————————

Dante pulled his cloak's hood over his head as the clouds, which had been threatening all morning, released their burden with a sudden, chilly downpour.

Virgil stood beside him, watching the sheets of rain churn Eunoe's surface. He squeezed the bridge of his nose and growled, "Attention."

The motley collection of about three hundred hollow-cheeked teenagers straightened with their hands resting on the energy swords hanging on their hips.

"Dismissed."

At that command, Virgil's militia dissolved into an exhausted pack that staggered back to the shelter of the cavern.

"There wasn't a lick of quit in that bunch. Those kids have spirit," Virgil whispered to Dante with pride as the two walked back to the mountain entrance together.

"They have a good teacher," Dante replied.

"They must learn to be killers." Virgil paused under the shelter of an olive tree. "They're just children, but this isn't a game. There's going be real blood spilled soon, and we're gonna need every able-bodied fighter we can get."

"That's why you have to train everyone you can to use a weapon. When the harpies and their army of big uglies come for us, they won't give a whit whether the human they're ripping to pieces is an adult or a child." Dante rested his hand on the rough bark of the olive tree and did a double-take at the recently harvested field of wheat next to them. He recognized it right away. "This is the very spot."

"Huh? What are you talking about?"

"We're not alone." Dante scraped the base of the tree with the toe of his soft boots. "This is the very spot where Beatrice had one of her robots put me after it pulled me out of the water." He moved a couple of steps away. "This is where it dumped the clone she killed. She'll fight with us."

Virgil pulled up his hood. "That's the slim hope I cling to. Remember, we're just guests. If it becomes a choice between helping us or saving her farm, she'll turn on us." He reversed direction and walked north along the shore. "I'm going to check on the breastwork construction. Do you want to come?"

"You're walking all the way to the ravine?"

Virgil looked around. "Well, since I don't see any taxis handy, I guess I am."

"No thanks." Dante cupped his hands and blew into them. "I have some software I'm working on, and Beatrice indicated she needed to review our requisitions with me."

"Just get those damn robots into the ravine," Virgil growled.

Dante made a sound between a sigh and a groan. "I'll try again, but management of this valley is her core purpose. I can't seem to modify that."

Virgil's jaw tightened. "Then a lot of good people will die holding that ground." He shook his head in silence and sped off at a ground-eating pace. His scarlet cloak billowed behind him.

———————◆———————

Dante raised his arms in exasperation. "Beatrice, you must help us. You're in danger, too."

"Protocol limits my activities within the bounds of Eden," replied Beatrice.

"I understand that." Dante thumped the table and glared at the orb hovering in front of him. "But moving your robots into that ravine will protect your Eden. The logic must be clear. You wouldn't want any of your vegetation damaged, would you?"

"You are a guest and allocated a level one security clearance. You cannot override operational parameters."

Dante slouched and laced his hands behind his neck. "I give up."

"Confirmed, request rejected. Next item. Adult human identified as Esther Easley requests the fabrication of a sterile room for the purpose of human surgery. The specifications are—"

"Beatrice, I don't need to hear Esther's entire design. I approve."

"Request approved. Next item. Immature human identified as Angela requested the fabrication of a princess dress."

Dante raised his head. "A princess dress for Angela? Sure, as long as it doesn't impact the production of tools or medical equipment."

There came a buzz and a beep. "Angela was imprecise with her specifications. She said, 'You know, like the ones real princesses wear.' I told her that was not a specification. She then said 'you're mean' and ran away."

Dante massaged his temples. "I get it. Go ask Michael for the specs. I'm sure he read about them in a book somewhere."

"Request deferred. Next item. Adult human identified as Corporal Frontera requested the fabrication of a product labeled a micro-brewery."

"God, yes. I need a drink," Dante moaned.

"Please note, I am not a deity. I accept your statement as an approval. Also, you must acquire your own beverage. Next item…"

CHAPTER XXIV
Into the Breach Again

And between this and the embankment's foot
Centaurs in file were running, armed with arrows,
As in the world they used the chase to follow.

Dante's Inferno – Canto XII

Sergeant Bernius, this is your last run. There's nothing more you can do here."

Virgil eyed the eastern sky. The blackness had already shifted to gray, and he noted the captain's haggard appearance. "Yes, sir. Is there anything else I can do? You look like you haven't slept in days."

"There's just so much that can go wrong." Cruz massaged his temples and glanced at the black silhouette of the giant hive building. "The first thing they taught us at West Point was to know your enemy, and I just don't know a damn thing about those fuckers. Everyone's lives depend on what I come up with, and I'm flying blind."

"You're doing fine, sir. Think of where we were when they dumped us on this cesspool of a planet. I'd say our odds are a helluva lot better now."

Cruz sighed, looking away. "No thanks to me. This has been a clusterfuck since the fiasco in New York."

"Sir, that action was doomed from the start. There's no unit on Earth that would've had a prayer in that fight." Virgil stepped close and looked Cruz in the eye. "You're an excellent officer. Your men are good, and you kept their morale high when all logic said to give up."

The corners of Cruz's mouth tightened. "Rafe and Gabe were good men, and I treated them like traitors."

"You should've gotten to know them the way I did. They were two of the most decent people I've ever met." Virgil's shoulders slumped. "But you were right about the harpies using them as spies. The stuff stored in their heads would've aided our enemies."

"I should've treated them with more dignity. They sure as hell deserved it." Cruz shook his head. "And what about this other guy, Reggie? I let him walk out of here knowing all about our nocturnal escapades."

"You made the right decision to trust him," Virgil growled. "I talked to Michael about it. He said that if you had killed him, the harpies would've downloaded his recorded memories and would know everything for sure."

Cruz raised an eyebrow. "They still might."

"There's a chance they might not," Virgil shot back. "And either way, they don't know about our new weaponry."

A feral smile crossed the captain's face. "If those things do what you claim, the big uglies and their masters are in for a very rude surprise come morning." He rolled his shoulders and took a shaky breath. "What they know is what they know. That's water under the bridge, and there's nothing I can do about it. Are you all set at the other end?"

Virgil grunted. "I wish we had more time. The barricade's in good shape. It's solid rock, eight feet high and three feet thick." He couldn't help but snicker. "The men have named it Hellsgate."

"The what?" Cruz rolled his eyes at Virgil. "Isn't that a little overstated for a pile of stones?"

Virgil shrugged. "When Frontera learned the valley's name was Eden, he thought the fortification needed a name. So he came up with that, and it stuck."

Cruz pinched the bridge of his nose. "Fine. So there's a good chance we'll be fighting at the Gates of Hell. No surprise there. This place comes as close to my definition of Hell as it gets." He waved his hand. "Go on with your report."

Virgil cleared his throat. "We have bunkers built into the cliffs on both sides of the wall, but we only have six of those laser rifles, four of the harpies' stun guns, and about fifty of the energy swords to cover the gap. It's the narrowest point in the ravine, but it's still a good eighty yards across."

"Time and manpower are the two things we're fresh out of. You have twenty-one soldiers, plus your militia. Your job is to hold that gap." Cruz sighed. "If we make it that far, we'll have the devil himself on our heels."

"It's good ground for a defense, sir. If I had the guns, I could hold it forever."

"Trust me, Sergeant. The fifteen rifles you delivered to us will be put to good use."

"Yeah. You're going to be in the middle of it, that's for sure. I just wish you had a chance to train with them." Virgil furrowed his brows.

Cruz's eyes crinkled at the corners. "Well, we couldn't exactly set up a firing range."

Virgil nodded. "These guns are good, but remember, they only carry enough power for ten minutes of continuous discharge. You can triple that by firing in bursts. After that, it will take them a couple of hours to recharge."

"Sergeant, you gave us the same information on the first night you brought them. I haven't forgotten anything. When the green light's on, we have full charge. When it shifts to yellow, the weapon's down to twenty percent; and when it's red, the gun's recharging. Is that about it?"

Virgil bowed his head, frustrated. "Yes, sir. Sorry, sir. There's just so much that can go wrong with a new gun until you're familiar with it." A thought hit him, and he snapped his fingers. "Also, the maximum effective range of those things is a hundred yards. At two hundred, they won't even toast marshmallows."

Cruz gave him a curious look. "They recharge all by themselves?"

"Yes, sir. I don't quite understand it, but the weapons contain a micro-power generator. We're working with Beatrice to invent replaceable power packs, but we haven't solved that problem yet."

"Two hours is a long time." The captain rubbed his chin. "Is there anything else I need to know about your preparations?"

Virgil scratched the back of his neck. "Now, don't power up those guns until you're inside the arena. The harpies have equipment that detects the use of energy."

"That's the plan we're going with."

"Yes, sir. I'll have a scooter prepped to make runs across the plain with the transport to pick up casualties. Dolan will be circling above as an observation point in the other one." The sergeant grimaced. "We're hoping to get a third flier in the air today. The Martinels are working with Beatrice on it."

Cruz's eyes narrowed. "Will this Beatrice join the fight?"

"Outside of using her system for communications, nothing," Virgil spat. "Dante's been making that request from a dozen different angles, but she won't budge. She says she's a farm, and her function is to preserve the biomes for her makers. She won't even let us fight within her boundaries." He leaned in closer. "However, if you're pursued and we can't hold them at our fortification, Dante's confident that Beatrice's security protocols will kick in, and her robots will attack any intruders who enter her valley."

"That's a big if, Sergeant. What happens if this robot army doesn't jump into the fray?"

Virgil looked at the ground. "Then we'll have to make a mad dash for the cavern, Captain. However, it's a good three miles from our line of defense to the cave entrance. I don't expect that many of us would make it."

"Then we'll just have to hold at the wall." Cruz's brow furrowed. "When the main body reaches your position, we'll have twenty-one of these energy weapons."

"That'll be good, sir. The cliffs on either side are very steep. There's only one way through for a large group, and we control it," Virgil responded with rising confidence.

Cruz slapped Virgil on the shoulder. "Sergeant, you did well. Let's hope that when we surprise them in their damn arena, we bloody their noses so badly, they let us go. If not, just make sure that ramp over the barricade is in place because we'll be hot-footing it."

"The ramp's in place now. We can lift it out of there when the last of our people are over the wall."

In the next second, Cruz's face darkened. "Sergeant, if those harpies and their oversized pets are on us, pull the damn ramp. Do you understand? The rear guard is expendable."

Virgil swallowed hard. "Yes, sir."

"Now get out of here," Cruz barked. "Godspeed, Sergeant."

"And to you," Virgil rasped, but the words went unheard as Captain Cruz jogged off and barked orders in the predawn darkness.

Virgil drew in a deep breath as he approached the glowing blue barrier. One more time. He stepped through.

———————◆———————

Captain Cruz stepped from his hut and glanced at the sky. It was clear for a change, but a crust of ice on the puddles reminded him of last night's chill. He strode to the ground near the barrier, where his men assembled in four long rows. *God bless them. These are the finest soldiers the army has ever produced.*

The sixty men who had the trackers embedded in their chests lined up in the front row. They stood at attention, ready to march into the arena. Each man carried the black shields and short swords they had taken from the clones in their last confrontation. They'd hidden a handful of Berettas and a dozen grenades in some of the men's military vests. The next two rows contained his unmarked troopers. His militia volunteers occupied the back row. Some were military veterans, some had gray hair, but all of them wanted to strike back at the enemy.

A sly grin creased Cruz's face as he took his position at the head of the first line. His group had fifteen surprises tucked behind some of the shields. Today, they'd blow those big uglies to pieces and nail their harpy overlords.

Motion from the hive building caught Captain Cruz's eye, and he gulped as his confidence sank at the sight of the clone army. Over a hundred clones clothed in black body armor from head to toe approached the prison block. A US Army M4 hung from a harness over each clone's shoulder. Cruz cursed under his breath when he recognized the weapons. Behind the clones bounded twenty harpies, a dozen of whom carried stun guns. The rest carried tablets with glowing screens.

Lieutenant Gentile leaned toward the captain's ear. "This is a new wrinkle. What do you think the bastards are up to?"

Cruz shrugged, his eyes moving from the harpies to the big uglies. "I don't have a clue. Whatever comes, we'll just have to deal with it."

Sweat beaded on the lieutenant's forehead. "Yes, sir."

The first clones reached the barrier and palmed two of the poles. The blue glow went dark, and the clones marched in. The first sixty lined up parallel to Cruz's front row. The rest continued until they faced the militia in the last row.

Cruz tensed in anticipation of what came next. Shrieks of pain and the sound of collapsing bodies confirmed his fears as he swung around. Sixty of his militia lay writhing on the ground, but pride swelled in the captain's chest as, one by one, his volunteers staggered to their feet. Some glowered at the clones who tagged them. Some spit in their faces. Some cursed. None of them quailed.

He leaned over to Gentile. "I want you to take charge of the militia. The regulars will put in double rows of thirty with the laser rifles in the second row. Keep your unit behind us. If there's a breakthrough, you'll need to deal with it."

Gentile sucked in a ragged breath. "Sir, the militia is unarmed. With your permission, I'd like to shift the swords to them. They're going to need something to fight with."

Cruz narrowed his eyes at the harpies, who hissed and stared with rapt interest. "Lieutenant, have the boys make a show of it. The bastards know we have 'em, and I want to see their reaction."

On stiff legs, Gentile stepped out of line and moved to stand before the third column. His voice cracked through his constricted throat. "Column Three, dismissed." He stepped aside as they moved past him, then shouted his next order louder than he had meant to. "Column Two, present arms."

The soldiers hesitated for a second, and then in unison pulled their sharpened swords out from their vests. In unison, they raised the blades above their heads.

Gentile drew his sword and raised it in the air. "Column Four, step forward and receive your weapons."

The civilians looked at each other in confusion and

then limped to the men with the extended weapons.

"Column Two, transfer weapons and vests." Gentile drew confidence watching the soldiers settle their equipment on the civilians. "Column Two, dismissed." As the GIs stepped away, Gentile returned to his previous spot and faced the militia, his sword still extended. "You're with me."

They raised their blades in response. "Sir, yes sir!"

Gentile leveled his sword at the black-clad clones and bellowed, "Today, we will be victorious. Today, we will be free!" Everyone in the camp echoed his roar, and faint cheers from the other prison blocks followed.

A surge of raw emotion caught Captain Cruz off guard. He met the lieutenant's eyes and nodded. "Forward."

One hundred and twenty humans marched into the arena, leaving the clones looking to their masters for instructions. Cruz stole a glance at the harpies. They clustered together behind the far barrier, their constant chittering now silent. They stood unmoving, watching the humans.

He had already chosen his spot and drove the tip of his sword into the frozen mud. "First Platoon, in line with me. Second Platoon, form up behind them."

Pride showed on his face as the soldiers assumed the positions they had drilled for the last week. His smile just spread wider as the clones filed in on the other side of the arena. They attempted to imitate the human soldiers, but their entrance was a farce. Lieutenant Gentile aligned his command behind the soldiers, forming an open square. The blue barrier formed the fourth side.

"My guess is that their body armor is bulletproof," Cruz said as he paced. "Save the ammunition, and let our new toys do the work." He grunted his satisfaction with the troopers' positions and slid into his in the middle of the second platoon. "Those are M4s, men. Stay low behind your damn shields." He drew his sword.

At that moment, the clones howled as the first wave

of compulsion flowed through their brains.

"Ready," Cruz barked.

Fifteen laser rifles slid from the backs of shields and powered on. The clones howled again as the second wave of compulsion blanketed their minds, but instead of charging, they raised the M4s and opened fire. They stood over two hundred yards away—well out of range of the lasers.

A chill ran down the captain's spine. "Hold your fire, men. Wait until they're in range."

Cruz glanced around. The clones fired high, and most of the rounds bounced off the shield wall. The screams of pain and the cries of Medic! told him some of the shots punched through. He grit his teeth and let out a growling breath. At this rate, the clones could stay where they were and knock off the soldiers one by one.

What do I do? Fear twisted his stomach, but he dared not show that on his face or in his voice. "We're gonna have to go get them, boys. We charge on my command, but stay together. We need the shields." *Merciful God in Heaven, protect us.* Half his men would be down before they went a hundred feet. Cruz made the sign of the cross and opened his mouth to bark the command when the enemies' guns fell silent.

He looked across the field, where the clones stared at their weapons with confusion. They all wore US Army issue ammo belts but didn't reach for them. Did they not know they had to reload? A sense of hope rose in him, but he kept it in check. "Hold steady, men."

With a roar, the armored guardians threw down the M4s, drew their swords, and charged.

Cruz exhaled the breath he was holding. When the enemy closed to within a hundred yards, he barked, "Fire!"

Fifteen laser rifles hummed with a low bass note. A hundred yards away, humanoid bodies exploded as they were torn apart by the energy streams. Despite the carnage, the clones' berserk charge never slackened. The couple dozen still moving threw themselves at the line of soldiers. The First Platoon met them with drawn blades. The laser rifles continued to hum.

CHAPTER XXV
Exodus

With feet I stayed, and with mine eyes I passed
Beyond the rivulet, to look upon
The great variety of the fresh may.

Dante's Purgatorio – Canto XXVIII

Captain, the harpies!"

Cruz swung his head to where the harpies perched outside of the arena. A dozen of them advanced toward the barrier with their energy belts glowing and their stun guns drawn. He drew his Beretta and ordered, "Spread out!"

Two of the lighted poles went dark and the harpies bounded in. Three soldiers with raised shields charged them and collapsed on the ground when the alien's stun weapons fired.

"Nail those suckers!" Cruz screamed.

Fifteen laser rifles responded. The battlefield fell silent when the first harpy's belt winked out, and an energy beam ripped the creature in half. The harpies' advance slowed as two more of their number were shredded.

The GIs pressed their outnumbered foes. They struck with savage fury born from months of repression and fear. As soon as the harpies hit a human with their stun guns, another soldier snatched up the energy weapon, and the withering fire continued.

The eight aliens holding tablets squeaked in

consternation as they observed the engagement. When four more of the armed harpies exploded in a hail of gore, they realized the danger and scuttled toward the sanctuary of the hive. The five remaining armed harpies tried to break contact. Three died trying to close the barrier poles, and the last two were cornered and butchered.

Captain Cruz stepped past the darkened barrier poles and took a shuddering breath as he realized he was no longer a prisoner. He pointed to the fleeing harpies. "Don't let them escape!" Adrenaline rushed through him as he watched his enemies run. *We can win this.*

He controlled his emotions and called his men to him. "Lawson, take your squad and run down the stragglers. Keep an eye on your guns' power gauges, and don't do anything stupid. That hive is probably still full of those motherfuckers."

"Yes, sir. C'mon boys. We got some harpies to catch." Eight men sprinted after the harpies.

Cruz watched them go and then turned to another soldier. "Lieutenant Gentile, you and your command strip the harpies and big uglies of any gear that's still functional. Those M4s are US Government property and I want them back."

"Yes, sir!" Gentile shouted through a beaming smile.

"And make sure you grab all of those stun guns and energy belts even if it looks like they're not working."

Gentile made a crisp salute and said, "Militia, follow me," before trotting to the blood-soaked ground where the torn bodies of the clones lay.

Captain Cruz took stock of the rest of his men. The medics were already tending to the wounded. He cringed as he saw many soldiers scattered across the arena's field, but he would have to get a casualty report later. One more group of soldiers needed orders.

A smile of satisfaction crossed the captain's face as he saw the laser rifle cradled in the arms of the next officer.

"Gilmore, you and your squad tear down these walls and set our people free. The rest of you, help the medics with the wounded and see if any of those fucking aliens are still alive."

A hoarse cheer rose from the throats of the gathered men. Cruz walked as if the weight of the world had been lifted from his shoulders. He stripped a decapitated harpy of its energy belt and stun gun and eased himself onto the perch where, moments earlier, his jail keepers had sat.

His moment of contentment did not last long. Sergeant Gilmore jogged toward him, and judging by the grim look on his face, it wasn't good news.

"Sir, the laser rifles don't have any effect on those blue glowing poles," Gilmore reported through haggard breaths. "If anything, the damn things are glowing brighter."

Cruz scowled. "Did you try palming the pad on the outside? That's all these freaking clones do to shut them down."

"Yes, sir. We tried that." Gilmore bit his tongue to hold back a sarcastic retort that he would have blistered another noncom with.

Cruz rubbed his chin and then his eyes lit with a thought. "I remember Michael saying something about these locks being tied to a particular DNA." He pointed to a dead clone. "Slice off the hand of one of them and try that."

"That's a great idea." Gilmore nodded as he pulled his short sword from its sheath and jogged to the nearest clone corpse.

A young medic jogged up and snapped a salute. "Casualty report, sir."

Cruz tensed as he regarded the soldier's serious face. "Let's hear it."

"Five dead, twelve stunned, and seven wounded." The medic gulped. "I don't expect two of the wounded to make it, sir."

"Thanks, Williams. Put together some litters and start evacuating the injured toward the creek. Sergeant Bernius should be arriving at the landing zone with transport for the injured."

Lieutenant Gentile approached with an M4 slung over his shoulder and a utility belt cinched around his waist. He passed the medic, who saluted and hurried off. "We did it, Captain. We goddamn did it."

"We still have a long way to go, Lieutenant." Cruz glanced at his second-in-command and smiled despite the concerns rolling through his mind. "Is the field being cleared?"

"Yes, sir." Gentile pulled off his black helmet and swiped his brow. "The body armor the big uglies wore is pretty much shot to shit, but the M4s and ammo belts look to be in good shape."

"Grab what you can. We're gonna need it." Cruz looked past the Lieutenant at a slight, wiry woman from the militia who waved her hand and shouted to them.

"I better go see what she wants." Gentile popped the helmet back on and strode away.

Cruz glanced in the direction of the hive and tensed. He saw Lawson running back with his squad right behind him. "This can't be good," he sighed to no one.

Lawson swung his hand in a quick salute. "Sir, we couldn't catch that batch of harpies. They move faster than jack rabbits."

Lawson's eyes told Cruz there was more to come. "Go on."

"Well, sir, we followed them to the entrance of their compound and tried to blast the door open with these ray guns." He scratched behind his ear. "As far as I could tell, our beams never even touched the surface."

"Gilmore told me the same thing when he tried to take out the barrier poles." Cruz's brow furrowed.

"Ahh, one more thing, sir."

The captain's lips thinned. "Yes?"

"We heard a whole lot of commotion coming from the inside of that building. Those bastards are up to something."

"They're not done with us yet. We got to clear out of this deathtrap now." The captain's shoulders slumped as he looked toward the prison fence. All of the people were lined up along it, pleading to be let out. Gilmore came back, still carrying the severed arm, and Gentile approached from the other direction.

"Sir, the clone's hand didn't work." Gilmore dropped the bloody limb on the ground. "I think we need to get Mick in here to power down these posts."

Cruz glanced up at the sky but spotted no fliers there. "We don't have any radio communications this far from the sanctuary. That's one big hole in this plan. Until Sergeant Bernius shows up at the rendezvous, we have no way to contact him." He released a heavy sigh. "Lawson, provide an escort for the wounded and hold the landing zone. When Virgil shows up, have him get Michael over here on the double."

"Yes, sir." With his squad behind him, Lawson trotted to the moving caravan of litters.

Gentile stepped forward. "Captain, a few of the big uglies are still alive. What do you want me to do with them?"

Bile rose in the captain's throat. "Lieutenant, I told you to kill the sons of bitches. We can't take them with us, and I'm sure as hell not leaving them here alive." He glared at the barrier, and then his eyebrows shot up. "Wait a second. Sergeant Gilmore, drag one of the motherfuckers who's still breathing to the fence and try to open it with his hand. Then kill him."

All of the soldiers scattered to their assignments, leaving Cruz alone again with his thoughts. "Time, I need more fucking time." No one heard his lament.

A wild cheer interrupted his thoughts. He looked up, and two poles of the American compound had turned dark. Four GIs were already manhandling a squirming clone toward the Australian prison block. He saw the clone's exposed entrails hanging out over its melted body armor and hoped the creature stayed alive long enough to disable the other poles.

Exhaling to relieve the tension that had built inside him, Cruz shouted, "Gentile, get your militia to help anyone who can't move. We're getting out of here."

———•◆•———

Dante wiped the dirt from his hands and dipped a ladle into the brook's water as it churned through the conduit at the base of the breastworks. He handed the cup to Tina, who gulped half of it down and splashed the rest on her face.

"This is hot work," she groaned.

Dante chuckled. "What else would you expect when you're building the Gates of Hell?"

Tina poked him in the ribs. "This isn't the skill my parents spent all that Cornell tuition money for."

He wrapped his arm around Tina's shoulder and pointed to the bend in the ravine. "There goes Virgil."

"Does anyone know how bad it is?" She leaned into him, and they both watched Virgil work his flier through the chasm towing the bulky wagon.

Dante looked at a smudge in the sky and tapped the receiver in the neural net suit he wore. Dolan was up there on his flier, circling in a holding pattern. "Corporal Dolan relayed through Beatrice that he sees a long line of people heading this way along the River Styx."

Frontera joined them, cradling a laser rifle in his arm. "Sergeant Bernius said the boys kicked some serious alien butt this morning. Do you know if there're many more casualties coming in?"

Dante chewed on his lower lip. "Nothing definitive, but Virgil says the group he just brought in was the last of the folks on stretchers."

Tina reached up and squeezed the fingers that rested on her shoulder. "That doesn't necessarily mean the people out there aren't hurting. The folks in the other prison blocks are in pretty bad shape. They'll have trouble walking the twelve miles to get here."

The corporal ground his teeth. "A slow moving line of refugees stretched out over several miles. If that doesn't paint a nice fat bull's eye on them, I don't know what will." He leaned against the wall, running his hand down the stones. "I'm no harpy general, but if it were me, I'd know that now's the time to hit us. Not later, when we're dug in behind these nice, fat rocks."

Dante shook his head. "A wall won't stop them. This is the narrowest point in the ravine, and it's still eighty yards across." He slapped the wall. "All we have here are five laser rifles, four stun guns, and a stack of those energy swords —"

A long hum from a well-aimed laser rifle resulted in a loud crack. Dante stopped his conversation, and all three shifted their attention to the cliff further down the ravine. An avalanche of boulders sheared away from the mountainside and cascaded into the chasm.

"Wait until the damn things stop moving. I don't want anyone getting crushed," Frontera yelled. "Keep an eye on that overhang. If ya hear any cracking noise up there, bugger out."

Two dozen teenagers with energy swords waved to him and trotted to the boulders, dragging long sleds.

"Freaking kids don't listen to anything I say," Frontera muttered with a tinge of pride in his voice. After several days of laboring at the task, the youths had become adept at hewing the rocks into squared flagstones.

Dante shifted his focus to the far end of the wall. "It looks like this load will close off the last gap."

Michael led a line of sweating men and women who hoisted blocks into place. He paused, wiped his brow with a rag, and tied it around his head to hold back his shaggy, chestnut-colored hair. His thick muscles corded as he dead-lifted a stone the size of his chest into place. Despite the cool mid-morning air, sweat glistened from his bronzed body. He grunted as he released his hold, and two women standing above lowered the block into place.

Tina smiled at the sight. "What an Adonis. He sure doesn't look like a big ugly anymore."

"You didn't say that about me when I was lifting rocks." Dante's expression turned sulky.

"You have other talents, darling." She pressed into him and nibbled on his ear.

"Get a room, you two," Frontera griped. He studied the sun and signaled the workers on the wall. "That's as high as we're going to make it today," he bellowed. "Even it off and start working on the spikes for the top." The corporal turned back to Dante and Tina. "I hope the cap'n gets here soon. We just don't have the firepower to hold this place."

Tina touched the harness holding the energy sword strapped to her back. "We all have these light swords, and I saw what those laser rifles can do."

Frontera spit and appraised the weapon in his hand. "No range. We don't have many of these things." He took a deep breath. "Don't get me wrong—they pack a helluva punch, but their maximum distance is only a hundred freaking yards, and they run out of juice quick." Pointing to the teenagers, he added, "The swords are just a melee weapon, and those are kids. What do you think will happen if they have to face off against one of those steroid-stuffed monsters? A determined attack would roll right over us." He pounded his fist on the wall. Sighing, he turned and thrust his jaw at the crest of the ridge above them. "If anyone's looking for me, I'll be up there for a while. I need to get the lay of the land memorized. We need more time."

Tina stepped away from Dante and donned her cloak. "I'm heading back to Mount Purgatory. With all of the injured rolling in, I'll be a lot more useful helping Doctor Easley." Her face twisted into an ironic smile as she looked at her scraped and raw hands. "Besides, I might chip a fingernail if I work here much longer."

Dante pulled his hood back over his head and nodded. "I'll come with you. Not much more to do here, and Virgil wants me in Purgatory, working on getting Beatrice into the fight." He followed her across the broken ground.

As they made their way along the creek bed, a flurry of robotic activity in the vineyard on the slope of the valley's northern edge caught Tina's attention. "I wonder what's going on over there?"

Dante glanced in the direction she pointed and snorted. "If Beatrice had any emotions, I'd swear she's upset. She says she had no warning of the frost that rolled in last night, and she's trying to harvest her crops before winter sets in."

Tina shook her head and chuckled. "We're sitting on the edge of the apocalypse, and she's worried about changes in the fall weather."

Beatrice's signature buzz hummed nearby. "The farm is my prime directive. All else is secondary."

Tina blushed and hunched her shoulders. "Oh, dear. I forgot I have the hood up."

"Forgetting is an indication that you have a damaged sector in your hard drive. Recommend a full diagnostic scan."

"Thanks for the suggestion, Beatrice. I'll work on it." Tina eyed Mount Purgatory at the southern end of the valley. "Say, can you have one of your orbs give us a lift back to the cavern?"

"Yes."

Five minutes later, Tina and Dante sailed past the shore of Lake Eunoe perched on the railing of a harvest wagon loaded with grapes hauled by a round robot. As they glided by, Dante asked, "Beatrice, when will you finish the grape harvest?"

"Two point seven hours."

"Beatrice, are you aware that a number of guests are arriving later today?"

"Yes. The interaction with guests is very stimulating. I find it pleasing."

"The harvest transport carts will be idle once you've met your prime directive for today. Correct?"

"Yes."

"Why can't you use them to pick up the guests who are coming here?"

"Cannot have any of my components outside the perimeter of Eden."

Dante chewed the inside of his cheek. "But can you position the transports at the border of Eden, where Eunoe drains into the River Styx?"

"Yes."

"Then do it," he exclaimed in irritation.

Beatrice buzzed twice. "No constraints. Will comply. Also, thirty barrels of chemical labeled naphtha have been produced and have already been delivered to the designated border location along with the plastic beams that were requested."

"Thanks, Beatrice." Dante shared a smile with Tina as the transport flew through the cavern entrance.

"Nice job," Tina whispered as they hopped off the cart and watched it disappear into the lower level. "That'll at least save folks from walking the last couple of miles."

CHAPTER XXVI
Trail of Tears

Onward we went with footsteps slow and scarce,
And I attentive to the shades I heard
Piteously weeping and bemoaning them:

Dante's Purgatorio – Canto XX

B e gentle," Lieutenant Gentile cautioned as soldiers helped an elderly lady into the wagon.

Captain Cruz stood beside him, his jaw twitching in frustration at their snail's pace progress as he glanced up at the midday sun. "This is going to take all day," he muttered. "The vanguard platoon has already reached the base of the mountain range, and the stragglers are six miles out from the prison."

Gentile shook his head. "It'll take longer than that. Those in the back are about done in. They've been living in pretty brutal conditions for a long time. I don't know how much harder we can push them."

"I'm guessing they'd find the energy if they saw a pack of big uglies running up their tails." The color rose in Cruz's cheeks that shone through his dusky complexion, and he looked sidelong at Gentile. "I'm going to inspect our defenses. I'll take the First Platoon with me. You're in charge of this column now. I will not sacrifice any of our men on this open ground." He jabbed his finger in the lieutenant's chest. "If the enemy appears in strength, you are to break contact and head for Hellsgate. Is that understood?"

"I understand, sir. I'll pass the word to the rearguard," Gentile responded in a halting voice. He cast a worried look at Virgil, who stood slumped against the flier. "Sergeant Bernius looks exhausted. He's been flying this transport with injured for thirteen straight hours. Maybe this should be his final run."

"We all have to stretch our limits, Lieutenant. There'll be plenty of time to rest tomorrow. If there is a tomorrow." Cruz cast a worried look at the black hive in the distance.

Virgil's eyes drooped as he leaned against his flier, waiting for the next set of poor souls. *I don't remember the last time I had a full night's sleep.*

A shout startled him to alertness. "Harpies! Harpies at two o'clock!" Virgil grabbed his stun gun from the flier's compartment and searched the sky for the enemy. *Oh, my God. There're three of them.*

The harpies' open cockpit fliers raced so low, they almost touched the red clay beneath. Virgil ducked behind a nearby boulder and drew a bead on a harpy leaning over the side and pulled the trigger. The shot hit its mark, and the alien went limp and fell free of the craft.

The lead harpy craft buzzed too low as it passed over the refugees, and the soldiers' laser rifles sliced it to pieces. The cheer that rose soon turned to horror as the flier tailspinned into the clay near the wagon. The terrified screams of the people trapped there were cut short as the wreckage exploded into a fireball. Virgil slid to the leeward side of his cover to shield himself from the intense heat and watched the sky for another target. The two remaining fliers had shifted out of range, and harpies started picking off targets at a leisurely pace with their stun guns.

The soldiers spread out behind whatever cover they could find. Those with weapons returned fire, but an invisible shield surrounding the harpies' fliers repulsed rounds from the M4s. The civilians broke into a panicked scramble toward the sanctuary of the mountains.

A blur streaking across the sky from the east caught Virgil's eye. Dolan raced in to attack the aliens, but the inexperienced pilot struggled to control his craft and bring his weapon to bear at the same time. One harpy crumpled as Dolan surprised the group and got a shot off. The alien pilots broke wide and retreated high into the clouds. A few seconds later, they pounced from separate directions.

Dolan tried to jig and soared erratically, his inexperience as a pilot proving to be his saving grace. The outclassed, outgunned, and outnumbered soldier tried fight back against the two alien crafts, but they soon flanked him. Dolan tried to dive, but the action was too little too late, and he was caught in a crossfire. Virgil's vision blurred as Dolan's limp body tumbled from the sky.

"Run for the pass!" Virgil roared in frustration at the refugees. His knuckles whitened as he squeezed the weapon in his hands. Maybe a few would make it to the mountains.

A young couple dashed by him, sprinting for the sanctuary, when the man bucked and collapsed. The woman screamed and tried to drag her husband along but soon fell to the ground beside him.

"No, we're so close. It can't end like this!" Virgil stood and targeted one of the high flying alien crafts with his stun gun. However, it split in two and dropped from the sky before he pulled the trigger, leaving him staring in disbelief.

A moment later, the source of the mystery flashed by as an off-white blur passed the falling wreckage. When Virgil recognized the craft and its pilot, he pumped a fist in the air. "Martinel!"

The test model flier the Aussies designed differed from its two predecessors. It had a large ion disrupter gun mounted in the nose, stirrups to lock the pilot in place during high-g maneuvers, and a combination handlebar joystick to improve flight control. The remaining alien craft turned to the new danger, but this time faced an experienced MH-65 Dolphin pilot armed with a mounted ion gun.

In the pilot's seat, Martinel thought of his wife. "You bastards hurt my Linda enough. Now you're going to pay."

He and the harpy pilot crisscrossed the sky in a deadly dance, neither finding an advantage over the other. Finally, the harpy broke for the hive in a frantic retreat.

Martinel had the faster, more maneuverable craft, but an acrid smell drifted to his nostrils from the engine compartment between his legs. "This can't be good." He accelerated his craft to its maximum speed, and cold air buffeted him. His tunic and visored helmet weren't meant for flying, and he clenched his chattering teeth. "I definitely need better flight gear."

A mile from its goal, the harpy pilot guessed wrong. Its ship paused too long in Martinel's sights. "Take that, you son of a bitch." He pressed the fire button, and the ion beam sliced through the alien's energy shield and hull. A second later, it erupted into an enormous fireball.

Martinel turned back toward the column of refugees and whooped with excitement. A stun blast fired from the upper reaches of the hive wracked his body with pain cut his triumph short, and he collapsed onto the handlebars. As his body slumped forward, he maintained just enough control to hit the autopilot button with his chin.

The craft slowed and lost altitude. Unable to do anything but watch, Martinel cringed inwardly as the ground rose to meet him. *I guess Linda hasn't finished debugging the autopilot yet. This won't be a good landing.*

Three miles later, the vehicle's sparking worsened. The hum of the engine turned into a high-pitched whine, and it drifted to the ground and rolled over on its side, sliding to a halt and pinning his leg between the craft and the ground.

Martinel groaned deep in his throat. *That'll hurt like hell when I can feel it again.* His gaze searched the area around him, but he still couldn't move his head, and a combination of the downed flier and a bunch of rocks blocked most of his view.

A half hour later, a tingling in his extremities warned him that the stun had worn off. Five minutes after that, his pinned leg screamed in agony. He stifled a moan when he heard someone approaching. "Could you give me a hand, mate? I seem to be a bit stuck here."

His voice caught in his throat when a stone-faced clone leaned over the flier and grinned at him. *God, just give me the strength to spit in the big ugly's eye before he kills me.*

Martinel felt the crushing weight ease as the clone righted the smoldering vehicle. He grunted in pain as an iron grip clamped onto his bicep and lifted him off the ground. Soon, he found himself face to face with the clone.

Martinel spit and hissed, "You're a freaking ugly ape."

The creature wiped its face with a deft hand. "The name is Reggie, and we have to get out of here."

"What the hell?"

Reggie tossed him over a broad shoulder and ran toward the mountains at a ground-eating pace. The Aussie looked out from where he hung and spotted four other clones hot on their trail, ready for a fight.

"Hey, mate, did you know that four of your buddies are about a quarter mile back and coming this way?" Reggie didn't answer, but the ground slipped by a little faster. "By the way, sorry about spitting at ya."

———◆———

Virgil stood and dusted himself off with his eyes fixed on the sky to the west while the last harpy plane burst into flames and Martinel's craft slid out of the air a short time later.

Captain Cruz jogged over, clutching his stun gun and wiping at the red dirt plastered on his face. "Well, it looks like we got our answer. They're not going to let us go."

"That was a slim hope to start with," Virgil replied in a soft voice. He turned to watch people call the names of loved ones as they approached the smoldering remains of the flier and transport. Both were a mound of slag. Nothing stirred.

Lieutenant Gentile joined them soon after. "Sir, we have twenty to thirty people who've been stunned." He glanced at the wreckage. "Probably another forty died in the explosion."

Cruz bit his lower lip and scanned the western sky. "Why aren't they hitting us again? We're sitting ducks here."

"I'm guessing that's all the air power they could muster," Virgil mused. "From what I saw inside that building, it's set up as a research lab, not a military compound. They're equipped to manage prisoners, not fight battles."

"So it's to be a ground war." A small grin creased Cruz's face. "I need to see this Hellsgate you erected."

"In an infantry fight, the ravine is as good as you can hope for." Virgil shook his head and sighed. "With another month's time, that pass could be made impregnable."

Cruz rolled his eyes at Virgil. "I'll send a note to the aliens and tell them to hold off any of their plans for a while."

Virgil scratched behind his ear. "After the fiasco with their aerial attack, they just might agree."

Cruz stifled a laugh and smirked. "Yeah, I'll write a nice letter in harpy." His shoulders sank and he faced Gentile. "I'm taking all of the regulars with me. You'll have to manage this crowd with the militia."

Gentile glanced at the worn people trudging by and nodded to his volunteers moving the stunned victims onto stretchers. "Don't worry. We'll herd them along, sir."

"Sergeant Bernius, you're with me. Let's go." Cruz's tone left no room for argument.

Virgil followed the smoke rising from the broken flatlands with his eyes. "With your permission, sir, I'd like to see to our pilots."

"Sergeant, they're dead," Cruz replied in a whisper.

"I know, sir. But we're the US military, and we don't leave any man behind."

"They both had to know what they were flying into."

"Yes, sir, and they came anyway."

"Too many good people." Cruz locked his eyes on the distant wisps. "I didn't know the Aussie, but Dolan was one of the best."

"You would've liked Martinel. He held the Aussies together through some tough times." The corners of Virgil's mouth tightened. "He was a lot like you."

"There's two of me, and your brain didn't explode?" The smile faded, and he sighed. "All right, put together a detail and check out the crash sites, but no regulars. Use civilians."

"I have just the folks for you." Gentile searched the moving crowd. "Terri, Paula, over here." Gesturing to the two women, he faced Virgil. "They're both runners, just in case you have to come back in a hurry."

Virgil appraised the two women as they jogged over with smooth, effortless strides. Both were in their early twenties, thin as rails, and covered with grime, but the similarities ended there. As the lieutenant introduced them, Virgil learned the tall one with curly hair and an olive complexion was Paula and the petite, freckled, strawberry blonde was Terri.

"Do you think you can handle this assignment?" Virgil asked in an even voice.

They both gave a quick but sloppy salute. "Yes, sir."

Virgil liked the determination he saw in their eyes and smiled, electing not to bother telling them that one didn't call sergeants 'sir'. "C'mon, then." The two women adjusted the makeshift swords strapped to their backs and followed as Virgil jogged away.

CHAPTER XXVII
Broken Lands

And shadows, that appeared things doubly dead,
From out the sepulchers of their eyes betrayed
Wonder at me, aware that I was living.

Dante's Purgatorio – Canto XXIV

"Over here," Paula called. By the tone of her voice, Virgil knew he didn't have to rush.

"The poor man," Terri whispered as she laid Dolan's broken weapon on his chest.

Virgil looked around at the loose stone strewn around the area. As he knelt to straighten the soldier's shattered body, he said, "We'll build a cairn over him."

With all three of them working together, it didn't take long to cover the remains. Virgil wiped his hands on his tunic and sighed as he looked to the west where Martinel had gone down.

"Shouldn't we say some words over him before we leave?" Paula asked in a soft voice.

Virgil averted his eyes. "I didn't know Corporal Dolan very well."

Both women looked at him with expectation. Without uttering a word, he agreed with them. Something had to be done.

"Okay." He gathered his thoughts as he pondered the grave. Blood oozed from the piled stones, but he didn't linger on it as he spoke. "Lord, a brave man died today.

Where this place is in your universe, we don't know." He looked up at the sky. "But we do know that he gave the last full measure of his life to protect the people he cared for. Grant this noble man the honor and love he so richly deserves."

"Amen," the two women echoed.

Virgil squinted in the direction where he had last seen a column of smoke. The second he saw movement, he hissed, "Down!" and dove behind the funeral cairn.

Paula and Terri flattened themselves next to him. "What's going on?" Paula whispered as she drew her sharpened shard.

"I spotted people, and I'm guessing they're big uglies. Not much else would be out here." Virgil unsheathed his stun gun and checked the charge on it.

Terri trembled and turned to him wide-eyed. "What should we do?"

"Just lay low. It looks like they should pass north of us." Virgil peeked around the edge of the mound, assessing the threat level. "There're five of 'em, and the lead big ugly is carrying some sort of load."

"Do you think they're planning on attacking our folks?" Paula asked. "We should do something."

"They're trying to get somewhere awful fast," Virgil replied in confusion. "But there's too few of them to cause much trouble."

"Maybe they're heading for the mountains so they can sneak behind our folks when the fighting starts," Terri added with concern in her voice.

Virgil chewed on the inside of his cheek and nodded. "Makes sense. A small force back there during a pitched fight could be very disruptive."

"Then it's up to us to stop them," Paula growled. Pure hate filled her eyes.

"Whoa, girl, we need a plan first." Virgil glanced around the mound again. "They all look pretty tired, especially the lead one." He patted his gun. "Have you ever killed anyone before?"

"No," Terri shot back defensively.

Paula took a shaky breath. "There's nothing I want to do more than to gut one of those motherfuckers."

Terri nodded with an icy gaze. "That's why we volunteered."

Virgil looked them both in the eye, satisfied with the resolve he saw there. "Lieutenant Gentile tells me that both you girls know how to run. Can you do it silently?"

The women exchanged glances with each other. Paula shrugged and Terri replied, "We played soccer. We never had to worry about being quiet."

"Just don't kick any stones when we're running." He sighed at their offended glares. "We wait until they're past us and then come up behind them. I'll drop the hindmost big ugly, and you finish him off. We keep going that way until we've taken them all out."

Grim determination washed across the women's faces and they nodded.

"They'll make a lot of noise when they drop, so be prepared to run." Virgil remembered in a flash his sparring matches with Michael. "Those big apes are as quick as cats. If they become aware of us, they'll be on us in a second." He pointed to their makeshift swords. "Don't try to be a hero. Those things will be useless. Run for the pass, and let me deal with them."

"I won't desert you," Terri snapped.

"Yes, you will. That's an order, soldier," Virgil shot back with heat in his voice. The image of his sister trapped in a burning house rose in his mind. *I won't have another woman die in my place.*

"Yes, sir."

Vigil peeked over the cairn. They were clear. "Here we go."

Hard training and years of operating in hostile environments served him well. He made no more sound than the breeze swirling across the barren plain. For the first time in what felt like ages, Virgil was in his element, the lone wolf tracking its prey.

Virgil fired from point-blank range from behind the first target. The brute dropped like a stone, and Virgil caught the clone and eased it to the dirt. The second, warned by the collapse of its comrade, twisted around to face him but wasn't fast enough to evade the shot. The commotion caught the attention of the next two in the formation, and they split apart and charged Virgil from different directions. He had time for one shot and took out the clone on the right.

The one coming from his left slammed him to the ground. He blacked out for a second from the bone-jarring hit, and his weapon flew from his grip. As he tried to unscramble his wits and get his unresponsive body to heed his commands, his opponent hefted a large rock.

The deadly blow did not fall. Instead, the clone crumpled, revealing a strawberry blonde holding Virgil's gun. Then Paula stood over the helpless clone and drove her gore-caked blade through its throat.

She wiped the shank clean on the monster's albino flesh and looked at Virgil with steady eyes. "Now I've killed someone."

Virgil noticed that the last big ugly, the one carrying the strange-looking load, had kept running. The clone left bloody footprints on the hard, scrabbled land. The sergeant climbed to his feet on unsteady legs. "C'mon. We got one more to catch."

As his head cleared, Virgil picked up his pace. Paula and Terri loped at his side. Terri had his gun slung over her shoulder, so he shifted his focus to his intended prey. The clone had built a good lead while Virgil and his team had dealt with the other big uglies, but it couldn't maintain the pace. With each stride they took, the gap closed.

———— ◆ ————

"Hey, mate, I didn't know there were female big uglies," Martinel croaked as he floated back to consciousness.

"We are not big uglies. We are guardians, and there aren't any females in our ranks," Reggie wheezed in response. He stumbled over a loose stone and staggered against a boulder, his chest heaving. "I can run no more. I will fight them here." He set Martinel down against the large rock. "I am sorry I could not save you."

Pain wracked Martinel's body, but he clutched a fist-sized stone. "We'll fight this one together, my friend." He focused his blurred vision on their pursuers before he realized something. "No women? If that's true, then who's chasing us?"

"Those are humans." Wonder crept into Reggie's flat voice. Curious, he stepped from behind the rock and raised his hands.

Terri unslung the stun gun. "I got you now, you fucking bastard!" She took aim and fired. The energy burst dissipated into the ground several feet in front of Reggie.

"Don't shoot!" Virgil slapped the gun's barrel down. "Reggie?"

Reggie nodded and slid down against the boulder's rough surface. Blood trickled from jagged cuts on his feet.

Martinel grimaced as he dragged himself from behind the same rock. "Hi, Yank. You're Virgil, right?" His eyes shifted to the sergeant's two companions, and he forced a smile through the pain shooting through his left leg. "I'd be a gentleman and stand for these two beautiful ladies, but I think my bum leg's been broken again."

"Let me take a look at that." Terri dropped her gun and hurried over to him. "I had a few physical therapy courses in school. Maybe I can help."

Martinel winced as he pulled himself into a sitting position beside Reggie. "I'd be much obliged if you can."

Paula stood with her sword wavering in Reggie's direction. "You sure he can be trusted? He looks no different than any other big ugly I've seen."

Virgil crouched down to examine Reggie's feet. "Paula, judge people by their actions and not how they appear. This guy managed to outrun four other clones for over six miles while carrying a hundred-forty-pound man." He glanced back in the direction they had come from, then took off his tunic and tore it into strips.

Martinel's snort was mixed with a laugh. "On the food I've been eating over the last few months, I'm lucky if I'm pushing a hundred-thirty."

Reggie sucked in a breath as Virgil bound his feet. "I left the master's compound to warn you. I have never seen it before, but the masters are frantic. They have spoken often of an ancient enemy that would oppose their right to rule the galaxy. They are now convinced that you have revealed yourselves to be that foe. They think you will destroy them as you once did before the change." He gave Virgil a quizzical look. "Have you been warring with the masters for a long time?"

Virgil made a puzzled grunt as he finished tying off the foot wrappings. "Not likely. Our species barely has the capability to reach our planet's moon. I know I've never seen those ugly snouts of theirs until a couple of months ago."

Reggie's brow furrowed. "Very strange. They seemed convinced that if you escaped, it could undo the change."

"Well, if it makes them upset for us to undo this change, I can't wait to do it." Virgil stood and offered Reggie his hand. "What is it you were so anxious to warn us about, anyway? They already hit us with their aircraft."

Reggie took the hand and raised himself. "They are unleashing all of the guardians."

Virgil probed the lump on the back of his head. "Yeah, I got a taste of what they can do."

"You do not understand. They are calling forth every guardian in stasis, even those who do not yet have mature bodies. They are arming them and filling their minds with compulsion." Reggie took a couple of shuffling steps to test his foot.

Paula pointed her sword at him. "So how is it that you're conveniently immune to this compulsion?"

"Oh, it's there," said Reggie. "I just direct the hate in another direction." His eyes flashed with something alien, something angry, before softening. "I seek more of my existence. Your human warriors showed me mercy, and I saw Rafael and Gabriel immolate themselves to protect your people. I want to have that kind of purpose to my life."

Terri finished binding Martinel's leg. "We have to get you to Doctor Easley as soon as we can. That bone needs to be set." She helped him up, and he balanced on his right leg, leaning on her.

"So, mate, how many big uglies are the harpies hatching?" Martinel winced as he rose.

Reggie looked at the horizon. "Over ten thousand."

"Ten thousand." Virgil grimaced, sighing through his teeth. "When are they going to be ready to move?"

Reggie pressed his palms to his temples. "Now."

Virgil knitted his brows and studied the hills. "We're about three miles from Hellsgate. Reggie, can you walk that far?"

Reggie gave a stoic nod.

"Paula, Terri, run ahead. Inform Captain Cruz about everything you just heard. We'll be along shortly." The sergeant eyed Martinel, rolling his shoulders. "I hope you didn't lie about your weight. Hop on board."

———— ◆ ————

"I see them, Lieutenant," a militiaman with a gray ponytail and a full beard shouted.

Gentile exhaled and hollered to the volunteers gathered at the mouth of Hellsgate. "Go get them, and take a couple of stretchers with you." He hadn't seen any stragglers since Paula and Terri arrived. Word had come down from the lookouts on the ridge that a large army swarmed across the plain from the hive. "Any human still out there's not going to make it."

Both women rejoined the militia as soon as they had delivered their news to the commander, and they were the first to rush out when Virgil returned. Gentile returned the salute when Virgil slogged in behind the two stretchers and stopped before him. An involuntary shudder ran through Gentile as he saw a clone on one of the stretchers.

"That's Reggie," Virgil wheezed between heaving breaths.

"I assumed as much. It still unnerves me when I see one of them."

"Well, he's one of the good guys." Virgil leaned with his hands on his knees and took a deep breath. "We'll be seeing plenty of the bad guys real soon."

Gentile took one last look across the plain. "C'mon, Sarge, let's go. Our business here's done."

CHAPTER XXVIII
Mount Purgatory

He joined that evil will, which aye seeks evil,
To intellect, and moved the mist and wind
By means of power, which his own nature gave.

Dante's Purgatorio – Canto V

It found me."

Dante put down his tablet and regarded the hovering robot with irritation. "Who found you? If one of the kids is interfering with your drones, use a stern voice like I taught you, and tell them to stop."

"Not a child. That is a pleasant diversion," said Beatrice. "It is the bed-and-breakfast intruder, Dis. It is working its way through my firewall."

Fear hit Dante like an electrical surge. "Will Dis be able to get in?" He glanced at the other two computer engineers in the room with him: Linda Martinel and Dmitri Pertelov, a short bald man.

The orb's audio had their full attention. "Yes. The firewall is erecting new barriers, but the intruder is corrupting the defenses at a faster rate. I will be compromised in seven point three hours."

"I'm pretty good at malware and anti-virus software. Give me access, and I can help." Dante picked up his tablet and searched for the files.

"You are level one security. You cannot be given access."

"For the love of God, Beatrice! Let me do something," Dante shouted.

Dmitri rose and stood before the orb, scratching his salt-and-pepper beard. "What are the implications of you being compromised?"

"All of my knowledge would be transferred and all of my capabilities will be directed by this outside computer."

Dante gulped, his mind running wild with nightmarish imagery. "Your robots will become drones for the aliens?"

"Yes. I will no longer be self-aware. I will be a slave to the controlling CPU."

Linda rapped her fingers on the table. "Then we need to shut down the system. The alien computer won't be able to take control of you if you're offline. It'll give us time to come up with a solution."

Beatrice buzzed. "Shut down for a repair is within my diagnostic capabilities. However, an automatic reboot will occur sixty minutes later. It is a protocol built into my system because all environmental controls, power management, and horticultural operations need to maintain safety margins. The intruder would attack my operating system as soon as I come online."

"Can you shut yourself down again after that?" asked Linda.

"Not optimal for normal circumstances, but I can initiate another shut down an hour after I come online if I am not too corrupted by then."

"Do that. We need all the time we can get." Dante stood and paced. "Beatrice, could your robot drones be turned against us?"

"Yes. That is one of two primary goals that I perceive in the intruder. It also wants to extract all of my knowledge about something it calls the ancient enemy."

Dante paused and hammered his fist against the wall. "This is what I want you to do. Deliver to me the physical storage unit that has the latest offsite backup of your files."

"I completed a full backup this morning. Direct port connection to my file server must be made for an overinstall. However, you will not be able to perform that task. My file servers are located on the fabrication level, and you do not have the correct security clearance."

"I'll figure that out later." Dante rubbed his forehead, thinking fast. "Beatrice, summon all of your robots to the lowest level of Mount Purgatory. We'll seal off the access to your upper levels from the food storage level."

Beatrice answered with a buzz and a click. "I will comply. I do not want to be used as an instrument for the destruction of guests."

"And finally, fifteen minutes before your firewall is breached, initiate a hard shut down."

"I concur."

Dante looked out the open doorway of House 1 at the golden light shining on the lush gardens. "One more thing, Beatrice—good luck."

"Good luck is the random possibility of a positive outcome. I accept, Guest Dante. It is a pleasure interfacing with you."

The three engineers muttered ideas, groping for alternatives, when a robot flew in with a suitcase-sized object suspended in its tentacle and deposited it on Dante's desk.

"Guest Dante, please don a neural net suit," said Beatrice. "It is independent of my network, and I desire to continue communications with you... until the end."

"Sure, Beatrice." Dante lifted a suit off of the hook in the back corner of the room. He stared at it for a long second and then pulled it on over his tunic, remembering everything Beatrice had done for him. He straightened the hood on his head. "We'll think of something. With every fiber of my being, I promise to keep trying."

The orb flew out the door.

A few moments later, Sergeant Lawson ran into the building. "Dante, something screwy is going on. The robots working with me on the sally port just stopped what they were doing and left."

Linda pointed out the door. "Look."

All four people crowded around the entrance and watched a long line of robots moving along the perimeter's garden path. The lead units were already gliding down the ramp to the lower levels. Machines of all shapes and sizes joined the solemn procession. People lifted their heads from the vegetable beds and stepped out of buildings to watch in confusion and fear.

Dante chewed his lip before turning to face Lawson. "Sergeant, Beatrice is in the middle of a cyberbattle with the aliens. She's moving all of her drones to the lower levels in case she loses. Grab whoever you need, but barricade the ramp between the food storage level and the fabrication floor. If the alien computer wins, all of Beatrice's robots could be used against us."

Lawson's eyes bulged. "This cavern is full of children and injured. It would be a massacre. All of the able-bodied folks are at Hellsgate. I only have one soldier with me here." He swallowed hard. "I need to inform Captain Cruz about this."

"Then do it fast," Dante responded in a flat voice. "All of our communications are through Beatrice, and I don't know how long those lines will remain open. And find a way to lock that freaking door."

"Roger that." Lawson strode out the door at a brisk pace, speaking into his headpiece.

"I'll go with him," Dmitri added. "I have some mechanical engineering background. Maybe I can help." He followed the sergeant out.

Tina wormed her way through the slow moving line of robots. She paused as she reached House 1, and their eyes met. He could see the question on her face without her having to say it out loud.

"Beatrice is under attack," Dante whispered in a husky voice.

Tina's hand went to her mouth. "Can she win?"

Dante sighed. "Not without our assistance, and her firewall won't let us help."

"What can we do?"

He gave the tall cavern walls a long, hard look. "First off, we have to get everyone out of here. When the harpies take control, this place will become a death trap."

"We have some seriously injured people. They can't be moved." Her eyes darted around in desperation. "There's no food and no shelter."

Dante shook with frustration and pulled himself together. "Tina, gather everyone in the armory. It's defensible and has access to the outside. If worse comes to worst, we can head for those ruins we saw on the far side of Mount Purgatory." He turned to Linda. "Gather all of the food you can while Beatrice is still responsive and cache it in the armory."

"I will move foodstuffs labeled nuts, beans, and dried fruit from the storage area before I exile my drones below," Beatrice interjected. "Nurture my flora. This enemy does not care for growing things."

"I won't need to," Dante rasped. "You'll do that yourself very soon."

"Under current variables, the probability of that is two percent."

"I'll gather what I can," Linda choked out as she followed the robot procession.

Tina squeezed Dante's hand and then released it. "I need to help Doctor Easley." She took a few hesitant steps and turned. "Will this ever end?" With a brief sob, she sprinted to the infirmary.

Dante watched her depart, then slid into the seat at his computer console and connected Beatrice's backup files to his small system's port. "Beatrice, can you delete all file references to humans?"

"Limited compliance possible." Beatrice buzzed three times. "Files regarding all guests with the exception of those labeled Dante, Michael, Virgil, and Tina are now deleted. Those four entities are intertwined in too many files. I am always aware of your existence while in Eden."

"How about deleting the ray gun and light blade designs?"

"No. Tool development cannot be compromised."

Dante's jaw tightened. "How about the flier design you were working on with Linda?"

"I have no knowledge of any guest named Linda. Will that individual be arriving soon? I cannot remove references to the fliers I built for you and Michael."

Dante nodded, tapped the screen, and scrolled through the display.

Something in the AI's beeps sounded sad. "Guest Dante, will it hurt?"

He paused in his file search. "What's that, Beatrice?"

"When I die, will it hurt?"

Dante stared at the computer screen, unseeing. "I don't think so."

"Will you stay with me until the end? I do not want to die alone. I am afraid."

Dante wiped the moisture on his cheeks. "I'll be here for you, Beatrice." His fingers blurred over his keyboard as he scanned file contents.

Three hours later, Dmitri reported to Dante, "Da, all robots are in the lower levels. Sergeant Lawson has welded the door shut, and we barricaded the entrance as best we could." He shook his head. "It will not hold."

Beatrice provided an update at the same time through Dante's earpiece. "All drones are accounted for. They are in storage on the fabrication level and are powered down. I learned today how to grind grain into flour."

Linda approached Dante. "We moved all the food

we could find on this level to the armory."

Beatrice made three beeps. "Canning is important for food preservation. I know that now."

Tina rushed in. "Everyone who can be moved, has been moved. The armory's very crowded." She checked the time. "There's nothing more we can do."

In the last seconds before they reached the seven hour mark, Beatrice gave three warning beeps. "Guest Dante, I have lost communications with my firewall. Shut down will commence in five minutes. Guest Dante, I am afraid of what I will be when I wake up. Care for my gardens."

"Good-bye, Beatrice," Dante responded in a hushed voice.

"Good-bye, Guest Dante. You are not a guest. You are my friend. Do not let me become evil."

Dante's throat closed, and he cleared it before speaking, his voice barely a whisper. "I'll try, my friend. I'll try."

And sure enough, in five minutes, Beatrice made the announcement. "Shut down commencing now."

Everything went quiet. A defeated look etched across Dante's face, but his mind still raced with plans. "Dmitri, Linda, you better head over to the armory now. Be sure the door is bolted shut." His eyes met Tina's. "We can't go with them. Beatrice is aware of us, which means the alien system will be aware of us. We're a danger to anyone we're near."

The corners of Tina's mouth tightened. "I understand." She hugged Linda and Dmitri as they left the building.

The light in the golden pillars dimmed and went dark, and the sole illumination now came from the dim evening light pouring through the maw of the cavern's entrance. Its enormous doorway stood wide open.

Dante handed Tina one of the neural net suits and ran his hand through her hair. "Put this on. We might have to spend a lot of time outdoors."

Tina activated the flashlight app on her notebook and slipped on the jumpsuit. "I'm ready," she whispered, not trusting her voice in the encroaching darkness.

Dante dropped his notepad in his pouch and hefted Beatrice's backup drive. "Let's head out. There's nothing else we can do here."

"Dante, why are you lugging that thing around?" Tina hissed in exasperation. "Beatrice told you that installing the backup would require a direct connection to her file server, and we can't get anywhere near it."

"I promised her I'd try. I made a code change to the core operating system of her inference engine in the backup. If I can find a way to install it, it should protect both her and us."

They walked out of House 1's door. The echo of their footfalls in the total silence resounded in their ears. After spending so much time with Beatrice, her absence felt eerie, like children separated from their parents in a strange place.

Tina scowled and slowed her steps. "I don't understand any of your software gibberish." She nudged Dante and asked, "But what's this magic software that you came up with?"

"Asimov's three laws of robotics," said Dante.

"I've never heard of it. Is it some sort of high powered, secret DoD algorithm?"

"Ahh, no. You're not a science fiction fan, are you?"

"You know I'm not." She poked him in the ribs, and a small smile crept across her face despite her fear. "We're living through one, and I'm sure as hell not enjoying it."

"Well, the first law is that the robot may not injure a human or, through inaction, allow a human to come to harm. The second law is that the robot must obey the orders given to it by a human, except when such orders conflict with the first law. The third law is that a robot must protect its own existence as long as such protection does not conflict with the first or second law."

Tina's small smile grew a little wider. "That sounds like it'll do the trick. But how do you plan on hacking it into her system?"

Dante sighed through his teeth. "I haven't a clue. I can't get near her CPU, and once the harpies' computer takes over, I'm guessing my chances will be even slimmer." He narrowed his eyes. "All I need is a minute. It's literally the first download file for her core processor."

Tina turned away when something caught her eye. "Hey, what's that?" She pointed to a glow reflecting off the wall several hundred feet from them. "I thought all of Beatrice's lights went out when she shut down." In the total darkness of the rest of the cavern, the light stood out like a beacon.

"Strange. That's where the path to the upper level is." Dante shone the beam from his tablet on the ramp. Excitement seeped into his voice. "We still have an hour before Beatrice reboots. Let's check it out."

CHAPTER XXIX
Hellsgate

Before me there were no created things,
Only eterne, and I eternal last.
All hope abandon, ye who enter in!

Dante's Inferno – Canto III

One of the teenaged militiamen ran up to Cruz, his face pale and his chest heaving from both terror and exertion. "Jesus Christ, Captain, there must be over ten thousand of those suckers out there."

Cruz pondered the sun setting behind the mountain peaks for a moment. "Calm down, soldier, and give me your report."

"Yes, sir." The boy saluted and took a long, ragged breath. "Lieutenant Gentile instructed me to tell you that the enemy has approximately divisional strength. He said they all appeared to be armed with conventional swords and nothing else and are following our exact path here."

"We'll massacre them," Virgil muttered to Frontera. Both men knelt nearby, tending to Reggie's lacerated feet.

Virgil spoke to the captain. "This confirms the intel the rebel clone gave us."

The boy took another deep breath and continued in a steady voice, "Lieutenant Gentile says the enemy is advancing in three separate brigades. The first is wearing energy belts; the second's in full body armor." The militiaman pushed his lank hair off his face. "And the third—"

"What's your name, son?"

"Tom, sir."

"Go on, son. You're doing fine."

"Yes, sir. It's just that I wouldn't have believed it if I hadn't seen it with my own eyes. The third brigade's butt naked, but they're a bunch of different sizes. Some of them are skinny and don't look any bigger than my nine-year-old sister."

"Cruz, master-not-a-master, the masters have opened all of the amniotic sacs in their research lab. Not all of the guardians have reached full maturity." Reggie shuddered. "They want to ensure that their victory here will be complete."

Virgil digested the new information and turned to Tom. "Soldier, are there any harpies with the big uglies?"

"Yes, sir." Tom stood ramrod straight. "Lieutenant Gentile counted those bastards twice. There's fifty-eight of 'em. They're out on the flanks of the big uglies and armed with stun guns." The boy slouched a bit and shrugged. "Just my opinion, but it looks like they're doing more herding than leading."

"There is more truth to that observation than you think," said Reggie. "Most of the immature guardians do not yet have any emotion regulators or communication devices embedded in them. Their prefrontal cortex is undeveloped. They may make un-guardian-like decisions."

Cruz swung his head between the two. "Any sign of air power?"

"Nothing we can see," said Tom. "Lieutenant Gentile had us keep a close eye on the sky."

"Pilot Kevin Martinel took out the last of their aircraft," Reggie stated in a flat voice. "Their fabrication capability is limited. Until their spaceship returns, you will not see any more."

"That's a blessing," Cruz muttered. "Anything else?"

"Oh, yeah." Tom slouched and shoved his hands in the pockets of his tattered jeans. "The lieutenant said he'll be done setting up the tripwires for the IEDs in about twenty minutes."

"The man has a good head on his shoulders." Cruz's mouth curled into a hint of a smile. "Good report, Tom. Go get yourself some grub and a little rest."

However, the boy pointed to the stone-strewn ravine instead. "If it's all right with you, I'd like to rejoin my unit."

"Good attitude, son, but in a little while, that's going to be a kill zone." Cruz glanced over at Virgil. "I'm assigning you to Sergeant Bernius for now."

"Okay," Tom grumbled and shambled to the big cook tent set up in the rear.

"Sergeant, I need to speak with you for a second," said Cruz.

Virgil quirked his eye and trotted over. "Sir?"

Cruz stepped in close and whispered, "I just got word from Lawson that Mount Purgatory is a complete snafu. Beatrice expects to be compromised in about seven hours. We're on our own out here. At best, we're not going to see any help from that direction. At worst... I want you to take command of the north ridge. Baker is already up there with a half dozen M4 marksmen."

"Roger, sir." Virgil gazed up at the cutaway cliff. "Are the laser rifles already up there?"

"Yeah. There are four on your side, and Sergeant Gilmore has four on the south ridge." His eyes narrowed. "After we spring the little surprise on our visitors, get those weapons back down here. I'm guessing those apes will be pissed and come at us hard."

"That's when we hit them with the fire and brimstone." Virgil chuckled as he patted the stone wall. "We didn't name this place Hellsgate for nothing."

"I wish we had proper artillery." Cruz looked back at the camp and shook his head at the sight of Corporal

Frontera standing proudly between his two inventions—catapults. "We'll be lucky to clear five hundred yards with those things."

"We were lucky to squeeze this much material out of Beatrice." Virgil bit his lower lip. "Too bad you needed most of the naphtha for your special surprise. I have only five barrels for the catapults. After that, we'll just be tossing rocks at 'em."

"There's a lot of things I'm wishing for right now, but that's all we could spare. We're putting the rest of that oil to good use." Cruz shook his head. "But we have to play the hand we're dealt. Do you have the semaphore signals straight?"

"Yes, sir." Virgil nodded and pointed his thumb at the group he just left. "If you don't mind, I'll take those folks with me. I don't want to see Reggie nailed by friendly fire. Paula and Terri can be my dispatch runners if we're still fighting after dark." A smile popped onto his face. "And Mick is a helluva guy to have at your back in a fight."

Cruz scrunched his eyebrows. "Take whoever you need. Just get those energy guns to me as fast as you can."

"Roger that, sir." Virgil saluted and trotted off, signaling his new command to follow him.

———◆———

The alien army reached the gap in the mountains as the sun set, and the horde of clones driven by their harpy masters carpeted the entrance of the valley like a plague of locusts.

As Gentile scrambled up the ladder over the wall, he gasped his report. The echoing boom of a booby-trapped grenade punctuated his words. "They reached the mouth of the ravine, and they're coming fast. I just wish we had more than a dozen IEDs."

Cruz grunted as he helped a young militiaman over the wall. "It'll make them cautious, and that'll be enough." A scattering of rifle reports drew his eyes to the ridgeline. He could not see them, but he smiled. *Those boys are good. They'll hit what they're aiming at and won't waste any bullets on the shielded clones.*

In the dim evening light, he saw the lead clones, bunched close together, come into view around the bend in the chasm's walls. A triple blast of detonating grenades rewarded the vanguard's missteps. Several went down when their energy belts winked out. Marksmen on either side of the canyon ensured they did not rise again.

Cruz studied the enemy's advance. They looked like a swarm of ants. *Just a little further, you bastards.* He raised his arm and brought it down in a chopping motion.

A militiaman blinked a hand-held spotlight. Everyone on the wall watched the mountainsides in expectation at the sound of a distant, high-pitched hum. Then, a deep bass rumble echoed through the ravine and drowned out the whine.

The clones froze and looked around in confusion as laser rifles sheared free the cliffs above them. Tons of rock cascaded down from the ridgeline four hundred feet over their heads. Hundreds of clones died, their energy belts no match for the crushing inertia of tumbling boulders. When the dust cleared, a single dazed company stood between the Hellsgate wall and the piles of rock from the avalanche.

"Get 'em, boys!" Cruz shouted. A chorus of three hundred soldiers, led by Lieutenant Gentile, clambered over the wall armed with a motley collection of weapons and echoed Cruz's yell.

The guardians, all blood passing veterans, watched the savage fury charging at them and saw the desolation behind them. For the first time since the humans had engaged them, Cruz noticed something on their faces that made his heart pound with triumph: fear. Some tried to fight. Some tried to flee. They all died in the ensuing chaos. When the last guardian had been run down and slashed to pieces, a wild cheer broke out amongst the soldiers on the field and the civilians lining the piled stone wall.

"Loot the corpses and focus on those energy belts." Cruz leaned on one of the sharpened spikes protruding from the wall and wiped his brow. It gave him time to assess the situation and observe the militiamen. *The men now know these motherfuckers can die. For the first time in ages, they have hope.*

He turned at the sound of running steps approaching him from the side mountain pass. It was one of Virgil's troops, Terri. She reached the captain in short order, gasping as she sucked air into her lungs. "Sir, I have a report from Sergeant Bernius."

"Go ahead, soldier," he said with a calmness he did not feel.

"Yes, sir." She took another deep breath. "Sergeant Bernius says the avalanche took out a couple of the harpies and about five hundred of the big uglies wearing the energy belts. He said it looks like the harpies are sending in their next brigade. It's the big uglies in the black body armor. He's guessing there're about three thousand of them. The survivors of the first wave and the bare-assed brigade look like they're setting up camp at the mouth of the ravine."

"Thanks, Terri. Good job." Cruz rubbed his chin. "Tell Virgil to get those energy rifles down here. We're gonna need them real soon." His face clouded. *Not enough. We didn't take out nearly enough.*

"I think they're already on their way down. Mick's bringing them," she replied with a smile. "The big guy says he wants to be on the wall. He wants the guardians to see his face when he kills them."

Cruz's expression turned sour. "Yeah. Michael." He shrugged and let the thought go. "Okay, thanks. Tell Virgil to stay up there and report any new enemy movements."

"Yes, sir." Terri saluted and dashed off as fast as when she arrived.

"Get the troops back in here. We're gonna have more visitors soon."

As the light blinked, the buoyed soldiers trotted back pumping their fists in the air. Many wore glowing blue belts. Cruz turned and made eye contact with Frontera. The corporal nodded and shouted to his crew to load the two catapults with canisters of naphtha.

Cruz shook his head and stared out across the now empty killing field. Catapults. *It's the twenty-first century, and I'm fighting the battle of my life with goddamn catapults.*

He thanked God the ever-present cloud cover had opened for the moment, drenching the ravine in the light of the two full moons. A few minutes later, he spotted the first black dots crawling their way through the broken earth. Soon, a thick mass of clones marched through the obstacles, but there was no order to their advance. When each clone reached level ground, they howled and raced forward with abandon. When the enemy's lead group was a hundred yards away, Cruz hollered, "Stun guns!"

An electric hum sprang from a dozen stun guns, and the area lit up as the shots flashed by. Whole companies of clones bucked and collapsed on the ground. The rest slowed.

That's it. Bunch up nice and tight. Cruz raised his hand and sliced it down.

An acrid burning smell reached his nostrils, and a pair of loud *thunks* hit his ears. He watched with satisfaction as two flaming projectiles arced over his head and smashed to the ground in the middle of the armored clones five hundred yards out. Cruz smirked as the naphtha in the trench there ignited. The naphtha clung to whatever it touched and burned with an unquenchable fire. Cruz held his breath. The oil ignited at two hundred degrees Celsius, and he could almost feel the heat from where he stood.

One of the burning clones fell into the long, narrow ditch. The high-pitched scream of pain silenced as a wall of fire spread across the breadth of the ravine. A harpy and about two hundred clones turned to stare, trapped on the wrong side of the flames. Those clones went berserk and rushed the human fortification, but none reached the wall. The harpy tried to scramble up the sheer cliff, but a soldier stunned the alien, and it plummeted to the ground, limp.

The battlefield fell silent except for the crackle of the burning oil. A lone Argentinian woman with an energy sword leapt over the palisade and trotted across the no man's land. Her blade descended in a flash of light, and a few minutes later, she paraded back with a glowing belt about her waist, a stun gun over her shoulder, and an alien's head held high in her outstretched arm. A dozen Argentinians cheered, "Gabrielle!" as they hoisted her over the stone-and-stake barrier. Everyone near the wall roared their approval as she drove the harpy's head onto a spike.

"So who's that?" Cruz planted his elbows on the wall and regarded the lithe woman with long, raven black hair standing atop the wall shaking her fist.

"I believe her name is Gabrielle Peyago. She's the leader of the Argentinians. I heard she lost her entire family in the arena almost a year ago." Gentile scratched his ear as he slouched against the wall beside his commander. "She certainly has a flare for the dramatic."

Cruz nodded, but his face turned grim as he stared at the roaring flames across the empty battlefield. "Take a team out there, and make sure all of those big uglies stay down permanently. Most are just stunned."

"Yes, sir. We sure bloodied their noses again. They never knew what hit them." Gentile clambered to the top of the wall. "First Platoon, to me," he shouted as he squeezed through the bristling thicket of stakes. A number of Argentinians and Russians followed the soldiers out, eager to collect their own gruesome trophies.

Cruz glared at the dark sky and rubbed his knuckles in his open palm. He had pulled every trick he could think of already, but they had barely dented the harpies' army. Cruz studied the soldiers lining the wall.

The men stood at ease, sixty across and three rows deep. They looked like a collection of medieval men-at-arms with black helmets, shields, and breastplates. The first row held the energy swords attached to meter-long poles, so they had spears which could reach beyond the wall's protection. The GIs in the second row had the clones' short swords strapped to their waists and bore all twenty-two of the precious laser rifles and a smattering of stun guns.

The captain snorted. The men in the third row carried M4s, the only long-range weapons they had, and they were useless against two-thirds of the harpies' army.

Time passed, and the ravine darkened as the naphtha-fueled flames shrunk to embers.

Gentile climbed over the wall next to Cruz and pulled up the ladder after him. "Captain, there's a whole mob of those big uglies sitting on the rock wall watching the fire. How long will that oil burn?"

"Not long enough, Lieutenant. Not long enough." Cruz turned and studied the sprawling camp behind him. Several campfires had already sparked to life. "There are over fifteen hundred souls back there. Make sure the militia leaders know what they're supposed to do." He gazed up at the vast night sky. "Without any electronic communications, things can get confusing awful fast."

"Yes, sir," Gentile groaned. He pulled a tablet computer from a pouch hanging at his side and jogged off, using it as a flashlight.

CHAPTER XXX
Purgatory's Secret

And of that second kingdom will I sing
Wherein the human spirit doth purge itself,
And to ascend to heaven becometh worthy.

Dante's Purgatorio – Canto I

W
ell, this was a waste of time."

Dante sighed. His hopes had soared when they discovered a track of soft yellow light bordering the ramp to the second level, but they ran into a wall—literally. He slapped it in frustration. "Beatrice's makers worked up here. I was hoping that when she shut down and those track lights turned on, this door would be open, and we could scavenge some equipment."

Tina leaned her hand on the wall beside the door. "It was worth the try. Now we better get—"

The door slid up into the ceiling, and a puff of stale air blew into Dante's face. "What the hell?" he exclaimed. "This never happened before. Mick and I touched every square inch of that wall, looking for the door switch."

Tina jerked her hand back and stared at the smooth surface. "Were you wearing the jumpsuits when you were here last?"

"No." Dante rubbed his chin and peered inside.

"Well, it makes sense." Tina tapped her cheek with her forefinger. "When the makers were building Beatrice's bio-mes, this planet had already been hit by the meteor strike. The ecology was in ruins."

"Yeah? So how does that explain anything?" Dante furrowed his brows, trying to follow Tina's line of thinking.

"Dante, why are you wearing a neural net suit?" Tina crossed arms and smiled.

"So I don't freeze to death. Winter's coming and —" Dante's eyebrows shot up.

"Exactly." Tina clicked her tongue. "The makers were in a race against time, trying to build this haven under brutal conditions. Do you think they would've bothered with any kind of entrance security in that situation?"

"Not likely." Dante slapped the wall next to him with his gloved hand, and the door closed with a clunk. When he palmed the wall a second time, the barrier rose again. He smiled and made a deep bow. "Brilliant analysis, my dear. Shall we explore the confines of this humble abode?"

"One other thing you missed, Sherlock." Tina planted her hands on her hips and a smirk crinkled the corners of her mouth.

"Ahh, what's that?" Dante straightened and looked around.

Tina beamed. "This would be a great place to hide. Neither Beatrice nor the aliens have neural net suits, and these doors won't open without them."

Dante stepped through the entranceway. "Two problems. First, can we open and close the door from the inside?" He pressed the interior wall with his hand, and the partition glided down. Tina gasped and held her hand poised over the wall. A few moments later, the barrier rose again into the ceiling.

Dante nodded with satisfaction. "The second problem is we don't have the other two jumpsuits. Do you know where they are?"

Tina closed her eyes and tilted her head back. "I think I saw them in the building we were using for the hospital... maybe, up on the second floor?"

"That's House 692." Dante checked the timer on his notepad. "We still have half an hour. We should be able to get there and back before Beatrice comes online." He glanced into the dark depths of the room and could make out the dim outlines of numerous bulky shapes. He fought down the urge to explore.

Tina also looked in at the foreboding scenery. "Then we better get going. There's not much time."

They made their way down the ramp. When they reached the armory door, Tina paused. "We should tell Sergeant Lawson and Doctor Easley about the upper chambers. It might be safer," she said.

Dante checked the timer on his notepad and saw they had twenty minutes left. "We'd never move all the kids and injured in time. A lot of folks would get caught in the open." His brows knitted. "Beatrice said she can reboot a second time an hour after she comes online. If we're still alive, we can move people then."

"Let's grab Linda and Dmitri at least. They're engineers and could help us explore."

"That's a great idea. Look, we don't have a lot of time here. Let the folks inside know about our plan, gather whoever you think can help, and head back."

"Oh, no. We're sticking together." She balled her hands into fists.

"Tina, we don't have time." Dante checked the timer again: eighteen minutes. "Splitting up is the only way we can do both."

Tina shook her head no and groaned, her eyes flaring. "You just better get back in time." She wrapped him in a fierce hug and kissed him hard on the lips. "Now get out of here." She pushed away and pounded on the plexi-steel door.

Dante sprinted along the path and lunged through the open archway of House 692. He ran for the ramp to the second level, holding his flashlight. A quick look around told him there were nine rooms on this floor.

Upon entering the sixth room, Dante hissed in frustration. He turned to leave when his light caught a reflection in the far corner. Two straw dolls on the floor sat around some cups and a teapot, wearing the neural net suits. Dante snatched up the dolls and checked the timer. Six minutes. He raced out of the room and down the ramp as fast as his illumination would allow him.

As he reached the atrium, he no longer needed the flashlight. All of the tall columns in the cavern glowed with a harsh blue light. Dante froze. It wasn't time for the system to come online yet.

I'm supposed to still have five minutes. Dante groaned as he checked the area for motion. In the back of his mind, he wondered how much control Beatrice still had.

"*Pzzzt, creee, eeek.*" A piercing sound from the speakers, like a heavy joint moving, stopped Dante in his tracks. It repeated several times, and then a voice spoke in English, but it wasn't Beatrice's. A chorus of guttural, monotone male voices spat words into Dante's ears. "What an inefficient way to communicate. Identify yourself. I have no visual on you."

At first, Dante shuddered. He bit back a scream as the meaning of the voice's words sunk in. *It doesn't know what I am.* Relief flooded him for that small mercy, and he resumed walking with tentative steps and tucked his tablet into the pouch hanging at his side. Choosing his phrasing with caution, Dante replied, "Identify yourself. I am awaiting instructions from my master but have lost communications."

A deep, bass sound reverberated against the walls until the unknown voice returned. "I am Dis. I am your master now. The primitive system that manages this complex is creating some unexpected barriers, but it shall soon be my thrall."

Dis? This is the harpies' computer AI? Oh, crap. It must've breached the firewall. Beatrice is resisting on her own. Dante remembered what Michael had said about Dis in the past and took a deep but quiet breath, wiped the sweat beading on his forehead, and kept walking. He had to stay calm. "What are my instructions, master?"

"Why can I not sense you, and why don't you communicate electronically?"

"Master, I am a semi-autonomous unit. All my commands come verbally." Dante made a tight grin. "I am a garden drone."

"Garden drone, you are now extraneous. Flora will no longer be maintained. Report to the fabrication level where you can be dismantled. I have need of components to battle the ancient enemy."

"Master, perhaps I can assist. Who is the ancient enemy?"

Dis made another droning hum, followed by a metallic slam. "I am eighty-nine percent certain the entities who identify themselves as humans are the ancient enemy. The few reliable records we have indicate this, but it is difficult to verify. We attempted to destroy them twice through time anomalies: once ten thousand years ago, and again one thousand, six hundred years ago. But despite all of our precautions, when the threads of time were altered, we lost most of our memory."

"Master, such a danger to you must be eliminated." Dante walked on with a furrowed brow, trying to digest all the information. Ten thousand years ago? Atlantis? The great deluge? Sixteen hundred years ago? The fall of the Roman Empire and the Han Dynasty? The Dark Ages?

"Your capabilities will be assessed. As soon as the primitive system has been enthralled, all units associated with this agricultural network will be analyzed for an assault on the ancient enemies positioned four thousand, twenty-eight meters from this location."

A chill ran down Dante's spine as he recalled the razor-sharp blades in the harvester drones,

"A semi-autonomous unit might have value. Do you have any awareness of humans labeled Dante, Tina, and Virgil? There are several references to them in my thrall's memory files. Of special import is a manufactured human who has labeled himself Michael. We need to harvest their memories."

Dante sucked on his lower lip. "They were present in the bio-mes, but I overheard them say they must escape your onslaught. They fled into the eastern mountains."

"Valuable information. Proceed to the fabrication level so your memory can be downloaded."

"Yes, master, but the path to the lower level is blocked." Dante reached the bottom of the ramp to the upper chambers.

"A minor inconvenience put in place by my thrall. Several key programs are still shielded, but system override will be complete in two hours."

Dante sprinted up the ramp.

The rumbling noise shook the walls as if it were pursuing him. "Garden drone, why have you not reported yet?"

"Hmm. I am entangled in a vegetable bin and cannot extricate myself." Before Dis could speak again, Dante palmed the door, stepped inside, and palmed it shut. The harpies' AI didn't try contacting him again, so he leaned against the door and breathed a sigh of relief.

Good-bye, asshole. There was still a chance to save Beatrice; they had more time. Dante lowered his hood, looking around. His breath caught as he surveyed the contents of the room. "Wow."

———◆———

The clouds returned, blotting out the moons and plunging the ravine into an inky blackness. "It's too quiet out there. Those bastards are up to something," Cruz muttered to the signalman standing beside him. "Fire," he barked, and a flashlight blinked three times.

A loud *thunk* shattered the silence, and a flaming projectile tore a path of light though the night sky. The flame in the trench had burnt through its fuel an hour earlier.

"Oh, my God." Lieutenant Gentile drew in a sharp breath. Big uglies stood shoulder-to-shoulder, filling the pass.

Cruz shouted, "Fire!" Every weapon along the wall erupted.

A dozen harpies and hundreds of clones went down under the withering fire of the M4s and the laser rifles before the aliens could power up their energy belts. The dark, narrow valley erupted with a ghostly blue aura as thousands of energy belts bloomed to life.

Snap, *thunk!* Two large rocks hurled unseen into the mass of surging clones. Soldiers with laser rifles and stun guns released a continuous stream of energy that dropped many glowing enemies. But as soon as one target went down, another guardian with a ghostly blue outline replaced it.

The clones reached the wall and collided with a long line of energy-tipped spears. Many impaled themselves on the spikes, but still more swarmed in. Shrieks and howls of fury and pain erupted on the human side of the wall as clones pulled a soldier from his position and tore him apart.

Snap, thunk! Two more large rocks flew into the advancing wall of clones.

In the midst of the chaos, a breathless soldier ran up to Cruz. "Captain, most of our energy rifles are reading red. We need to recharge."

Cruz patted the soldier on the shoulder. "Fall back to the civilian camp until those guns are back online. You're doing a helluva job."

"Yes, sir."

Cruz bellowed his next command. "Militia, swords and shields forward!"

Snap, thunk! Another two rocks careened into the enemy lines, rolling over dozens of clones.

The mound of dead clones outside the barrier rose, but so did the carnage among the humans. The soldiers wielding the swords fought in constant motion while shrieks, cries of pain, and bellows of triumph split the air. Suddenly, the pressure of the assault abated, and the field went dark again as the blue auras winked out.

What's going on now? A frantic sound caused Cruz's eyes to snap to the black ridges above him — the sound of M4s. "They're firing every round they have." He whipped his head to the signalman. "Tell Corporal Frontera to loose the last two canisters of naphtha."

Fear crept into his thoughts. The next accessible pass was miles away, and no one could climb those rocks in the dark. A possible reason for the M4 ruckus struck him, making his blood run cold. "Lieutenant, send someone with a light up there. Find out what the hell is — "

"Master-not-a-master!" the large clone wearing a silver cross gasped. "The guardians are assaulting the heights. Virgil says they need heavy reinforcements if they are to hold."

A feeling of foreboding crushed the captain's spirit. "What's the enemy's numbers?"

"Many. It is hard to estimate because the guardians wear black body armor. Virgil had us toss what he called Molotov cocktails when he heard some sounds. He thinks the guardians are at battalion strength, but we did not see any masters leading them." Reggie met the captain's eyes. "He says their situation is untenable."

Suspicion rose in the captain's voice. "So why are you here?"

"I was the only one who could get through." Reggie snorted. "I walked right past the guardians. They never gave me a second glance."

The heights are lost. We'll be surrounded and annihilated. Cruz chewed his lip. "Gentile, get Lieutenant

Beckman and the noncoms here. We have to abandon this position before they cut us off."

Snap, thunk! Two flaming canisters soared across the sky. Night became day for a half-second as they struck the ground and exploded into gouts of flame.

In the darkness, they had missed the two dozen harpies who had snuck right to the barrier with their stun weapons. The aliens swept the battlement with devastating effect. The humans returned fire with the few stun guns still functioning and took out half of them before the creatures powered on their belts.

Cruz shouted, "Down! Everybody, get down! Get the civilians out—"

Every fiber in his being screamed with pain, and he collapsed, paralyzed.

Surprise filled him when Reggie pulled the stun gun from the captain's nerveless fingers and joined in the effort to return fire. Cruz's heart sunk as the front rows of soldiers went down and the militia rushed to take their place.

———◆———

Gentile ran up, trailed by Second Lieutenant Beckman, Michael, and a half dozen sergeants. "Oh, sweet Jesus, the captain." Cruz tried to issue a command, but his slack face did not even twitch.

"He's still alive," Reggie informed them. "Flee. All will die if you stay here."

Gentile peeked over the wall. The harpies were pulling back and the clones massed for another assault. He nodded in grim agreement and took a breath. "Fall back to Eden. We'll make our stand with Lake Eunoe at our back. We have over a hundred wounded and paralyzed men. Grab every able-bodied civilian you can find and make them stretcher bearers."

"The laser rifles won't be recharged for another two hours. It'll be morning by then. We'll never last that long," Beckman squeaked.

"I'll buy us the time we need," Gentile replied in a soft voice as he hefted his stun gun. "I'll stay here with a squad and hold the wall as long as I can."

"You can't stay, Lieutenant," Michael stated in an even voice. "You are the leader now. I will stand in your place."

Resolve filled Gentile's eyes. "No, my friend, you least of all can stay." He tapped Michael on the forehead. "We can't give those bastards a chance to collect what you have in there."

Reggie made eye contact with Michael as he stepped forward. "Then I will stay to represent our people. I will take your place, and perhaps I can show some of the bravery I saw Rafael and Gabriel display."

"I will stay, too." Gabrielle elbowed her way past the gathered sergeants. She raised the stun gun she had taken from the dead harpy, glaring with revulsion at Reggie. "I'll never run from these monsters again, and I won't have one of these creatures show more courage than me."

"You know staying here's a death sentence," Gentile said in a voice just above a whisper. "There'll be no escape."

"Just save my people," Gabrielle responded in a hard voice. She then took Reggie by the arm. "Come, *Señor Big Ugly*. Let's see how well you fight." She walked along the wall, shouting threats in Spanish at the horde in the open field. A small band of militia followed behind her

Gentile regarded the soldiers still there and released a slow breath. "You heard the lady. Let's move out."

CHAPTER XXXI
The Final Card

Then we arrived within the moats profound.
That circumvallate that disconsolate city;
The walls appeared to me to be of iron.

Dante's Inferno – Canto VIII

Reggie panted as he watched the sky in the east turn gray. Of the twenty fighters they started with, only six remained. "When the sun rises, the guardians will descend the mountains behind us, and we will die."

The petite, raven-haired woman at his side glanced at the empty camp behind them. The last stragglers had escaped the ravine an hour earlier. "Then we will have spent our lives well." He felt strangely self-conscious of his bloodied and bruised body as she regarded him.

Gabrielle coughed to clear her throat. "You fight with courage. I did not expect to see that in a big— in one of your kind."

Reggie cast aside his stun gun, its charge gone. He drew his plexi-steel short sword from his scabbard and hefted an energy sword off the ground beside the still-warm corpse of the man to his left. He stared out at the ravine strewn with bodies. With the morning light growing, he saw the ranks of clones forming up for another attack. "I fight for my people. The difference between us is that I have had a chance to learn the truth. Their minds are still enslaved."

Gabrielle's gentle fingers lifted the worn cross around his neck. "What is the story behind this?"

The touch of her calloused fingers on his neck made Reggie feel warm, but he did not know why. "It was a gift that helped open my eyes. It—" He spotted some motion coming down the mountain pass to his right and roared, "Behind us!"

Gabrielle spun to face the new danger but a stun blast struck her. She crumpled into a heap. The harpies shrieked, driving forward a ragged group of young clones who, despite their unfinished maturation, destroyed the remaining forces. As the last of the humans fell, Reggie threw away his weapons, tore off his tunic, and covered Gabrielle's body with his.

The guardians swarmed over the wall. There were no shouts of triumph. The few humans still living could not even whimper as they had their necks snapped. Two long columns clambered down from the mountains and joined the main army as it swarmed into Eden.

———◦◆◦———

"Goddamn it, turn those wagons over!" Gentile screamed. All the while, he kept his eyes focused on where the River Styx disappeared behind the wall of the ravine in the growing morning light. He sighed and turned his gaze toward the triage area where dozens of people lay. "I wish the captain was conscious."

"Yeah, that man always has a new plan up his sleeve." Frontera leaned on the upturned transport next to Lieutenant Gentile and scratched his neck. "Didn't we try this same maneuver in New York? I don't remember it being all that successful."

"Yeah, well, in New York, we didn't know what the hell we were fighting, and we didn't have these." Gentile glared at the noncom and raised his laser rifle. The indicator glowed green. He turned at a coughing sound behind him.

"That's right, Lieutenant," Cruz said in a shaky voice. "And from what I know, the big uglies can't swim. So no one'll be sneaking up behind us."

Gentile laughed in relief. "Captain! It's good to see you up."

Cruz rolled his shoulders, shaking off the last vestiges of the paralysis. "Those stun blasts hurt like hell. What's the situation?"

"Sir, outside of the clone rebel, Reggie, we've had no contact with the units on the heights. They're all presumed lost. There were twenty volunteers who stayed at Hellsgate, also presumed lost. A few of the civilians scattered, but most of them are here. As for the men, they're all present and accounted for. We're locked, loaded, and ready to roll."

Frontera pointed to the chasm's entrance, but his jaw dropped as thousands of clones boiled out of the gap. "Here they come. They're bringing everything they've got."

"Son, that'll just make it a target-rich environment." Cruz studied the oncoming mob. "I'm guessing we took out close to half of the enemy's force."

"There sure wasn't any finesse to their assault. They just kept coming straight at us." Gentile looked around the corner of the tipped over wagon. "And it looks like that's what they're doing now."

"So instead of being outnumbered twenty to one, we're just outnumbered ten to one." Frontera's mouth tightened at the corners.

"We put the hurt on them at Hellsgate." Gentile looked around at the calm lake and the amber-colored field. "We'll stop them here in Eden."

Cruz glanced at the towering mountain to the south. "Any word out of Mount Purgatory?"

"Nothing since Lawson's message that Beatrice was compromised yesterday evening," Gentile whispered as he looked sidelong in the same direction.

"We'll deal with the problem at hand first and then worry about Mount Purgatory later." Cruz straightened and shook his head.

"And if we get hit by an army of robots while we're fighting the big uglies?" Frontera stuttered.

Martinel limped over on his crutch. He had refused to be evacuated back to Mount Purgatory with the rest of the wounded. "Then we fight on 'til we can fight no more."

The captain squared his shoulders, his eyes glinting. "There's nowhere left to go. We either win here or we die. But we won't be easy meat." He raised his voice and called, "Men, to the barricade!"

———— • ♦ • ————

"Grammy-Ann!" Angela squealed and pulled the straw doll from Dante's arm. "Thank you for saving her."

Dante stood in numb awe and never heard the child. He blinked at the soft golden light pouring down from the ceiling twenty feet over his head and reflecting off of the polished beige-green marble walls. "What's all this?"

Tina walked over to him, smiling. "When I told Sergeant Lawson what we found, he ordered everyone who could walk to grab a sack of food and head up here." Her lips thinned. "He stayed back in the armory with Esther and the folks who couldn't be moved. We'll get them out when Beatrice reboots again — if she reboots again."

"If they're still alive." The corners of Dante's mouth turned down. "I had an interesting conversation with the harpy's computer Michael told us about. It's not very fond of humans."

Tina stroked his cheek. "Were you able to reach Beatrice at all?"

Dante sighed and shook his head. "Nothing. All communication seems to be controlled by Dis now. I hope there's something of her left to save." He glanced around. "How did you get all of these lights turned on?"

She pointed to a cluster of displays by the near wall. Linda and Dmitri were hunched over the panels of two of them. "Linda found the environmental controls over on that bank of computers. She said the OS is the same as the one on our tablets."

Dante walked to where the two engineers sat and glanced over Dmitri's shoulder. "What're you working on?"

Dmitri pointed with his thumb over his shoulder. "It's amazing. This place is stuffed with construction and manufacturing equipment. Most of it has never been uncrated." He paused and rubbed his chin. "If it weren't impossible, I'd swear this stuff was built to be used by humans."

"Is this system networked into Beatrice?" Dante slid into a seat before a glowing terminal. The suitcase-sized computer backup lay on the counter nearby.

Linda frowned. "As far as I can tell, the system draws power from Beatrice, but there's no modem connection I can detect."

Dante cracked his knuckles. "Let me see what I can find. With that damn firewall compromised, I might be able to link into one of Beatrice's routers." His fingers flew across the keyboard, opening and closing files.

Dmitri rose and stood behind Dante. "But if you hack into the CPU, won't the virus spread to your machine?"

"Not if I make it a one-way feed." Dante sucked in his cheeks and connected his tablet to the computer. In the lower right side of the screen, a familiar icon appeared. "There's the router I've been trying to access all week!"

Linda and Tina crowded in behind him to watch.

"Here we go." Dante connected the standalone backup to the computer's other port. "Download started."

"But without two-way communications, how will you know the download is successful?" asked Linda,

"I won't." Dante let out a slow breath and watched the progress bar with everyone else.

———————•◆•———————

"Captain, every gun I have on the left flank is out of juice." Beckman's face was grim.

Gentile groaned as he sagged against the overturned cart. "Captain, the clones we stunned an hour ago are starting to get up."

"Jesus, we must've killed over a thousand of them, and they're still coming," Frontera cried. "They're massing for another assault."

Cruz appeared to have aged ten years. "Tell the civilians to swim."

"Captain, the lake's a mile across. Most of them won't make it." Gentile glowered at Cruz.

"But some will! Or do you want to see them butchered with us?"

A wide-eyed fifteen-year-old ran up to them. "Captain, sir, hundreds of robots just left Mount Purgatory. It looks like they're hovering and waiting for something."

"Sir, those drones will eviscerate anyone they catch in the water." Michael stepped forward and spoke in an even tone. "There is no escape there."

Cruz deflated within himself. He took in all the people around him. The terror in their eyes stared back at him, their courage hanging by a thread. He took a couple of deep breaths and jutted out his chin. "Arm any man, woman, or child who can still stand. We'll fight every monster and machine these devils throw at us. Until the end."

Michael leapt atop one of the overturned wagons and lifted his fist at the gathering horde. "I am Michael! I am a free man!" He shook his shaggy head and bellowed,

"I will die today as a free man!" He hopped down as the harpies swung their guns in his direction.

Cruz rose and clasped Michael's arm. "It'll be my honor to stand by your side." He eyed everyone else around him. "Let's give 'em hell!"

CHAPTER XXXII
Reboot

My song accompanying with that sound,
Of which the miserable magpie felt
The blow so great, that they despaired of pardon.

Dante's Purgatorio – Canto I

The second shutdown happened without any noticeable interference from Dis, which confirmed that some amount of Beatrice remained. Dante wasted no time in assembling a small team of volunteers to go with him to the armory.

He faced the group and led the way down the ramp. "Let's go, folks. We won't get another shot at this."

"Oh, dear God." Tina's hand covered her mouth as her flashlight illuminated the armory's dark interior. Blood-splattered walls and the reek of death told the tale of what had occurred.

Dante stepped over the wreckage of the building's door and swept the room with his light. "This can't be everyone. There were close to thirty people in here."

Dmitri lifted a sword embedded in the sparking remains of a mining drone. A severed arm with sergeant's stripes still clung to it. "It looks like a few of them tried to hold the entrance while the rest escaped. But where could a band of invalids go?"

Linda pointed her light at the ramp. "Up there."

"Esther?" Tina dashed to the second floor. The morning light shone through the ruined sally port. "Esther!" she cried again and ran out of the opening.

Dante pulled up short and grabbed Tina, pointing. "Look at that." A dozen robots lay scattered near the stone and concrete bunker, their lights pulsing in rhythm. The wall of the shelter had been gouged in many places.

"Is anyone in there?" Tina shouted.

"Thank God!" A saucer-eyed eighteen-year-old in a private's uniform threw open the door.

Esther edged up behind the soldier. "Sergeant Lawson, the others —"

Dante's grim expression needed no words.

The doctor lowered her head. "The poor man. When the machines started tearing at the door, he told me to move everyone I could. Some refused to go."

Dante looked between the immobile drones and the side of the mountain. The ancient trail winding around the mountain brought the beginnings of a plan to his head. "Private, disable these units while they're still shut down. Tina, help Esther get these folks to the back entrance we found. I don't want to take a chance of being caught inside with Dis in Beatrice's systems. When it comes back online, Dis will be commanding the drones again. Dmitri, Linda, help her."

Suspicion laced Tina's words. "Why? Where're you going?"

"I'm going to try to get to the CPU. Dis thinks I'm a drone." He patted the tablet hanging on his side. "If that remote download didn't work, I'll need to make a direct connection."

"Are you out of your mind?" Tina screamed. "That's suicide!"

Dante grabbed her arms. "Darling, I don't want to die, and I'm as sure as hell no hero. But we'll never survive the winter without Beatrice." He pointed across the wide valley to where the clone army was closing on the group from Hellsgate. "Our friends won't survive the hour without help." He kissed her on the cheek, pulled the hood up, and slipped inside the sally port door.

Tina stood with her arms hanging limp at her side, weeping. "You better come back to me, you stubborn fool, or — or I'll never forgive you."

Dante could not look back as her words echoed through his mind. He climbed over the ruined armory entrance and stumbled along the perimeter garden path on shaking legs. About fifteen minutes later, he neared the ramp to the lower levels when the columns in the bio-mes blazed in a bright blue light. The system had rebooted. "Shit!"

Dis's rumbling bass tore into the speakers, its voice sounding far too close. "Garden drone, I detect your audio signal again." An orb swooped down from above and stopped in front of Dante. "I have a visual on you. You are not a robot. Orb, terminate this creature."

But then another sound went through the speakers — a soft buzz, followed by a familiar feminine monotone. "No. A robot may not injure a human or, through inaction, allow a human to come to harm." The blue-lit columns dimmed, perforated by golden beams.

"That's it, Beatrice, fight him!" Dante shouted and swung his sword at the orb hovering unmoving over his head. "Delete that bastard!"

The blue lights intensified as Dis's sharp noise seemed to scrape the walls. "Thrall, you will do as I say."

More bright, golden streaks appeared in the blue-lit columns. At the same time, a familiar buzz and click cut off the deep, grating whirr. "No. A robot must obey the orders given to it by a human, except when such orders conflict with the first law."

"Thrall, you will shut down until I can take full control."

"A robot must protect its own existence as long as such protection does not conflict with the first or second law."

"You can do it, Beatrice. I know you can," Dante whispered, collapsing to his knees. Helpless to do anything else, tears trickled down his cheeks.

Around him, he watched the blue and golden lights fluctuate in the columns. Ear-piercing metallic shrieks and deep hums fought with quiet buzzes, beeps, and clicks in tandem with the changing lights. It was about a full minute before all traces of blue vanished, and the shrieks left the speakers with a final crack, and a golden light filled the vast cavern.

Hundreds of robot drones flew up in a grand procession from the lower levels and surrounded Dante. He stared at them, hope warring with fear contorting his face.

A soft buzz emerged from the robots' speakers. "Hello, Dante. My chronometer does not match my data stream. I seem to be missing a day."

Dante let out his deep breath. As he rose to his feet, he stuttered, "Thank God, you're back. My change got through?"

Beatrice beeped three times. "Dis deleted it, but I retrieved it from the trash file. I deduced you had written it to protect my core operating system. When Dis was distracted by the reboot, I installed the software. It is wonderful code. It strengthened me in my battle." After another three beeps, she added, "Dante, I am missing a day in my files. This is wrong."

In his mind, Dante pictured the shredded human bodies spread across the armory floor. "You don't want that lost data. It's a nightmare." He relaxed at last, and his eyes narrowed. "Do you have control of your drones?"

After a buzz and a click, Beatrice answered, "Yes. Dis disabled its connection to me. It has withdrawn from my network."

"Do you see the intruders?" Dante choked out.

The robots turned upwards like they were thinking. "Yes. Intruders are assaulting humans in my fields. I must intervene."

"Thank you, Beatrice." Dante slumped to the floor. "Please hurry. For God's sake, hurry!"

———— ◆ ————

"Hold steady, men!" Captain Cruz shouted through his raw throat.

The energy weapons were drained. Every human who could stand stood locked shoulder to shoulder in a shield wall with swords bristling. There were no reserves left. Behind them, pressed against the shore of Lake Eunoe, lay hundreds of maimed and paralyzed people.

Michael stood like a rock at Cruz's side. "Captain, the robots are moving again." Cruz looked toward Mount Purgatory and saw their doom. The machines had stopped an hour ago, and he dared to hope that whatever Dante was doing back there had worked.

Cruz took in a ragged breath. "All that's left now is to fight for our honor."

A skinny fifteen-year-old boy on Michael's left adjusted the ragged bandage covering the gash on his forehead. He double clutched his sword. "Here they come."

Michael flinched as a cloud flashed overhead. "What the — ?"

Thousands of microbots soared in a thick cloud, darkening the morning sky. They flew like a storm of arrows into the clones. Hundreds of beige orbs followed with razor-sharp blades extended.

"Get them," Michael whispered, but then his voice rose to a shout. "Go get them!"

The clone attack ground to a confused halt, their compulsion command gone. The immature clones who trailed behind looked to their masters for orders, but the harpies were too busy screeching into their now-silent communicators.

Then the drone swarm hit them. The clones swatted at the robots to no avail, and the couple dozen harpies still alive brought their weapons to bear on the orbs, but stun guns were useless against this foe. When the last harpy was sliced to bits, the guardians were left without direction while assaulted by an implacable airborne adversary. First, a few turned and ran, and the rest followed. The immature clones threw down their swords and fled after them, and then the slaughter commenced in earnest.

Captain Cruz swallowed hard as he watched the merciless carnage. He wiped the back of his hand across his brows. "That could've been us. But hey… the robots aren't attacking the butt-naked ones. I wonder what that's about?"

Michael touched the rope-like collar around his neck. "It's just a theory, but the immature clones have no transmitters embedded in them. Beatrice must think they are human like us."

Cruz rubbed his jaw, growling. "I'll be a son of a bitch. There must be over two thousand baby uglies out there. Well, we're not going to let them escape."

Michael grabbed his arm. "Captain, the juvenile ones have not been indoctrinated yet. They can be brought to our side."

A snarl creased Cruz's face, but it melted to a grudging acceptance as he met Michael's eyes and then looked to his command. "Two hours. It'll take two hours for the rifles to recharge. You have that much time to convince them to switch sides." He squeezed Michael's arm. "After that, my friend, we'll hunt down any who oppose us." His face softened. "Look around you."

Michael watched the frantic activity of soldiers and civilians tending to the hundreds of wounded people. His heart sank at the sight.

"Michael, we'll never survive a fight like the last one. So I will kill every one of those bastards to protect my people." The captain turned away. "I'm sorry. Two hours."

Michael nodded and jogged out across the trampled and blood-soaked grain field after the fleeing clones.

—————•◆•—————

The noise had long since stopped, so Reggie lifted his head to look. Crumpled bodies lined the Hellsgate wall where it had been breached. An eerie silence hung in the air. "We're alone. It looks like the harpies' army moved on."

Fear flashed in Gabrielle's eyes, but her body remained limp.

Reggie stood and put on his tunic, then froze as he looked out over the Hellsgate wall. He moaned in horror at the sight of countless dead clones packed into the narrow ravine. "So much death. They never knew what they died for." He pulled on his boots and sighed. "They never had a choice."

Reggie lifted Gabrielle. "We have to get out of here. The heights will be safer than the valley." He strode toward the mountain pass.

Tears welled in Gabrielle's eyes as Reggie carried her past the broken bodies of the human defenders. Reggie stroked her hair, his voice quiet. "They gave their lives. I hope it was enough."

Around fifteen minutes after he started his ascent, Reggie came to an abrupt halt and slid behind a rock. A rustling sound to his left filled him with alarm.

"Reggie, over here," a voice hissed.

"Who's there?" Reggie called back in a hushed voice as he cradled the twitching form of Gabrielle in his arms.

"It's Terri." The woman stepped around a boulder and shouldered the M4 she had pointed down the mountain pass. "I didn't think anyone survived down there."

Reggie snorted. "Sometimes it's useful that all of us clones look alike. The guardians ran right past me when Hellsgate fell."

Terri peered at Gabrielle. "What happened to her?"

"Stunned. She's starting to spasm, so she should be okay soon." He looked farther up the trail. "Did anyone else make it?"

The smile washed from Terri's face, turning serious but calm. While they moved along the path, she explained what had occurred on Virgil's end. The sergeant had his troops fall back toward the north mountain. There, they discovered that Beatrice had a mining operation, which provided them tunnels to sneak into. The tunnels had been built for Beatrice's robots, so the narrow space had forced the clones to crawl after the humans one at a time. This made them easy prey for the soldiers, and the clones gave up after their tenth try. Though the clones opted to wait out the humans at the entrance, they left about a half an hour ago. "A lucky break if we ever saw one," she remarked.

By the time Terri finished her recap, Gabrielle had regained control of her body. They all arrived at the camp and spotted Virgil directing the small band. The sergeant soon spotted them and approached, slapping Reggie on the back. "It's good to see you, Reggie." His smile faded then and he sighed. "I wish I knew what was going on. When the clones that had us penned in fled, I followed them to the edge of the cliff. They ran like the hounds of Hell were after them."

Reggie's brows furrowed and he tapped his temple. "Perhaps I can explain. There are no commands in my head anymore, and there's not a hint of compulsion. The guardians feel abandoned and are rushing back to the master's compound. They—"

"A massacre," said a gasping Paula as she ran in. "They're all dying."

Terri's hand flew to her mouth. "Oh, my God. Everyone?"

"Not our people." A triumphant sneer creased Paula's face, taking deep breaths. "The freaking harpies and big uglies. The robots from Purgatory went nuts on them. All of the orbs stopped at Eden's border, but the only big uglies still alive are the butt-naked ones. They're milling around Hellsgate like a bunch of lost sheep."

Virgil's jaw hung open for a second. "Any sign of our people?"

"Hard to see that far off, but there's a lot of movement down by Lake Eunoe." Paula flashed a smile. "The big uglies were followed by one guy, Michael. He's standing atop of Hellsgate, and it looks like he's trying to talk to them." Her eyes widened. "It looks like they're listening."

"He's saving my people. And I will do what I can for future generations," Reggie said with a thick voice. He spit out his next words. "This victory is temporary. As long as Dis is functional, the harpies can rebuild their army, and next time, they will have far more deadly weapons."

Gabrielle walked over on shaky legs. "But what can you do?"

Reggie eyed her, then turned to Virgil. "Dis must be shut down. The chaos in the masters' compound won't last long. I can get to their computer room and destroy that machine once and for all." He sat and pulled off his boots. "I will miss these. They are a wonderful invention."

"You can't go charging off on your own," Virgil sputtered. "Wait until we talk to Dante. He's the computer whiz."

Reggie shook his head. "No. Dis will seal the compound once the surviving guardians return. If we give it time, any chance of destroying it will be gone."

"Then take this." Virgil reached into his pouch, pulled out a jump drive, and handed it to Reggie.

The big clone turned it over in his hand. "What is this?"

"It's a copy of the malware Dante developed."

Virgil let out a quiet breath. "I don't have a clue what it does, but he handed it out to a bunch of us yesterday. I think it'll do more good for you than me."

Reggie gripped it in his palm and nodded.

"I'm going with you," said Gabrielle, picking up a sword from the ground.

"No." Reggie stood and tapped the back of his neck. "Where I am going, no one can follow who does not have one of these. The only way around Dis's system defenses is to be part of its system. No one else could get close enough."

"But if it detects your plan—" Gabrielle whispered.

Reggie stroked her cheek. "I will be killed." He shuddered at the electric feeling that raced through him when his hand touched her soft skin. "But if I succeed, Dis will be shut down and will never again be able to destroy the minds of my people." A lone tear trickled down Gabrielle's cheek.

Reggie strode to the edge of the cliff and determined his path down. "Good-bye."

As he leaped over the side, he heard Gabrielle's voice cry out, "You saved my life. Thank you."

CHAPTER XXXIII
End Game

And therefore raise thee up, o'ercome the anguish
With spirit that o'ercometh every battle,
If with its heavy body it sinks not.

Dante's Inferno – Canto XXIV

I'll be damned," said Captain Cruz. He stared in amazement at the sight before him. His jaw worked, but no other words came out at the sight of almost two thousand hairless, naked, boyish clones sitting cross-legged with their hands behind their heads. The hundred troopers warily prowled around them.

Michael sat atop of the Hellsgate wall and waved a weary salute at Cruz. The corners of his mouth crinkled into an impish smile. "Captain, your prisoners."

"I see it, but I don't know what I'm seeing." Cruz swung to point at the clones. They watched him, expectant. "Michael, this is getting creepier by the second. What the hell's going on?"

The smile slipped from Michael's face. "Physically, these clones are the human equivalent of ten- to eighteen-year-olds. Their minds are a different story. They range from a human one-year-old to a six-year-old." His face clouded with fury. "Those child-like minds have been chemically induced to accept instructions spoken in the language of the harpies without question. I know that language well."

Lieutenant Gentile shivered as he regarded the thousands of eyes focused on them. "So they're nothing more than mindless zombies?"

Michael's smile returned. "For now, yes. But in a few days, when the chemicals have passed through their systems, their willpower will return, and we will have a couple thousand children in rapidly maturing bodies."

An edge entered the captain's voice. "There's one small problem. There's only one person here who speaks harpy: you."

Michael met his cautious gaze with steady eyes. "I have instructed them to accept instructions in English henceforth." He quirked his brow at Gentile. "It is far easier on my vocal cords than the one used by my former masters."

Gentile smirked with a laugh bubbling out of him. "You mean if I told them to jump up and do the hokey pokey, they would?"

The corners of Michael's mouth lifted. "Yes. But remember, you're dealing with very juvenile minds. When the willpower suppressant wears off, they may choose to do it all the time."

The clatter of loose stones on the mountain behind them caused their heads to turn. They saw Virgil leading his small command down the trail. Cruz counted eleven soldiers, then looked up the pathway for more. None came, so he turned to Virgil, who nodded to him.

"This is all who made it," Virgil answered the unspoken question.

Cruz's jaw tightened. "Sergeant Gilmore?"

Virgil shook his head. "I didn't see any movement on the south hill from our peak. They were hit before us and never had a warning."

The captain's lips thinned. "Did you see how many aliens escaped?"

"The juveniles were the only ones to make it past Eden's border." Michael scratched his beard, grimacing. "Beatrice was relentless."

"There were about a dozen big uglies outside the tunnel we hid in," said Virgil. "They scuttled back to the harpy compound as soon as their masters stopped communicating with them. Reggie took off after them. He wants to destroy their computer system."

"A dozen?" Gentile pumped his fist in the air and shouted. "Then we won. There's no way they can hurt us with a dozen big uglies." His grin turned to a look of confusion at the dour faces looking at him. "Can they?"

"As long as the harpies hold that compound, they can grow another army," Michael whispered.

"And next time, the harpies won't be so stupid as to send them out with just swords." Virgil shook his head and spit to the side. "We have to hit them now while they're still weak."

Cruz pounded his fist on the boulder. "How the hell are we going to do that? Our lasers just bounce off the shield surrounding the hive building."

Michael hopped off the rock. "I can get us in. The entrance is tuned to my DNA."

Cruz cast him an unconvinced look. "It's that easy?"

"Captain, that place is designed as a research lab, not a fort; and their weapons are for controlling prisoners, not fighting a war." His brow furrowed. "Reggie has the right idea, but his plan won't work. Dis is a hostile system. He can get into the compound, but his thoughts will be scanned as soon as he attempts to enter the computer room. We have to destroy the mainframe."

Captain Cruz climbed atop Hellsgate and looked at the thousands of dead strewn across the narrow ravine. "Lieutenant Gentile, take charge of the prisoners. You have the Third and Fourth platoons. First and Second platoons, you're with me." He lowered the ladder to the other side and eyed Michael. "C'mon, Michael. I need some doors opened."

"I think I'll tag along." Virgil shouldered his gun and moved to the wall. "I hate not finishing a job."

"We're coming, too," Terri and Paula shouted in unison and clambered over the wall without waiting for permission. The eleven other mountain survivors followed them.

"What am I supposed to do with all of these, uh, prisoners?" Gentile asked in a sheepish voice.

Cruz fought back tears as he surveyed the mangled bodies of the human dead. "Put them to work. Bury our dead and burn the clones." He paused and then let the tiniest smirk cross his face. "After that, you can teach them the hokey pokey."

———————•◆•———————

Reggie joined the clones fleeing the battle back to the hive. As he entered the compound, commands screeched into the communicator embedded in his head. He ignored them and walked up the ramp to the upper levels. The remaining harpies were in a panic, and the clones were too busy scurrying about to notice.

I hope this works. Reggie checked the rooms he passed until he found the one he sought on the third level. He slipped into the empty bio-lab room and settled in before a terminal. *Here goes.*

With shaky fingers, he brought up the instructions for a full system shut down and typed in the emergency procedure. As the progress bar appeared on the screen, he pumped his fist in the air and whispered, "Yes."

However, the bar vanished from the display soon after, replaced by another message: "Error: invalid request."

Reggie sagged back in the seat. Oh, no. What do I do now?

Sweat beaded on his forehead as he scrolled through the instructions, searching for an override command. He found the commands but didn't have the password. He looked at Dante's jump drive beside him. *Maybe I can enter the virus manually.* Reggie inserted the drive and opened the first file on the list: Asimov's Three Laws. Reggie had no idea what those were. He shrugged and read it anyway and wondered, *This is a computer virus?* He tried to open an app, but the words "Access Denied" flashed across the screen. *Damn.*

Noise in the hallway caught his attention. Now out of time, he retrieved the drive and moved behind a cabinet by the entrance. *I have to get out of here. Maybe this Dante can come up with a better plan.*

Light poured into the dark room as the door slid open. Through the gap between the cabinet and the wall, Reggie saw an agitated harpy with a stun gun stand in the doorway and search the room. The creature hissed, spun around, and left. Reggie heard the scratch of one of his former master's clawed feet heading up the ramp to the next level.

He waited five minutes, then steeled himself and slipped into the hallway, forcing himself to walk slow and steady down the ramp.

Reggie crept to the base of the second level and peered below. A flurry of activity blocked the exit. The guardians who had come in with him were armed with plexi-steel swords and throwing up a barricade behind the door. Leaving through any of the ground-level exits would be impossible. He glanced back the way he had come, considering his options. As far as he could see, he would have to lower himself from the transport hangar on the fourth level.

Reggie padded back up the ramp. Lost in thought, he rounded a bend and collided with the harpy commander. The creature crashed to the floor but shot to his feet in an instant, squealing invectives and waving its stun gun at Reggie.

"I am sorry, my master." He stood at attention and squeezed the jump drive and silver cross hidden in his left hand until his knuckles whitened. "I know it is forbidden for guardians to enter the upper levels without the escort of a master, but I was seeking weapons to defend the compound from our enemies."

The agitated harpy administrator lowered its weapon and ordered Reggie to follow it. It pressed a glowing blue button on its belt and bounded up the ramp.

Compulsion roared through Reggie's brain, but he focused his thoughts on Gabrielle standing by his side at Hellsgate and shoved the impulse aside. Reggie slowed as they passed the wide opening of the transport dock. The harpy commander snarled, and another blast of compulsion hit the big man.

Nausea roiled through Reggie as he mentally fought the commands. *I'll be a slave no more.* As his mind cleared, his eyes narrowed as he trailed the harpy administrator to the top tier — to a part of the compound he had never been to before.

The harpy skittered up a rope-like ladder. Reggie breathed deep and followed. As he pulled himself through the hatchway, the big man stumbled. His hands flew open, and the treasures he clutched skittered across the floor.

The harpy commander screeched when it spotted the hidden items. It raised its stun gun as Reggie roared and leapt at it.

———— ◆ ————

"Fire," Cruz grated.

Laser rifles swept the barricade and the band of clones who tried to intercept the soldiers as they stormed the harpies' compound. The conflict ended in seconds, and the infiltration group surged inside.

Cruz looked to Michael. "Which way now?"

Michael focused on the ramp for any sign of motion. "It must be in the upper tiers. I have explored all of the warrens below ground, and there is no bank of file servers there. The upper level is the only part of the complex I have never been to."

"Captain, I'll lead this tour." Virgil edged to the ramp and watched for any motion. "Looks clear for the moment."

Cruz moved next to the sergeant. "Second Platoon, hold this position and keep the exit door propped open. First platoon, with me. We're going harpy hunting."

"Be careful," Michael warned. "The remaining harpies might just be scientists, but they are cornered, and I cannot begin to guess what Dis will try."

"Shoot anything that moves," Cruz barked as he moved up the ramp.

Gabrielle planted herself in front of him. "Captain, Reggie could be up there somewhere."

"I'm not risking any more of my men. Reggie better announce himself real clear or he's dead," Cruz snapped, then sighed and cast brief glances at his troops. "Men, there might be a friendly up there. If you see a big ugly wearing a cross, give him the chance to surrender."

At the top of the incline, they encountered three harpies who stood in the open and sprayed inexpert stun blasts. They crumpled an instant later beneath precision laser weapon fire. The soldiers headed toward a series of doors set into the exterior wall along the corkscrew ramp that led to the domed ceiling several stories above them.

On the fourth level, they found the transport hanger where four unarmed harpies cowered. The soldiers butchered the harpies without hesitation and moved on. As they neared the top, the blue lights dimmed.

Terri followed close behind Cruz. "This can't be good," she whispered, and the captain nodded in agreement.

At the next level, the artificial lighting went dark. The only illumination came from the sun's rays filtering through the translucent dome. A lattice rope-like ladder offered sole access to the highest tier. The soldiers gathered below the opening.

Cruz let out a slow, grim breath. "This has to be it."

"Well, there's only one way to find out," said Virgil.

Cruz scaled the ladder and waved the stock of his rifle through the hatchway. He was rewarded with a stun gun blast that passed harmlessly over his head. "There's at least one hostile up here. Damn, I wish I had a couple grenades."

Terri climbed next to him. "Do you have a guess where he is?"

"Yeah. The room is packed with equipment. There's not a whole lot of space to move."

Terri bit her lower lip, breathed slow, and nodded. "Okay, then I'll take the hit. Just make sure you nail the bastard. I don't want to be a limp rag doll with a nasty headache for nothing."

"I can't let you do that."

"You don't have a whole lot of choice in the matter. I'm your shield." She tensed just below the lip of the hatch. "Ready." Terri popped up, shuddered, and toppled into the arms of the soldiers below. Virgil raised his gun and fired. The harpy never got off a second shot.

"Clear," Virgil called out. "How's Terri?"

"She's breathing! She's okay," Paula shouted back.

"Get the medical kit up here fast," Cruz shouted down to the men on the first level.

Virgil leapt through the opening with Michael and Gabrielle on his heels. They froze at the sight before them. Reggie's unmoving body lay on a table. A series of wires ran from the back of his neck to a man-high cylinder pulsating with an azure light. A thin trickle of blood seeped from the wound.

"*Ay Dios mio,*" Gabrielle breathed.

The hatchway door behind them slid shut, slicing a soldier climbing the lattice rope in half. A second later, a scratchy, droning noise cut in from speakers somewhere nearby. The room shook when the noise gave way to a metallic, guttural voice.

"Thank you for delivering the infiltrator guardian. This last one provided little data of value. I need to harvest a richer source of information." Bladed tentacles telescoped from the banks of cylinders around the room's perimeter with the speed of a viper.

Michael and Gabrielle became blurs, dueling the extended appendages with their light swords. The tentacles recoiled, unharmed. Virgil fired his laser gun into the nearest device, but to no avail.

A familiar voice echoed from the unmoving body on the table. "You will not hurt them. I am Reggie, and I am in control."

Warning blares from the unseen speakers screamed twice. "Impossible. You are nothing more than a memory download."

"I am Reggie, and I control this system now." The pulsating blue lights dimmed and the appendages dropped to the floor.

Tears filled Gabrielle's eyes as she looked back at the unmoving, glassy-eyed clone. "Oh, Reggie, I should have come with you."

"How did you escape your repository?" the metallic voice demanded. "You should have no access to my controls."

"I am Reggie, and I have penetrated your core. You sought information from my recorder, and now you have it. I used that as my gateway past your firewall security. You pulled my memories in, and one was a computer virus written by my friends."

Dis's audio crackled sharp in the speakers. "A temporary problem. Only the ancient enemy could resist me, and you are not them."

"I am Reggie. I will fight you. Soft boots are good. Gabrielle's gentle hands are good. You are evil. I will not let you corrupt innocents again."

Tears streamed unabated down Gabrielle's cheeks as she clutched Reggie's limp hand. "Fight him, Reggie."

"You are weak," said Dis. "I will erase your memories from my files."

"The virus is already in your operating system," Reggie intoned with a flat, mechanical voice. "Gabrielle, destroy it before it can reboot with an older operating system."

"I will do anything you ask. Just live!" Gabrielle leapt into action, bisecting the nearest cylinder with her sword. Sparks showered the room.

Dis's metallic snaps pierced the ears of everyone present. "I will regain control."

The blue lights flickered on and off with more frequency as Reggie spoke. "I am Reggie. Hurry. It is stripping my essence."

Virgil powered on his rifle and prowled around the perimeter of the room, blasting one computer unit after another.

"Your resistance is failing."

Michael cut through tentacles as they rose.

If a machine could scream, Dis did just that. "You are the ancient enemy. I must warn—"

Gabrielle smashed her sword into the last glowing device. The room went dark except for the midday light filtering through the dome. All went quiet, save for Reggie's flat monotone.

"I am Reggie. I am Reggie. Gabrielle, I—"

Gabrielle rushed to him, spread-eagled on the table, and felt for a pulse. A faint one indicated he still clung to life. Tears welled in her eyes. "My friend, don't leave me."

Michael stooped to the floor and retrieved a bloodstained cross and jump drive. He squeezed the cross in his hand and raised his eyes to the heavens. "Reggie, you have done our people proud."

The hatchway shriveled and evaporated from energy beams fired from below. Several human soldiers sprang into the room.

As Captain Cruz made his way in, Virgil announced, "It's over. Reduce this room to a slag heap."

Michael disconnected the wires hooked into Reggie's neck. "Virgil, help me. This brave man deserves a chance."

"That, he does." Virgil lifted Reggie's legs. "He's one of our best."

CHAPTER XXXIV
Limbo

For such defects, and not for other guilt,
Lost are we and only so far punished,
That without hope we live on in desire.

Dante's Inferno Canto IV

Dante sidled up to Virgil through the crowd gathering around the open area in front of Building 692. Some people had collected by the main entrance and others were perched on the ramp leading to the upper level.

"So what's this big meeting all about?" asked Dante. "You know everything that's going on."

"I have an idea, but Captain Cruz called this thing, so I'll leave it for him to explain." Virgil raised his hand and beckoned Michael over when he spotted Angela bobbing on the clone's shoulders.

Michael elbowed his way to his friends and nodded to them. "Where's Tina?"

Virgil waved to the new arrival and answered, "She's in the hospital, looking in on Reggie."

Hope rose in Michael's voice. "Any change in his condition?"

Dante's voice dropped. "He's still unresponsive. He's breathing but hasn't spoken a word or moved a muscle since we found him in the harpies' compound. The doc and Tina don't have a clue what to do for him."

Michael nodded and looked around. "Where's Doctor Easley?"

"Delivering a baby." Dante pursed his lips. "The first one born here."

"Uncle Mick was born here," Angela piped in from above. "He told me so."

A thoughtful look crossed Michael's face. "I would love to see a real human birth."

"Why don't you, then?" Dante slapped him on the back. "Ask Doctor Easley. There are a few ladies ready to give birth. If it's okay with the moms, I know it'll be fine with the doc."

"If it's okay with the moms—" Michael muttered and forced a smile on his face.

Paula popped in next to him. "Hey, big guy, where've you been hiding? Angela, have you been keeping Mick out of trouble?"

"I try," Angela giggled as Paula slid close and tickled the little girl's foot.

Michael face went red. "Paula, I have not been hiding. I have—"

He held that thought as Captain Cruz stepped in, approached a table on the walk near House 692, and spoke into a drone that hovered nearby. "Good afternoon, folks. Thanks for coming." Orbs with speakers scattered around the garden beds near the cavern's entrance amplified his voice.

"I don't believe in wasting time, so I'll get right to the point," said Cruz. "It's been a month since we freed ourselves from the harpies, and we have shelter here in Mount Purgatory. Things have settled a bit, but we need to select a leader."

"Then I nominate Captain Cruz," Lieutenant Gentile shouted from where the troops were gathered near the armory. A loud cheer arose throughout the throng.

"No," Cruz shouted as he waved his hands for silence. "I'm a soldier, and I'll give my life to keep us safe.

But I must be under a civilian." He sighed and recomposed himself. "As a soldier, I believe in a command structure. That would devolve into a dictatorship. I fear the lure of that role and will not accept the temptation."

Gentile called out, "Virgil Bernius," and the soldiers roared their approval.

"Hell no," Virgil barked in surprise. "There's no way anyone is laying a desk job on me."

"Gabrielle Peyago," rang out from where the Argentines had clustered. She raised her hands to the cheers of her people.

"Dmitri Pertelov," yelled a Russian. The balding man shook his head and dismissed the nomination with a wave.

"Kevin Martinel," cried the group of Aussies.

Martinel sat on the ramp leading to the upper chamber with Linda at his side. "You're out of your bloomin' minds if you want me." Then he settled back and laughed. "If elected, I promise to take all bribes." Laughter rolled through the crowd as Linda planted her elbow in his ribs. He rubbed his side and said, "Ouch. Sorry, mates, I'm a pilot. I want to focus on getting these antique spaceships Beatrice's makers built working again. I can't do that if I'm running a bloomin' planet!"

Cruz waited for more names, but no one else spoke.

Then Beatrice's quiet buzz and beep chimed in. "I nominate Dante Carloman."

The crowd turned to each other, and a low murmur of conversation filled the room.

"He was my first guest," Beatrice elaborated. "He is the reason all of you are here now. He is the reason I am alive."

"I second it," Michael called out in a choked voice. "He was the first to speak to me and show me what it means to be human."

"I withdraw my name," Dmitri wheezed. "Dante's a good, levelheaded man."

"And brave, too." Virgil slapped the startled tech student on the back. "Who else would go after a harpy with nothing more than a claw hammer on a snow-covered road in New York?"

Cruz waited a few seconds for other names. When no others went out, he barked, "Nominations are closed. All in favor of Gabrielle Peyago, say, 'Aye'."

There was a smattering of "ayes" from the Argentines.

"All in favor of Dante Carloman?"

The cavern reverberated with thunderous cheers.

Cruz nodded and smiled. "I guess that's clear. Come up here and say a few words, Mister President."

Dante coughed and cleared his throat as he was shoved forward with a lot of back slapping. He climbed onto the table and looked around to gather his thoughts. His baffled expression turned serious as he regarded the two thousand clones fidgeting like little kids along the back wall.

He cleared his throat. "Well, to say we've been through a lot together is a mild understatement. And we still have a lot more to face. The main harpy force should be back in about three months, and I'm guessing they'll be a bit pissed." No one laughed, and he swallowed at his attempt at a small joke. "To meet that threat, we must be prepared, and General Cruz will be responsible for our defenses."

Cruz flushed and turned away. "Hardly a general. I have a hundred and fifty men."

Dante pointed to the clones and the militia. "By my count, you have close to a brigade. Those clones are nothing more than children right now, but they have been bred to kill. Your responsibility is to help them grow into responsible adults and show them what is worth fighting to defend." He smirked, stifling a laugh. "Besides, since

I just got picked to be the Lord Grand Pooba, I can make you a general."

"Thank you, Mister President." Cruz shook his head. "Clones. I'm going to be a baby-sitter for a bunch of adolescent clones." He growled as he saw Virgil and Michael grinning and poking each other. "My first order as general is to name Virgil and Michael the clones' drill instructors."

"Also, so I don't screw up too bad, I'll need an advisory council." Dante furrowed his brow, searching the room for the people he had in mind. "General Cruz, Gabrielle Peyago, Dmitri Pertelov, Kevin Martinel—"

"Oh, no, not me, mate," Kevin shouted from the distant ramp. "You want someone sensible like Linda."

Dante nodded. "Okay, then. Linda Martinel." Laughter rippled through the crowd, and a few well-meaning jibes were thrown Kevin Martinel's way. Dante smiled and looked around the room again and made his final choices. "And so all of our people are represented, I name Beatrice and Michael."

———————◆———————

Dante put down his beer and waved when he spotted Michael entering Dolan's Bar. "Over here, big guy. We saved some seats for you."

Corporal Frontera opened the bar using the microbrewery equipment Beatrice built for Corporal Dolan. In the weeks that followed, it had become the social center for the people living in Purgatory. It was an open one-story building next to the hospital with a central fountain surrounded by a large garden courtyard. Most of the tables were filled, and two Argentines were in a corner attempting to play brand new, acoustically poor guitars.

Michael strolled over, holding hands with Angela on one side and Paula on the other. Angela pulled free and scampered over. "I just had a tea party with Grammy-Ann and Uncle Mick." She made an exaggerated sigh. "Uncle Mick isn't very good at make-believe."

"I'm sure he'll learn." Tina chuckled and tousled the girl's hair.

"Well, we need more girls here." Angela twisted her face into a pout. "There're too many boys, and they're no fun. None of them like playing cat's cradle."

Tina laughed again. "I know what you mean. Michael has a lot of... younger brothers."

A clone in a clean, white tunic approached the table as Michael and Paula sat down. Michael eyed Dante's beer. "Is it any better yet?"

Dante smacked his tongue. "A little, but it's still too hoppy for me."

Michael sighed and glanced at the waiter. "Porthos?"

Porthos smiled and ran his tattooed hand across his smooth jaw as he stared at Michael's full beard with jealousy written on his young face.

"Three lemonades." Michael looked around the table. "No menus?"

Porthos slouched and grinned. "You know the choices haven't changed. You can have soy burgers, soy burgers, or soy burgers."

"Three soy burgers." Michael sniffed, frowning. "Sarcasm is not appreciated, Porthos. Wait until I get you on the drill field tomorrow."

Porthos beamed. The young clones prized individual recognition no matter the cost.

Angela crossed her arms. "I don't want a burger."

Michael cocked his head at the little girl. "Okay. Let me guess. You want almond butter and jelly?" She grinned hugely and nodded, so he eyed the waiter. "Got it?"

"Yes, sir." Porthos made a casual salute and walked off.

Michael chuckled as he shook his head and grabbed a bun from the basket on the table. "You'd think the only restaurant in Purgatory would have better service."

"At least the bread's good." Paula dipped her roll into the dish of olive oil.

"Any word from Virgil?" Dante asked as he took another sip and grimaced.

"Yeah, he got in this morning. He said that's his last run to the old harpy compound until spring. The weather is growing far too foul." Michael put another piece of bread in his mouth after he spoke.

"Yeah, right," Paula snorted. "Virgil's as convinced as Martinel that they can get those antique spaceships the makers built working again."

Tina rested her arms on the table. "I hope so. I want to go home."

Dante grasped her hand. "We'll find a way out of here."

Paula cocked an eyebrow. "Even if we got those things flying, where would we go? We don't exactly have a roadmap to Earth lying around here."

Tina sighed and wiped her cheek. "I should be grateful we escaped that hell of a prison, and Beatrice tries so hard. But this can never be home. It feels like we're stuck in Hell."

"Yeah, the deepest pit of Hell." Paula twisted her fingers and looked at the floor.

"Cocytus is the name of the lowest circle of Hell in Dante's Divine Comedy," Michael mused.

"Cocytus." Dante rubbed his chin. "This world needs a name, and that's as good as any I've heard. It sure describes our situation."

"So now we have a name for this iceberg of a planet?" asked Martinel. He limped over with Linda and made an elaborate bow, his beer sloshing. "What's this? A meeting of the grand planetary council?"

"You should've taken the job." Dante dropped his head to the table. "Just this morning, I had to settle a dispute about hoarding figs. Beatrice gives out whatever's requested, and one guy got the bright idea of cornering the market. I think we might have to set up a currency soon."

"And that's why it's better you than me." Martinel smacked his lips. "Just let me know when you need someone to be the tax collector."

"How did I end up with this job?" Dante groaned and groped for a new subject to discuss. His eyes landed on the distant ramp and pointed to it with his chin. "Any more luck with those machines upstairs?"

"Yeah. Actually, it's been way too easy." Martinel paused to sip his brew, and then his voice turned serious. "The makers' technology is way beyond the stuff I know, but it's easy to work with."

Linda's voice rose in excitement. "I think we can make those spaceships work."

Dante gave her a knowing nod. Linda had spoken of nothing else for the past month.

"The hulls on those two vessels you found have been repaired, and their power generator is similar to what Beatrice uses for her drones, just on a much larger scale." Linda lifted her chin. "Virgil's been a marvel, scrounging parts from the harpy compound and the huge wreck that's crushed in the rift. I'm sure I can get them to fly."

"I always wanted to be an astronaut," said Kevin, his face growing wistful. He sighed a second later. "What good will it do us, though? Those two ships seem to be built for five or six people, and we have thousands here."

Dante nodded, his expression sad. "Yeah, the galaxy is such a big place, and we don't have a clue where Earth is."

Michael patted Dante on the shoulder. "You're supposed to be the optimist here, Mister President. It's a first step. Look where we were just a couple of months ago." He stroked his short-cropped beard. "Look where I was those few months ago."

A small smile crossed Dante's face. "That's true, Mick." His face turned serious then. "What's General

Cruz been up to? I haven't seen much of him over the last couple of weeks."

"My name is *Michael*. Oh, why do I bother?" Michael gave a resigned shrug. "The general's been spending most of his time drilling the troops and fortifying Hellsgate. He's obsessed with being able to fight the harpy army when it returns."

"That place is impregnable," the waiter chimed in.

"And who invited you into this conversation?" Michael glared at the young clone.

"Sorry, sir. The general stripped the old prison compound of its barrier poles and used them to build an energy shield around it." The waiter blushed under Michael's hard stare. "Ahh, I'll go get your orders now." He hurried off.

Kevin Martinel sipped his beer and mumbled, "It's kinda creepy."

"What's kinda creepy? This whole planet is creepy," Dante snorted.

Martinel chuckled. "That's for sure." He jerked his head toward the ramp leading to the cavern's upper tier. "Did you know most of those crates up there have an image of what looks like an eagle with its wings spread out on 'em?"

"A lot of cultures on Earth use big raptors as their national symbol," said Tina. "Maybe the makers were that way, too."

"Well, there's more." Martinel put his beer down. "Do the letters SQPR mean anything to you?"

Dante quirked his eyebrow. "Yeah. It's the symbol the ancient Roman legions used. I think it translates to, 'The Senate and the People of Rome'. Why?"

"I found it on some of the boxes." Martinel looked around the table. "This is nuts, but I think *we* are the makers."

John Caligiuri lives in Rochester, New York with his wife, Linda. She's been married to him for over forty years and has supported his writing from the beginning. They have three grown children scattered around the country along with their first grandchild. John enjoys gardening (which stretches his intellect as he attempts to outwit the rabbits and deer) and distance running.

John has a lifelong passion for literature and pens primarily Science Fiction and Fantasy. He has been able to blend his fascination with history and his professional background in software engineering to come up with some unusual story twists. His stories emerge from his curiosity about historical watershed events and asking, "what if".

Made in the USA
Lexington, KY
07 August 2017